THE SUFFERING TREE

THE SUFFERING TREE

ELLE COSIMANO

HYPERION

LOS ANGELES   NEW YORK

Copyright © 2017 by Elle Cosimano

All rights reserved. Published by Hyperion, an imprint of Disney Book Group. No part of this book may be reproduced or transmitted in any form or by any means, electronic or mechanical, including photocopying, recording, or by any information storage and retrieval system, without written permission from the publisher. For information address Hyperion, 125 West End Avenue, New York, New York 10023.

"The Answer" poem © SEPS licensed by Curtis Licensing, Indianapolis, IN.

First Hardcover Edition, June 2017
First Paperback Edition, April 2018
1 3 5 7 9 10 8 6 4 2
FAC-025438-18054
Printed in the United States of America

This book is set in 11-pt. Adobe Devanagari, Engravers
Gothic BT/Fontspring; Bell MT Pro/Monotype
Designed by Maria Elias

Library of Congress Cataloging-in-Publication Number for the Hardcover Edition: 2016037233

ISBN 978-1-4847-8750-2

Visit www.hyperionteens.com

SUSTAINABLE FORESTRY INITIATIVE

Certified Chain of Custody
Promoting Sustainable Forestry
www.sfiprogram.org
SFI-01054
The SFI label applies to the text stock

For Florrie and Bob, who seasoned my imagination
with a little pepper and salt

THE SUFFERING TREE

THE BONFIRE DANCE

The dances were always secret, cloaked in darkness and distance, hidden from the master's eye. Fiddle tucked under my arm, I held the bow in one hand and fought off the brambles with the other. A bold moon illuminated the summer sky, but it was barely enough to light my way under the thick canopy of leaves as I pressed on, dripping sweat and swatting mosquitoes. I passed through three fields and two long stretches of wood before I heard the first note. Ignoring the stiffness in my shoulders and the ache in my feet, I walked faster, glad I hadn't missed it.

Slaughter had been host to a party of his own...mead and food and dancing in celebration of his appointment to the role of sheriff, a position he'd been chasing for years. All of his men had been there—all of his neighbors and friends, drunk and fat and lazy with the heat. I had played the music fast and light, to keep their feet moving and to keep them thirsting for wine. They'd all been too tired to walk far in search of trouble that night.

It was near midnight now. The full moon was a reckless time for this kind of foolishness—the smoke from the fire would be too easy to see, all of us dancing like demons around it—but Slaughter's party, a distraction that tipped the odds of being caught in our favor, had presented an opportunity too tempting to pass up.

We were all exhausted. From the heat, the bugs, the blistering labor of planting and harvesting. Soon we would be exhausted from trying to keep warm. An endless cycle of struggle against nature and work and our own despair. But nights like this were for casting off cares. For losing ourselves and closing our eyes to our stations. And as the moonlight and music parted the trees, as the bonfire sent up sparks into the night sky, as the clapping and stomping of feet found the rhythm of my own heart, I was ready to risk everything and be forgotten.

I stepped out of the trees into the cornfield, dodging through a maze of stalks far taller than my head. Tall enough to conceal the sight of us, but not the song. I inhaled wood smoke and relief. At the end of the path between the corn, Slaughter's slaves—men, women, and a few small children—danced in a circle around the fire. Emmeline was there too, her fair face against the night sky as radiant as the moon. She laughed, her head thrown back as she danced, her black spill of curls clinging with sweat to her pale shoulders. Stripped down to her shift, she held the ends up above her knees, her filthy feet kicking up clouds of dust.

She was entirely bewitching. More so in that moment than maybe ever before. Her cheeks glowed with sweat and firelight, the thin cotton clinging to her breasts and her hips, to the slight roundness of her belly....

Emmeline laughed, mimicking the stomps of Samuel's huge black feet in front of her, demanding he teach her the steps. And as she circled the fire again, her gaze fell upon Ruth where she sat outside the light of the fire, curled in on herself, watching Emmeline dance as I had been. Emmeline bent low to grab Ruth's begrudging hand, dragging her to her feet and pulling her behind, until Ruth had no choice but to join in. Emmeline's eyes met mine through the opening in the corn, and she faltered, as if I'd stumbled upon a secret. Emmeline had always been full of secrets. My eyes drifted to her belly. A smile gathered across her face, wide and fearless.

With a seductive curl of her hand, she gestured for me to join her. I swallowed back the knot in my throat and lifted my fiddle, stepping into the music, toward the heat of the fire. I closed my eyes and pulled all my fury through the bow. I didn't care how loud it rang or who might hear it, so long as it drowned out every other sound in my head.

Tomorrow, I would talk to her. Tomorrow, we would come up with a plan. But tonight, I wanted only to forget.

I hit the water with an icy crash.

It pours over me as I sink down below the surface, the face above me silhouetted by a circle of light and wavering farther and farther from reach. I can't get any air. My arms are heavy and my clothes weigh me down and I can't kick my way to the surface. The walls of my chest press in until black and white stars twinkle in front of my eyes. I scream, a muffled sound that's lost in the rush of cold water pouring into my lungs, bubbling up and away from me toward the light. And I sink down, down, down until darkness closes in all around me.

●   ●   ●

Tori sat bolt upright in bed, gasping for breath. A cold wind blew through her open window, and the sound of the neighbor's dogs barking in the distance cut through the night. The air smelled like rain. She got up fast, catching her toe on an unopened moving box of bathing suits and summer clothes and swearing quietly to herself in the dark.

Tori shut the window just as the sky flickered behind the tall branches of the old cemetery oak. She sat down on the edge of her mattress with her head in her hands, pushing away images of a dream that was already beginning to fade.

The pale pink walls of her room felt tight, the air constricting. Like this room wasn't really hers. Even her dreams felt like they belonged to someone else, like she was peering through the black-and-white lens of a camera. The nightmares had started when Tori's family had moved here, and they were always variations on the same theme. Underwater. Sinking. Unable to move or breathe.

She raked her hair from her eyes and rubbed at the dark smudges underneath them, avoiding her reflection in the mirror over the dresser. Looking at herself in this quilted, pink room gave her the same out-of-place feeling she got whenever she saw herself in a family portrait. She was supposed to belong in this house . . . in this room. Her mother said it in the same emphatic way she used to reassure Tori she belonged in this family. That it was hers. Most days, Tori believed it. But sometimes that wasn't how it felt.

She slid open her night table drawer and quietly dug around for a paper clip or a pen with a metal pocket clip—something with sharp edges. Anything to relieve the pressure building in her chest. There was a razor blade hidden in a cardboard box, but it was buried inside her closet behind an old milk crate full of swim trophies she didn't want to think about, and it would make too much noise to dig it out.

A toilet flushed down the hall. A door clicked open and shut again. Her mother. She must have come in while Tori was sleeping and opened the window. Her compulsive check-ins were getting old. Tori did a quick search of her drawer and came up empty-handed, making her wonder what else her mother might have opened. There was no lock on her bedroom door, and even if it was just a coincidence that the previous owners hadn't bothered to install one, it felt more like a punishment.

Tori scrambled out of her pajamas and into a pair of jeans, grabbed her T-shirt off the floor, and drew it over her head. Then she pulled on a dark hoodie, stuffed her phone in her pocket, and listened through the door. It was quiet on the other side. She cracked it open, checking for light down the hall. Her mother's and brother's rooms were dark through the gaps beneath their doors. So she crept down the stairs, cringing when she hit a squealing creak she hadn't committed to memory yet. She treaded lightly through the hallway, careful to avoid the stack of unpacked boxes along the wall, and paused in the kitchen for a flashlight.

Tori's hand hovered over the utensil drawer. Her mother had been counting them—the knives, the peelers, the skewers, and scissors—and if she woke up in the night and found Tori gone with a single piece of cutlery missing, Tori would be lucky to wake up with a door on her bedroom at all.

She bit her lip, weighing the risk against the pressure steadily building in her chest. With a whispered swear, she reached for the flashlight and slipped out of the house before she could change her mind, pulling the front door shut behind her.

ountry dark was total and complete. So dark, it was impossible for Tori to tell if her eyes were still open. Not like the city dark that was always half-awake, pink and twinkling around the edges. She'd stumbled most of the way. Even with the flashlight, the trail to the cemetery still felt vague and unfamiliar at night. She missed home. She missed the bustle of the sidewalks and the honking horns on M Street, the hum and sway of the Metrorail and the flashing lights as it rushed underground. She missed living in a place so flooded with people—with so many faces coming and going, it was impossible to focus on one. Where everyone was so different, it was hard to tell who didn't belong.

On the surface, it seemed like Chaptico, Maryland, should've been just as easy to get lost in—a wisp of a nothing town insulated in endless acres of soybeans and cornfields. But even after four long weeks here, the grocery baggers and bank tellers in town seemed to stare at Tori's family sideways, and all the busybody neighbors still wanted to peel back the Burnses' thin curtains and peek inside their lives as if they were some kind of spectacle.

Tori shivered in her hoodie. She couldn't shake off the dream. Couldn't shake off the near-constant feeling that she was being watched. Her mother (and the therapist she'd hauled Tori off to before they'd left the city) thought Tori hadn't gotten over the fact that her father was gone. They thought maybe Tori was imagining him. That this feeling she had of being haunted was just her own wishful thinking, grief conjuring memories of him from the grave. But Tori knew better. She used to feel her father's presence in every room of their apartment. The smell of him clung to every surface, and her memories of him were so clear and alive, sometimes she imagined she could pull back the comforter from his side of her parents' bed and the sheets would still be warm and rumpled where he'd been. That had all stopped the day she and her mother and little brother, Kyle, left their apartment in DC for an old farmhouse in Chaptico. And if they were all being honest about it, it was also probably one of the reasons *why* the Burns left their home in the city. Because if there was one thing Tori was certain of, it was that her father sure wasn't here.

When she finally reached the huge white oak near the edge of their field, she sank to the ground between the headstones, staring up into the starless black sky and cranking the volume on her music loud enough to drown out the ceaseless barking from next door and the chorus of crickets in the brush. She traced her fingers over the tree's gnarled roots. In the daylight, the ground was barren here, a perfect circle of dirt and brown, straw-like grass surrounding the tree's craggy, sun-bleached trunk. Beneath its long, twisted branches, a cluster of grave markers leaned, forgotten and tangled in the brittle weeds. The field just past it was left unplanted, overgrown with high green grass and fenced by a thick strand of maple and pine. It was almost as if no one—not even the grass in the field—wanted to get too close.

This place had always felt strange to Tori. When her mother had asked about it, the neighbors had joked that the tree was cursed. But their smiles were thin and tight when they spoke about it, like maybe somewhere down deep, they believed it was true.

Maybe that's why Tori felt drawn to it. This weird tree no one wanted to come close to, surrounded by dead people no one seemed to want to talk about. To her, it felt like the only place in this town with a lock on its door.

Her fingers closed over a fallen branch. She peeled away the loose bark with her fingernails, picking the tip into a jagged point. Then she drew up the sleeve of her sweatshirt, bit down hard, and pressed it into her skin. Tori's breath hissed between her teeth with the rush of pain as she dragged it across her forearm, careful to control it. Careful not to cut too deep.

Then she shut her eyes, letting the pain drown out everything else. Warm blood pooled in the crease of her arm, dripping from her elbow. Her heart rate slowed and her muscles unwound. She took a deep, trembling breath.

A cold, wet wind carried the reek of river silt and decaying fish over the field. Lightning sparked in the distance and she counted through the roll of thunder the way her father had taught her when she was little, back when she'd thought the echo of thunder off apartment buildings was the worst thing she would ever be afraid of—*one-Mississippi—two-Mississippi—three-Mississippi.*

Another fork of lightning struck beyond the field, and she closed her eyes, letting it flash against the inside of her lids until she could almost pretend she was somewhere else—someplace with streetlamps and neon signs and traffic lights. ... *One-Washington, DC—two-Washington, DC*... Closer now, the ground rumbled, deep enough to rattle her bones.

A fat raindrop plunked down on Tori's cheek and she wiped it away. Her fingers were warm and sticky. Blood smeared her hands. Her entire arm was drenched in it. She prodded the broken skin. The cut was deep— too deep.

She plucked out her earbuds and swore under her breath. Bending her elbow and raising it over her head, she held the skin together and waited for the bleeding to slow. The stick had been a stupid substitute, too hard to control. Next time, she'd be more careful. Tori checked the cut one more time, but it was still bleeding faster than it should be. *There shouldn't be a next time at all.*

A slow, steady rain was beginning to fall, and she shut her eyes, listening to the patter of drops against the headstones. To the steady trickle of blood, falling from the crook of her arm. She looked up through the trees toward the house. Her mother's bedroom window was still dark. If she was quiet, her mother wouldn't have to know.

She stood up, careful to keep pressure on the wound. Her head swam, woozy and light, and she focused on the trunk of the tree and waited for the feeling to pass. Slowly, like a curtain being drawn wide, the sky drenched the field in a cold, hard rain, and she hunkered down, waiting for this to pass too. Her clothes were heavy, plastered to her skin, and the farmhouse felt a million miles away. The bleeding would stop, eventually. It always did. It was just taking longer than usual. *Too long*, a voice in her head whispered as she considered curling up on the ground to wait.

But the ground seemed to move. Not in her head. More like a rolling pressure under her feet. She sank to her knees, feeling queasy and weak.

The dirt crumbled under her hands, a mound of it rising up through her fingers.

She crept back from the newly formed hole, cradling her arm and waiting for some furry country animal to slink out of it—for the yellow night-eyes of a groundhog or gopher to find her and scuttle off into the woods.

The dirt shifted again.

"Be a good little critter and go away," she whispered.

Lightning flashed and Tori froze, blinking against the afterimage of something that had begun to surface from the ground.

She scrambled backward, tripping over the earbuds hanging loose from her pocket.

Whatever it was, it stilled at the sound of her voice. Tori inched closer on all fours to see. A twig snapped under her knee and she held her breath, recalling something her father had said once—something about the squirrels and pigeons she'd been scared of when she was a child being more afraid of her—and wondered if it was true. She skimmed a tentative hand over the ground.

Dirt erupted in a sudden spray. Something clamped around her wrist. She yelped, pain shooting through her arm as cold fingers dug in and pulled. She pushed herself to her knees and leaned away, groping for a headstone, for anything solid to hold on to, but the nearest one was too far to reach. Her wrist strained. Her skin stretched painfully. The hand was strong, calloused, struggling to hold on as Tori wrenched against it.

An arm emerged.

Tori faltered, breath held. This . . . this *thing* inside the ground wasn't trying to pull her down. It was using her to pull itself out.

She stopped fighting. Stopped pulling. Her flashlight . . . it was somewhere behind her. If she could just reach it . . .

Lightning struck close. She twisted, fumbling blindly for the handle, struggling to stay upright as the hand gave a sudden hard tug. A shoulder breached the hole.

Shaking, her fingers closed around the flashlight. She flicked it on and swung the beam at the ground.

At the face coming out of it.

The man's long hair clung to pale, muddy cheeks and eyes caked shut with red clay. His mouth opened, gasping for air, as he shook the dirt from his eyes. Tori struggled to pull away, but he only gripped her wrist tighter, blinking against the flashlight with green, bloodshot eyes.

Tori's scream stuck in her throat. She jerked back hard, feeling the edges of her cut tear. Half out of the ground, the man gritted his teeth, leveraging her weight to work the rest of himself free. Frantic, Tori swung the light at his head. He dodged the blow, knocking it from her hand. It landed beside the hole, casting shadows as he climbed out of it and stood over her, raining dirt and breathing hard, clutching her wrist so tightly she couldn't feel her fingers.

Sparks burst at the edge of her vision. She felt herself sway. He turned her wrist, making the cut gape open, and Tori cried out with pain as her arm finally slipped from his cold grasp. She staggered back, and as he reached to grab her, the world, the field, the cemetery, his face, dissolved into a kind of darkness she'd never known before.

LOST & ALONE

I was a boy of only ten when I first met her. We were crammed together in the belly of a ship full of children and criminals bound for the colonies. If I had seen her before in passing on the streets of Bristol, I didn't recall. Children weren't allowed to roam so often then, and certainly not after dark. The spirits were everywhere, they used to tell us to scare us into staying indoors. Avoid the alleyways, they told us. Don't play near the wharfs. I asked her once what she was doing when she was taken. She refused to answer.

She was filthy the night they carried us, wriggling and wrapped in brown sacks, onto the ships. Her hair was tangled and dotted with lice, and her clothes weren't much more than a collection of old rags stitched together. I wondered why she never cried that night, like so many of the rest of us did. If there was anyone at home who would miss her. Or if her family had sold her to the ships simply to be rid of her. One less mouth to feed.

As for me, I wasn't supposed to be outside after dark. My mother would never have it. But that night, my father was late getting home. Too many children had gone missing—too many neighbors and friends mysteriously vanished with every ship that left port. He had gone with their families to stage a protest at the town hall, to force the governor's hand into starting an inquiry. My mother stood close, watching me eat my supper as she rubbed her huge, round belly. I remember how her eyes crinkled with worry, fretting over when my father might return. How she suddenly doubled over with pain and called out my name, and the gush of water from between her legs. How I was the only one home to fetch the midwife.

I followed my mother's instructions, careful to avoid the alleys and the dark and shadowy paths. Careful to avoid the wharfs and taverns where the ship's men drank long into the night between passages. But as I rounded the last corner, a figure leapt into my path, and another behind me. I never made it to the midwife's house. And I never saw my mother again.

It was little more than four months later when we were the last two children left on the ship. I only know because she used a splinter of wood from the lid of the crate we sat upon to etch hash marks into her skin, one for every day we spent at sea. At each of the recent dockings, we had been quickly passed over in favor of others who were older, stronger, or (in my case) more impressive in stature. Finally, we stood on the wharf, wincing against the brightness of a world so unlike the one we'd lived in below the ship's deck.

We wobbled and swayed, our legs unaccustomed to dry land. The captain's huge, calloused hand was firm on my shoulder, holding me in place. I held her hand, our fingers clasped tightly together. The captain, the crew, they all refused to touch her. Rumors had started mere days after we'd cast off from Bristol. About the bewitching lightness of her eyes, her unusual fondness for the ship's cat, and the strange way the clouds seemed to grow dark and threatening whenever any of the men looked at her. I had always thought that was her intention, deliberately playing on a sailor's superstitions, but now? I'm not entirely sure.

A man strode onto the wharf. He was tall and stately, wearing a gentleman's clothes. The captain nudged me in the back, forcing my spine straight as he approached, and it was all I could do to keep from falling over.

"Good to see you, Slaughter," the captain greeted him. "I see life in the colonies is treating you well."

"You're delayed. I was expecting your arrival weeks ago," the man said curtly.

"We were set back by a nasty squall." I could feel the captain shift anxiously. "But your goods are well and accounted for." The captain gestured behind him, where the crew hefted large wooden barrels and crates down the plank to the wharf. "And I brought two fine young redemptioners for you. I'm sure you could use another set of strong hands in time for the harvesting. This one seems sturdy enough." The captain clapped me hard on the back, nearly knocking me off my feet.

The man gave me a cursory glance, his distaste clear in his grimace. His eyes lingered a moment longer on her. "I've no need for any more redemptioners. I've just purchased six Negroes from a captain on his way north from the Caribbean."

The captain faltered. "Are you quite certain, sir? This is my last stop in the colonies."

"Which only speaks to the fact that no one wanted them. I see no benefit for me in relieving you of your orphans."

The captain cleared his throat, his face reddening. "Given that we set sail back to England tomorrow, I'd be willing to negotiate a very fair price."

"They come with papers signed by their parents, then?" the man asked, raising a brow. "You know, the governor has been under quite a bit of pressure about this. I will be forced to register them with the magistrate."

I opened my mouth to speak, to tell him my father would never sign such a paper. The captain's fingers dug into my shoulders. "Of course, I could sign a contract for you...assuming, of course, the price was fair," he said. "Two barrels of tobacco each."

The man called Slaughter stood in front of her. He grabbed her by the chin and forced her eyes to his, turning her face from side to side, his critical gaze traveling down to her bare, blackened feet. "I'll give you one barrel. For the girl."

"But the boy," the captain said. "He'd make a fine field hand."

"I've no use for the boy."

The captain blurted, "Two barrels for the both of them, then."

"One barrel. I'll take the girl." The man took her by the shoulder, as if to lead her off. "I'll have one of my men pick up the girl's contract within the hour. Come, then," he said to her. "My man, Thomas, will deliver you home and see that you get cleaned up." At the head of the wharf, a scruffy middle-aged man wearing muddy boots and a murderer's brand stood waiting beside a cart loaded down with barrels.

Her hand clenched more tightly to mine. The harder Slaughter pulled, the more she refused to let go. The captain held me firmly in place so our fingers strained between us.

Slaughter glared at our clasped hands, then at the captain. "Are they siblings?"

"If ye like," the captain said. "I can't keep the boy. Can't afford another deckhand to feed. Take him. I'll give you the both of them. What's your name, boy?" the captain asked gruffly.

"Nathaniel Bishop," I croaked, my throat so parched I was barely able to speak.

"And you, girl. What's your name?" Slaughter asked.

She cast her pale gray eyes on him and refused to speak. He regarded her with thin, tight lips.

"Her name is Emmeline," I rushed to answer, before he or the man they called Thomas got any ideas about whipping her. "Emmeline Bishop."

The man called Slaughter looked at me, his head cocked with amusement, as if he could see through my lie. But I had made her a promise.

A promise to keep her safe. And for most of our long journey, that hadn't been an easy promise to keep. She'd come dangerously close to being thrown overboard by the crew, who were fearful of the cold willfulness in her eyes that suggested she might conjure a storm and drown them all. Slaughter, on the other hand, seemed to have none of the same reservations.

"I expect their contracts within the hour. You'll have your barrel then. Come with me," Slaughter said, striding back up the wharf with a gait that said he was confident we would obey him.

The captain shoved me after him, and because I went without a fight, Emmeline followed.

GAPING HOLES

Tori's eyes snapped open.

Her clothes stuck to her skin, her chilled body curled to fit on the wooden bench beside her front door. Pins and needles pricked her arms and hands and feet. She scraped at the hair that clung to her forehead and lashes to find a light rain dripping softly from the eaves of the porch. Lightning flickered far off in the distance.

She sat up too fast. Her head pounded and the bench swayed. A dull throb had taken root in her arm. She drew up her wet sleeve to find her forearm wrapped with a torn piece of fabric, the unraveling hem of what, up until now, had been her favorite T-shirt. The hair on the back of her neck stood on end as she looked out across the porch over the lawn, peering into the shadows. The sky was dusky and violet, still too dark to see. She couldn't be certain that everything she remembered from last night wasn't just a hallucination or a really weird dream.

Tori eased off the bench, gripping the rusted arm to keep her balance. She crept to the door and pried it open, listening to be sure the house was still asleep before stepping inside and sliding the chain in place. Careful to avoid the creaky middles of the steps, she darted up the stairs and into the bathroom, falling back against the locked door. She looked down at herself, at the smears of mud on her jeans and the dried blood under her fingernails.

It was almost sunrise. She could run the faucet. If her mother heard, she would only assume Tori was getting ready for school.

School. The thought sent a fresh shudder through her. Maybe she could crawl in bed and tell her mother she was sick.

She splashed handfuls of water over her face. It trailed down her arms, tingeing the sink with dirt and blood. She popped a couple of pain relievers and tipped her head to take a swig from the tap. The well water smelled strange, faintly earthy and metallic, but she didn't realize how thirsty she was until it was running cold down her cheek and she gratefully gulped it down.

When she finally came up for air, the room seemed to wobble. She held the sides of the sink to keep herself upright. And that's when she saw them.

The dark, fingerlike bruises circling her wrist.

Hands shaking, she stripped off her sweatshirt and reached for the makeshift bandage below her elbow. The knot looked complicated and secure, but it released with a surprisingly light pull. She peeled it away from the inflamed skin. The cut was bad. Worse than she'd thought. And somehow, the terribleness of it was comforting. *I must have lost a lot of blood. I must have passed out and imagined horrible things.* She had probably treated her wound and wandered home, too weak to have a recollection of any of it. The bruises on her wrist were probably marks left by her own hand when she'd tried to stop the bleeding.

But the knot . . .

She stripped off her remaining clothes and buried them under the pile in the hamper, discarding the bloody rag and the remains of her T-shirt in the bottom of the wastebasket. Washing the laundry and taking out the trash were Tori's chores anyway; she'd get rid of the whole mess after school.

She brushed her hair from her eyes and examined herself in the mirror. She looked as terrible as she felt. But playing sick wasn't an option. If her mother took her to the doctor, or even just took a close enough interest, she'd never be able to explain the cut and bruises. She'd just end up in another therapist's office. Instead, she pulled the iodine and hydrogen peroxide from the medicine cabinet and grabbed the first-aid kit from under the sink. Teeth gritted, she poured the peroxide over the length of the gash and watch it bubble over, pink and speckled with dirt. Every muscle inside her clenched with the sting. She ran the shower and climbed under the hot water, letting it steam the chill from her bones as she scrubbed herself clean.

When she was done, she opened the curtain and stared at herself in the mirror. At the pink and purple lines crisscrossing her arms and thighs, visible in the steamy glass against the winter-pale skin she always kept covered. Turning away from them, she snatched a towel from the cabinet and got down to the business of covering them up.

Tori had become good at this, slathering angry wounds with antibiotic ointment, stretching butterfly strips over the length of a fresh cut and hiding it under a thin layer of loose gauze and bandages that no one would notice through the sleeves of her shirt. Always black. Always long-sleeved.

Tori jumped at the bang on the bathroom door. "Quit hogging the bathroom, Tori! You're going to make us late for school." Pulling her towel tighter around herself, she checked the lock, but Kyle didn't try to come in.

"I'm almost done!" she called back, cringing when her sore throat cracked on the last syllable.

Breath held, she listened for the sound of his retreating feet on the hardwood. Kyle was ten, and keeping secrets had never been his strong suit. When she was sure he was gone, Tori scrambled, burying the bandage wrappers in the wastebasket and checking the shower and sink for signs of blood. She waited for the slam of his bedroom door before creeping across the hall to her room.

The pink walls were too bright and her room was freezing, the lace curtains wavering in the damp breeze. The window was open again, a wet spot darkening the floor where the rain must have blown in during the night. But she'd closed it last night, before she'd left. She was certain of it. She slammed the window shut and examined the springs. They seemed fine. Tori, on the other hand, was far from it.

The sheets and blankets were still peeled back on her bed, and she thought hard about climbing under them. But even if she crawled under the covers and closed her eyes, she wasn't sure she'd be able to sleep. She massaged the lingering marks on her wrist, then drew the curtain closed and sat in her damp towel on the edge of her bed. Just another bad dream. Just shock and blood loss and an overactive imagination. That's all it could have been.

Groggy and sore, she put on her school uniform, pulling the sleeves of the thick dark emblem sweater over the collared shirt all the way down past her wrists. Everyone assumed Tori's wardrobe was a fashion statement, including her mother. That the black sweatshirts she wore regardless of the season was a dark mood she'd eventually grow out of, like her hair. She'd cut it short when she'd started swimming, into a cute blunt bob that fit easily inside her swim cap. But for the last year, she'd kept it cropped close, trimmed tightly around her ears. She dragged her fingers through it, hardly checking if it fell in place.

She headed downstairs and peeked around the door frame into the kitchen. Her mother dug noisily through cabinets in a paint-spattered smock, mumbling to herself about a pan that had been missing since the move. After a while, she gave up trying to find it. She splashed coffee over the sides of her mug while she busied herself making Kyle an overly complicated breakfast of dippy eggs in maple toast. Her mother coddled him too much, making excuses for his bad attitude and the long, silent stretches he spent in front of a game console, saying he was too young to know how to cope with so many transitions after the death of their father a little more than a year ago. But sometimes Tori wondered, however juvenile it might be, if her mother paid Kyle more attention because he was actually *hers*. Tori's parents were convinced they couldn't have children, so they'd arranged to adopt. They *chose* Tori. But then a few years later, much to everyone's surprise, her mom got pregnant with Kyle, and he fit in every way that counted—he had their mother's hair and eyes, and their father's freckles and protruding ears that looked fun and eager on Tori's father's face, but looked a little ridiculous on Kyle. Or at least, they used to. Tori darted a quick glance where he sat at the table, hunched over his hot chocolate, not bothering to look at her. The older he got, the more striking the resemblances.

"Can I make you a plate?" Her mother's spatula hung almost hopefully over the pan. The butter began to sizzle and burn. Her expectation that a change in Tori's breakfast choices, like a change in her hair or clothing choices, might be indicative of an improvement in her mental well-being set Tori's teeth on edge. But she forced herself to smile back, grateful her mother didn't know she'd slept on the front porch.

"No, thanks." She reached up to the top shelf of the pantry for a box of Cheerios and felt her bandages pull. The small effort made her woozy. She poured herself a glass of orange juice, remembering something from eighth grade health class about blood loss and shock, and orange juice being good for that. She sucked it down in four big gulps, then refilled her glass.

They all paused at a hard knock on the door. Tori's mother rushed past, muttering about it being too early for visitors. Tori and Kyle listened from the kitchen as she struggled with the chain.

"Alistair, good of you to drop by," her mother said in an overly cheery voice she usually reserved for people she wasn't sure she liked yet. Alistair Slaughter was their neighbor on every side, and the thing Tori liked least about living here. It was his late father's land they were living on now, a fact Alistair hadn't seemed to come to terms with, given the frequency of his unannounced visits.

Tori peeled back the curtain and saw Jesse Slaughter through the open window of the passenger seat of Alistair's truck. "Good morning, Jesse," her mom called out to him. He looked up and waved at her. His eyes found Tori's through the kitchen window. He pulled the bill of his ball cap lower over his eyes and raised a couple of fingers to her in a half wave, biting back a cocky smile. Tori let the curtain fall closed, feeling the blood rush to her cheeks. "I wasn't expecting company," her mother said.

"Mrs. Burns," Alistair said. "Sorry to interrupt your breakfast."

"Please, call me Sarah."

"I'd rather not." Alistair cleared his throat sharply and continued before Tori's mother could catch her breath to answer. He spoke in a worn, leathery drawl. Even though her family had already been here for a month, the thick, scratchy dialect was still rough against her ears. "Just wanted to let you know that I came by this morning to pick up the last of my father's equipment from the shed. Had to cut the padlock, seeing how you already changed the keys. Anyhow, we're done here . . . for now. Whatever's left behind ain't worth much good, so I guess you'll welcome yourself to it." *Just like everything else* went unspoken, and Tori could picture her mother pursing her lips.

"Thank you."

"There's been a disturbance over in the northwestern field. In the cemetery."

Tori set her glass in the sink and crept into the hall behind her mother.

"Looks like someone dug up a hole. May be just neighborhood kids. But I plan to find out who did it, and when I do, they'll answer for it." Alistair's gaze turned on Tori. She lowered her head at the mention of the cemetery. Did Alistair know she was there last night? Could he have been the one to tie that knot on her arm and leave her on the front porch? Not likely. If he'd found her there, he would have banged down her mother's door and made sure she (and everyone else) knew about it. There wouldn't have been any thoughts on privacy, or polite conversations to spare anyone's feelings. Tori tossed her bangs out of the way and looked the man straight in his eyes. "Anyhow, I figured you probably didn't know. You might want to get down there and take a look."

"Thank you, Alistair. It was very kind of you to come by," her mother said. She moved to shut the door, but Alistair braced it open with the toe of his boot. His pinched smile revealed tightly gritted teeth. Hospitable enough on the surface, but not so welcoming once you got past that.

"I couldn't help but notice you don't have any equipment of your own. How do you plan to fill it?"

Tori's mother tucked an errant curl behind her ear and turned up the wattage on her uncomfortably bright smile. "I appreciate you thinking of us, Alistair, but we're pretty resourceful. I'm sure we'll figure something out."

A muscle ticked in Alistair's jaw. "I'm sure you will," he said crisply. "It's your land. You can do whatever you like with it. For now." He reached into his pocket and handed an envelope to Tori's mother. She hesitated before taking it. With a grumbled good-bye, Alistair plucked at the brim of his hat, and his muddy boots clunked down the porch steps and disappeared into his pickup where Jesse still sat, pretending not to watch them. Rifles hung in a rack across the truck's back window, and as they drove away, Tori had to look through them to see Alistair eyeing her disdainfully in the rearview mirror.

She didn't have to guess what was inside the envelope—probably the monthly land lease payment Alistair had grudgingly agreed to pay them in exchange for letting him farm two of his father's old fields—but Tori's mother didn't open it. Drained of color, she tucked it into her pocket and disappeared into the house without a word.

Alistair was wrong. This wasn't the Burnses' land. The longer they were here, the more Tori was convinced she couldn't possibly be any farther from home.

Tori's mother retreated to her bedroom with Alistair's envelope and closed the door. Alistair might have said he was done here, but Tori didn't believe him. He'd cut her mother's padlock. Had tromped all over her property and raided her shed before her mother could even finish her coffee. And Tori didn't trust him not to keep snooping around, looking for someone to blame for whatever he'd seen in the cemetery that morning.

Tori raced upstairs and tore a sheet of stationery from her desk drawer. Then she scratched out a letter in loopy cursive letters. Scurrying down the stairs, she called out a quick good-bye through her mother's door and chased her brother down the long, gravel driveway to where he waited for the bus.

When she finally caught up with him, she was winded and dizzy and her shoes were soaked through to her socks from all the puddles after last night's rain. She hesitated before giving him the letter.

"What is it?" he asked, eyeing her suspiciously—Tori never rode the bus.

"I'm going to be late. Give this to the attendance office at school." Tori thrust the note she'd forged into his hand. It was written in a close impression of her mother's handwriting and signed, "Sincerely, Sarah Burns," but Kyle didn't look fooled. "If anyone asks, tell them I'm sick."

"Where are you going?"

"None of your business," Tori replied.

Kyle's brow wrinkled. She could see the worry burrowing under his skin. Which made Tori worried too.

"On second thought . . ." She reached to snatch back the letter. "Never mind. It's fine. I'll go to school."

"I can do it," he said.

Tori paused, torn between putting it in her pocket or trusting him not to snitch. "Swear you won't tell Mom?"

"I can keep a secret," he said, trying to look offended. But his brows knit deeper, like maybe he wasn't so sure.

Down the road, the Slaughters' dogs started barking. School bus tires crunched over the gravel toward Tori and Kyle's house, and Tori knew it was too late to take it back. She shoved the letter in Kyle's hand and retreated behind the bushes, out of sight of Mrs. Butts, the driver. The people who lived in Chaptico had too many eyes and ears, and everyone talked too much. Even the bus drivers gathered in the school parking lot every morning to gossip over coffee.

Kyle didn't look back as he climbed the bus steps, and Mrs. Butts pulled away down Slaughter Road, leaving a cloud of exhaust behind her. When the bus was out of sight, Tori texted Drew and Magda, telling them she wouldn't need a ride and hoping neither of them would bother to ask why.

WHY? came Magda's immediate reply.

Headache, Tori texted back, feeling guilty for the lie, even if it wasn't entirely untrue. A pause followed. Tori could picture Magda reading her reply to Drew, who was probably driving and already on his way. She didn't think they'd bother to come to check on her. But just in case, she added, *Going back to bed.*

K. Text us before 2nd if you're feeling better. Drew had study hall during second period, and after he'd signed in, it was easy to slip out unnoticed.

Thx. Tori waited a minute, and when they didn't reply, she circumnavigated her house where her mother's car still sat in the driveway. If she stayed out of sight until her mother left for work, her mother would never know she'd ditched. Her mother called it work. But it wasn't really. Not the kind that paid. She volunteered, teaching painting at the senior citizens' home in town. It gave her something to do, and a long, sterile hallway with crappy lighting where she was allowed to showcase her paintings. For today at least, Tori was glad her mother had somewhere pressing to go.

Tori picked her way through the woods toward the cemetery.

Avoiding her mother wouldn't be hard, but avoiding Alistair might be. The Burnses' twenty acres sat smack in the middle of the two hundred that made up Slaughter Farm, a peculiar tract of land that made little sense to Tori and her mother. The northwest corner was marked by the overgrown field—the giant dead oak and the small cemetery plot. The southwest quarter was densely wooded from the field all the way to the river's shore, sheltering the remains of a few long-abandoned wooden structures that looked like old barns and sheds. The east side of the property was mostly soybean fields, and through an arrangement suggested by Alistair's father in his will, Tori's family was paid a nominal fee each month to continue allowing the Slaughters to farm it. Since Tori's dad had no life insurance and her mother had never worked a paying job outside the home, the monthly check they received from the Slaughters was all that sustained them now. The house, the Burnses were told, was paid for, free and clear. But it didn't feel that way when they had to cross someone else's property just to walk to their own front porch.

When Tori's mother first received the letter from Al Senior's attorney, telling her she'd been granted this strange piece of land, her mother had combed through the will—through every document and letter she could find—searching for an explanation. As far as they knew, their family had no roots in this town. No connection to its people. Why them? Why here? When the Slaughters had so many family members with a rightful claim to it?

And then they'd found it: a clipping of her father's obituary from the *Washington Post*, citing the names of his surviving family members and a request for donations to help support them. Al Senior had included it in a letter to his attorney before he'd died, "bestowing" Tori's mother the property. The house had been a gift. A charitable donation, pure and simple. Al Senior had died less than a week after he'd requested the amendment to his will, before anyone in his family knew what had happened. Before any of them had a chance to argue with him.

Tori followed a thin footpath through the woods and emerged at the edge of the cemetery field. She looked around for signs of Alistair, but it was empty, so she stepped out from the cover of the trees. The dead grass formed a distinct brown ring around the cemetery that crunched under her feet. In the dark last night, she hadn't noticed, but it seemed to reach farther than it had last week. Probably from the cold.

The graves were scattered in a loose circular pattern, as if the old oak was the center of a forgotten clock, the hours marked by headstones around the circumference of its trunk. They leaned in places and heaved up in others, the roots having grown through and around them. Tori could only guess how long the tree had been here by the dates on the stones. The oldest one she could decipher was over a hundred years old, and others . . . probably older . . . had worn so thin, few legible markings remained at all.

As Tori came closer, her toe connected with something hard. She stooped to pick up her flashlight. It was solid and heavy and covered in frost, and the longer Tori held it, the more real her memories of the previous night felt. But they couldn't be real. It was blood loss. She'd been disoriented and dizzy and she'd imagined the entire thing. Hallucination. Plain and simple. It was the only explanation that made any sense.

Tori took another few steps, shaking the flashlight. It was still switched on, but the batteries were dead. When she looked up, it left a smear of blood on her hand as it fell to the ground.

Inside the ring of headstones was a hole.

A large hole. Dirt caved in around the edges, where it looked as if someone had climbed out.

No shovel marks. No tracks left by any farm equipment or digging tools. Just a recess in the ground about as deep as a shallow grave.

She crept to the edge of the hole. The roots of the oak snaked through it like veins.

There was no way . . . no possible way she saw someone crawl out of it. Tori touched her bandage through her sleeve, willing herself to remember tearing her favorite shirt. Desperate to remember herself binding the dressing over the wound. She searched the muddy ground for signs of her own footsteps, impressions of her sneakers pointing toward the house. Proof that she'd walked herself home.

Because if she hadn't done these things, who had?

Tori's breath caught.

A chill snaked up her spine as she knelt over a pair of large, bare footprints in the mud.

The footprints sank deep and clear in the ground. They wound through the cemetery.

Tori followed them, occasionally pausing to pick up the trail where it was lost in wet leaves or around a headstone. The trail disappeared into the trees. Toward her house.

Brush crackled somewhere close and Tori froze.

Her breath came fast, hot anxious puffs against the cold as she searched the tree line for the source of the sound.

And then she saw him.

A young man, standing at the edge of the wood. His long hair fell limp around his face, and two vivid green eyes peered through the tangled strands. He was shirtless, his pants caked with mud and hanging low on his hips. He stared vacantly at the tree, heavy-lidded and swaying.

Tori stood no more than a few yards away, but she couldn't be sure he was even aware of her. Stumbling through the cemetery, he dropped to his knees in front of the oak to the carvings in the trunk—initials in hearts scratched deep into the wood with dates spanning decades. Tori watched as he traced them with shaking, dirt-caked fingertips. Streaks of thick mud covered his shoulders and back and the soles of his bare feet.

Relieved, she choked back a strangled bubble of laughter. She'd come back in the daylight searching for an explanation that made sense, and she'd found it. Whoever this guy was, he was clearly high, or at the very least, mentally ill. She should go. She should call someone. The police? Her mother? Alistair? She wrapped her arms around herself against the cold and held her breath as she walked away, cursing the mud that sucked at the soles of her shoes.

"Is this how it ends, then?" he asked.

Tori nearly tripped when his voice broke the silence. It was low, scratchy and cracked, like maybe he hadn't used it in a long time. Or maybe he'd been crying.

"Who are you?" Tori called back, not wanting to get close. Whoever he was, he was trespassing. She meant to sound authoritative and commanding. But she couldn't seem to find enough air to play the part.

He turned sharply to look at her, his green eyes widening when they found her. They flickered over her, confused.

"This is private property," Tori said, louder this time. "What are you doing here?"

His gaze drifted to a headstone, then another. He touched his throat. "Emmeline," he said in a gravelly voice. "Is she dead?"

Tori had a sinking feeling, like concrete in her belly. Everybody in the cemetery had been dead nearly a hundred years. Some probably longer.

If this Emmeline person was here, whoever this young man thought he was grieving for was long dead by now. Which meant he was sicker than Tori had thought.

Tori shifted from foot to foot, trying to figure out what to do. What to say. But she knew better than most people that there was no right thing to say in a cemetery.

"I think you might be lost."

"Lost?" He wiped his cheek with the back of his arm, smearing mud across his jaw. His green eyes turned on her, incredulous. "I know *exactly* where I am. I spent days chained to this bloody tree. I'd know it blind!"

"Okay." Tori held up her open hands to show she meant no harm. There was a hospital in town, about twenty miles or so from here. Maybe he'd escaped and hidden in the field. Maybe he'd dug himself a hole under a bed of weeds and shallow dirt to keep warm. Maybe she'd startled him last night, and that's why he'd grabbed her. If he was the one who'd put the tourniquet on her arm, maybe he hadn't meant her any harm either. "I believe you," she said in a low, calm voice, the way the nurses had spoken to her the night she'd been admitted the last time she'd cut herself too deeply, when her mother had found her bleeding in the tub. She'd been terrified and confused. She'd wanted to be left alone, and at the same time, she was afraid they actually might.

The young man knelt by a faint inscription in a headstone, touching the dates the way he had touched the carvings in the tree, as if he wasn't sure they were real. Or maybe they were too real. 1885–1935. His brow crumpled. He rose slowly to his feet.

His hand curled into a fist. His shoulders trembled as he looked up into the tree. Tori remained quiet, afraid anything she said might set him off.

"Slaughter once told me the fires of hell burned for each man's individual sins. Is this place to be mine, then? Tell me!" he shouted, as if the tree was actually listening. Tori jumped as he kicked a spray of mud at the trunk. "Leave me to hell! I have no regrets!"

She waited for his tantrum to end, watching silently as he paced before the tree until his shoulders finally slumped, the last of his anger spent.

He sank to the ground and pulled at the dead grass. "Keep quiet, Nathaniel. You mustn't tell, Nathaniel. You'll heal, Nathaniel," he muttered under his breath.

He was definitely crazy. Tori was certain of that. But whoever this boy thought he was, at least he knew *where* he was—Slaughter Farm. Maybe he knew Alistair's family. And if so, maybe they could take him home.

"Do you know who you are?" Tori asked. "Do you know how you got here?"

He looked up at the tree and his eyes clouded over. His voice was brittle and thick. "My name is Nathaniel Bishop. I was murdered on the twenty-first day of September—"

A frustrated laugh slipped out of her.

The boy turned and bit out, "In the year of our Lord, seventeen hundred and six." His eyes were like daggers, steady and unflinching.

He was serious.

The laughter dissolved in Tori's throat. "I think you must be confused. That's just not possible."

He mumbled to himself and scrubbed his hands over his mud-caked hair, letting out a long, resentful sigh. No steam. No white clouds formed from his mouth. And something about that seemed very wrong.

Tori fought back a chill that had nothing to do with the temperature outside. "Aren't you cold?" she asked, recalling the way her swim coach used to nag her about her breathing in the pool, that she was holding it too long. She'd insisted she wasn't, but her exhale—the information hidden within a single breath—always managed to give her away.

The boy's laugh came out as a choked sob and Tori looked sharply to catch the curl of warm air from his lips. But there was nothing to see.

"I asked you a question! Are you cold?"

Nathaniel swallowed hard. His face sobered. "If I am, I don't seem to feel it."

"But that's..." Tori argued with herself—with the crazy, nagging voice at the back of her brain that couldn't seem to just walk away. "Your body is ninety-eight degrees. It's barely forty-five out here. The air should feel cold to you. Your skin should feel warm. And your breath..." She couldn't make herself finish. He was looking at her. The color of his eyes was as impossible to grasp as everything else about him.

His hollow gaze came to rest on the hole behind her. Tori sucked in a breath as Nathaniel stumbled to his feet and stepped close. Close enough for her to catch the faint earthy smell of him as he passed. He stared down into the opening, then at his hands, at the dirt caked under his fingernails.

When he spoke, his voice was hardly more than a whisper. "Dear God, Emmeline. What have you done?"

A low fog rose off the field, the sun warming the wetness and cold from the ground. Alistair would probably come back to investigate the hole like he'd promised. Nathaniel sat on the muddy ground beside it, barefoot and hardly clothed, with his head buried in his hands. If Nathaniel waited here long enough, Alistair would find him. Maybe Alistair would know what to do with him. The way Nathaniel had almost spit the Slaughters' name suggested that might not be a good idea, but Tori didn't know what else to do.

She started to walk away. But after three steps, she swore quietly to herself and turned back. She couldn't leave him alone out here. And given how angry Alistair had been about the hole, she didn't feel right about turning Nathaniel over to him and letting him take the blame either. Alistair said it himself. This was her family's land and she could do whatever she wanted with it. "Do you have a place to go?"

Nathaniel shook his head.

"I'm going home. You can come if you want," she said, before she could change her mind. He looked up at her with those strange, piercing eyes. "Or don't. I don't care." She turned too quickly, almost tripping over a headstone. Then she tromped through the muddy grass, into the deep shadows of the trees between her house and the field, without looking back.

Great. She'd just invited a lost, possibly schizophrenic boy who'd climbed out of a hole in a cemetery to follow her home. Maybe *she* should be the one committed.

She listened for the crackle of his feet behind her rather than check over her shoulder, afraid she might lose the nerve to do the right thing. Nathaniel followed, and she sensed more than heard the falter in his step when the Slaughters' dogs started barking again.

When Tori reached the old wooden toolshed behind the house and opened the door, Nathaniel lingered in the tree line.

The air inside the shed was warm and musty. Dusty sunlight filtered through a tiny skylight, revealing walls of jumbled shelves teeming over with rusty gardening tools and broken farming equipment—all the stuff the Slaughters didn't want and Tori's family would never use—and trails of muddy prints left behind by Alistair's boots. Tori's eye caught on a small carpenter's knife and she wondered if maybe this was a terrible idea, leaving Nathaniel alone in a shed full of sharp objects.

No—if he'd wanted to hurt her, he would have done it last night. She shook off those thoughts and tucked the knife in her hoodie pocket.

"I can't take you inside," Tori called out to Nathaniel where he still waited, standing away from the shed. "My mom's home." That was a lie. Her mother's car was gone. She would already be at work by now, but Tori wasn't sure she wanted him to know that. "You can wait in here. It's warm, at least. I'll be back in a few minutes with some towels and dry clothes for you, but after that I've got to go."

Nathaniel gave a small nod, his face downcast as she turned for the house. "Wait," he said quietly. His expression was heavy as he gestured toward her arm. "You should change the dressing, if you haven't already."

Nathaniel's confession knocked the wind out of her.

Tori gave a small nod back, feeling the outline of the knife in her pocket, unable to meet his eyes as she walked away.

Tori told herself she would make the call to the crisis hotline first, but when she got inside, she ran for the bathroom and locked herself in. She clenched her teeth against the rising wave of panic. The cresting feeling that everything was out of control. She unzipped her hoodie, ripping it off with shaking hands, the carpenter's knife clattering out of the pocket to the floor. She tore open the medicine cabinet and fumbled with the top of the peroxide bottle, pouring half the contents over the blade, waiting impatiently until the bubbles begin to dissipate before yanking up her sleeve. With her thumb, she pressed hard on the gauze, making the cut from last night scream. Then she pressed the tip of the blade just below it, drawing it over the unmarked skin, careful to make a shallow cut that would heal quickly on its own and letting the pain from last night fool her body into quieting itself. Blood seeped through her bandage, and the new slice beside it beaded red.

The pain subsided to a dull ache, and Tori's chest began to loosen. She took a long, deep breath and slid to the floor. It was as if every muscle in her body had been wound to the point of snapping, and suddenly, they'd all let go. She watched the new cut carefully to make sure the bleeding was under control, then she pulled on her hoodie and hid the knife behind the dresser in her room.

She reached for her phone, her hand hovering over the keypad, replaying what Nathaniel had said, her resolve crumbling. Before, calling the hotline and reporting Nathaniel had felt like the right thing to do. Now, it felt more like a betrayal. She bit her lip, checking the time on her phone. A text from Magda was illuminated in a chat bubble on her screen: *Everything okay? Need anything?*

It was almost second period. And she'd kept Nathaniel waiting too long. Tori didn't want him to come to the house looking for her. She felt guilty as she sent a quick text to Drew, asking if he would mind picking her up. She'd hardly known him long enough to expect any favors, but aside from calling her mother at work, she didn't have any other choice. She set down the phone, her mind made up. She'd bring Nathaniel some food, a blanket, and some clothes, and then she'd figure out the rest after school. Maybe Magda would know what to do.

Tori tiptoed through the house, even though it was empty. Her father's clothes were stored in a trunk at the bottom of the guest room closet. When they'd packed for the move, her mom hadn't been ready to get rid of them, and while she pretended to have forgotten them, sometimes Tori thought maybe she wasn't the only one who snuck in here once in a while, just to hold one of his old sweaters.

A musty mothball smell greeted her as she cracked the closet door, and then the subtler scent of her father underneath: leather-bound books and strong black coffee and the fabric softener that still clung to his soft flannel shirts. The scent of chlorine lingered in the soles of his shoes, coaxing memories to the surface of him watching her swim laps with a stopwatch in his hand, cheering for her from the edge of the pool.

Every time she opened this trunk, she was thrown back in time—nine years old again, sitting on his lap in her swim cap, blue-lipped and shivering, wrapped in an oversized towel in his arms, her pruned hands pressed up against his. He called them her fins, and when her face fell and he asked her why, she wondered out loud why he didn't have any. Fingers twined, he pointed out the shape of their knuckles and their nails, the lines in their palms, how similar they were. How they both chewed their cuticles. How they fit perfectly together. And then the memories would fade, like they always did, and he'd be gone and she'd have nothing left to hold on to.

Tori pulled out a pair of khaki cargo pants, a knit button-down, and a large wool sweater, inhaling deeply before folding them into an empty duffel. Then she stuffed in some socks and an old pair of her father's brown loafers. Nathaniel was tall, like her father had been, but his build was long and lean. She tucked a belt in the duffel too. It was discomfiting, the idea of letting a stranger wear her father's clothes, but her dad had been a kind and charitable man. If he had still been alive, she imagined he would have approved.

She grabbed a handful of granola bars from the kitchen and a fresh towel from the linen closet and threw the duffel over her shoulder. Then she returned to the shed, trying to think of something to say. She approached the shed with heavy steps, intentionally snapping twigs. "Nathaniel?" she called out. Slowly, she pushed open the door. He wasn't inside, and part of her was grateful. The other part set the clothes and towel just inside the shed door, hoping he might come back.

LOVE & LOATHING

Emmeline ran to the shoreline, and I paused in the thicket, pretending not to watch her when she reached for the hem of her skirts. I picked at a twig, catching long glimpses out of the corner of my eye as Em stripped the dress over her head, not bothering to fold it before tossing it to the ground. My face grew hot when Ruth caught me staring.

"Come on, then, Ruth!" Emmeline called over her shoulder. Ruth sat far from the shore with her back to the wide waters of the Wicomico River, her long arms curled around her knees, glaring at me. "It will soothe your calluses." Em lowered her voice and grinned at me. "And if we're lucky, perhaps her disposition."

Ruth may have been Emmeline's friend—she'd arrived at Slaughter Plantation a few months before us and had been placed in charge of teaching Emmeline her tasks—but she was also a slave. The rules for her were different, the punishments more severe, and I didn't begrudge her reluctance to join us. And yet, at Emmeline's insistence, she'd followed us here.

"I won't!" Ruth said, hunkering down stubbornly and pulling her feet in close until they were completely hidden beneath her skirts. "Not while that boy's here."

"He's not a boy. He's my brother. Aren't you, Nathaniel?" Em winked at me.

"I am no—"

"Even the master says so," Em said, cutting me off.

"That boy's no more your brother than I am. He looks at you too much," Ruth said, making the blood race to my cheeks. I stared at the ground, pretending to ignore her.

"Nathaniel won't look. Will you, Nathaniel?" Emmeline turned to find me still wearing my trousers, my face growing hot again when she put her hands on her hips and stared at me impatiently. There was nothing to look at. We were hardly eleven, our bodies still lanky and smooth, clumsy and curious. And maybe this, more than the promise of spending time with her, was the reason I had agreed to come. And I disliked Ruth even more for being right about that.

Emmeline huffed to the water's edge, testing it with a toe before leaping in. With a quick glance to make sure Ruth wasn't watching, I yanked off my shirt and trousers and raced in after her, wincing when the salt water found the welts on my backside where Slaughter had ordered me striped for failing to finish my chores the day before.

"Why are you so slow?" Emmeline called over her shoulder, too eager to wait for me.

But I was reluctant to slide in any deeper until the sting wore off. "It burns."

"It will cure you."

"Like a salted fish," I muttered. It was the same thing she'd said right before she'd convinced me to abandon my chores yesterday. Right after I'd told her we were sure to get in trouble. That there wasn't enough salt in my blood. That I was too pure. Too compliant. And that a little rebellion would be good for me. But it wasn't her blood staining the end of that switch. I hadn't seen any stripes on her back through the fabric of her shift.

Suddenly, Emmeline surged forward, the water claiming her narrow shoulders and clinging to the ends of her long, dark hair.

"Wait! You mustn't go too deep!" I called after her. With a careless smile, she sucked in a mouthful of air and held it, her cheeks near to bursting. Then she fell under, her body disappearing into the river.

"Em!" I cried out, rousing Ruth's attention. Behind me, I could hear her scrabble up, her feet rushing through the high, dry grass toward us.

"Where is she?" Ruth asked, a touch of panic in her voice.

"I can't see!" I called back, my heart thundering in my chest. A burst of laughter rang out somewhere in the channel. Emmeline surfaced just long enough for Ruth and me to spot her before filling her lungs full of air and diving under again, making a game of it, wading out a little farther from shore every time until I couldn't follow her.

The cold water reached my chest and I stood on my toes, shivering, wondering what I would do if she went under again and didn't come back up. I reached a foot blindly, feeling for the steep drop-off beneath my toe.

"This isn't funny, Em!" I listened for the sound of her exhale, of her body breaking the surface.

"Of course it is," she laughed, somewhere to my right. When I found her, only her nose and eyes and the top of her head were showing, the rest of her still completely submerged, her shining hair masked by the glitter of the sun against the dark water. Em was so much like the sea—always moving, her moods swinging like the tides.

Ruth looked anxiously over her shoulder, ducking low and waving frantically from the safety of the shore. "Emmeline Bishop!" she yelled through a whisper. "You come out of that water right now! If Thomas catches you—"

"What then?" Emmeline fired back defiantly, unconcerned by her own volume. She rolled over onto her back, moving her arms out to her sides and kicking her feet, sending a spray of water in my direction. Ruth gasped and muttered under her breath, wringing her skirts in her tight little fists.

I grinned in spite of myself. Emmeline had told me she could swim. She had confessed it that first night on the ship, when she suggested we pitch ourselves over the side and take our chances on making it home. And I had only partly believed her. I believed in her willfulness, if not her skill. Everyone knew women didn't swim. Not unless they were possessed by the devil. And no matter how hard I looked at Emmeline, no matter how mischievous and secretive she was, I could never see any real evil in her.

"Show me!" I called out to her. She had been watching Ruth, relishing Ruth's hand-wringing and worrying. But now, Em's face snapped to mine. Suddenly, she was swimming toward me, showing off with long, arched strokes, her arms and legs slicing through the water with great flourishes. Ruth stomped a foot and turned her back to us, returning to sulk on the ground where we'd left her, leaving me blessedly alone with Em. "Teach me," I begged her, thinking only of dragging out the time we had before Ruth made Emmeline return home to their chores.

"Will you trust me?" she asked, her arms paddling the water and the sun kissing her cheeks. I nodded, unthinking. Trusting Em had always been such an impulsive thing, something I couldn't dwell on much, lest I think better of it.

She swam closer, resting a hand beneath the small of my back and giving me a gentle push until I was off my feet, my breath hitching and my eyes wide with alarm, paddling frantically to keep myself above water. "Shhhhhh . . ." she said, quieting me and pressing a hand against my forehead. "Lie back. Put your ears in the water and look at the sun. I won't let anything happen to you." My heart was a flutter of wings, panic, and joy, my body floating, supported by the soft touch of Emmeline's hand.

"Where did you learn to do this?" I asked, euphoric, not caring if she learned from the devil himself. I wanted to swim with her like this every day. In that moment, I was sure I could make it all the way back to Bristol, with just the press of her hand at my back.

"My mother taught me," she said.

"Do you miss her?"

"No," she said through a dismissive laugh. "I talk with her all the time."

I stood on my toes in the water, lifting my chin to keep my mouth from filling up with salt. "What do you mean?" Emmeline was wily, tricky with words. Surely she was only playing with me.

"Precisely what I said. I talk to her all the time. She teaches me all kinds of things."

"Like what?" I demanded to know. "What do you talk about?" I was certain that if I listened hard for the sound of my own mother's voice, my mind would only echo with my own disappointment. Our mothers were gone. Our lives were an ocean away. We were lost to them, and them to us. And no amount of imagining or swimming would bring them any closer. "You're lying!" I said, before I even gave her a chance to answer.

Her face fell, the quiver in her lip teetering between disappointment and anger. "Why would you say such a thing?"

"If you really do talk with your mother all the time, then why hasn't she come for you?" I backed away from her into the shallows, until I could stand. Until I was tall enough to look down on her.

Ruth stirred in the grass behind me. I felt her critical stare.

Emmeline sank away, looking as though I'd slapped her. She didn't even take a breath, diving under the water before the tear in her eye could fall. The sun slipped behind a cloud. And if Emmeline came up for air, it was far enough from both Ruth and me that neither of us were there to see it.

Tori waited for Drew's Mazda in a cluster of trees near the road, poking her head out only when she heard him downshift at the bottom of her driveway. Tori had never taken her driver's test. Her father had been teaching her how to drive, and after he'd died, she'd never got back behind the wheel.

Magda waved from the passenger seat. Magda had Statistics and Probability second period. And Tori guessed that it probably wasn't a class she liked to miss.

"Thanks. I owe you," Tori said, sliding into the backseat. It had been a weird morning, and even though she hated the smell of Drew's car, disappearing inside it was a welcome relief. As usual, Drew's swim bag was in the hatch behind her seat. It reeked of chlorine and bad dreams and the shoes she'd left in the shed. She took a deep breath, trying to ignore it, determined to put last night out of her mind.

"Hope you're not ditching because of me," she said to Magda.

"I'm not ditching. I'm taking an extended bathroom break." She held up a hall pass and then zipped it back into her purse. "We have a substitute today and I was worried about you."

"We were both worried about you," Drew said. "You're still coming to my meet this afternoon, right? You can ride with us. We're leaving right after seventh period."

"I can't," Tori said too quickly, before she had time to come up with a reason. She hadn't shown up to a single practice to watch him since he'd befriended her on her first day at the Academy, and she was running out of excuses. She didn't need to know Drew very well to know why he kept inviting her anyway. There was something about seeing a familiar face at the far end of the pool—the sound of someone calling your name, counting down the seconds until you reached them—that had always pushed her to be better. Stronger. Aside from Magda, Drew didn't seem to have many people in his life cheering for him. And the fact that Tori couldn't even tell them she had been a swimmer, or why she wasn't anymore, after Magda and Drew had tried so hard to help her feel like she fit in here, made her wonder if she deserved either of them. "I'm watching my brother after school," she said, the lie sticking in her throat. "For my mom. She's got something to do. I can take the bus home."

Drew made a face, as if he wasn't sure what was worse—Tori missing the meet, or Tori stuck on the school bus. She definitely didn't deserve them.

"Your loss," Drew said, shaking it off. "I'm taking the fifty yard freestyle in under twenty-two seconds."

Tori couldn't help it—she raised her eyebrows. Drew saw her in the mirror. "No, really. Everyone is going to worship me. They'll all want me to drive their sorry asses to school. But I promise, I won't forget the little people," he said, holding up a royal hand. "I might even need some help carrying my trophy. You can be in my celebrity entourage with Magda. I'll let you both pose with me in my Speedo."

Magda snorted.

"Wish I could be there to see it," Tori told him, shooting for sarcasm and coming up short. Probably because she really wished she could.

Tori looked out the window, watching the stubby cornfields and the yellowing soy plants roll by, the occasional tiny rambler or ramshackle trailer floating like lawn ornaments in the middle of flat, manicured yards. She didn't like lying to Drew. He tended to want to believe the best in people. Even ones he didn't know very well, who weren't always as honest as they should be.

And lying to Magda was just pointless. As far as Tori could tell, she had an uncanny ear for omissions and could smell a lie a mile away. Magda scrutinized Tori over her shoulder, then turned thoughtfully back in her seat.

"I ran into your brother this morning," she said. "He was on his way to the attendance office. With a note." Magda let the statement hang, like she was waiting for Tori to incriminate herself. Magda watched way too many reruns of *Law & Order*, Tori thought. Magda cracked a smile. "You know, a surefire way to get caught breaking the rules is to leave a paper trail, so I took it upon myself to dispose of the evidence for you."

Tori's stomach dropped into her shoes. "What do you mean?"

"I convinced your brother you'd be in a lot less trouble if he gave your little forgery experiment to me. I assume you don't know that the front desk receptionist at the senior center is the attendance secretary's sister?"

Tori cringed and slumped in her seat. That meant her mother would definitely find out Tori wasn't in school. "Is there anyone in this town that isn't related to everybody else?"

Drew snickered.

"You can thank me later," Magda said. "You know, Kyle was kind of adorable. He was so nervous. I think he was afraid he was going to get you in trouble."

"Some accomplice, huh?" Tori muttered.

"I knew it!" Magda said, holding an open hand out to Drew. "You owe me five dollars. I told you she was up to something."

"I'm not up to anything!"

"The need for an accomplice suggests otherwise," Magda said.

"You just cost me a Starbucks, missy." Drew reached into his pocket, keeping one hand on the wheel, and slapped a five-dollar bill in Magda's waiting palm. Some days, watching them banter felt like being a spectator at a Ping-Pong match. They always seemed able to finish each other's thoughts, and she wasn't even sure what she'd done. "Why were you late this morning? No fibbing."

Magda snapped the bill between her fingers and did a victory dance in the front seat.

Tori thought about telling them the truth—that she'd found a homeless, paranoid schizophrenic teenager sleeping in the cemetery, and oh, by the way, what should she do with him? But Magda was on her game today, and she'd probably want to know A) what Tori was doing out there in the middle of the night, and B) why Tori didn't call the hotline to begin with. And as much as Tori wanted to be able to confide in them, she couldn't tell them about the cutting. No one knew about it, aside from her mother and Kyle . . . and now Nathaniel. She liked Magda and Drew, but liking and trusting were two different things. And she hadn't known either of them long enough for that. She needed time to come up with a story that didn't include Tori nearly bleeding to death and the disturbed homeless boy in question dumping her body on the porch.

"There's nothing going on," Tori said, pushing Nathaniel's face out of her mind. "I didn't sleep well last night. Like, hardly at all. And I really did have a headache. I might be coming down with something." Magda threw her a skeptical look, but let her off the hook, shoving the five back at Drew.

The fields gave way to a few small shopping centers the closer they got to school. Clustered at every street corner were small picket signs promoting candidates for the upcoming elections. JACK SLAUGHTER FOR COUNTY COMMISSIONER blared brighter than all the others.

"Someone else was looking for you this morning," Drew said when they pulled up to a stoplight. He was waiting expectantly, like Tori should know the answer, but the only people she hung out with at school were the ones sitting in his car.

"Who?" she asked when he didn't cough up an answer.

"Jesse Slaughter." Drew eyed Tori suggestively in the mirror. "He was waiting at your locker before class. A little birdie tells me he's going to ask you to Homecoming."

Tori thought back to that morning in the kitchen, to the smile he had given her from the passenger seat of his truck, and her stomach did a small flip. She wasn't sure exactly what it meant—the smile *or* her reaction to it.

"Where did you hear that?"

"We overheard it in the cafeteria. People are talking," Magda piped up.

"Whatever you heard, it's not true. Nobody's asked me to Homecoming. It's just a stupid rumor."

Drew shrugged. "You know what they say about a kernel of truth."

"That it doesn't grow in any of the cornfields around here?" Tori muttered. For a small town, people sure came up with big gossip.

"Whatever," Drew said. "I'm shipping you two, and this ship sails on faith."

"I thought he was going out with that girl Lisa," Tori said, determined not to believe him.

Magda scrolled through her phone. "Not according to her Instagram. Looks like Lisa's got a new profile pic, and Jesse isn't in it."

"That doesn't mean anything."

"Not yet," Drew said, swinging the car into an open space near the back of the school. "The rumor mill may exaggerate from time to time, but it sure as heck don't lie."

Tori sat up in her seat. If everyone around here knew something about everybody, then maybe they knew someone who knew Nathaniel. She leaned forward between the seats. "Have you ever heard of someone named Emmeline?"

"You mean the Chaptico Witch? Who hasn't?"

"Obviously Tori hasn't," Magda said. She pivoted in her seat. "It's an old local legend. Why do you want to know?"

Tori ignored her. "How old?"

"Really old. Like three hundred years or something. Apparently she was accused of witchcraft and driven off into the woods, but not before she scared the bejesus out of everybody in town. No one ever saw her again. But that doesn't stop people from talking about her. Everyone loves a good ghost story."

And, apparently, so did Nathaniel. Only he may actually have believed this one was true.

They all climbed out of the car. Drew and Magda locked arms and headed to the side door nearest the gym, which was usually left unlocked for the PE classes.

"Thanks for the ride," Tori called awkwardly behind them. "I'll catch up with you at lunch." She'd have to sign in at the attendance office anyway if she was going to mitigate the damage with her mom. Even so, Tori watched them go with a pang. They fit at the Academy about as well as Tori did. Magda Schiller was a transplant—that's what the locals called people who couldn't trace their lineage back to the area at least two generations—having only moved to Chaptico in kindergarten when her father's law practice moved. She was also the only Jewish kid in their Catholic school. And while Drew had lived in Chaptico all his life, he definitely understood what it felt like to be on the outside at the Academy. Magda said even before Drew knew he was gay, the kids at school knew he was different, and that was enough reason to pick on him. In the short time she'd known him, Drew had always seemed comfortable in his own skin, but that didn't keep the bullies from finding their way under it.

Even though Magda and Drew didn't fit in, they managed to fit together. Which made Tori feel better about being here, but also made her feel a little lonelier somehow.

"*Plessy v. Ferguson.* The answer is *true*," Magda shouted back across the parking lot. Tori turned, startled, and Magda laughed at her puzzled look. "Guess you didn't do the reading assignment last night?"

Oh, shit. The reading assignment. The one she'd planned to do during first period study hall.

"Just trust me," Magda said with a knowing smile as she disappeared into the gym with Drew.

Tori headed to the attendance office and signed in, then slid into her seat in third period History a second after the bell rang and a second before Mr. Harper set a pop quiz down on her desk. Tori's heart stopped. Until she read the first question. *Plessy v. Ferguson.* A single true-or-false question, and a space for a brief opinion essay about why she felt the decision was right or wrong. She sent up a silent thank-you to Magda for bailing her out for the second time that morning.

Then she took out her pencil and wrote her name at the top of the quiz.

Someone kicked the back of her chair, making the *i* run off the edge of the page. Tori turned back to find Lisa's best friend, Kim, head down and focused on the question. But her foot was still resting against Tori's chair leg. A few rows behind her, Lisa was watching. Her lip quivered with a suppressed laugh and she turned back to her paper. Kim snickered into her hand. Tori bit her tongue and turned back to her quiz with Drew's tiny kernel of truth stuck between her teeth.

M agda and Drew left straight for the swim meet after school, and Tori caught the bus home. Kyle was already sitting in one of the front rows, sandwiched between another kid and the window, by the time she climbed in. At first, he looked surprised to see her, but when she paused beside his seat, he quickly turned away, pressing his forehead against the window glass and pretending to ignore her. So she headed down the aisle toward the back of the bus, and claimed an empty seat for herself.

Tori set her backpack on the bench beside her as if she were saving the seat for someone, and sank into the sun-warmed vinyl, her thoughts consumed by the previous night. She chewed on her nail, watching the fields blur past the window, wondering if Nathaniel had come back to the shed. She should have told Magda and Drew the truth. She should have asked Magda what to do. A big part of her hoped Nathaniel was gone. That he'd wandered away into someone else's yard. Because if he hadn't, she would have to face the half-naked, delusional boy waiting for her in her toolshed. And then she'd have to figure out what to do with him.

The bus rolled to a stop; Kyle was out of his seat and scrambling down the steps before the doors were even open. By the time Tori had grabbed her bag and maneuvered down the aisle, her brother was already halfway down the road to their driveway. It didn't use to be like this. They'd been close back in DC. Even closer after their dad had died. Things were weird after he'd caught her cutting and told her mom, just before they'd moved, but he'd still looked at her then. Still talked to her. Still picked fights after school when their mom wasn't around, and made the occasional effort to get under her skin. Even when he was being a royal pain in the ass, she'd always known where she stood with him. But ever since they'd moved, she wasn't so sure anymore.

The bus pulled away, and when the exhaust settled, a flash of white caught Tori's eye. The edges of a flyer stapled to the stop-sign post turned over in the breeze. The word MISSING had been printed below a color photo, and she stepped closer to get a better look at the boy's face. He was familiar in a faraway sort of way she couldn't place, and it left her feeling a little uneasy.

William Slaughter. Thirteen years old. Last seen yesterday morning. The boy was probably one of Jesse's cousins; she felt a pinch of remorse for being grateful that Jesse hadn't been at school that afternoon. He and his cousins had probably been hanging these flyers.

"You that new gal?"

Tori turned. A woman stood hunched on the rickety front porch of an old bungalow across the road. The house sat in the shadow of a large walnut tree, and the roof was sprinkled with dried yellow leaves and wrinkled nutshells. Peeling and splintered, with warped siding and missing shingles, the old place looked as if it could blow to the ground with the next stiff breeze.

"You that gal lives in Al Senior's ol' house?" She pointed a knobby, arthritic finger at Tori.

Since the move, Tori had grown accustomed to greetings that said welcome on the outside and felt more like a rejection in her gut. But the woman on the porch smiled, and it seemed warm and genuine. Her rich umber skin creased deeply around her eyes. Tori felt them focus on her, but she couldn't be sure. They were clouded with a silvery film that matched the woman's thinning tufts of hair.

Tori nodded and kept walking past the lopsided mailbox that said MATILDA RICE.

"I always knew he'd come back." The woman's brittle voice carried through the air.

Tori turned, shielding her eyes from the afternoon sun, uncertain who the woman was speaking to. Matilda Rice stood bowed in the shade of her porch, her clouded eyes watching Tori. She must have seen Tori reading the flyer.

"Did they find him?" Tori called to her.

"That boy," the woman said with a shake of her head, "he wasn't supposed to die like that."

A cold weight settled in Tori's chest. "What?"

The old woman's gap-toothed grin melted into a thin line. She looked hard at Tori. "Emmeline always said that boy would come back. He's got business here. Old business. You mind yourself 'round that Bishop boy. It's dark magic brings him back."

The hairs on the back of Tori's neck prickled as the woman's bent frame disappeared into the house.

* * *

Tori was still standing in the road, staring at Matilda Rice's empty porch, when a big blue pickup truck pulled up alongside her. Jesse rolled down his window. "Hop in. I'll give you a ride home."

Tori turned back toward the direction of her house. It was a long walk to her driveway, and she couldn't think of any excuse to turn him down that wouldn't make her seem rude or ungrateful. With one last look at Matilda's porch, Tori climbed in. The cab was high and she struggled to keep her skirt from riding up. Yanking it back in place, she rested her backpack on her lap. Her eyes slid to Jesse. He wasn't wearing his uniform, just a soft-worn University of Maryland sweatshirt, some muddy work boots, and a faded pair of jeans.

He plucked off his ball cap and brushed his sweat-slicked hair from his forehead with a grin. The bench seat between them was piled with missing-person flyers weighted down with a staple gun. The rear of the cab was full of wooden pickets and election signs with Jack Slaughter's face on them, and a big rubber mallet rattled around in the back. Jesse was driving slower than he normally did on this road, slow enough that the silence seemed to drag out between them. He stretched and relaxed, resting his right arm across the back of the bench seat. Then he threw her a sideways smile and cleared his throat, like he was getting ready to say something.

"I noticed you weren't in History today," Tori blurted before he could gather his thoughts.

The truck lurched over a pothole. Jesse's eyes darkened and he put his hand back on the wheel. "I was hanging flyers with Mitch and my dad."

Tori took one of the flyers from the stack on the seat and studied it, just to have something else to look at other than Jesse or the road. The bright blue shade and shape of Will's eyes reminded her of Jesse. "Is he your cousin?"

Jesse nodded, gripping the wheel. "He didn't come home last night. His teachers said he wasn't in school. Everyone's starting to worry," he said, frowning at the road.

"You can borrow my notes if you want." She backtracked quickly. "I mean, they're probably not that good."

"No, that'd be great." Jesse smiled, bigger this time, his dimple cutting into his sun-kissed cheek. Not the fake-bake people wore in the city. Jesse's tan was warm and uneven from hours spent outside. Tori quickly looked away. "I can use all the help I can get. That last test killed me." He took the bend in the road even slower, and Tori felt his eyes skip from the road to her face a few times. "What happened to your friends? I thought you usually catch a ride home."

"Drew had a swim meet today. And I had . . . something I needed to do," she added awkwardly.

"You must be pretty busy. I never see you around on the weekends much. You probably go back home to visit your friends?"

Tori ignored the sting. She didn't keep in touch with anyone back home. They'd all stopped calling even before she'd left. And this—this pitted dirt road winding through Slaughter Farm—was home now. "I haven't been back to DC. Not since we moved."

Jesse's brow lifted. "You don't miss it?"

Tori shook her head. It was easier than trying to explain that going back wouldn't bring her any closer to what she missed most.

"I'd probably be up there every week if I were you. One more year," he said, his foot on the accelerator hinting at his eagerness. "One more year and I can get out of here."

"You? Why would you want to get out of here?" Tori asked, not bothering to mask her surprise. Jesse raised an eyebrow and looked at her sideways. "I mean, you've got so many friends and family here." *You've got everything*, is what she'd wanted to say.

Jesse shrugged. "Sometimes there's a lot of pressure being part of a big family. I mean, how are you supposed to figure out who you want to be when everyone's trying to tell you who you are?"

"What do you want to be?" she asked, curious about this side of Jesse she'd never seen.

"I don't know," he said, thinking. "I want to go to college. Preferably someplace where nobody knows me." Jesse stared out the windshield with a faraway look. And something about that made her feel a little closer to him.

He eased to a stop in front of the cluster of mailboxes across from Tori's driveway, and Tori threw open the door. "Thanks for the ride." She slid off the bench and shut the cab. But his truck didn't pull away. Instead, Jesse killed the engine and got out.

"Hey, Tori. Wait." He crossed to her side, and Tori tried to think of some polite way to excuse herself before he could ask her anything else.

He stood in front of her next to the mailboxes, his hands jammed in the pockets of his jeans. He raked his hands through his hair and flashed her a dimpled smile.

"I heard you don't have a date to the Homecoming dance," he said, cocking an eyebrow. "I thought maybe you'd want to go with me." Tori opened her mouth to speak, but seeing the look on Tori's face, Jesse added, "It'll be fun. I promise. Bobby's girlfriend's parents are renting us a limo, and a bunch of us are riding together—"

Her palms were sweaty around the straps of her backpack, and her pulse felt quick. "Can I think about it?"

Jesse looked confused. "Sure." He nodded, rocking back on his heels and scratching his head. "Sure, I guess you probably need to check your schedule. Or ask your mom or something."

Tori gave a noncommittal nod. They stood there for a minute, not saying anything. Finally, Jesse turned and opened his family's mailbox. Feeling stupid for still standing there, Tori turned and opened hers too. Beside her, Jesse thumbed through a stack of letters. Something in the shift of his posture made Tori glance up at the envelope in his hand. University of Maryland Office of Student Financial Aid. It was thin.

He folded it into his pocket without opening it, as if he already knew what was inside. "I'll see you around," he said stiffly. Without looking at her, he climbed into his truck and drove away.

THE BELLOWS

Emmeline and Ruth were bent close together, giggling softly when I entered the scullery, my arms laden with kindling for the fire. I dumped it beside the hearth, startling them so their heads snapped up, eyes wide with surprise.

"What are you doing?" I asked, angling to see what they were hiding behind their backs.

The mangy gray cat that had hugged Emmeline's heels since we'd arrived here weaved around her back, peering out from under her arm at me. "That's none of your concern," Emmeline teased, jutting her chin high and looking down her nose at me with an air of authority, even though I was the one who was standing up. Being six months my elder, she had already turned twelve, and lately she refused to let me forget it. "It's a secret," she said, winking at Ruth. I made a fast reach behind Emmeline's shoulder, startling the cat and snatching the small wooden figure from her hands. Em swatted and grabbed as I held it away from her, examining it over her head while she took only half-serious swings at me. It was a carving, a small doll with a sullen face and high cheekbones and a narrow chin that looked uncomfortably familiar. I turned it over in my hand. There were small puncture holes in the doll's back. "It looks like Missus Slaughter," I said, narrowing my eyes at them both. "What are you playing at?"

They fell upon each other in a fit of giggles, and the cat darted out the door.

"What's going on in here?" a stern voice called from the pathway to the scullery. Emmeline and Ruth scrambled to their feet. In a panic, I tossed the doll into the fire, not a second before Elizabeth Slaughter darkened the door of the room. Ruth covered her mouth, stifling a gasp. Her other hand searched blindly for Emmeline's, their fingers barely touching behind their skirts.

"You shouldn't have done that," Ruth whispered, her eyes wide with fear.

I turned to face Mrs. Slaughter, brushing my hands together. "I was just delivering the wood, ma'am."

She pushed me aside, her gaze hard on Emmeline and Ruth. "I asked you a question," she snapped at them.

"We've just finished the washing, ma'am," Emmeline said, a hint of bitterness on her tongue. Mrs. Slaughter surveyed the work, and finding nothing to criticize, she said, "Then go tend to the master's study."

"Yes, ma'am." Emmeline started for the door.

"No," Mrs. Slaughter said, with a sharp and pointed look that froze Emmeline where she stood. "Ruth will do it. You will stay here and work on the mending. When you're finished with that, you can feed the hounds." Mrs. Slaughter turned and paused at the door. "But not too much, mind you. My husband plans to hunt this afternoon."

Ruth squeezed Emmeline's hand behind her skirt, then hurried off to the study. Mrs. Slaughter braced herself in the doorway, one hand on the wooden frame and one hand clutching her lower back, as if she had a crick in it. Emmeline's shrewd gray eyes fixed on her. A bead of sweat slid down Mrs. Slaughter's face.

"You, boy," she said without looking at me. "Come and walk me to the house. I'm unwell."

I took Mrs. Slaughter's arm and walked her slowly through the door, risking a glance backward at Emmeline. She had turned to the fire, reaching desperately for the hearth tools. I prayed she would use the tongs to fish the doll from the flames. Instead, she took up the bellows and began fanning them.

SOMETHING BROKEN

ori walked up the front porch steps like she always did after school, inadvertently scanning for an eviction notice taped to the door. She'd been the one to come home and find the notice from the sheriff, ordering them to vacate their apartment, and even though they'd moved someplace new—and the house was unequivocally supposed to belong to her mother and not a bank—she didn't necessarily feel any more secure.

She pushed open the farmhouse door and dumped the mail on the hall table. The TV in the living room was on so loud, she suspected Kyle hadn't heard her come in. He slouched low on the sofa, all she could see was the top of her brother's head. Even when she slammed the door harder than usual, he still didn't bother to move. She kicked off her shoes and ran upstairs, ready to change out of her uniform and head to the shed to see if Nathaniel was still there. But when she reached the top of the stairs, the abrupt drop in temperature sent a shiver up her spine.

The hair rose on the back of her neck as she approached her bedroom door. She remembered the sheen of frost that had covered her window when she'd left for school that morning. She knew she'd closed it. Creeping closer, she threw open the door and scanned her room. Her window was shut, the curtains still, and the radiator ticked quietly on the far wall. She dumped her backpack on the floor and walked slowly down the hall, pushing open her brother's door. His room, as usual, was a complete disaster. Toys and graphic novels and clothes piled everywhere.

But her mother's . . .

Her mother's curtains snapped in the breeze, sunlight catching the broken glass scattered across the hardwood. Her closet door was cracked, a dresser drawer slightly open, and the stack of magazines and books on her nightstand beside the window was toppled across the floor. Tori checked inside her mother's closet. Her mother's winter clothes hung neatly, her spring clothes still packed in taped, marked boxes, unopened since before they'd moved. Nothing appeared to be missing or out of place, but she couldn't be sure.

Tori moved to the open window. A single pane was broken, the one closest to the lock. A trail of red clay shoe prints cut across the black asphalt shingles on the roof of the front porch below it, and the aluminum rain gutter was dented where somebody must have climbed over it, catching it with a foot. The mulberry tree at the corner of the house stretched a sturdy arm over the porch, littering the roof with brightly colored leaves and broken twigs and smaller branches that had been shaken loose.

Someone had climbed the tree to the porch. They'd broken the window and let themselves in.

Tori felt sick. Nathaniel. Nathaniel must have done this. What had she been thinking, letting him stay?

Tori looked around the room, trying to see it anew . . . the way he would have. Her mother's bed was rumpled, but that was nothing new. Her mother never made it in the morning before she left for work. And, even on her second scan of the room, Tori didn't think anything was gone. Maybe he hadn't stolen anything. Maybe Nathaniel had only wanted a warm place to sleep.

Tori quickly changed out of her uniform into a pair of jeans and returned to her mother's room to sweep up the glass. She duct-taped a plastic trash bag and some cardboard over the broken pane before her mother could get home and see it, struggling to come up with a story. A branch must have blown in. She would tell her mother that's how it broke. Her skin crawled at the thought of a stranger creeping around in her mother's room. But if she reported it, she'd have to explain to the police (and her mother) how she knew Nathaniel, why she'd given a complete stranger a duffel bag of bedding and clothes, and why she'd invited him to her house to begin with.

She finished cleaning up the mess, then set out to find Nathaniel herself.

●   ●   ●

When Tori arrived at the shed, the duffel bag she'd left for Nathaniel that morning was gone, and the pillow and blanket were missing. The muddy boot prints Alistair had left behind on the floorboards earlier that morning hadn't been disturbed. Wherever Nathaniel had spent the day, it hadn't been in here.

A freshly trodden path cut through the rustling grass, leading to the river—away from the road or the cemetery. She followed it, trying to keep her feet quiet and her unease at bay, until the trail became a narrow swath through the underbrush in the trees.

A soft splashing sound reached her. Through the branches, sunlight shimmered on the river and Tori peered out, keeping herself hidden.

An oddly disquieting feeling passed through her as she looked down the tangled slope of the riverbank. Not the usual anxiety she felt when she was close to the water. This was more like déjà vu, the sight of the river dredging up vague impressions of her dream last night, then pushing them back down again, just below the surface.

Careful not to get too close, Tori followed the jagged shoreline until her shoulder caught on something heavy and wet—a pair of drenched, dripping pants, slung over a sapling to dry. On the ground beside it, her duffel bag lay open. The pillow and blanket were gone. He must have taken them someplace else. Maybe he'd camped in the woods. She knelt and searched inside the duffel, looking for anything he might have taken from her house, but all she found were the towel and clothes, still folded exactly as she'd left them. She took out her father's shoes, but the soles were clean. And the only thing in the duffel she hadn't put inside it herself was a small wooden figurine. She turned it over in her hand. It was old, roughly cut. The contours of a woman in a bell-shaped dress. She worried it between her fingers.

If Nathaniel hadn't climbed her porch and broken into her house, then who had?

Tori turned at a close splash, dropping the figurine. Nathaniel stood, waist-deep in the murky green river with his back to the shore, throwing handfuls of water over his face. Tori watched, feeling the familiar swell of panic in her chest as he dove under and kicked toward deeper water. She closed her eyes, but all she saw were flashes of her nightmares. Being pulled down below the surface.

Instead, she focused her thoughts. Focused on his stroke. The mechanics of staying afloat.

Nathaniel had the lean, muscular body of a swimmer, but the movements weren't precise enough to be anything other than self-taught. Even with his height, she could have lapped him without much effort.

She hated herself for standing there, far from the edge of the shore, struggling to breathe, counting his strokes, clutching a bag of her father's things. The rhythm of his breaststroke was a niggling earworm she couldn't make herself tune out as he got closer to shore. She set the duffel down and fished the towel from it, prepared to announce herself.

Nathaniel paused, standing in the waist-deep water to watch an oyster boat motoring upriver with its haul. It sliced through the glassy surface. As he stared after it, water rolled down his back. The layers of mud had all washed away, but the streaks were still there.

Only they weren't streaks at all.

Thick, raised scars cut across his skin, crisscrossing the width of his back and disappearing under the water around his waist. When he turned back toward shore, she saw another scar, circling his throat.

Suddenly Nathaniel yelped and jolted, making Tori flinch. He brought up his knee and hobbled toward shore to sit in the shallows. Cradling his foot just beneath the water, he pulled a shard of glass from his heel. As he inspected the wound, his spine stiffened. Whatever the damage, Tori knew it wasn't good. The shard Nathaniel held was sharp and clear as he lifted it against the light, turning it this way and that. Then, before Tori knew what was happening, he pressed the point of it against his palm and dragged it hard across his hand.

Tori didn't move. Didn't breathe. She felt like she was standing outside her own bathroom door, and she wasn't sure she wanted to be the one to open it.

Nathaniel stroked the cut with his thumb, and even from where she stood, she could see his hands shaking. Then he raised the shard again, jaw clenched as he pressed it to his . . .

Tori stumbled out of the thicket.

Nathaniel dropped the shard and scrambled naked to his feet. She covered her eyes and thrust the towel in his direction.

"I'm sorry. I didn't mean to scare you," she said.

For a moment, everything was silent. Then she heard the soft splash of his feet, and the crunch of roots as he climbed the bank. He ripped the towel from her hand, and she waited a moment longer before blinking her eyes open.

Nathaniel stood close to the river's edge with the towel around his waist, clutching it in place with one hand and hiding the other behind his back. As they stared at each other, Tori could name every emotion that crossed his face. Fear. Shame. Humiliation.

"Are you okay?" She stepped closer.

"It's nothing."

"You're hurt." She leaned toward him, straining to see without getting too close. He angled away from her. But she was here now. She'd seen him. And there was no taking that back. "Look, you did the same for me. At least let me repay the favor." She reached for his arm, catching a glimpse of the clean, deep slice in Nathaniel's palm. He snatched it away, making a tight fist so all she could see was a scar in the shape of a *T* at the base of his thumb. It reminded Tori of the *s*'s branded on the ears of Alistair Slaughter's cows, and the sight of it stole her breath. "You have a lot of scars."

"So do you," he said sharply. It was the same way she'd talked to her brother when she'd come home from the hospital. Like her shame had teeth.

"Please. Let me see," she said, firmly this time. His lashes were wet and dark, and against them, his irises were a shade of green common in nature, yet completely unnatural in the context of a human face. Her mouth went dry under his stare.

She took his hand, grateful for an excuse to look away. It was cold and pale, reluctant to open. She peeled back his fingers. They were as thickly calloused as the hands of every farmer she'd met here, but long and delicate, like an artist's or a musician's.

"I'm fine . . ." he said. But there was a tremor in his voice.

Tori held fast to his hand when he tried to pull away. The palm should have been dripping with blood, but there was none. None at all. Instead, a shallow cut seeped a sticky, clear-gold fluid. Tori's breath caught. As she watched, the wound—smaller than it had been a moment ago—knitted itself closed, the skin on both sides sealing together until a faint pink line and the sticky yellow residue it left behind were all that remained.

Tori looked up at him, eye-level with the marks on his neck. Close enough to see the impression of a rope. His eyes were wide and terrified.

It's dark magic brings him back.

Skin crawling, she scrambled away from him and took a deep, unsteady breath, wiping her hands on her jeans. But the sticky fluid wouldn't wipe away. Instead, it grabbed at her clothes.

"Who are you?"

"I already told you."

"Then *what* are you?"

"I don't know!"

Nathaniel blinked back angry tears. He eased away from her, darting desperate glances into the woods.

Tori risked a quick look at her fingertips. Her thumb and index finger stuck together, reluctant to pull apart. One eye on Nathaniel, she lifted a finger cautiously to her nose. No coppery tang. It was earthy and woody, and faintly sweet. Familiar. She backed slowly toward the tree line, to the trunk of a maple, careful not to turn her back to him as she reached to touch a trail of shimmering yellow beads. They morphed into stringy webs when she pulled away, the same color and texture of the blood on her hands.

"You bleed sap," Tori whispered. "How is that possible?"

Nathaniel swallowed. He snatched the wooden figure from the ground and held it, guarded against his chest, every muscle in his body poised as if ready to run.

Emmeline always said that boy would come back.

"Is that her . . . Emmeline?" It felt ridiculous to ask this out loud, to acknowledge that any bit of his story might be true. But after what Matilda

Rice had said . . . after what Tori had just witnessed, it felt more foolish not to.

Nathaniel glared at her. Tori was afraid of him. Afraid of what she had just seen happen to him. But she was more afraid of what she might say. That the wrong question might scare him away.

"Who is she?" she asked. He stroked the wooden doll absently with his thumb. "Is Emmeline a friend?" She waited through a silent pause. "A girlfriend? Your sister?"

"She's no one of concern to you." Nathaniel's expression hardened, as if Tori had overstepped some boundary. Definitely a girlfriend, Tori thought. And definitely time to change the subject.

"Where did you go?" she asked. "I went to the shed after school. I couldn't find you." At this, he risked a quick look at her face, but didn't answer. His jaw clenched and his eyes flicked to his pants, still dripping from the branch nearby.

She tossed him her father's khakis and shirt, and he caught them against his stomach with a look of surprise. Tori turned her back to him, sneaking just one glance as Nathaniel pulled the shirt over the tangle of scars on his back. His chest was smooth with the exception of the mark at his throat. She looked away again.

"You're wearing trousers." His voice was low and steady, but his hands were shaky on the buttons of the shirt when she faced him again.

"So?"

He picked up the towel and rubbed it over his wet hair, watching her sideways. "It's the kind of thing Emmeline would do. She'd wear trousers and swim the river every day if—"

"I don't swim," Tori said sharply, cutting him off.

"Don't you, then . . . ?" His voice trailed off and he looked hard in her eyes, like he could see the lie inside them. He rubbed the towel over his hair again. "My apologies. It's just that you remind me of her. Last night, in the dark, I imagined..." Something in Tori's face made him abandon his thought. "Forgive me," he said with a glance at her arm. "I hope I didn't hurt you."

She tugged at her sleeve, remembering the relentless grip of his hand, the bruises it had left on her wrist when she'd pulled him out of the dirt. "I'm fine," she said, trying to mask a shudder. "You didn't hurt me."

Before she could think to stop him, he reached for her arm and gently pulled up her sleeve. Tori winced as the fabric chafed the fresh cut. The crease in Nathaniel's brow deepened as he opened his mouth to speak, then shut it again. Tori jerked her arm away, wondering how many lines he'd been able to see.

"This has happened before?"

"It's none of your business!" She tugged her sleeve back in place.

He reached again, this time for her pocket.

"Hey!" Tori snapped, sidestepping away. She threw her father's sweater at his face and he caught it with a pained expression. She felt the heat flood her cheeks as he stared at her.

"The knife you took from the shed," he said softly. "I thought you took it because you were afraid of me."

"Maybe I did."

"Then why isn't it in your pocket?"

Tori turned and reached for the duffel. Nathaniel caught her wrist. "Is that what you were doing last night, when I found you? Is that how...?" He leaned down until she had no choice but to look him in the eyes. They were piercing and bright, and they cut right through her. When she didn't answer, he released her.

She took a step away from him. "You won't tell anyone?" she asked brusquely.

He thought about that for a moment. "I would ask you the same."

"Are you hiding from someone?" She looked pointedly at the scar around his throat.

"I'm..." He touched it as though she'd brought up a painful memory. "It is as you said before. I'm...lost. And I'd rather no one know I'm here. Not yet anyway."

Tori nodded, because on some level she understood. And because he had left her little choice. Nathaniel was hiding a very big secret—but he wasn't the only one. Nathaniel knew the Slaughters. The Slaughters knew her mother. If her mother found out Tori had been cutting, then she would end up back in therapy. Or worse. He was offering her a bargain. Her silence for his.

Nathaniel looked down at his bare feet. Then at the shoes Tori had lent him. "I haven't even asked your name."

"Tori." Her voice cracked. "Tori Burns."

"Burns," he said, as if he was rolling it around in his mind for some sign of recognition. He pulled the sweater over his head. "I saw it on the sign posted outside your home, and I wondered..." Tori felt the blood rush back to her cheeks. "I had you mistaken for a Slaughter."

Tori choked out a harsh laugh. "No, I am most definitely *not* a Slaughter."

"Then I like you better already." His smile was tentative, shy and curious. And maybe it was nerves, but Tori couldn't help but smile a little too.

"Are they gone, then?" he asked.

Tori was still lost in thought, and it took her a second to figure out what he was asking. "The Slaughters? No, they own everything past our property."

Nathaniel sobered. "The cemetery?" he asked in a rough voice.

"No, that's ours now. Our land runs all the way to the edge of the field." Tori paused. "How do you know them?"

He bent, thoughtful as he wiped the mud from his feet before pulling on the socks and slipping into her father's shoes. "We had an arrangement once. A contract the Slaughters failed to honor. It's nothing you need concern yourself with."

But everything about this concerned her. Her mother had an arrangement with Alistair Slaughter. Their house and their income was part of that contract. And even though the lawyers insisted that it belonged to her family, no strings attached, it felt like they were living on borrowed land. She worried that somehow, one day, the Slaughters would pull this rug of soybeans and cornfields right out from under them, leaving them homeless in a town that had never wanted them anyway. And if Nathaniel didn't trust the Slaughters, she wanted to know why.

They both turned at the distant bark of Slaughter's dogs.

Nathaniel swallowed hard, his eyes searching for the source of the sound.

"Come on," Tori said, a strange foreboding in her chest. Nathaniel didn't belong here. He shouldn't be here. And she didn't want to think about what Alistair Slaughter might do if he found him.

HIDDEN IN THE BARN

Tori led Nathaniel back toward the shed, unsure where else to take him. Nathaniel, careful to stay a few paces behind her at first, now ambled beside her, his eyes downcast. They walked for a while, the crackle of brush and twigs under their feet filling the silence. At a break in the path, he paused.

"What is it?"

Nathaniel hesitated. Then he pointed off in a different direction, into a tangled stretch of wood Tori had never ventured into before, dark and thick with ivy and brambles. Through the trees, she could just make out a thin crushed path in the underbrush.

"Is this . . . Is this where you were today? In there?"

He nodded and took the lead into the woods, his long legs navigating the path effortlessly.

Tori leaned on her knees, breathless from the walk, her duffel flopping off her shoulder as he began to fade from view. She was out of shape. But more than that, she was out of her mind to consider following him. The shed was safe. Close to the house and exposed on all sides, sitting in plain view.

Which was probably why Nathaniel had chosen this route.

Tori whispered a swear and trudged into the trees after him, following the soft sounds of his feet and the narrow trail left behind by her father's shoes. She pushed the low branches from her face, the brambles snagging and pulling at her stockings. Up ahead, a structure emerged through the trees.

The old tobacco barn was hidden deep in the woods, overgrown with ivy and buried in a dense thicket. It resembled a toothless old man, the wood siding aged to a smoky gray and riddled with gaping holes. Nathaniel opened the door, which creaked and groaned on rusted hinges. Inside, the walls seemed mostly sturdy and the dirt floor mostly dry. The pillow and blanket Tori had given him rested in a bed of leaves and straw, and a small ring of stones circled a stack of kindling under a jagged hole in the roof.

"It's perfect," Tori said, almost to herself as she eased her duffel to the floor. The air inside was warmer, shielded from the wind. She peeled off her sweater and tossed it beside the bag, comfortable in the collared shirt she wore underneath. There was no lock on the door, but there might as well have been. She couldn't see her house from here. Couldn't hear the road. The only sounds were the caws of crows and the chittering of squirrels. They were so far into the woods, she wasn't even sure they were still on her property. "How did you know this was here?" The barn was old. At least fifty years. But nowhere near as old as Nathaniel claimed to be.

"I got lost," he said with a sheepish grin.

"That's a bit of an understatement."

At this, he laughed a little. And Tori couldn't help but smile too.

"Just don't wander too close to the house. My mom will be home soon, and she can't see you in my dad's old clothes or she'll have a total meltdown. I'll try to find you something else from the lost and found at school tomorrow."

Nathaniel looked down at the clothes and shoes, abashed. "Perhaps it would be best if I go."

"Don't worry. My mom's never stepped foot in the woods. She's not exactly the outdoorsy type."

"I'm a runaway servant. A squatter at best. Surely your father—"

"My dad's not here." It stung to say it out loud, like pouring peroxide in an open wound. "It's no big deal." Tori turned her back, pretending to check out the rest of the barn to keep from having to talk about her dad anymore. "Why did you call yourself a servant?"

"I am. . . ." He paused, adjusting the neck of the shirt, but it wasn't high enough to conceal the marks on his throat. "I was a redemptioner." At the puzzled look on Tori's face, he added, "A laborer, indentured to a man named Archibald Slaughter. It was supposed to be a seven-year contract. We were barely ten when we were taken from Bristol and sold to the ship. We had nearly finished our term, Emmeline and I." His brows knitted together and his eyes took on a faraway look. "We were to have ten acres each plus provisions, but our papers. . ." His voice drifted off, leaving a heavy silence in the room.

"Thank you," he said too softly.

"For what?"

"You've been very kind to me."

A wave of guilt rolled through her. She looked around the dusty barn, at the cobwebs in the rafters and the thin blanket on the floor. None of this felt kind.

"Are you hungry? Can I get you something to eat?"

He shook his head and turned his eyes to the floor.

"What about more blankets? You might get cold."

"I won't get cold," he reassured her with a sad smile.

She fought the urge to smile back. Maybe it was hysteria. Maybe it was fatigue. But the more she tried not to, the wider it grew. "Is there anything you *do* need?"

"Maybe . . ." He paused. "Maybe you could stay for a while?"

Something in his expression felt so lonely. So utterly lost. The way

Tori had looked in the mirror in that awful pink bedroom, the day she'd moved into the house on Slaughter Road.

Tori sat down beside him on the blanket, just close enough to be polite. She wrapped her arms around herself, her nerves still crawling whenever she thought about the sap under his skin. For a while, neither of them spoke, but then the silence grew too awkward.

Nathaniel opened his hand. The faint pink line was gone, and the earbuds Tori had lost in the cemetery lay curled in his palm. "I found these. After I carried you home." Tori took them from him, and Nathaniel looked down at the empty space they left, rubbing the strange scar beneath his thumb.

He reached back for the earbuds and she felt her breath catch at the cold brush of his fingers. "What is this?" he asked.

She fished her phone from her pocket and plugged in the headphones. Then she reached up awkwardly to put the earbuds around him. Even sitting, he was tall. She barely reached his shoulders, and he hunched toward her with a cautious expression as she tucked the buds in his ears.

She pushed the PLAY button and watched his face. Sitting this close, when he was so still, she noticed all the little details she had missed before. The hints of gold and copper in his hair, and the strong cut of his jaw. After a moment, Nathaniel's nose scrunched up. There was a small knot at the bridge where maybe it had been broken before. He braced his hands over his ears.

"What is it?"

"It's music."

"You call this music?" He plucked out the buds and held them out to her, the faint, tinny sound still playing in his hand. Tori looked at the screen.

"Hey," she said, a little defensively. "This song is timeless."

Nathaniel rubbed his ears. "I was acquainted with an Irishman once. His wife wailed like a banshee at funerals. It was a bit less terrifying than this."

"Oh yeah?" Tori snatched the earbuds away and tucked them in her pocket. "What kind of music do you like?" She hadn't realized they were sitting shoulder to shoulder until he turned, his face suddenly close to hers.

"Give me a fiddle, and I'll show you." His eyes were gleaming and eager, more hopeful than she'd seen them since they'd met. It felt like a challenge, to give him a reason to smile.

"Maybe I will."

His eyes drifted to her lips. And for a moment, Tori forgot to breathe. She cleared her throat and leaped to her feet.

"I should probably go. I've got a ton of studying to do and my mom's probably wondering where I am. She'll have a fit if I miss dinner."

Nathaniel stood up slowly and followed her to the barn door.

"I'll come back after school tomorrow . . . to see if you need anything . . . if you want me to."

"I'd like that," he said quietly. And before she could look at his face again, she turned and ran out the door.

THE BLOOD WE BLEED

We were thirteen years old when I knew in my heart I had lost Emmeline. She had outgrown me. Not because she was six months older (as she'd always claimed), or necessarily any wiser. Not because she didn't still enjoy sneaking off to the river on Sundays to pick wild berries and torment the crabs that burrowed in the mud. But for the simple fact that her body had conspired against us.

It seemed to me that womanhood was a certainty. An event that was thrust upon her, leaving no room for questions of readiness or consent. Whereas manhood—the milestones that marked it—remained elusive and unclear.

I remember it so clearly. It was a crisp and perfect day, and the sweet aroma of corn pudding carried on a cool breeze. I was always hungry then, it seemed, my rations of salt fish and porridge never quite curbing an appetite that had grown as unmanageable as my bones. Thomas had assigned me the task of delivering firewood to the kitchen. The missus was host to a party that night, and preparations were already underway. I was grateful for the excuse to see Em there, where she'd sometimes been known to sneak me a biscuit or some other rare treat.

I peeked my head inside, savoring the scent of scalding oysters, roasting beef, and the fresh bread baking over the fire. Em and Ruth were too busy to notice me at first. Em looked lovely—not at all like the filthy, tangled girl who'd come off the ship from Bristol. She was freshly bathed, her clean hair tied back in a bright white-laced cap, a few silky black curls having fallen loose and trailing over the shoulder of a cornflower-blue dress I'd never seen her wear before. Probably for the party. Mrs. Slaughter liked her house servants to "be presentable," she often said. Which is why I was never permitted in the main house during such events.

I snuck quietly inside, resting two armfuls of kindling and wood beside the hearth. Then I snatched at a chunk of carrot from the pile of vegetables on the table. Em slapped my hand before I could grab it, leaving a bright red mark.

"Nathaniel Bishop! Don't you dare!" she scolded. "Your hands are filthy!"

"Aye? Well... so's your dress!" I snapped back, grabbing a warm piece of bread where it rested near the window, simply to spite her. I hadn't planned to say anything about the stain on her dress. But if she was handing out insults, I was happy to repay her.

Em put her hands on her hips and scowled at me, her cheeks flushed pink with anger, which only made her look more lovely. Which only made me feel filthier by comparison.

"What's that supposed to mean?" she barked.

Suddenly, Ruth froze behind her with a small gasp. She turned on me, pushing me toward the door.

"Shoo!" Ruth whispered harshly, waving me away. But I wouldn't be dismissed from my duties by a house slave, and certainly not by a girl. I stood my ground beside the door, my filthy hands folded under my arms around fistfuls of cooling bread. Emmeline looked down at her skirts, her lip trembling.

Ruth inspected the small rust brown stain spreading through the fabric. "Oh, your dress..." she said softly.

"What have I done?" Em whispered, a tear brimming over as she looked over the surfaces of the tables at all of the food she'd been preparing, as if searching for the source of the stain. Her face paled and she clutched at her stomach. "Mrs. Slaughter...She'll be furious...."

"You're bleeding, is all. Go on and take care of it. I'll stay and mind the kitchen."

"Bleeding?" Em said, looking down on herself with such an expression of horror and disbelief that I immediately regretted bringing the stain to her attention. A sudden understanding seemed to dawn on Ruth's face, which made me feel all the more confused. She placed a hand on Em's shoulder and looked around with worry at the half-chopped vegetables and half-baked bread and the cooling corn pudding that had yet to be stirred.

"Are you hurt?" I asked, watching helplessly as a tear spilled down Emmeline's cheek and Ruth rushed to cover the puddings and take the unfinished bread from the fire. "Should I call for the missus?"

"No!" they both shouted in unison, their heads snapping to me. Ruth pointed a hard finger at the door. "Out with you. Go on!" she commanded me. "This is no place for a boy." Then she turned to Emmeline and whispered in a low, soothing voice, "Come with me, girl. I know what to do," she said, tugging Emmeline behind her toward the scullery.

And somehow in that moment, Ruth pushing me out the door and standing between us, shielding her from my curiosity and concern, I knew that Emmeline had grown away from me. That she would suffer wounds I didn't understand and couldn't protect her from. Suddenly, we were different. More different than Ruth and Em from each other. Everything between us felt changed, divided in ways that felt fated and permanent. Emmeline would be stuck in this world of kitchens and sculleries, washing blood from her skirts, and I would be stuck outside, hungry for the warm, soft pieces of her I remembered, my unworthy fingers pressed against the glass.

A man hangs from a tree. His legs dangle, motionless. His chin rests against his chest, as if he's asleep.

Through the black-and-white lens I see his face: Nathaniel.

A seething rage burns somewhere inside me. Like my soul is on fire. Like everything inside me is on fire. A scream tears itself from my throat. Every person in the crowd turns toward me, pointing, whispering, their faces long and terrified.

I feel my lips move to the rumble of thunder. I hear the words in someone else's voice.

> "Warned be the wicked who would harm those bound to me,
> Should the blood of Slaughter spill the blood of mine own,
> The tree will bear witness against him.
> Tragedy will befall him, suffering and fire.
> And my curse will not quiet until Slaughter blood is shed."

My eyes dart from one face to the next.

"All of you!" I shout, the vision clouding with tears as I point at them. "All of you will suffer for this! All of you will burn!"

The wind stirs, kicking up dust devils across the ground. The skyline flickers. The scent of smoke is so clear and thick it's almost real.

I turn. Up the hill. Flames lick through the windows of a house, and I laugh and laugh, tears blurring the roof as it catches.

The crowd gasps and shouts. The fire jumps across the grass, as if riding a trail of gasoline. It slithers to a shed, and I choke out another surprised laugh and point to it, my head thrown back as if I'm hysterical.

The laugh is not mine, these hands are not mine, I remind myself. But I feel powerful. As if I am controlling the flame. And I cry out, victorious, as sparks rise white-hot against a smoke-darkened sky.

The lens swings back to Nathaniel. Back to the crowd of men gathered around him. Some of them are running up the hill toward the fire. The rest run with buckets toward the river. One man is left, standing alone with Nathaniel, stone-faced and slack-jawed, his long hair blowing across his face as he watches the house crumble and burn.

A raucous laugh bubbles out of me. The man turns to face me, fists clenched at his sides, and I hurl myself into the darkness of the woods.

●   ●   ●

Tori lurched awake before her alarm, drenched in sweat. Her bedroom was still dark. She eased back on her pillow, unable to close her eyes. Someone else's cries haunted her mind, yet her throat burned as if she'd been the one screaming. She stared at the ceiling, hoping the tightness in her chest would pass on its own, but her heart refused to slow and the air in her room was hard to breathe.

She got out of bed and peeled back her curtain. Then she threw open the sash, letting the cold air wash over her. The sun had barely broken the horizon. Beyond the thinning woods, she could just make out the sprawling gray limbs of the oak. And through them, a pair of lights coming from the cemetery.

Tori shut the window, threw on her school clothes, and slunk quietly down the stairs. Her mother was already awake in the kitchen, staring absently into a mug of coffee. Tori crept past the opening, hoping her mother wouldn't notice as she slid the lock on the front door free.

"Where are you going?" she hollered as Tori slipped through it. "It's not time for school yet. And you haven't had breakfast!"

"Not hungry," Tori called over her shoulder. "Going for a walk!"

"Not so fast, young lady!"

Tori froze on the top step with a heavy sigh. She turned to find her mother holding the door open, and she stepped back into the foyer. Behind her, Tori's brother descended the stairs in his pajamas and sank into the sofa in the living room, close enough to overhear.

"I got an e-mail from the attendance office at school. What's this about you being late to school yesterday?" Kyle slouched deeper into the cushions. He put the TV on, but not the sound.

"It was nothing. Just a headache."

She pressed a cold hand to Tori's forehead, and Tori pulled away. "I'm fine," she said, even though her head felt woozy and she had a case of the chills. Her arm itched and burned under her sweater, and Tori thought of the rusty knife, hoping her cut wasn't infected.

"Maybe I should call the doctor. You look feverish. I can take the day off work and stay home with you." Her mother was hovering, her eyes narrowing with worry over every inch of her. There was absolutely no way Tori was going to a doctor.

"I'm okay," Tori insisted, pasting on a smile. "I slept with too many blankets on. I just need some air. I'll be back in time for school." She gave her mother a quick peck on the cheek, but her mom caught her by both shoulders. She pressed her lips together and looked deep into Tori's eyes.

"I still have the number of that therapist we talked about."

Tori couldn't hold her mother's stare. "I said I'm fine." She made another break for the door, launching herself down the porch steps and across the lawn, checking over her shoulder to make sure her mother wasn't watching. Then she headed for the cemetery.

Through the trees, the sun crept over the horizon. Tori could begin to make out the brown ring around the cemetery, the lighter green and gold of the field, the trunk of the oak. . . .

And a big green tractor.

It was parked at the edge of the cemetery with its digger facing the graves. Its motor was running, a low rumble she could feel as much as hear. The smell of exhaust was suffocating.

She walked faster. No one sat in the driver's seat. She looked past it to the deep ruts where the tractor had churned its way through the fallow field. Alistair had no contract to farm this field. There was nothing in it to harvest. But that hadn't stopped him from destroying the padlock on their shed, leaving his muddy footprints behind, and taking whatever he wanted. The closer she came, the bigger the digger seemed—a giant green lock-cutter ready to break into the only piece of sacred ground she had left.

Alistair stood beside Nathaniel's grave with his thumbs hitched in the pockets of his jeans. His wife stood with him, the heels of her shoes sinking in the dirt, and her arms folded against the cold. Tori had seen Dorothy Slaughter plenty of times but had never been formally introduced. From a distance, she didn't look a thing like Jesse. He was the shape of his dad, the muscular build and the same squared shoulders. But this close, Tori could see their similarities. Jesse's mother had the same high cheekbones and the same light eyes that crinkled around the edges. She compulsively smoothed her hair back as she talked, the way Jesse fidgeted with his cap when he was nervous.

Tori stood in the trees and listened. "For all we know, Will was the one who dug it!"

"What if it was someone else?" Dorothy asked.

"It had to be Will. The kid's been digging up holes all over the god-damn place!" Alistair shook his head. He stepped in close, standing over the hole with a clenched jaw. "When I get my hands on that boy—"

Dorothy shuddered. "Let's just fill it and be done with it, Alistair."

He heaved an angry sigh. "This field is blighted. Look at it! Last thing we need is to stir up more of whatever's causing it."

"I don't see that we have much of a choice," Dorothy said, shifting her back to the wind. She stared down into the hole as if it were some kind of burden. "If we leave it like this, someone else is bound to come poking around wondering what it is."

Alistair pulled off his cap and scratched his head, frowning at the brown stretch of ground. "Must be some kind of bug or a mold." Tori dragged her attention from Alistair to the blighted ring, only it wasn't shaped like a ring anymore. The wintry dead fingers of grass she'd seen just yesterday had spread almost all the way across the field, and to the road. He stared bitterly at the long stretch of dying grass. Then he mopped his brow and put on his hat, pulling it low over his eyes. "I'll fill the damned hole. But that Burns woman can come here and figure out how to fix this blight for herself. She thinks she's worth a piece of this farm, then let her prove it."

"That's exactly what we're trying to avoid, Alistair." Dorothy sighed. "For that matter, we should take down that damn tree while we're here."

Tori felt something snap inside her. She stepped into the clearing. "What's that tractor doing here?" What were *they* doing here? Why couldn't they leave her family alone?

They turned at the sound of Tori's voice. Dorothy darted an anxious look at her husband. Alistair stared coldly at Tori, refusing to answer.

Tori wrapped her arms around herself and pinched the bandage under her sleeve. "I'd like you to go now," she said past the lump in her throat.

Alistair started toward her, his hard finger pointed at her face. "You think you've got the right to tell me—"

Dorothy caught him gently by the arm. "Victoria, is it?" she asked, as if Tori's name had never been worth committing to memory. Her smile was tight, her eyes barely crinkling at the edges. "We just came by to help. We'll fill the hole and be on our way."

Tori raised her voice. "I said I'd like you to leave."

A vein bulged in Alistair's temple. Dorothy held fast to his sleeve. "I see," she said calmly. "We were only trying to be neighborly. But if our help isn't welcome, we'll just go. Come on, Alistair. Clearly the Burnses can manage on their own."

Alistair spit on the ground, glaring at Tori until Dorothy pulled him gently away. Tori watched the big green tractor drive off, leaving its ugly deep tracks in her field.

⁂

Tori watched them go, waiting until Alistair's tractor was gone before sprinting back up the trail to her house. The closer she got, the more the rage and pressure built. After throwing open the front door, Tori raced up the stairs. Her mother's bedroom door was closed. The *tink-tink-tink* of the pipes carrying hot water to her mother's shower echoed softly in the hall.

She thought of the broken window, and a fresh ripple of anger rolled through her.

Alistair. Alistair had climbed the tree to the porch, broken the window, and let himself in. The same way he'd cut the padlock on their shed. Probably to intimidate them. Just to show her family how useless their locks really were. That nothing inside this house belonged to the Burnses, and he could *take* whatever he wanted if their mother didn't agree to give it to him.

Tori darted into the bathroom and slammed the door. She ripped open the cabinet, the medicine chest, the shower curtain. Her whole body was shaking as she searched for something she knew wasn't there. Something pointed and sharp to ease the pain.

The hallway floor outside creaked.

For a moment, Tori didn't move or breathe. Kyle and Tori were both silent, listening on opposite sides of the door.

Tori waited for him to say something. To bang on the door, or run and drag their mother from her shower to check on his sister. But all Tori heard was his quiet retreat and the soft click of the lock on his bedroom door. She slid to the floor. She should have been relieved. Instead, she curled into herself and squeezed her arm until her cuts began to scream.

ori was silent through most of the ride to school that morning as Magda and Drew regaled her with a lap-by-lap description of the previous day's swim meet. She stared out the window at the long stretches of green, her thoughts festering on her conversation with the Slaughters.

"Drew did great," Magda said. "Everyone said his times were incredible!"

Drew blew on his fingernails and rubbed them on his shirt. "I took first in the two hundred with a minute and forty-two point five..."

Tori cocked her head.

"...and first in the fifty with twenty-one point four..."

"Those times are good. You could probably qualify for state," she said. Magda turned in her seat, just enough to glance curiously at Tori. Tori pursed her lips and sank lower into the backseat.

"But I keep screwing up the butterfly. I came in fifth." Drew's brow crinkled in the mirror. "Coach says I can't compete in medley until I get my times down." He tapped the steering wheel, thinking. "I've got to work on my setup. My breakouts suck and my kicks need work."

"It isn't your legs," Tori blurted. The secret to a fast butterfly was back strength, not just the kick and the stroke. He focused too much on his limbs and his chest, and not enough on his back and his core. It's what made him fast at the freestyle, but slowed his butterfly to a crawl. Tori's thoughts ran to Nathaniel. To his bare back in the river ... The shape of it, strong and straight with broad shoulders and a narrow waist, probably carved from years of balanced endurance and resistance training. With a little coaching, he could beat out Drew's time.

Tori looked up to find Magda staring at her. Drew drummed his fingers on the steering wheel, his thoughts probably lost in a replay of yesterday's meet. "You're right," he said absently. "Definitely gotta work on my breakout."

Tori bit her lip.

They pulled into the school parking lot. Missing-person flyers hung on every light post, flapping in the breeze, and Tori tried not to look at them.

Magda was still watching her.

"Text us if you see Jesse in first period," Drew said when they hit the front doors of the school. Tori didn't bother to tell them he'd already asked her to Homecoming and it hadn't exactly gone well. Drew gave her arm a playful punch, awakening the sting beneath her bandages. She hid a flinch under a tight smile, rubbing her arm as she watched them head the other direction down the hall.

The bell rang, and Tori sat in a cubicle at the farthest corner of the library. She pulled a Pop-Tart from her backpack and took discreet bites as she thumbed through her textbook, grateful for first period study hall. She was two days behind on homework, and she'd been determined to use this period to catch up, but she couldn't focus on school. Her skin still crawled at the memory of Alistair's tractor in her cemetery, and his finger in her face. She hated the thought of him nosing around in her mother's room. But if she reported the break-in, they were sure to send the police out to investigate. And if they stumbled on Nathaniel, she'd have a lot more explaining to do.

Tori's eyes snapped open at the sound of a book slamming onto the desk on the other side of the bookshelves. Through the spaces between the shelves, she could just make out the sweep of Jesse Slaughter's blond hair and the black-and-red lettering on his varsity jacket. She inched her chair back a few inches until she could see him clearly through a gap between the books.

"Anyone heard from Will yet?" She recognized Bobby Coode's orange hair through the stacks. His family's farm was adjacent to the Slaughters', which meant they were most likely cousins. The Slaughters had been careful to make sure every inch of land they abutted was owned by relatives. Every inch but Tori's.

"Nothing yet."

"How about Aunt Francine? How's she doing?"

Jesse shrugged. "About as well as you'd expect. Dad says she spent all day yesterday staring out the kitchen window, waiting for Will to come home."

"Mitch is a mess over it. I don't think he's coming to school today. He was supposed to be watching Will when he took off. And now Mitch is all in his feelings." Bobby shook his head. "You think we oughta ditch and go see him? We could probably get a pass from the office."

"No," Jesse said, digging around in his backpack. "In case you weren't paying attention last week, we've got a Chemistry test in third period."

"So we'll make up the grade next week."

"College recruiters coming next week. I can't afford to miss any practices."

Bobby was quiet, yanking his jacket zipper up and down.

"Quit worrying," Jesse said. "Will can't have gone far. He'll come home when he's ready."

"What the hell are we gonna do, Jesse?"

"About what?" Jesse asked, his voice tight with annoyance. "We go to school. We ace our Chem test. We go to practice. That's what we do."

"I mean about the bonfire."

Jesse dropped into a chair and flipped open a textbook. "Relax. I'll figure it out."

Bobby slumped down beside him and leaned toward Jesse with his elbows on his knees. "If I don't get polluted and laid by Halloween, I'm going to throw myself into the river. All this stress is killing me."

"I told you I'll handle it," Jesse said, angling away from Bobby and burying his nose in his book. "We'll have the bonfire at the cemetery, same as we do every year. Nothing's changed."

"What the hell do you mean, nothing's changed? Come on, man. Didn't you get the memo? The transplants live there now. It's not your daddy's farm anymore."

"Just because they're living in that house doesn't mean we can't do what we've always done," Jesse snapped. "Besides, it's not like it's forever. My dad says he's getting it sorted. It's just gonna take a while."

"Homecoming is less than a month away."

"Relax. I've got my own plan in the works." But Jesse didn't sound entirely confident.

"You're not seriously going through with that, are you?"

Jesse turned a page of his textbook.

"That's the dumbest thing I've ever heard!"

"If I wanted your opinion, I would have asked for it," Jesse said, snapping another page.

"The transplant. You're seriously taking the transplant to Homecoming. What the hell?" The librarian shushed him from across the room.

Tori felt all the color drain from her face.

"You wanted a solution? There's your solution."

"Jesse, look at what's wrong with this picture! You are supremely popular. With the exception of me, you're the best-looking guy in school." Jesse threw Bobby a sideways look. Bobby rolled his eyes. "I'm serious. You're captain of the baseball team. *And* the freaking debate team, whatever the hell *that* means. You're junior class president, for Christ's sake! You could take any girl you wanted to Homecoming, and you're going to ask *her*?"

"I already did," Jesse muttered into his book.

Bobby buried his face in his hands. "This sucks. She's gonna ruin everything. And Kim's gonna be pissed. We were supposed to double."

"Don't go telling everybody just yet."

"Why not?"

Jesse hunkered over his schoolwork. "She said she needed some time to think about it."

Bobby's eyes flew open wide. He guffawed loud enough to draw the librarian's attention again.

Jesse's neck flushed red. "Shut up. You know she's just being coy. She's going to say yes. You should have seen her in my truck yesterday. She couldn't keep her eyes off me."

Tori mashed her face into the desk to keep from blurting out something she'd regret. Up until this minute, she'd thought maybe he was a nice guy. And maybe any *other* girl would jump at the chance to go to Homecoming with Jesse Slaughter. But Tori refused to let herself be used just so he could have a stupid party.

"Lisa's gonna kill you when she finds out."

Jesse rubbed his eyes and slouched back in his chair. "We were probably gonna break up anyway. Everybody knows she's been flirting with that guy from Calvert."

"But Burns? Seriously? She's always wearing black like some kind of crazy goth chick. And my mom says she heard she was in some hospital up in the city last year. Tried to kill herself after her dad died." Bobby rested a melodramatic hand on Jesse's shoulder. "Come on, man. You don't need that kind of negativity in your life."

Tori cringed. She hadn't been trying to kill herself. It was an accident, but try convincing anybody else of that. . . . And what the hell would a guy like Bobby Coode know about what she'd been through?

Jesse shook him off. "You shouldn't go spreading that shit around. Last thing I need is for *that* rumor to start running around school. How's that gonna make me look? She's supposed to be my Homecoming date, asshole."

"Some date," Bobby muttered, shaking his head. "If you ask me, she's flat and her hair's too freaking short."

Tori hunched in on herself, her face growing hot.

"Whatever. I caught you checking out her legs during Pre-calc last week." Instinct, or maybe self-protection, made Tori reach down and hold them. Even though she hadn't been in a pool in a year, they were still muscular and defined, and she hated that the heavy wool tights did little to conceal them. "Admit it, she doesn't look bad in a skirt."

"She probably looks just like Lisa when it's hiked over her face."

Jesse snorted and shoved him, but the effort seemed half-assed. Bobby hardly moved.

No way. No way was she going to let Jesse Slaughter and his friends have a kegger in her cemetery. And as for the dance, she'd chew off her own arm before she'd go anywhere with any of them.

The bell rang. Bobby gave Jesse another playful shove. "Guess Chaptico's got itself a new witch. Good luck with Morticia, man."

"I don't need luck. Tell everyone the bonfire is on."

THE LONG RIDE HOME

Drew waited until all three of them were safely inside his car at the end of the day before firing a barrage of questions. As soon as the car doors shut, he and Magda pivoted to look at Tori, so their heads brushed together between the front seats.

"The rumors are out of control. We've been messaging you all day. What is wrong with your phone?" Drew plucked it from Tori's hand and began tapping into her apps like he owned stock in them. He turned the phone to show Magda the screen. Tori *had* been getting their messages, every hour . . . every period . . . always same question: *Have you answered him yet?*

Apparently it hadn't taken long for the rumors to start flying.

"Nothing is wrong with my phone!" She reached between them to snatch it back.

"What? What is it?" Magda asked.

Tori swallowed an angry lump in her throat. "I overheard Jesse and Bobby talking. He only asked me to Homecoming because he wants to have a party in my cemetery."

Magda and Drew exchanged a look. "The bonfire," she said, sinking in her seat.

"I've always wanted to go," Drew said with a hushed reverence. Magda elbowed him hard enough to make him flinch.

"What?" Drew rubbed his shoulder. "I don't see the problem."

"The problem is that this place was supposed to belong to *my* family!"

"Try telling the Slaughters that," Magda muttered.

"It's one night," Drew said. "Why not go with him to the dance and let him have the bonfire?"

"No way!" Tori wrapped her arms around herself, hating the warmth that pricked at her eyelids. She looked out the window and blinked it away. "He's just using me."

"So? Two can play at that game. And you might even have a good time!"

"I'm with Tori," Magda said gently. "She should forget Jesse. There are plenty of other guys she could go with."

"Like who?" Drew asked, pausing to let the silence that followed prove his point. "Believe me, if there were all kinds of mature, eligible, halfway attractive boys running around the Academy, I wouldn't be going to Homecoming with you."

Magda ignored him. She tapped her lip, slower and slower, as if eliminating possibilities. Finally, she said, "She can be *our* date." She threw Tori an encouraging smile.

Magda and Drew had been each other's dates to every school function since the beginning of time, or at least since their first sixth-grade dance. It was one thing to tag along in the backseat for school carpool. But to be the third wheel at a dance was just awkward.

"No, thanks," Tori said. "I'm not going."

"Don't be ridiculous. You're coming with. We already picked out your dress," Drew insisted. "We found it during fifth period. They've got one left in your size at that cute little bridal shop at the mall in Annapolis. Totally worth the drive."

Magda turned to peek at Tori around the seat. "It's sapphire and strapless. It's perfect for you."

Tori's skin felt hot and her bandages itched under her sweater. "Can we please just go?"

Drew sighed and put the key in the ignition. Tori was grateful when the roofline of the school disappeared behind her. She had more important things to worry about than Homecoming dresses, like how to keep tractors and drunk people out of her cemetery. And what to do about the dead boy who'd recently climbed out of it.

*   *   *

When Drew slowed at the turn for Slaughter Road, Tori sat up, pressing her face against the glass. A U-Haul truck sat in Matilda Rice's short driveway. A stack of boxes waited, piled on her front porch.

"Can you let me out here?" Tori asked, slipping her backpack over her shoulder before she realized what she was doing.

Drew made a face. "I get that you don't want to talk about the dance anymore, but isn't this just a little dramatic?"

"That's not it. It's just..." They rolled slowly past Matilda's yard. A cascade of yellow leaves fluttered down from the branches of the walnut tree, gathering around a FOR SALE sign in the little square of grass on the other side of the truck. Matilda stood on the porch, leaning on her cane, her wrinkled face crumpled and misty eyes furious as a woman carried another box down the rickety porch steps. "I know the woman who lives here. It looks like they could use a hand."

"You know old Mrs. Rice?" Drew asked, looking surprised. And maybe a little scandalized.

"I've met her." Matilda's filmy eyes swung to Tori's through the car window, making the hair on Tori's neck stand on end.

"That woman is batshit crazy. I bagged her groceries last weekend. She spent the entire time in line talking to herself." Drew shook his head as he eased to a stop, and Tori jumped out of the car before they could offer to help. Though judging by the look on Drew's face, he wasn't planning on it.

Tori leaned in Magda's window and pasted on a smile. "Thanks for the ride. I'll see you tomorrow."

Magda leaned closer, lowering her voice like she could tell something was bothering Tori. "Don't worry about the dance. We'll figure something out."

Tori watched them drive away. The missing-person flyer rustled and flipped in the wind. Tori hiked her bag higher on her shoulder, took a bolstering breath, and walked toward Matilda's driveway.

"Quit messing with my things, Lorraine! You put that back! This is *my* house! You hear me? My. House!" Matilda banged the floorboards with her cane and hobbled after the woman as she loaded another box into the back of the U-Haul. The younger woman—Lorraine—put her hands on her hips, catching her breath beside the truck while Matilda let loose a long and heated argument with herself. It was only when Tori got closer that she started to see the resemblances between them. The similarly shaped nose and cheekbones and ears. Only this woman's eyes were clear—a deep, dark brown.

"Hello?" Tori said, pausing in the street and feeling like an intruder. "I'm Tori Burns. I live down the street. I just stopped to see if everything is all right."

"Ain't nothin' all right!" shouted Matilda from the porch. She clutched an old bible and pointed her cane at the truck. "Al Senior gave me this house! And I ain't leaving just because that nasty twat down the road thinks I'm crazy! I might be old, but I ain't crazy! And I ain't going into no assisted living." Matilda set down her cane and leaned against it, catching her breath. "More like assisted dying if you ask me," she muttered to herself.

The woman beside the truck shook her head. "You'll have to excuse my mother. She hasn't been well lately." She brushed the dust from her hand and extended it to Tori. "It's nice to meet you, Tori. It's kind of you to stop by and check on her."

Tori shook Lorraine's hand, but her gaze slid back to the porch.

"You know what Emmeline would say! She's been talkin' to you, even if you ain't been listenin'." Matilda's clouded eyes shone right at Tori until a knot twisted in her gut. A man, probably Lorraine's husband, emerged from the house and took Matilda gently by the elbow, guiding her back inside, which only made her start shouting again. "She'd be mad as hell. That's what she'd say! The nerve of that woman, tellin' everybody we're crazy." Matilda banged her cane hard as she made her way slowly back inside.

Lorraine let out a long sigh as she watched her mother's hunched back disappear into the house. She looked tired as she picked a fallen walnut from the back of the truck and tossed it into the yard.

"Where's she going?" Tori asked with a pang of sympathy for both of them.

"We put her house up for sale. We've been getting calls from the neighbors. They're concerned about her."

"Why?" Aside from all of Al Senior's relatives, Tori's family were the only neighbors, and she couldn't imagine her mom complaining.

"She's old. Too old to stay alone in this house anymore. Her dementia's getting worse. She's been irritable and confused, hearing voices. Sometimes I think she's paranoid," Lorraine said through a broken laugh that sounded like it came from a despondent place. "My husband and I can't take her, but we can't let her live alone here anymore either. We're moving her into the senior center in town. I think she'll be in good hands there." Lorraine nodded reassuringly to herself and tried to smile.

"My mom teaches art classes there. It's not so bad." Tori doubted her smile was any more convincing than Lorraine's. She hated the senior center. It felt like a hospital and it smelled like dying things. And she felt a pinch of sadness for Matilda, that she couldn't stay in her home. Tori knew what it felt like to watch someone carry your boxes and stuff them in a truck, to open them in a stranger's room, in a place where you didn't want to be.

Lorraine grimaced. They both heard Matilda through the thin walls of the house, still talking to herself and spewing rage at her son-in-law. Lorraine was right. She did sound paranoid. Tori took comfort in the fact that everything Matilda had said to her the other day—all those things about Nathaniel being dangerous—was just the rambling of a senile old woman.

"Why don't you go on home, sweetheart," Lorraine said, pulling Tori's attention from Matilda's door. "We're almost done here. Thanks again for stopping by."

Tori nodded, and with a small wave turned down the driveway. Will Slaughter's face stared back at her from the stop sign.

"Did they find him yet?" Lorraine called to her. The moment felt eerily familiar. Too similar to the way her conversation had started with Matilda just yesterday. That déjà vu feeling crawled over her skin.

"I don't think so," Tori said.

Lorraine hugged herself, a flash of worry behind her eyes. "I hope he's all right. My mother's convinced..." She pressed her lips together, holding back the rest of her thought. "Well, like I said, she's been a little paranoid lately." She offered Tori a sad, almost hopeless smile. "I'll pray he turns up soon."

SHAME & SCANDAL

Emmeline's arms were full of linens as I followed her down the first few narrow stairs from Archibald and Elizabeth's quarters, careful to avoid the third step from the top and its telltale creak. She had dragged me up here on the promise that no one was in the house and we wouldn't be caught snooping, when we'd heard the door open downstairs. She'd snapped up the linens from the bed, even though they didn't appear to need washing, presumably so she would have some reasonable excuse for being there. But my own hands were empty, and my heart hammered at the thought of Archibald finding me in his quarters, alone with Em.

We reached the turn of the landing, where the stairs below us opened into the master's study, pausing to listen to the murmur of voices on the other side of the wall. Emmeline leaned to glimpse around the corner. I crouched on the step behind her, trying to listen, but my curiosity got the best of me, and with a hand upon Emmeline's shoulder, I peered cautiously around her. Elizabeth stood behind Archibald's desk with her hands on his back. Her lips were puckered and thin, her head tipped in thought, giving her the appearance of a curious bird.

"What is it?" she asked, rubbing the tension from her husband's shoulders while looking over them at the open letter in his hand. Slaughter folded it closed and laid it on his desk, frowning at the broken wax seal.

He rubbed his eyes. "The governor's magistrate from Annapolis will be here in a fortnight. He'll be staying at the ordinary in St. Mary's for three days, hearing cases. They've a mind to appoint a new sheriff while he's here. The journey has become too long for him. They wish to hear only felony trials at the capitol, and leave the minor charges to the local lords and sheriffs to handle."

Elizabeth squeezed his shoulders and bent low, pressing her cheek to his. "This is wonderful news, then! Why do you look so troubled, my love?"

Archibald stood, pulling out of her embrace and pacing to the window. I eased my nose a bit farther around Em's shoulder to see. "The magistrate requires every local lord to present his indentured charges in person. Any found to be under the age of sixteen will have their papers scrutinized."

Elizabeth laughed and rested a hand on his shoulder. "Why should this worry you? The children have papers."

"There is talk among the neighboring lords of a list."

Her smile fell from her cheeks. "What kind of list?"

"A list of names . . . of missing children. The trouble in England has escalated. Marches, strikes, riots at the shipping yards. Parents are claiming their children have been spirited and sold into the colonies under false papers. The penalties for such business are steep." Emmeline turned her face quickly to mine, her nose bumping my cheek in the cramped space. My stomach turned at the look on her face, her gray eyes wide and alert, her restless mind already scheming and planning.

"I told you," Elizabeth said coldly, "bringing those children here was a mistake."

"It was no mistake. Thomas was overrun with his tasks. He needed a stable boy. And you needed a house servant," Archibald said, avoiding her gaze.

"Thomas needs nothing. He's lazy. A stronger master could milk more effort from him. And as for a house servant, I have Ruth and she's quite competent. The girl, on the other hand, is irreverent and slow. She's proven herself to be nothing but trouble."

Emmeline's jaw hardened next to mine and I held her tightly by the shoulder to keep her from offering a reply. The stair creaked under my feet. We held our breaths and stayed perfectly still, praying neither Archibald nor Elizabeth had heard.

"She's young." Slaughter dismissed her argument with a wave of his hand. "Perhaps a stronger mistress could milk more effort from her," he said drily, easing back into his chair.

"She's fourteen. Hardly a child."

"Indeed." Slaughter angled his face from hers and repressed the edges of a smile. "Perhaps they've outgrown our expectations of them. The boy will be ready to take on several of Thomas's fields within the year. He shows promise."

"I can't say the same for the girl. She's a poor influence on Ruth." Elizabeth ran a finger over the length of the desk, checking it for dust. "I don't know what you were thinking, wasting a perfectly good barrel on the two of them."

"The captain was desperate to be rid of them. The fool made me a handsome offer. I could not refuse."

Elizabeth's lips twisted with disgust. "So it was the captain who was desperate, then? A wiser man would have seen why. Perhaps the fool was you?"

Archibald shot to his feet and slammed his fist on the desk, making Em jump. Elizabeth, apparently unmoved, paced the length of the room.

"Can the magistrate's silence be purchased?" she asked.

Slaughter thought about this for a moment before shaking his head. "I've met him once. He seems a righteous man."

"Then the solution is simple, my lord. The Bishop children will remain here when you meet with the governor. You need not present them at all."

Slaughter scowled, still seething. "If they are discovered—"

"We will tell the neighbors they are your niece and nephew, sent to live under your care."

"And if they're bold enough to suggest otherwise? If the local sheriff were to hear of them?" he snapped, cutting his eyes to her.

Elizabeth glided to stand in front of him, the long hem of her gown grazing the floor. She straightened his cravat with tender hands and gritted teeth, answering in a slow, deliberate tone. "If you were to become sheriff, I daresay little would trouble you anymore." She patted his shoulder and left him standing beside the window.

"I've enough responsibility lording over this plantation. I do not need the added burden of becoming an appointed man to the governor," he said to her back.

Elizabeth paused beside the door. "My lord." Her sharp eyes seemed to pierce him from across the room. "It is possible you misunderstand me. I will not tolerate shame on this family, nor will I allow scandal to tarnish the name of this house. At all costs, regardless of their burden upon you, I expect you to manage your affairs. My father's dowry will not be wasted upon steep penalties in payment for your mistakes." Her smile barely lifted the corners of her lips. "You will speak to no one of the children. And you will present yourself to the magistrate to petition for the position of sheriff with all of the ambition and statesmanship of a man worthy of the name Slaughter."

A red flush stole over Slaughter's neck and cheeks, and a vein throbbed in his temple. "And for your part, dear wife?" he asked venomously.

Elizabeth smoothed her skirts. "I'll speak with Goody Eldridge. Perhaps she can plant a seed in her husband's ear. His voice is loudest among the lords in the county, and he's far too old to seek such a position for himself. Leave it to me, my lord," she said, snatching the letter from his desk and folding it into her bodice. "I shall draw the reply for you. We shall simply explain that you have no new indentures to present to the magistrate, and that the lords and ladies of this county are all upstanding and abiding of the law, as are we. As far as it concerns the governor and Annapolis, there are no missing children here in Chaptico. And you," she said, planting a kiss on his rigid lips before walking away, "will have no one to answer to on the matter, or on any other from here on out. You, dear husband, will be a sheriff of St. Mary's soon."

Emmeline and I remained still, waiting for the door to close behind her, and I sent up a silent prayer that Archibald would follow her. After a moment, he swore under his breath, snatched up his waistcoat where it rested on the back of his chair, and stormed out of the room.

I let out a long-held breath and sank against the wall, relieved we had not been caught and subjected to every terrible punishment I'd been imagining in the long moments that passed. But Em...

Em's eyes were alight with plans. Inside them I could see every machination of her mind—a mind that had thought of nothing but flight since we'd stepped from the belly of that ship.

"How long do you think it would take to walk to St. Mary's?" she asked, so quietly I wasn't sure if she was speaking to herself or addressing me. Her gaze was distant, lost somewhere on the other side of the wall behind me, as though her thoughts were already mapping the way.

        ❀   ❀   ❀

Not a week later, I awoke to the steady clop of hooves and the snap of a crop in the back of a wagon cart, jostled between Emmeline and Ruth. My head throbbed with every bump of the road and my vision was slow to focus. Em and Ruth were tied at the wrist and ankle, and gagged at the mouth, the three of us filthy and bloody and rank with sweat. We hadn't made it as far as Newtown before Slaughter realized we were gone and sent Thomas to fetch us. And fearful of the wrath that awaited us, we hadn't come quietly.

I'd no idea what time of night it was when the horses turned into the manor, but Slaughter was waiting with torches lit and the farrier, Mr. Fredericks, at the ready.

"Where did you find them?" Slaughter asked Thomas when he pulled up on the reins.

"Just north of Newtown," Thomas replied, stiffly dismounting his post.

"Was anyone with them?"

"One of the slaves. The one they call Ruth."

"Present them."

Thomas dragged me from the cart by my ankles and dumped me to the ground while Emmeline and Ruth watched, wide-eyed over their gags. Thomas knelt over me on the pretense of checking my binds. He reeked of blackstrap and horses, and whispered, "Have I taught you nothing, boy? There's no sense in running. And taking a slave? It'll be a thief's punishment for you." He leaned close enough for me to see the *M* branded on his cheek. "Hold your tongue and don't do anything foolish. It'll be over soon."

He pulled me to my feet by my pants and collar and shoved me in front of Mr. Slaughter. My head rattled in my skull and I came dangerously close to vomiting on the man's shoes. Archibald looked me up and down with disgust.

"You mean to steal from me?" he asked.

"No, sir."

Slaughter sneered, and growled, "Liar." He turned to Thomas. "Brand the boy. And take the slave's ear."

The ground swayed as the farrier wobbled toward me with a long rod in a bucket of hot coals. My heart leapt as Thomas cut the bindings from my wrist, and I wrestled against him as the farrier took my right hand. Thomas grabbed me by the hair and the elbow and held me fast. When I cried out, he shoved a length of rope between my teeth.

Like a wild horse, I strained to see the glowing T emerge from the coals. I flinched as he brought it to my hand.

"I'm sorry, boy," the farrier said grimly, positioning the brand over the meat of my thumb. With a hiss it sank in.

My hand was alight with a searing fire. I cried out until I was hoarse. With every breath came the smell of burning flesh, and I gagged against the rope. My body sagged limp. Thomas let go and I fell to my knees.

I lifted my head at the sound of a scuffle as he dragged Ruth from the cart. Her face was smothered in his huge, filthy arms. One held her in place as she thrashed. The other stripped off her white cap and struggled to slip a knife behind her ear. Ruth whimpered, stilling at the touch of the blade. It flashed quick in the torchlight, and Ruth screamed through her gag, reaching for the empty, bloody place where her ear used to be.

"No!" Emmeline had shed her gag, and her desperate shout shattered the night. Slaughter threw Em over his shoulder. Her hair spilled around her face, her arms reaching and her cheeks streaked with anguish as she cried out for Ruth.

The sky swam, heavy with the scent of blood and pain, and in the moment before I collapsed to the ground, I dreamed I heard her call my name.

THE INVITATION

Tori jogged the entire way home from Matilda's house, fighting the start of a runner's cramp. Her thoughts lingered on the conversation she'd had with Matilda's daughter. When she finally hit the gold-green stretch of lawn around her house, beads of cool sweat had begun trickling down the small of her back and her heart was pumping hard against her ribs. She slowed her pace to a walk, struggling to catch her breath. It had been over a year since she'd last taken a lap, and the burn in her calves and her quads and her lungs felt good, overpowering everything else.

Tori rounded the corner of the driveway and stopped.

Jesse Slaughter stood on her front porch with her mother. Tori took the steps slowly. Her mother's eyes narrowed on her flushed cheeks, and Tori wiped the sweat from her lip.

"What are you doing here?" Tori asked, not bothering to mask her irritation.

"Tori!" Her mother shot her a look. "Jesse is a neighbor. Of course he's welcome."

"I just came to tell your mom that we're having a vigil at the house on Saturday for Will."

Tori glanced at her mom. Her mother's unspoken message was clear.

Be nice to him. Don't rock the boat, please. "They haven't found him yet?" Tori asked.

Jesse shook his head. "They had search dogs out earlier today, but the trail didn't hold up long enough to tell us much. We lost it down by the point. Too windy, I guess." Jesse stuffed his hands in his pockets and glanced between Tori and her mother through an awkward silence. "Anyway, we've invited all the neighbors. Guess we need all the prayers we can get."

"Of course, we'll be happy to come." Tori's mother gave Jesse a reassuring smile. Tori wondered if she would have done the same if it had been Alistair standing in front of her. Or if Alistair even knew Jesse was here.

Tori nodded, unsure of what else to say.

"Can I talk to you?" Jesse asked Tori in a low voice. He took off his baseball cap and held it in both hands. Tori's mom took the hint and slipped inside the house.

"Fine." Tori descended the porch steps heavily. Her mother was right. She should at least be kind. But it didn't change the fact that she knew exactly why he was here. "I'm sorry about your cousin," she said when they were standing in the shade of a tree in her front yard, far enough from the house that her mom and brother wouldn't overhear.

"They'll find him. We've got eyes and ears all over this town, and he can't have gotten far." Jesse looked down at his feet, as if to hide the pink flush on his cheeks, and Tori braced herself as he twisted his ball cap in his hands, wondering how much longer he'd ramble before getting to the real reason they were both standing here. "The kid's had a rough time of it. He was real close with my granddad. Al Senior was like a father to him, took him under his wing after Will's parents divorced and his dad left. He hasn't really been himself since Granddad's death."

"What do you mean?"

"Will used to talk everyone's ears off. Never could shut him up. But after Al Senior died, he just stopped. Started wanting to be alone all the time. Then these holes started popping up everywhere. First I caught him digging in the front yard under the magnolia. Then way out back behind a line of old cedars."

"Why?" Tori rubbed her arms, feeling the sting under the bandages. She understood the need to be alone. And maybe Kyle's silence lately was partly his own way of coping with their father's loss. But digging?

"Just something stupid my granddad said when he died. Something about answers being buried under the oldest branch of the tree."

"Answers to what?" Tori asked. The one question everybody in Chaptico had been asking—the question only Al Senior could answer—was why her family was here. And if he'd left behind an answer, she wanted to know it too.

"Probably nothing," Jesse said dismissively. "My granddad was going senile, but you couldn't tell Will that. The kid took everything Granddad said as gospel." Jesse shrugged. "It didn't make much sense to anyone else, but it stuck with Will." Jesse fidgeted, crushing a dead leaf under his shoe.

The tractor. The hole.

Will's holes.

Tori's mind spun back to the Slaughters' argument in the cemetery that morning. She cleared her throat, tucking that information away for later. "Well, I hope they find your cousin soon."

He nodded, looking around awkwardly and shifting his weight, like he was trying to find a way to change the subject. Another uncomfortable silence followed, stretching out a little too long between them.

"What do you want, Jesse?" Tori cringed. Every word came out more sharply than it should have.

Jesse plucked a fallen leaf from the neck of her sweater and she angled her face away. "Sorry. I just thought maybe we could get to know each other. I didn't mean to stress you out or anything."

"Why don't you tell me why you're really here?"

He scratched the back of his neck, shy and tentative, nothing like the boy she'd seen in the library that morning. "You haven't given me an answer to my question yet...about Homecoming. It's coming up in a couple of weeks and I was thinking maybe we should—"

"Thanks," Tori said. "But I'm not interested."

Jesse's expression teetered between amusement and surprise. Tori imagined he wasn't used to hearing the word *no*, and she felt a small satisfaction in being the one to say it.

Jesse recovered quickly. "We don't have to stay long if you don't want to. We could just go for a little while. Or...you know...we can go someplace else...that is, if you'd want to."

"Someplace else?" The suggestion caught her off guard.

He shook his head and laughed softly. "I'm really screwing this up, aren't I?" His smile was self-deprecating, the dimple cutting into his cheek so sincere, making Tori second-guess herself. What if there was more to the invitation than the part she'd overheard? What if he really had been just saying those things to get his friend off his back? She hadn't exactly been honest with her friends either.

"Like where?" she asked hesitantly.

Jesse's spine straightened and his whole face lit up. "If you're not into going to the dance, I was thinking we could come back here. See, we have this bonfire every year and—"

And there it was.

"I already know about the bonfire."

"How did you...?" Jesse studied her quizzically, then his shoulders sagged. "Right," he muttered. "This town's got eyes and ears, and big mouths too." He fidgeted with his ball cap. "Look, it's just that we have the bonfire every year, and I was really hoping you might want to come. I meant what I said about—"

"About how I look in a skirt? Or the part about me being a transplant and the cemetery not being mine?"

Jesse's jaw fell slack. "I never meant for you to hear any of that." He reached for Tori's hand but she stepped out of reach.

"Listen, Jesse, I'm sorry. But I'm not going to the dance with you." As soon as the words were out, she regretted them. She wasn't sorry. Not sorry at all.

Jesse bristled. "Why not?"

"Isn't it obvious? Why can't you just have the party somewhere else?"

"Why can't *you* understand it isn't up to you?"

A low voice broke through their argument. "Tori?"

Nathaniel stood a few yards away, holding her sweater.

"You left this," he said quietly. "I thought you might need it." Nathaniel's eyes flicked between Tori and Jesse. He didn't come any closer. Behind her, Tori could hear the soft crack of Jesse's knuckle, the smell of his cologne closer than it had been a moment ago.

Out of the corner of her eye, she caught the flash of the living room curtain closing. She crossed the yard toward Nathaniel and reached for her sweater, determined to get Nathaniel out of there before Jesse started asking questions. Before anyone else saw him.

"What are you doing here?" she whispered, Jesse's stare hot on her back. "I told you I'd come to the barn."

"I can stay," Nathaniel said in a low voice. "If you need me to." He glanced furtively at Jesse, his grip lingering on her sweater.

The screen door popped open.

"Kyle said someone's here?" Tori's mom stepped onto the porch, drying her hands on a dish towel and surveying each of their faces. Kyle peered around her shoulder. All eyes were suddenly on Nathaniel.

Tori grabbed his hand, anchoring it to her side. She repressed a shiver; it was as cold as she remembered.

"Everyone, this is Nathaniel Bishop." Tori threw a quick glance at Jesse, but he gave no sign that he recognized the name. "Nathaniel, this is my mom, Sarah. And this is my brother, Kyle." She glared at Kyle until he withered behind her mother's back. "And this is our neighbor Jesse Slaughter." Jesse started forward with a tight smile, arm extended. Nathaniel's hand tensed in Tori's. Before Jesse could cross the gap, she said, "Jesse was just leaving."

Jesse faltered. His jaw hardened.

No one spoke as Nathaniel and Jesse studied each other. "Slaughter, you say? I once knew a man by the same name."

"I don't doubt it. There are a lot of us here." Jesse lifted his chin as if trying to make himself taller, but Nathaniel stood over him by at least an inch, maybe two. "You don't sound like you're from around here."

"He's not from around here," Tori said quickly. "He's an old friend . . . of Drew's . . . from . . ." A wave of panic rolled through her. She hadn't thought this far ahead.

"From Bristol," Nathaniel said with a soft squeeze of her hand. Their eyes caught.

"That's right," Tori blurted, realizing her mistake too late. Now she would have to tell Drew, which also meant telling Magda, so they could back up her story, which was quickly spiraling out of control.

"England!" Tori's mother said. Hoping her mother wouldn't recognize any of Nathaniel's clothes, Tori held her breath as Sarah practically skipped down the porch steps to introduce herself. "How wonderful!"

Nathaniel dragged his eyes from Jesse. He took her mother's hand and kissed it, making her blush an embarrassing shade of red.

"Pardon my manners," Nathaniel said smoothly. "It is my sincere pleasure to meet you."

Tori's mother's jaw dropped and she fumbled over her words. "Oh, Victoria, he's absolutely charming. Where did you find him?"

"You seriously don't want me to answer that," Tori muttered.

Tori's mother gathered herself. "I'm making meatloaf, Nathaniel. Would you like to join us for dinner?"

He smiled at Tori sideways. His eyes were a warm hazel-green. She leaned into him and discreetly stepped on his toe. Nathaniel raised an eyebrow.

"Thank you for the lovely invitation, Mrs. Burns. It's a tempting offer—" Tori shifted more of her weight onto his foot. "Perhaps another time. It's getting late and I should take my leave."

Tori's mother turned to Jesse. "You're welcome to stay too, of course."

Jesse clenched his jaw, looking back and forth between Tori and Nathaniel. "Thanks, Mrs. Burns. But my mom'll be expecting me for dinner."

Tori's mother finally disappeared into the house, dragging Kyle with her. Tori dropped Nathaniel's hand. "Sorry, Jesse. Now's not really a good time to talk. I've got company."

A red flush crept up Jesse's neck. "We didn't really have a chance to finish our conversation."

"I already told you. My answer's no. Besides, I've got other plans." Tori held her sweater to her chest as Jesse's eyes turned cold. In that moment, he reminded her of Alistair. "I'm really sorry to hear about your cousin. I mean it. Let me know if there's anything we can do."

"Sure. Whatever," he said, his mouth turning up like he was trying to smile. He stalked away, got in his truck, and slammed the door.

Tori didn't like the way Jesse was looking at Nathaniel as he started down the driveway. And she definitely didn't like the way Nathaniel was staring back.

*   *   *

"I should go," she told Nathaniel when they had returned to the porch. "I promise, I'll come to the barn tomorrow. After school."

He nodded, thoughtful. "Of course. Your family . . . they must be waiting for you." He looked almost sullen as she watched him go.

When he disappeared into the woods, Tori climbed the porch steps and dropped her backpack in the front hall. She slid into her seat at the table as her mother set a steaming serving of meatloaf and potatoes in front of her. Tori and her brother locked eyes across the table, each silently daring the other to taste theirs first. It was the first time he'd actually looked at her in weeks, and for a moment, things between them felt normal.

Kyle picked up his fork and poked at his plate. Tori reached for the ketchup and squeezed out a large puddle of it. Their mother dropped into the empty chair between them, smiling down at her dinner and looking pleased with herself. Kyle and Tori both watched out of the corners of their eyes as she took her first bite, frowned, and reached for the salt before taking another reluctant taste.

"So . . ." her mother said. There was a leading lilt in her voice, and Tori knew exactly what was coming. "Nathaniel seems very nice."

Tori forked another mouthful in with a noncommittal shrug. Kyle looked up, curious and alert. Tori could feel them both watching her eat.

"Jesse was here for quite a while waiting to talk to you this afternoon. Must have been pretty important." She scooped up some potatoes, waiting for Tori to fill the silence. Her cheeks warmed under the beacon of her mother's radar. Every statement was more like a question. . . . *Are you out there, Victoria? Is everything okay, Victoria?* Her mother would keep pinging her with them until one bounced the right way, letting her know exactly where Tori's head was.

"It wasn't important," Tori said without looking up. She groped for a change in subject. "You know, his parents were in our cemetery this morning with some kind of bulldozer. They said they came to fill the hole." Tori couldn't help wondering about that. Jesse had said Will was digging holes under trees, looking for the answers Al Senior had left behind. She knew he hadn't dug that particular hole, but what if he was onto something? "I don't know why they're all so weird about it. Why can't they just stay out of it?"

"Maybe they have family buried there."

"If so, they must not have cared about them very much." The cemetery was unkempt, the moss-covered headstones in complete disrepair. She thought about her father's shiny marble marker in a sprawling cemetery just outside the city, where groundskeepers pruned the grass around his grave. The one she hadn't visited since the day they'd buried him. She pushed the thought away.

"Regardless, if any of the people interred there are Slaughters, they have just as much a right as you or I to be there."

That thought dug under her skin. If the Slaughters thought they had the right to barge into the cemetery and the shed . . . even her *house* . . . just because something in it belonged to them once, what was to keep them from trespassing everywhere else? Like the barn in the woods?

Tori grumbled a few choice thoughts about Alistair and where he could stick his digger. Kyle fought back a grin, wiping his mouth with a napkin to try to cover it.

Her mother pushed food around her plate. "I have another meeting with Bernie next week. I'll ask him what he can tell us about the people buried there."

Tori paused, her fork suspended halfway to her mouth. She set it down. Al Senior had said the answer was buried under the oldest branch of the tree. Could he have been talking about one of the graves under the oak? What if her mother was given the house because one of *her* relatives was buried there? Or, more likely, a lost relative of her father. Maybe that's why none of this made any sense, because her dad wasn't here to figure out the connection. If she could find the answer to why they were here—if she could *prove* her family had a right to be here—they could shut Alistair Slaughter up for good.

"Tori?" her mother asked.

"Sorry." She shook her head free of the thoughts. "A meeting?" Bernie Wells was the attorney that handled Alistair's father's will. If anyone in this town knew why they were here, it was Bernie. But when her mother had asked before, he'd refused to say. "What for?"

"Can someone pass the ketchup?" Kyle interrupted. Tori pushed it across the table, but he didn't touch it.

"Just some unresolved paperwork. That's all. It won't take long—"

"And the salt?"

"What kind of paperwork?" Tori asked.

"Probably nothing important—"

"Does anyone want to hear about my day?" Kyle asked. Tori shot her brother an annoyed look. He stared down at his untouched food, his palms flat on the table beside it.

"Can I come to the meeting?" Tori asked.

"No. You have school."

"But—"

"Jesse asked Tori to Homecoming," Kyle blurted.

Tori's fork scraped hard into her plate, and they both turned to stare at Kyle. He hunched low over the table with a sickly expression, too afraid to look at her.

"And I told him I'm not going!"

"I don't think you should go with either of them," Kyle said quietly.

Tori shot to her feet and snatched up her silverware and dish. "Nobody asked you! Why do you have to be such a snitch?" She stormed to the sink and dumped everything in with a loud clatter.

"Tori," her mother called after her as she raced up the stairs to her room. She slammed the door hard, fumbling for a lock that wasn't there.

THE MARKS LEFT BEHIND

Crack!

I open my eyes. Everything is blurred. Black and white and wavering. I blink away hot tears, and my surroundings come into focus.

A boy is tied to the trunk of the oak. I can't see his face. It's streaked with dirt and his long hair hangs over it. He's young. Not much younger than I am. His shoulders are broad, but his body is long and coltish. He's bare from the waist up. His back is tanned and smooth except for a few faded pink scars that dip down toward his backside.

I start when a man shouts beside me. "I asked you a question, boy! Where were you last night?" He's dressed in old-fashioned clothes. Long hair tied back in a plait and buckles on his shoes.

"In my bed, sir," the boy says, gripping the trunk and shutting his eyes tight.

Crack!

Out of the corner of my eye, a huge ugly man with a scar on his face snaps a switch against the ground.

"Liar!" the man beside me shouts.

I'm grabbed by my collar. I'm yanked to his side. "I know for a fact the girl was not in her bed last night. You and the girl! Where were you?" A vein bulges in his temple. Spittle flies from his lips.

"Don't tell him, Nathaniel, please," I plead through a choking sob. Only it's not my voice. The man shakes me silent.

Nathaniel.

He grits his teeth. "I don't recall being out of bed, sir."

"Then your silence comes with a price. Ten stripes!" he shouted to the scar-faced man. "Well laid on."

"No!" I shout. I don't know if the scream is mine, or if it belongs to the me in my dream. I'm swatting at the man's fist, but he doesn't let go.

"The girl can salt and straw him when you're through." The black-and-white picture wobbles. I'm thrashing, wavering on my feet. The man finally lets go and I fall to my knees.

"Should one of them choose to speak, you may suspend his beating and bring them to me. I am nothing if not merciful." But I don't see any mercy in the black eyes staring down at me.

The scar-faced man holds the switch. He hesitates, and turns his ugly face to me. "You heard the man. Anything you want to say?"

I dart a quick look down the hill toward the field. A black girl in a cap, and a tall, muscled black man, stand motionless at the edge of it, watching us. Nathaniel turns from the tree to look at me with the same fearfully terrified expression.

I shake my head. "We have nothing to say."

The man rubs the M-shaped scar on his face. "Ready yourself, lad. This is going to hurt."

Nathaniel shuts his eyes. The first stripe rips his back open and he screams. I put my hands over my mouth as the scar-faced man delivers another. Every lash is a terrifying black-and-white flash.

"That's ten. Come on, girl," the scar-faced man snaps at me. "Do it quick."

I'm unable to move. Nathaniel's back is soaked in blood, and he hangs limp against the tree.

"Now, girl!" The man drops a bucket of salt beside the pile of straw at my feet.

I dig my trembling hands into the bucket. "I'm sorry, Nathaniel," I say, everything becoming wavy with tears. I press my hands into his shoulders. I drag the salt down his back.

Nathaniel arches against the tree and screams, a hoarse, desperate animal sound.

My hands burn like fire against his broken skin. "There must be salt," I tell him. "Like the salt in the river. It will heal you. It will make you strong."

Nathaniel passes out against the tree.

●   ●   ●

Tori got up early the next morning, scarfed down a bowl of cereal, and walked to the cemetery before her mother could realize she was gone. Kyle had cracked the door to his room when he'd heard her emerge from the bathroom, fully dressed, her hair still wet from the shower, but he'd slammed it shut again before she could ask him why he was staring at her. Like if he kept shutting doors hard enough, maybe she would just disappear. It seemed like the longer they lived in this house together, the less like family they felt. It was too big, with too many rooms and too much history. Back in their old apartment, all four of them had managed to fit. Maybe the less space they had, the less room there was to argue about the reasons they thought they didn't.

She set her backpack down against the oak. She hadn't been able to get the tree out of her mind since she'd woken up that morning. Normally, being close to the old oak was a comfort. Today, it frustrated her for reasons she couldn't quite put her finger on. She shut her eyes, repressing remnants of a dream before rooting around in her backpack for a pencil and some notebook paper. Then she got to work, sketching out a rough map of the burial markers and copying the information she could read on the headstones. Most of them were worn down, difficult to make out. She held the paper flat against them, using the side of the pencil to capture an impression. Half an hour later, she had a stack of damp, wrinkled sketches. She'd hoped one might ring familiar . . . a maiden name of one of her dad's distant cousins or aunts. For the most part, the names were familiar, all local family surnames she'd heard in class at school, or seen on mailboxes along the road to town, or on name tags at the gas station or the bank or the grocery. Curiously, not a single headstone bore the name *Slaughter*.

Tori stuffed the paper into her backpack and ran to meet Magda and Drew at the bottom of her driveway. When Tori got into the car, they were already deep in conversation about Drew's next swim meet. Magda glanced back at Tori and did a double take. Tori was winded and red-faced, trailing cemetery clay from the soles of her shoes.

"Hey, Magda," Tori asked breathlessly, changing the subject. "I've been thinking . . . about the bonfire."

"Oh, thank God," Drew said.

"Jesse came by last night."

"And . . . ?" Magda prompted.

"And I told him I wouldn't go to Homecoming with him and I didn't want him having a party in my cemetery. He said something about how it's not up to me. But if my mom owns the land, what gives him the right to think he can keep tromping all over it?"

"It's called an easement," Magda said, sliding into lawyer-speak. "Family members can access a burial ground on private property, regardless of who owns it."

"But what if they're not family . . . the people in the graves?"

Magda frowned. "What do you mean?"

"Most of the headstones are so old they're hard to read. But I didn't see the name Slaughter on any of them."

Magda thought for a moment. She quickly typed something into her phone and scrolled down the screen. After a few taps and a long pause, she swiped it closed and dropped it into her lap. "Technically, if they don't legally own the land, and the people buried there aren't related to them, you could probably argue that they're trespassing. But," she said hesitantly, "you'd have to file a peace order."

"A peace order?"

"It's like a restraining order. You can use it to keep someone off your land." Tori waited for her to elaborate. Magda was quiet, thoughtful as she looked out the window.

A restraining order. It might be exactly what Tori needed to show the Slaughters she was serious. But how would she prove he'd been trespassing? She'd never filed a police report after the break-in. And the Slaughters never filled the hole in the cemetery, so she couldn't support a claim that they'd tried. Proving Alistair didn't belong on her land sounded as hopeless as proving that Tori did.

"What's the big deal anyway?" Drew asked.

Tori grappled with this. On the surface, Drew was right. What *was* the big deal? She refused to allow herself to be afraid of Alistair, so why was she so hell-bent on keeping him off her property? She had no proof that Alistair had been the one to break into her mother's room. And nothing had been taken. Her mother hadn't even blinked an eye when she'd found out Alistair had cut their padlock and helped himself to the items in their shed, probably because she hadn't cared about anything that was in it. So why was Tori so concerned?

"Because . . . there's something I don't want them to find."

Magda sat up in her seat, listening.

Drew weaved in his lane, his eyes glued to the rearview mirror.

She was going to have to tell them anyway. Jesse had already seen him, and before long, he'd start asking around.

"There's this guy ..." Tori started. "He's from Bristol, England ... and he doesn't exactly have a place to stay."

"Let me get this straight." Magda twisted in her seat, looking at Tori like she had two heads. "You're hiding a runaway from England in your house?"

"In my barn." Tori cringed. It had sounded fine in her head.

"What barn?"

"The one in the woods behind the cemetery."

"Is he hot?" Drew asked. Magda rolled her eyes at him.

"What if you get caught?" she asked Tori. "Do you even know what this guy's running away from? You could be harboring a fugitive or something."

"It's not as bad as it sounds."

"I knew it. He is hot, isn't he?"

"Jesus, Drew! I don't know!" Drew raised a skeptical eyebrow in the mirror and Tori slumped down out of view. "Fine, maybe he's a little attractive—"

"Are you guys, like ... a thing?"

"He has a girlfriend." Tori shut her eyes, trying to keep the lies straight in her head. "I mean, he *had* a girlfriend." Didn't he? She thought back to the way he'd held Emmeline's doll, so fiercely protective of it. The way he'd talked about her as if they'd been close.

"So which is it?" Drew asked. "Did they break up or are you harboring an illegal alien with a girlfriend in another country?"

"Undocumented migrant," Magda corrected him.

"No, he doesn't have a girlfriend. Yes, I told him he could crash in my barn. And I really don't want to have to explain him to my mom. She's got enough to worry about right now, and if Alistair finds him wandering around..." Tori didn't even want to think about it. "So I told her that Drew and Nathaniel are old friends and he's staying with you." She glanced up at Drew to see him tapping his fingers on the steering wheel.

"Well..." he said. "Your mom already thinks he's staying at my house...." More tapping. "And he needs a place to stay anyway.... Why doesn't he just move in with me?"

"That wouldn't be a good idea."

"I knew it!" Drew said. "You're keeping a secret boyfriend in that hidden love shack of yours."

"I am not!"

Magda peeked at Tori between her seat and the headrest, her pale blue eyes suddenly twinkly and hopeful. "Is he taking you to Homecoming?"

"What? No!" Tori almost choked. "I mean, I told Jesse I had other plans. And I might have accidentally implied to Jesse that those plans were with Nathaniel, but—"

Magda and Drew squealed.

"It's not what you're thinking. I only told Jesse I had other plans so he would leave me alone. Nathaniel was there, and Jesse came to his own conclusions."

"Nathaniel," Drew said, waggling his eyebrows as he pulled into a parking space in front of the school. "Our mystery boy has a name." Tori buried her head in her hands. "Don't worry. Your secret's safe with me." Drew held out his palm to Magda. Magda laid her left hand over it, and raised her right.

"Me too. So help me God. When do we get to meet him?" Magda asked, throwing open her door.

Tori pressed her fingers to her temples as she watched them climb out of the car. This was totally out of control. She scrambled out after them. "A minute ago you were worried that a wanted fugitive might be sleeping in a barn in my woods. Now you think I should go to the dance with him?"

"Who could resist being an accomplice to a subversive intercontinental romance?" Drew asked, plucking his swim bag from the hatch.

"Romance?" Tori sputtered. "There is no romance!" But her argument was drowned out by the warning bell, and Magda and Drew were already gone.

•   •   •

Tori slid into the library a moment before the second bell rang. She was supposed to be working on the history paper due next week. Instead, she grabbed a spot at an open computer station and searched for local history, pulling up everything she could find about Slaughter Farm and its inhabitants. Mostly, she was curious about the cemetery and what answers might be buried in it.

She scrolled past name-origin sites to a who's who of St. Mary's County, broken down by the surnames she'd seen so often on business placards, road signs, and county office buildings throughout town. She clicked on "Slaughter."

> *The Slaughter family of Chaptico, Maryland, is one of the oldest and most prominent families in the county. Their local ancestry can be traced as far back as the early colonies. They are known for their long history of public service, charitable contributions, and their generous efforts to help preserve the history and traditions of the area.*

Tori grunted and continued scrolling through a long list of names and dates, many of them hyperlinked to other surnames by marriage, looking for any that might match the sketches of the headstones she'd made that morning. She found one that made her pause. Archibald Slaughter. This name was familiar, but not from the cemetery. This was the name of the man Nathaniel had told her about. The one he'd said had broken their contract.

Archibald Slaughter, son of James R. Slaughter, lived from 1674 until 1726. He married Elizabeth Slaughter (maiden name Hawley), daughter of barrister Henry Hawley of London, with whom he fathered a son in 1707. Archibald was appointed the role of sheriff in 1704 and held several provincial offices throughout his lifetime. At the time of his death he owned 1,000-plus acres, including land tracts known to this day as Slaughter Manor.

Curious, Tori closed the browser and typed *Slaughter Manor* into the search bar of the library catalog. The results were filed under a special collection called "Local History." The Dewey numbers led her to a mahogany cabinet near the front desk. Above it, a gold placard read: *This collection generously donated to the Academy Library by Aloysius and Beatrice Slaughter.*

Al Senior's collection.

Tori chose several heavy volumes of Southern Maryland history, and a thin paperback from the shelf called *Images of Chaptico*, printed by the local historical society. Inside the latter, she found an old black-and-white photograph of a house that bore a similar shape to her own. The caption read: SLAUGHTER HALL. *The original house known as Slaughter Hall was constructed in 1683 on 1,000 acres granted to James R. Slaughter, and later passed to his oldest son, Archibald Slaughter. Destroyed in a fire in 1706, Slaughter Hall was later rebuilt and remains in the possession of the Slaughter family to this day.*

Tori slammed the book shut. "Like hell it does," she whispered. Tori cast it aside and opened another, which contained a collection of maps.

There were maps of the peninsula that showed the original Slaughter Plantation, from what was now the end of Slaughter Road to the end of Slaughter Point. She thumbed through a bunch of historic-looking hand-drawn maps, surprised to find no mention of the cemetery. Even the more official-looking scaled drawings didn't seem to show the graveyard at all. The thought of all those erased deaths gave her chills.

Tori pulled the headstone sketches from her bag. She opened a few of the books to their indexes and began searching for the names. She didn't even know what she was looking for anymore. Proof that the Slaughters had no right to visit that cemetery? Proof that one of those graves held the answer to the question of why Tori was here? What they had been trying so hard to cover in the cemetery the other morning? Was it the same thing Will had been trying to find?

. . . The answers are buried "under the oldest branch of the tree."

Tori traced the names with a fingertip, but none of them sounded remotely familiar. The only connection she had to anyone in that cemetery was Nathaniel. And the only other person she knew who might be buried there was Emmeline.

Emmeline.

Tori flipped to the letter *W*, searching the index for references to the "Chaptico Witch," surprised when Emmeline's name leapt off the page in a chapter called "Local Legends and Folklore."

Emmeline Bell (born 1689?–?) is thought to be the name of a legendary eighteenth-century resident of Chaptico, Maryland, who was said to have been accused of witchcraft and chased off by the local townsfolk. The story of "the Chaptico Witch" has survived for generations, though no historical record has been found to prove her existence and there is no known record of her death. Records from the colonial period are often incomplete, and after a county courthouse caught fire in 1831, many early documents were lost. Historical evidence includes a captain's log entry, citing an incident involving a young girl named Emmeline Bell who narrowly avoided being thrown overboard by the crew as she was transported to Chaptico Wharf in October 1699 on a ship commanded by Capt. William Stone.

The period between 1654 and 1712 marked the height of witchcraft trials in the Maryland colonies. Mary Lee, accused of summoning a storm, was hanged by the crew of a ship bound for Maryland in 1654. Moll Dyer of Leonardtown is said to have been found frozen to a boulder in the winter of 1697 after being accused of witchcraft and driven from her home, the grounds of which are said to be cursed to this day. Rebecca Fowler of neighboring Calvert County was hanged as a witch on October 9, 1685.

Local folklore suggests Emmeline's spirit continues to haunt parts of Chaptico. Various blights, fires, illnesses, and lightning strikes have been attributed to her ghost, though there are no firsthand accounts of any sightings on record. For generations, the Chaptico Witch was annually burned in effigy during a fall festival, the origins of which are unknown. This practice was discontinued in 1976 after a feminist group protested the event, drawing widespread media attention to the small town and some of its prominent residents.

Tori drew her finger down the paragraphs as she read. The page was covered in rubbery eraser dust and she swiped it from the crease. Leaning closer, she could see the faint indentations of letters, written sideways in the margin, but they'd been so thoroughly erased, she couldn't read what they said. Curious, she took her pencil from her bag. Holding the tip at an angle, she gently rubbed it over the page, capturing an impression. The letters coalesced like the whisper of a ghost: *Where's Nathaniel?*

A chill skittered over her skin. She flipped to the back of the book and searched the library card. It had been checked out a month ago, by Will Slaughter.

Tori felt someone behind her.

She shut the book and turned in her chair. Bobby and Jesse sat hunched at the next table, whispering to each other in low voices so the librarians wouldn't hear. Bobby fell silent, nudging Jesse with his elbow. Jesse turned, his expression almost hopeful when he saw Tori staring. His eyes fell to her pencil impressions. Tori scooped her drawings into a pile along with the book, and cleared the search history from the monitor. She caught a glimpse of his face as she stood to go, the hint of hurt in his frown. He wiped it away before turning back to his conversation with Bobby. But she felt him watching her as she checked out the book and returned the rest to the shelf, and she ducked out of the library just as the second period warning bell rang.

CASTING SPELLS

It was a Sunday when Emmeline turned fifteen. Or at least, that was the day she chose to celebrate her birthday each year. She never talked about her real birthday, the home or the family she'd left behind in Bristol, if that's even where she was from. Perhaps that was my fault. The one time she'd spoken of her mother, I'd called her a liar. And since that day, Emmeline's life—the one before we were taken—remained a mystery to everyone who knew her.

Except perhaps Ruth.

After my morning chores were finished, I ran to Emmeline's quarters, then Ruth's. Finding neither of them, I tore off into the woods, to a secluded spot near the river's edge where Emmeline and I used to steal away together to play when we were children.

As I neared, the smell of wood smoke reached me, and I followed it to a small clearing where thick, dark chuffs of it ghosted from under a small cauldron and curled over the banks of the river. Ruth and Emmeline sat upon their knees, watching it boil.

I peered from behind a dense pine as Emmeline poured a bright amber liquid into the pot. Ruth made a terrible face and leaned away, pinching her nose.

"What are you up to?" I asked, stepping out from behind the tree and startling them both. Ruth's spine went straight at the sight of me. Her eyes darted back and forth between Emmeline and me, like she was waiting for Emmeline to procure an answer.

Emmeline sighed deeply, as if I'd spoiled something. As if she'd expected no less. I was always interrupting something with these two, a tagalong to whatever secret plans they'd concocted. And I was tired of being left out.

"Nathaniel won't tell anyone. Will you, Nathaniel?" Em reassured Ruth without looking at me. She didn't expect an answer because it wasn't intended as a question. It was a directive. A command not to tell. And Emmeline never took no for an answer.

I came closer, recoiling when the scent of ammonia and sulfur gripped me. "Ugh! It smells awful! Whatever it is, I hope you don't plan to consume it!" I fanned away the smell, my face still pinched with it. Emmeline laughed out loud, tossing a handful of pins into the pot. Ruth seemed to relax at this, and she stifled a giggle.

"Of course not! Don't be ridiculous, Nat."

"Well, what is it, then?" Beside the fire lay two small stone flagons with odd patterns etched in the finish. An empty chamber pot, two corks, some bent nails and small dried bird bones, and two pieces of cloth, roughly cut in the shape of hearts. A chill rippled over me. This was no child's play. We were all too old for that. Whatever Emmeline was up to, it looked as off-putting as it smelled.

"It's a protective spell."

"Well, if you don't plan to drink it, then what do you plan to do with it?" I asked.

"I plan to bury it," she said snappishly. I pressed my lips tight against the multitude of questions bubbling up inside me, feeling like a fool.

Em dipped a ladle into the brew, carefully pouring it into one of the flagons. Ruth and I watched with raised eyebrows as Em added some nails and bird bones. Then she folded one of the cloth hearts and dropped it inside. She reached around the cauldron expectantly, extending an open hand to Ruth. "Go on, then. You know what needs to be done."

Ruth glanced up at me shyly, then back at Emmeline. Emmeline nodded. Ruth took a small blade from her skirts, and pulling back her cap, cut off a tuft of black curls near the smooth stub where her ear used to be, and dropped it in Emmeline's hand. Emmeline popped it inside the flagon with the rest of the strange mixture and stuffed in a cork, pressing it firmly in place and whispering a quiet incantation before testing the seal for leaks.

Satisfied, she set it down carefully in the grass and began preparing the next flagon. This time, she took Ruth's knife and snipped off several inches of her own dark hair, shoving it inside the bottle and corking it tightly.

"There, one for each of us. That'll show the old hag. Maybe she'll think twice before taking a switch to you again. We'll bury them beneath the garden at the far corner of the main house, the corner closest to her bedroom." Emmeline reached around the cauldron and took Ruth's hand. "It has to work. I'm certain I've done everything right," she said, staring into the pot as if recalling a faded memory. But her brow was creased with worry, and she chewed on her thumbnail as if maybe she wasn't sure at all. "If we bury them someplace safe—as long as the bottles remain intact—the spells should protect us."

"Protect you from what?"

Emmeline looked up at me, incredulous. "From the Slaughters, of course!"

"And you honestly believe a flask of hair and bird bones is going to protect you from the Slaughters?"

Em rolled her eyes, clearly losing patience with me. She rose to her feet and grabbed me by the arm, dragging me far enough from the fire so Ruth wouldn't hear. She leaned close and whispered, "Granted, I may have taken some liberties with the bones for Ruth's benefit, but I'm quite certain about the nails."

"And what exactly are they supposed to do?"

Em sighed and held up her hand, counting off on her fingers. "The piss represents the one casting the spell.... Blood would also do, but Ruth protested." She resumed counting aloud. "The hair and the heart, for the one I wish to protect. I've added iron for strength, and the bird wings"—she hesitated, looking up at me as if with a guilty conscience before speaking the last—"the bird wings will raise us up and carry us free from those who bind us."

I choked out a harsh laugh. My brand still burned, the phantom ache of a lesson seared into me. Ruth withered under my gaze and tucked her cap around her missing ear. I needn't remind either of them of our last failed attempt at escape.

Despite the ludicrousness of the spell, I felt a twinge in my chest. Emmeline had created a protective charm for Ruth, and for herself. But not for me. She had only brought two flagons, as if the thought of safeguarding me had never occurred to her. Who was I to her, then, but a boy she'd shared a journey with once?

I turned and stomped off back in the direction I'd come from.

"Nat! Come back!" Emmeline shouted behind me. "Please!" My feet slowed in spite of the more sensible demands of my head. Emmeline caught me by the elbow, forcing me to look at her. "Please, Nat. Don't say anything to anyone. It's all just..." She glanced over her shoulder at Ruth and pitched her voice low. "It's all just to make her feel better, you know. Elizabeth is just horrible to her. And I can't bear to see her suffer. Ruth didn't want me to make her a bottle. Honestly, I think she's afraid of it. So I made one for me too, so she wouldn't fear it so much. That's all." She brushed my hair back from my face and looked at me tenderly, as if my heart had somehow revealed itself to her. She cocked an eyebrow and a playful smile tugged at her lip. "If it will make you feel better, I'll boil some of my piss for you too."

I felt my face grow hot, and I threw a hand over her mouth to keep her from speaking, my shoulders shaking with laughter.

"Come on," she said, dragging me back to the cauldron and plopping herself to the ground, taking me down with her. Em looked from me to Ruth and then back again, her eyes lighting suddenly. "Ruth, dear! I think Nathaniel should come with us tonight."

Ruth's face was a mask of disbelief. "No!"

"Why not?" Emmeline argued.

"The others already have enough reasons not to trust me. Don't go giving them one more!"

"Just because you live in Slaughter's house doesn't make you a Slaughter."

Ruth buried her face in her hands. "Samuel will have my head."

"Ruth," Emmeline said gently, lifting her chin. "Sam is your family—"

"Only as much as Nathaniel is yours."

"Precisely! We can trust Nathaniel. He would never tell anyone. You have my word." Emmeline took Ruth by the arms and looked deep into her eyes. "Do you not believe me? Are my promises worth so little to you?" She gave her a quick peck on the cheek while Ruth scrutinized me, as if weighing my worth. It was everything in my power not to stick out my tongue at her behind Em's head. Finally, her shoulders fell, along with her resolve.

"Good!" Emmeline said, clapping her hands with delight. "It's settled, then. I'll bring him tonight."

"Bring me where?"

Ruth shook her head slowly. "Thomas and the other men. They must never find out. If it gets back to the master or his wife..." Ruth's voice trailed away, her eyes taking on a haunted shine.

"I swear to you," Emmeline said, taking Ruth's hand. "No one will know. I would never let anyone hurt you."

Em handed Ruth one of the spelled bottles, and she took the other. And I was left to carry the chamber pot home.

THE BOARDED WINDOW

Tori climbed her front porch steps and paused at a steady, loud noise coming from around back. She threw down her backpack and clomped down the steps. It had to be Alistair. First the tool-shed, then the cemetery and her mother's room . . . now what? Couldn't the man just leave them alone?

Tori stormed around the corner. Through the branches of the mulberry tree, she saw someone perched on the roof of her back porch.

"Nathaniel! What are you doing?"

Nathaniel stopped hammering just long enough to smile down at her, then resumed his work, nailing wooden slats over the sheet of plastic and duct tape across her mother's broken window. The boards fit snugly together, as if they'd been cut to fit the opening. Weatherworn and gray, they looked like they'd been stripped from the side of the barn. When he was done, he tossed the hammer to the ground and shimmied down the tree, brushing the dirt from his hands and frowning up at the window. "I noticed it was broken."

"It was the wind. A branch," Tori said, bumbling through the same lie she'd told her mother.

"I don't think so. The tree's not missing any limbs large enough to have caused this. And there's been some damage to—"

"Look," Tori said, "you shouldn't be wandering around in the open like this. Someone might see you."

Nathaniel looked abashed. "I was careful to stay behind the house. Besides, your mother isn't home."

"Forget about my mother. What if Alistair had seen you? Or Jesse?"

Nathaniel took a step back as if Tori had hit him. "And would that be such a terrible thing? For Jesse to find me here?"

"What's that supposed to mean?"

"I was only trying to be helpful," he said, bending to pick up the hammer. "Perhaps I should have left it for Jesse to handle. I near expected him to be here awaiting your return. He seems quite eager to impress you." He scooped up a pile of nails and poured them noisily into an old tin can.

"What does Jesse have to do with . . . ?"

The tips of Nathaniel's ears went pink, and he lumbered off toward the woods.

"Wait. Is that what this is about?" Tori asked, close at his heels. "Are you seriously worried about me and Jesse?"

Nathaniel didn't answer. He took the path to the cemetery with long, angry strides and dropped his tools at the edge of the wood. Tori followed him to the middle of the field, waiting for the tightness to leave his shoulders, but it didn't. She had always come to this place when she'd wanted to be by herself, when it felt like no one else could understand what she was feeling. As he stood with his back to her while she tried to make sense of what was wrong, it seemed she was now intruding on Nathaniel when he wanted to be alone. After a long silence, she turned to go.

"I apologize," he said stiffly. Tori paused. "I'm not quite myself. It's just that I've been feeling unwell." He stared out across the brown, blighted ground with his hands on his hips, looking defeated.

"I'm sorry too," she said. "I should have thanked you for fixing the window. It's just . . ." She struggled to put her finger on exactly what was wrong. "There's a lot about you I don't understand. There's a lot about this *place* I don't understand. I'm just trying to figure out what both of us are doing here." He glanced at her, something softening in his eyes. "And until I know, I think it would be better if you keep a low profile, okay?"

Nathaniel massaged the scar under his thumb and gave a single brief nod. Tori stared out across the field, trying to figure out what to say. He looked so tired. There was an emptiness in his expression, a hollowness in his eyes and cheeks that felt hungry and alone. He'd come to her house last night; her mother had invited him for dinner and she'd stepped on his foot, hoping he would just go away.

"Look, about what happened with Jesse the other day . . ." Tori said.

"You don't need to explain," Nathaniel said softly. "You let him believe I was courting you. But why?"

"Because he was being an asshole."

Nathaniel choked out a laugh. The tension finally eased from his shoulders and he shook his head, watching her sideways with an expression torn between incredulity and admiration.

"What?" she asked.

"It's just that you remind me so much of her sometimes." There was a hint of affection in his voice, that same light in his eyes she'd seen only once before, when he'd talked about the fiddle. And Tori hated the jealous curiosity she felt needling under her rib.

"How?"

Nathaniel raised an eyebrow. "Like you, Em was never one to mince words."

Em. It made her seem young and harmless, and he'd said it with such endearment. It painted such a different image of Emmeline from the one she'd been carrying in her mind since she'd left the library. "Is it true what people say about her? Was she really a witch?"

Nathaniel thought about that. He winced into the afternoon sun and scratched the shadow under his jaw. "I often thought she fancied herself one, though I never really believed it."

"And now?"

"Now?" he asked grimly, gazing up into the twisted branches of the oak, at the small green buds that dotted the branches that hadn't been there yesterday. "Now I think she's sitting back, quite pleased with herself over what she's done. I only wish I understood why."

What *had* she done? With his head tipped back, Tori could see the entire length of the scar around his throat. She thought about the sap that ran under it. It made her sick and angry and sad, all at the same time.

"Do you remember what happened to you?"

"Aye." His voice was gravelly and thick. "I remember the day Slaughter hanged me. It was here. From this very tree." He stared past her, his eyes clouded and distant. Tori's stomach turned. The Slaughters had killed him. "I only I wish I knew what happened to her. I told her to run, to take the contracts and leave without me, but she was so damned headstrong." Nathaniel rubbed the scar on his thumb like a talisman, as if somehow it could bring her back. "The last time I saw her, she was bleeding and terrified, and I feared Slaughter would . . ." Nathaniel swallowed hard. "I don't know what happened after that." He pressed the heels of his hands into his eyes and shook off the memory. Tori could see it in her mind. She knew. She remembered the black-and-white vision—the way his head hung against his chest and his body hung lifeless—and she wished she could push away those images too. "When I came out of the ground, I was so confused. I thought it was Em standing over me and it had all been a terrible dream."

"She did run." Tori felt a pang when Nathaniel's eyes snapped hungrily to hers. "At least, that's what the books say. I read about her in the library at school. There are stories. Not many, but a few. That she was chased away for being a witch. No one knows where."

"And the child?"

A child? Tori's mouth went dry. The book hadn't mentioned anything about a child. But the doll—the wooden doll with its rounded belly—the way Nathaniel was so protective of it. A lump formed in Tori's throat. It was more than the curve of a bell-shaped dress; Emmeline had been pregnant when Nathaniel died.

"There were no records of Emmeline after that. Or a baby," she said quietly.

"Was there any mention of me?"

She hesitated. "No. There was a fire. In a courthouse. A lot of records were lost."

Nathaniel stared at the ground with a hollow expression, and for a long time, he didn't speak.

"You should go," he said quietly. "It's getting late and your family..." Nathaniel's thought trailed. The air in the cemetery felt heavy with grief. There was nothing she could say. Nothing she could do to bring them back. So she left him to mourn them alone.

WHERE THERE'S SMOKE

When Tori got home from school on Friday, she raided the kitchen, stuffing her backpack full of sandwiches, cookies, and fruit, and filling an old milk jug with drinking water. She carried them to the barn, but Nathaniel wasn't there. She left the snacks and water and headed home.

She had a test to prepare for in Math and a paper to write for English, but she didn't feel much like studying. And she didn't want to sleep. Her nightmares had been riddled with blood, and fire, and drowning. And every time she woke from them, she felt like she should somehow understand why.

Instead, she put on her headphones and stretched out on her bed. Her playlist was loud and dissonant, and normally she felt better letting it drown out the world like white noise as it beat against the insides of her head. Tonight, it just made her irritable.

The playlist looped to the song Nathaniel hadn't liked, and he drifted back into Tori's thoughts, unbidden. She remembered the way they'd sat in the barn, nearly touching. And the way his nose scrunched up with distaste. How his smile had seemed to glow from inside him when he'd talked about playing the fiddle. And then again, when he'd compared her to Emmeline.

Tori rolled over on the bed to look out the window, searching the sky over the barn for a ribbon of smoke from his fire. She couldn't help but wonder if anything in that smile had been for her. Or if, like her music, he found her ugly and grating.

Tori jerked the buds from her ears and turned off her music. The sky outside had deepened to violet-gray. A breeze rustled the autumn leaves, and Tori cracked her window, letting the soft sound spill into her room. She sat on the floor, breathing it in. The scent of smoke carried in with it, too strong and close to be from Nathaniel's fire in the barn, and Tori waited for the smoke detectors to blare and the string of hushed swears her mother always uttered when she was burning something. But the house was quiet. Just the soft clatter of utensils being tossed in the sink and the *tink-tink-tink* of the water warming the pipes in her radiator. Even the Slaughters' dogs were quiet tonight.

Tori shivered and got up to shut the window, pulling the thick curtains closed, unable to shake the feeling that something was wrong. She headed downstairs, following the rich aroma of chocolate brownies wafting from the kitchen, surprised to find the air in the lower hallway clear. Tori sniffed. No smoke smell.

Tori opened the front door, and a thick, dry smoke blew in on the wind, the moon a dull sliver through a charcoal-gray haze. Black pillars rose to the east in the direction of Matilda's house.

Matilda's house . . .

Tori ran back inside and skidded into the kitchen.

"Mom, I think something's burning."

"What are you talking about? It smells great in here. You have so little faith in me." Her mother smiled sardonically as she washed a mixing bowl, not bothering to look up.

"No, outside. I think something's on fire."

"Alistair's been burning leaves."

"Mom!" Her mother's hands stilled in the sink bubbles. "I think you should come look."

Her mother dropped the mixing bowl in the water and rushed to dry her hands as she followed Tori out onto the porch, Kyle trailing behind them. Her eyes flew open wide as she took in the thick bands of smoke spreading over the horizon.

The smell of it was everywhere. All around them. A shrill whistle blared inside the house, where a thin gray line of smoke had begun to stream through the open door.

"The brownies!" her mother cried, rushing back into the house.

Tori and her brother stood side by side in the middle of the lawn, watching through the window as their mother shut off the oven and climbed on a chair, ripping the batteries from the smoke detector in the hall near the kitchen.

Through the ringing silence, Tori heard the whine of sirens in the distance.

The wind had died. Tori stood in her yard and watched the smoke settle like a heavy blanket in the air. Deep inside her, she could almost swear she heard someone laughing. She shut her eyes and shook her head, and when she listened again, all she heard was the wail of fire trucks as smoke climbed everywhere except the small stretch of sky above the barn in her woods.

NO ESCAPE

can't focus. The black-and-white lens is shaking, bouncing. I'm in some kind of wooden cart. A wagon? I hear hooves. I'm jarred and jerked with every rut in the road. A boy lies beside me in the dark.

Nathaniel. I try to say his name, but I can't form the sound. There's something gritty and coarse in my mouth, making me gag. He blinks his eyes open. His forehead's bloody.

Voices. Two men talking as the cart rolls to a stop.

Suddenly, Nathaniel is dragged by his feet from the cart. On the other side of him, a girl lies watching me, crying. She's bound at the wrists and ankles. There's a gag in her mouth, but her wide, terrified eyes are pleading, calling to me.

I hear a struggle I can't see. A hiss and a scream.

The girl squeezes her eyes closed. She's shaking.

I strain my neck, stretching against the cloth in my mouth, and I spit it free.

"I'm sorry," I whisper through a sob. "I'm so sorry. Don't be afraid. One day, the wings of a bird will carry us from our bindings and we'll be free of this place. I swear it."

Someone grabs her ankles and pulls.

●   ●   ●

Tori jerked awake the next morning and pitched forward in the bed to the smell of burning flesh. Her nightshirt was soaked through with sweat, and her throat burned as if she'd been screaming. But it was only smoke from last night's fire. The smell of it lingered in the room, in the clothes she'd taken off before bed last night. In her lungs and sinuses. It was even stronger downstairs in the kitchen.

When she came down for breakfast, her mother wasn't there. Her brother stared into his bowl, poking the frosted Os down with his spoon. The kitchen still smelled like burned brownies, the charred remnants of it clinging to the baking pan she'd left in the sink the night before.

Tori reached for a bowl. "Where's Mom?"

Kyle's eyes darted toward the porch, and she peeled back the curtain. Her mother stood just outside, still wearing her night socks and sweats, talking with a police officer as he scrawled notes, listening. Alistair leaned against his truck in the driveway, his hands jammed in the pockets of his hunting coat, and a scowl on his face, far enough that he wasn't part of the conversation but close enough to hear it.

Tori lost her appetite. The last time a sheriff had come to their home, it was to kick them out. And Alistair would probably love nothing better than to bear witness to that.

Tori turned the lock on the window and slid it open an inch. Kyle stopped poking his oats, his spoon suspended over his bowl, both of them listening. Alistair's hateful eyes cut in their direction, and Tori eased down in her chair.

"It seems the fire originated in a house adjacent to Alistair's property. The strong winds last night must have pushed it toward Alistair's fields. Burned right through them. You're lucky the wind changed direction before it reached any of yours." The officer scratched his head.

The fire. It had burned through all of Slaughter's fields, leaving their own untouched. Alistair would need the use of the Burnses' fields again next year, and now they would be worth more to him than before.

The officer continued. "Thank heaven Mrs. Rice's house was vacant. There's nothing left of the place." Matilda's house. Tori leaned closer to the open window, struggling to hear.

"We're waiting on the fire marshal's report, but it was an old house. Old wiring. Apparently, nobody was living in it. I'd like to think it was just neighborhood kids, smoking or messing around inside. But just to be safe, we're asking the neighbors to keep their eyes open and report any unusual activity."

"You think someone set the fire on purpose?"

"We don't know anything for certain. Alistair's voiced some concerns, but the fire marshal hasn't finished his investigation, and that could take a while, given the amount of ground to cover. He'll search for the presence of accelerants, any physical evidence that might point toward an intentional crime. If someone's behind it, we'll catch them. Meanwhile, the fire marshal's asked us to talk with the neighbors. Are you sure you don't remember seeing anything unusual last night?"

Tori's mother shook her head, thinking. "No. Nothing more than I've already told you. I was in the kitchen, and my daughter came downstairs and said she smelled smoke. We all went outside to look. And that's when we saw the fire."

The officer nodded, scratching more notes on his pad. "Do you recall seeing anyone strange, maybe in the earlier part of the day or the hours leading up to the fire? Anyone loitering around the farm you didn't recognize?"

"No."

Alistair pushed off from his truck toward them. "Jesse told me some kid's been hanging around with your daughter and he ain't from around here. You know anything about him?" It sounded more like an accusation than a question.

"Oh, you must mean Nathaniel. I've met him. He's a lovely kid. He's not staying here, though. I think he's staying in town with one of Tori's friends from school."

"So he goes to school with your daughter?" the officer asked over the click of his pen.

"I don't—"

"No," Alistair interrupted. "I asked Jesse. He said that boy don't go to the Academy."

There was a long pause. The scratch of pen on paper. "Do you happen to know this boy's last name?" the officer asked.

"Um . . ." Tori could almost picture her mother's face, her eyes squeezed shut and trying to remember, the way she always did when something was hiding under the tip of her tongue. "I think it started with a *B*? Or a . . . Yes! Bishop."

Alistair stilled. Was Tori the only one who'd noticed?

"Nathaniel Bishop," her mother said with more certainty this time. "But he couldn't possibly have had anything to do with this."

"That's probably true, ma'am. But depending on the results of the fire marshal's investigation, if he's been on the farm in the last few days, I may need to ask him a few questions. It's just standard procedure after something like this. We're just making sure we turn over any loose stones."

Tori cringed. If Nathaniel got dragged into their investigation, this could all go downhill fast. And Alistair looked a little too eager to find him.

THE BLOOD BOND

I tossed and turned that night, thinking about the spell bottles Emmeline had made for her and Ruth in the clearing that afternoon. About the mysterious place she wanted to take me. Thomas was passed out drunk, snoring in a pile of straw on the other side of our cramped loft. It was long after the Slaughters were asleep in their beds when Emmeline finally came for me.

"Bring your fiddle," she whispered. Thomas stirred, then resumed snoring again. Ignoring my perplexed reply, Em held the fiddle out to me. Shushing me quiet, she took my hand and led me deep into the woods, to the far edges of Slaughter's tobacco fields. Her hand was sweaty, sticky and hot, but I didn't dare let go. I watched the long waves of her hair bounce against her back, her skirts swaying with every step, and I longed to pull her in close and steal a kiss rather than endure the pain of waiting anymore.

Being close to her in the dark, touching her, ignited an ache that kept me awake at night and made it difficult to rouse myself from my dreams of her in the morning. I was a fool to think that if I stared at her long enough, dreamed of her hard enough, that some magic might happen to turn her heart to mine. That she might finally be moved to give me that kiss.

"Where are we going?" I asked when we were well out of earshot of the main house and the servants' quarters. Emmeline walked briskly, never once looking back, and I gave up on any notions that she'd forgotten our secret meeting with Ruth and dragged me into the woods to be alone with me. I clumsily adjusted my trousers as she pulled me down a narrow path through the trees, waiting for the longing to pass.

"You'll see," she said, skipping easily over a fallen sapling as if she knew the location of it by heart. As if she'd walked this path in the dark before.

When it seemed as if we'd traveled to the edge of the world, or at least the edge of Slaughter's property, I caught the flicker of a bright orange light, the thick smell of wood smoke, and the rhythmic beat of a drum through a break in the trees. Emmeline sped her pace, and her slippery palm was hard to hold on to as she pulled me with purpose through the snagging weeds.

She stepped out into a high field of corn, still dragging me behind her. A bonfire was burning. Slaughter's slaves were there, singing. Clapping and dancing around the fire.

Suddenly, they all stopped. It was as if a blanket had fallen over every sound in the forest, except for the crackle of the fire. Samuel, who had been sitting on the ground, smiling widely around a mouthful of salted fish and bread, swallowed slowly and rose to his feet. He stood as tall as an oak, his arms roped thickly with muscle. I'd once seen him carry two grown men across his back. His eyes darted to Em and then Ruth, where she cowered in the shadows, her head hanging low and guilt written all over her face. I wasn't supposed to be here. And now I understood why Ruth had been so terrified, knowing Emmeline planned to bring me.

"We should go," I whispered to Emmeline. I looked around the fire at the faces that had all been smiling a moment ago, now rigid with fear as they watched me.

"Thomas? Does he know?" Samuel looked back and forth between Ruth and Emmeline.

"No," Emmeline said, still holding my hand. "And Nathaniel would never tell."

But no one looked reassured by this.

"You have my word," I said. I let go of Emmeline's hand and reached out to Samuel, determined to assuage the doubt I still saw in his eyes. He considered me for a moment, his skeptical gaze coming to rest on my fiddle. Finally, he extended his hand, pausing before clasping mine. His eyes narrowed on my fingers, smeared wet with blood.

The sight of it stole my breath and I looked back at Emmeline. The gash across her palm glistened red in the firelight. Who? Who had done this to her? What could Em have done to deserve such a punishment? And why hadn't she told me?

Samuel took my hand and shook it, startling me back to the moment, forcing me to meet his eyes as the drums resumed their beat. Then he returned to his place beside the fire and belted out the first line of a call-and-response chant that seemed to ease everyone's tension, coaxing the dancers back to the fire, even as he watched me from the corner of his eye.

Everything in me told me to leave, that I was unwelcome here. If Slaughter were to find out—that his slaves were secretly congregating, indulging in such revelry under his nose—someone, maybe all of us, would suffer for it in stripes. Which is exactly why I couldn't turn around and leave. Ruth had trusted Emmeline. She'd trusted me. And Samuel had allowed me to stay, only because I had given him no choice. If I turned away now, they would all be left to wonder where I was going and who I might tell.

I looked down at my fiddle, unsure of what to do. This music was different than any I knew. Shaken, I looked to Emmeline, but she was already at Ruth's side, whispering as if to comfort her. She took Ruth's hand, turning it over to examine her palm. It was wrapped in a band of cloth as if she'd sustained a burn. Or a cut...

I clenched my hand into a fist. The skin was tight with Emmeline's blood. Emmeline's and Ruth's. Just one more part of her that Emmeline had chosen to share with someone else.

I stormed off into the woods toward the river. When I got to the water's edge, I dropped my fiddle in the grass and plunged straight into shallows until I was drenched to my knees. Frantically, I scrubbed the blood until my hands shone clean in the moonlight. An ache swelled deep in my chest at the soft splash that came from behind me. Emmeline wrapped her arms around my waist, her bosom pressed to my back. We stood for a while in silence. I closed my eyes, both savoring and resenting the warmth of it, knowing it would never be mine.

FOOD FOR THE DEAD

Tori had spent the rest of Saturday in her room trying to study, but her thoughts kept coming back to Alistair's angry red face. How he'd looked at her as if this had all been her fault. It hadn't been *her* decision to come here and move into Alistair's father's house. And she certainly didn't have anything to do with the fire. If anything, the fire seemed more like an accident. The police officer even said as much. That it had started in Matilda's house, and it was the wind that had carried the flames toward Alistair's fields. So why was Alistair so quick to point fingers? Why was he so desperate for someone to blame?

Unless it hadn't been an accident at all.

Al Senior gave me this house! And I ain't leaving....

Tori laid her pencil down and pushed aside her textbook, Matilda's words echoing in her brain. What if Alistair had set the fire? But what reason would he have? Matilda was already gone. His family had already made sure of that. Unless it was only to make sure she never came back.

Tori thought about the tractor in the cemetery and the busted padlock on the shed. She thought about Alistair's boot bracing open her front door and the broken window in her mother's room. Her stomach turned and her pulse became quick. She could imagine it all so clearly in her mind: Alistair sneaking into Matilda's house and lighting a match.

When it all became too much, Tori ran to the bathroom with the knife she'd hidden behind her dresser tucked inside her sleeve. After a few minutes, when her racing heart had finally quieted, she leaned against the bathroom door, applying pressure to stop the bleeding of a fresh cut and carefully inspecting the wound. She listened for signs of her brother snooping, but it was quiet until her mother slammed the front door and shouted up the stairs that dinner was getting cold.

At the table, she dared a cautious glance at her brother, but he didn't look back, and they ate their french fries one by one, as if they were both hoping to put off the inevitable.

Her mother was a whirlwind of frizzy curls and tension as she wet a washcloth and threw it in the dryer with one of her brother's school shirts to coax the wrinkles out. "Hurry up and finish eating. We're going to be late. And put on something a little more presentable. You can't wear sweatpants to a vigil," she said, pulling a broccoli casserole from the oven for Will's mother. It smelled too strongly of curry, and Tori was grateful she wouldn't have to be the one to eat it. She dragged the last of her fries through the pool of ketchup on her plate, put her dish in the sink, and headed to her room to get ready, dreading the night ahead of her. Jesse would be there. Alistair would be there. And everyone in town was probably gossiping about the fire.

The texts had started coming to Tori's phone around noon. First Magda. And then Drew. People already exaggerating the facts, making it sound like more than just a shift in the wind that spared her land and not Alistair's, as if Alistair had been the only victim. It didn't seem to matter to anyone that the fire had started in Matilda's house or that Matilda's home had been destroyed. Everybody was too busy spreading rumors about who might have wanted to hurt Alistair's family and why. And Tori seemed to be at the center of every conversation, everyone curious about the strange boy who'd been hanging around with the transplant on Slaughter Farm.

Tori shook off those thoughts and stood in front of the mirror. She turned sideways a little, looking down at her scars and her hair and her chest, hating herself for caring about Bobby Coode's opinion. She pulled on her tights and her skirt and tugged her school sweater over her head, careful to avoid catching the fabric on her bandages, determined not to care what anyone thought of her.

"Tori! We're late!" her mother called up the stairs.

By the time she tromped down, Mom and Kyle were already waiting in the car. Tori knew Alistair would be at the vigil, but she locked up behind her anyway. Though she was pretty sure it would take more than a lock to keep him out.

Tori had been to the Slaughters' house once before, the day they'd picked up their keys, but they'd never been invited inside. Her mother pulled into the long driveway. Last time she'd seen the lawn, it had been freshly mowed in diamond-shaped patterns, as lush and green as a photo in a home-and-garden magazine. As they rolled up the hill, Tori couldn't look away from a long brown swath of yard stretching up from the road, becoming a sickly yellow finger of dying grass. It looked like it was pointing up the hill and it made Tori shiver as they rolled past it, toward the familiar emerald lawn surrounding Jesse's house.

Tori shut the car door and stared up at the front porch. It was a farmhouse, like hers, but not like hers at all. It stood taller, wider, and newer . . . more stately. There were fluted columns and ornate carvings around the front door, and cool, crisp white siding and flower beds bursting with brightly colored marigolds. The smell of fresh mulch nearly choked her as she climbed the porch steps behind her mother. They didn't creak under her feet. And something about that felt off somehow. Like the house was waiting, silently watching them. Or like it was ignoring them altogether.

Dorothy Slaughter greeted them at the door, clearly surprised.

"I hope it's okay that we're here," Tori's mother said. "Jesse asked us to stop by."

"Of course he did," she said with a tight smile. Her eyes traveled up and down Tori's school uniform. Then her brother's. She took the casserole from Tori's mother and tried to disguise a grimace. "Thank you," she said sweetly. "I'll set it with the others."

They followed Dorothy inside. Her hair was tied back in a tight, neat bun. The few strands left loose seemed intentional, carefully curled so they waved gently around her face. She wore a silky blouse, a knee-length skirt pressed crisp, smooth stockings free of pills or snags, and dress shoes that shone with polish. Everything about her—her clothes, her home, her kitchen—was uncomfortably perfect. Family photos in ornate frames and antique-looking collectibles in glass cabinets were all neatly displayed. No clutter, no piles of loose odds and ends, nothing out of place. Tori and her brother walked stiffly, their hands close to their sides, afraid to touch or break anything.

"You have a lovely home, Dorothy," Tori's mother said in a small voice.

"Please, call me Dot." Dorothy set the casserole down amid a countertop already full of them. "We don't see much of you around here." Her words were honed with a judgmental edge.

"Oh, I put a lot of hours in at the senior center. I teach painting there."

"How lovely." Dorothy's smile mirrored Tori's mother's. It was almost blinding, how polite they were all pretending to be. "You know Jesse, my oldest," Dorothy said, pointing across a family room packed with neighbors and friends. Tori spotted Jesse's bright blue eyes and Bobby Coode's orange hair in the middle of it. "He and his cousins volunteer once a month at the senior center too."

"That's wonderful. I'm at the center almost every day, but I guess I haven't bumped into him there yet."

Mrs. Slaughter's smile pressed into a thin line and she snapped open a dish towel. "We were going to use the equity from his granddaddy's house to pay for his college tuition. Since you all arrived, he's had to spend a lot more time on his studies and sports to try to earn some scholarships. I suppose in some ways, we all bear each other's burdens, don't we?" She wiped her hands of Tori's mother's casserole and set her towel on the counter. "If you'll excuse me, I have family to greet. I'm sure you'll make yourself at home." She drew out the last bit as if it burned her to say it. Then she put her warm smile back in place and disappeared into the crowd of Slaughter-like faces. As she passed, a tall, silvering man in an expensive-looking black suit rested a sympathetic hand on her shoulder and kissed her on the cheek. It was Magda's father. He was talking to Jack Slaughter. Tori recognized him from all the election signs. Mr. Schiller spotted Tori across the sea of dark suits and church dresses. Tori gave a small wave, but he excused himself from Jack's side to take a call on his cell phone, pretending not to see her. The french fries Tori ate an hour ago hardened in the pit of her stomach. She looked the other way, only to find Jesse talking solemnly to a group of his cousin-friends, and she turned her back to the room, hoping none of them had noticed her.

Tori's mother took a deep breath, steeling herself before stepping toward the family room. "I'm going to pay my respects. Then we can go," she whispered. Tori and Kyle waited, grateful she didn't ask them to follow. For a moment, they stood awkwardly with their hands folded, trying to blend in without actually mixing with anyone. Tori listened, overhearing bits and pieces of conversations. There were no new leads in the search for Will. Cousin Maddie's basement had flooded that morning. Uncle Ray got bad news from the oncologist—he was no longer in remission. Little Jimmy was messing around in the yard, lighting aerosol cans on fire, and accidentally blinded the family dog. And just yesterday, Aunt Donna had caught her husband in bed with someone they went to church with . . . Tori couldn't hear who. There was plenty of talk of the fire, and the blight that had encroached into Alistair's fields. But no one seemed to care about Matilda's house at all.

After a few minutes, Kyle found a seat in the empty parlor by the front door and sat alone with his chin in his hands. Tori dropped stiffly into the chair beside him, feeling sick.

"Pretty depressing, huh?" Tori said, nudging him with her elbow.

Kyle got up and walked through the kitchen, where a line had formed around the casserole dishes, right out the back door.

Tori squeezed her bandage through her sweater until her cut began to throb. She listened to the slow tick of the grandfather clock against the far wall and the hushed conversation on the other side of it.

"What are those people doing here?"

"Dorothy says Jesse invited them." Alistair.

"I don't like it. They've got no business being here."

"I can't do nothin' 'bout it now, Jack. Not without raising a stink."

"You'd better get your boy in line. And make damn sure he stays on the right side of it."

She couldn't listen anymore. Tori got up and went to the kitchen, catching sight of her brother through the window over the sink. He was standing in front of the kennels in the yard. Four beagles—the dogs she'd always heard barking at night—jumped and howled, with their paws on the fence. He rested his palms against the chain-link, talking sweetly to them, hoping one of them would lick his hand. But they only howled louder, jumping higher. Tori went out to the yard and hollered for him to stop, but he couldn't hear her over the din.

"Don't worry about him," a smoke-husky voice said. "They're louder 'an hell, but they won't bother him. They're just not used to the attention." A woman close to her mother's age sat alone at a picnic table in the backyard, smoking a cigarette and tapping her ash into an empty cup.

"Why not? Are they in those cages all the time?"

"Not all the time. They're hunting dogs. Can't spoil 'em like house pets, or they won't hunt right." She switched her cigarette to her other hand and reached out to Tori. "I'm Francine. Don't believe we've met."

Francine. The name felt familiar, but Tori couldn't quite place where she'd heard it.

"I'm Tori Burns," she said, hesitating before taking Francine's hand. Tori waited for the look of recognition. For the usual cold stare she got from most of the Slaughters. But Francine didn't seem to register the name. Or maybe she didn't care. Her red-rimmed eyes looked swollen and tired. There was a disconsolate glassiness to them, a subtle slurred edge to her words that made Tori wonder what had been in the cup before she'd drunk it. And then she recalled Jesse's conversation with Bobby in the library. His Aunt Francine was Will's mother. Suddenly it made sense why she was sitting out here alone.

Tori recognized the plate of picked-over casserole in front of Francine. "You might not want to eat that," Tori told her. "My mom's not exactly the best cook."

Francine laughed halfheartedly, pushing it away. "I thought maybe it was just me. Nothing seems to taste right lately."

Tori looked at her feet, not really knowing exactly what to say. She knew what not to say—what everyone always said at things like vigils and funerals. Things like "I'm sorry"—vague apologies and awkward condolences that never came out right, somehow managing to do more harm than good. So Tori kept quiet. Her brother had given up on the dogs and wandered around the house toward the driveway wearing a long face, probably to wait for their mother in the car. Tori should have gone too, but it felt wrong to leave. She knew, because that was the other awful thing everyone always did after something horrible happened. They'd descend on your life out of nowhere with terrible food, say something stupid, and then they'd leave. And you'd be left to wash a million casserole dishes alone.

After a moment, the dogs started to settle. The sun was nearly gone and the dusky evening air was cold and humid, the first few stars twinkling through the clouds overhead. Francine rose slowly to her feet, steadying herself on the edge of the table. "I guess I'd better go inside with the others. It was nice meeting you, Tori," she said. And then the only Slaughter Tori had ever felt any connection with was gone.

Tori took the picked-over plate Francine had left behind and carried it to the kennel, past the soft glow of the porch lights, and used the fork to scoop the rest of her mother's casserole through the fence. The dogs fell quiet, ignoring Tori as they licked every drop from the kennel floor.

"You can't feed them that." Tori turned sharply as Jesse Slaughter reached around her, snatching the paper plate from her hands. "They're on strict diets." The dogs started barking again, lunging and pushing on the fence.

"So I've been told."

Tori and Jesse stood there, staring awkwardly at each other in the almost-dark. He wore creased black slacks and a French blue shirt that was probably the same color as his eyes, and Tori wondered if his mother had picked it out. The top button was loose at his throat, along with the knot of his silk tie, like he was ready for the night to be over. Tori couldn't get the conversation with his mother out of her head. That house . . . her house . . . was supposed to be his future. And now, for reasons neither of them understood, suddenly it had become hers.

"What are you doing here?" Jesse asked, startling Tori from her thoughts. It took her a minute to realize he was mocking her after their conversation a few days ago, when he'd been standing in *her* yard and she'd asked him the same question.

"Sorry," Tori said, cracking a smile in spite of herself. "My mom. She thought we should come. But I don't think it was a good idea."

"Why not?"

She could think of a million reasons. "That casserole is dangerous," Tori said, pointing to the empty plate. "You probably shouldn't eat it."

"And why's that?" He sniffed the mayonnaise and curry smudges left on the plate, his lip curling higher.

"Because my mom made it. And she's a pretty lousy cook."

Jesse laughed. And then everything felt even more awkward than it had before.

"I should go," Tori said, backing away from him. "I'll see you in school tomorrow. And for what it's worth, I really am sorry about everything that's happened. . . . You know, the fire. And Will."

Something shifted in Jesse's expression, and his warm smile cooled. He didn't answer, but she felt his eyes on her back all the way to the driveway. And suddenly, she felt like everybody else inside that house, descending on his life and saying all the wrong things.

THE WAYS WE BLEED

"I'm afraid," the girl says.

She kneels in front of me, our knees almost touching at the end of a short funnel of black-and-white light. A tear slides down her cheek.

The edges of the vision are fuzzy, blurring the leaves of the trees that frame us. The sky all around us is dark.

A hand ... my hand. But not my hand. It reaches toward the girl. "Don't be afraid. This will make us stronger. You'll see." I push the girl's cap back from her face. Gently push the tuft of curls back behind the small stump of dark skin that used to be the girl's ear. But there's no lobe left to hold her hair back, and it bounces forward against her face.

The girl closes her eyes. The moonlight casts shadows over her high, broad cheeks. She takes a steadying breath, then blows it out through trembling lips.

I take her hand. I hold her palm up against the moonlight.

Then I press a knife to her skin and cut it.

She gasps, squeezing her eyes shut. A steady trickle of dark blood drips down her arm and I pull her elbow toward me to keep it from reaching her skirts.

I take the blade in my hand. Close my fingers around it like a sheath, then yank the knife through.

I feel the hot burn it leaves behind in my skin.

I drop the knife to the grass. I take the girl's bloodied hand in mine.

"We are bound to each other. Always."

●　　　●　　　●

Tori woke to a painful pressure against her palm. Blinking against the lamplight, she oriented herself in her darkened bedroom. The house was quiet. It was dark outside. The clock flashed 2:00 a.m.

She'd fallen asleep holding her Pre-calc textbook, the sharp point of her pencil clutched in her hand. She shook it out, recalling bits and pieces of a dream as she sat up in the bed.

Loose papers and notebooks shuffled under Tori, and she scraped them into a pile and set them on the desk. She leaned against it, catching sight of herself in the mirror. Her hair stuck to her damp forehead and sweat ringed the collar of her shirt. The radiator was hot, the air in the room stuffy, and she wanted nothing more than to rip off her long sleeves. But there were three bandages hiding under them now and a trail of pink and purple lines, and she couldn't look at herself without clothes in this mirror and remember herself without those scars. Couldn't imagine swim meets and strapless dresses and everything else that came with them. Instead, she threw open her window and let the cold night air rush against her face. Then she crawled back into bed, turned off the light, and tried hard not to let herself dream.

●　　　●　　　●

Tori spent the morning trying not to make eye contact with Jesse. For the most part, she wasn't surprised that Jesse seemed to be doing the same.

He hadn't so much as looked at her during first period study hall, but Jesse's locker was inconveniently close to the gym, and their eyes locked when she'd come out of the lost and found between classes. Bobby wasn't anywhere around, and Tori rushed in the opposite direction when Jesse started toward her.

"Let me help you with that," he said, cornering her in the hall. He plucked her backpack from her shoulder and Tori snatched it back. It was heavy, full of other people's lost shirts and jeans she'd hoped were large enough for Nathaniel.

"I can manage," she said, putting it back on and locking both hands around the straps.

"Can we talk?"

"Now's not a good time," she said, stepping past him.

"We never got to finish our conversation the other day."

"There's nothing to talk about, Jesse. Find someplace else to have your party, okay?"

"I'm not talking about the party." Jesse took Tori by the elbow and pulled her up short, lowering his voice so he wouldn't be overheard as heads around them turned, trying to listen. "I'm talking about you and me. Not my dad. Not your mom. Not Bobby and Mitch and everybody else. Just me and you."

Tori wanted to laugh. Every time they talked, all she heard was what he had told Bobby in the library, about how she was all just part of a plan. How he had everything under control. "I'm late. I should go."

"Relax." Jesse's voice was suddenly hard as she began to walk away. "Bernie Wells is old-school. He doesn't charge by the hour. He won't care if you and your mom are late."

Tori faltered. Her backpack slid down her arm between them. Tori shook him off.

"How'd you know about that?"

"About your mom's meeting with Bernie?" Jesse chuckled to himself. "This is a small town, Burns. Too small. There are no secrets in Chaptico. At least none that stay buried for long."

"So I'm learning." Tori stormed down the hall with Jesse close at her heels.

He stepped out in front of her, forcing her to stop and look up at him. "Your mom might as well cancel the meeting with Bernie. He can't do anything for you all anyway. I've got a free period before lunch. Stay and hang out with me."

"What do you mean, he can't do anything for us?"

"My dad's not gonna let this go. My granddaddy wasn't right in the head when he wrote up that will, and everybody knows it. It was nice, what he was trying to do for you and all. But it was a mistake. He did the same damn thing with old Mrs. Rice's place. He gave her that dump five years ago and now we're stuck trying to buy the land back." A dark thought passed like smoke through Tori's mind, confirming everything she'd already suspected. Alistair had been the one to force Matilda out of her house. He'd burned it down to make sure she never moved back. "My dad's right. That house should have stayed in the family to begin with. Same with yours. But once Mr. Schiller proves to the court that Al Senior was incompetent, and everybody sees your family's got no real claim to the land, the judge'll make it right."

Tori felt the color drain from her face. Magda's dad was Alistair's lawyer. A fact she'd never bothered to mention to Tori.

"Your dad's taking us to court," Tori said through numb lips. Suddenly, her mother's appointment with Bernie made a lot more sense. There was no unresolved paperwork. Her mother knew, and hadn't wanted Tori and Kyle to find out.

Jesse paused. "You didn't know? Mr. Schiller's been building a case for weeks and my dad gave your mom the papers.... And, I mean, Magda... I thought you were friends...." Jesse whistled long and low, and the sound of it grated against her skin. She did her best to walk a straight line while her mind raced in circles. Jesse walked slowly beside her. "Look, there's no sense worrying about it now. My dad says the whole case could take months to sort out." He leaned into her, eager and hopeful. "Come to the dance with me. I promise, I'll talk to my dad. Maybe he'll rent the place back to you for a while until your mom can figure something else out."

"Like my mom rented you back your crops?" Tori snapped.

Jesse clenched his teeth. He looked around to make sure nobody had heard. But Tori didn't care. Her family couldn't afford any rent, which was the whole reason they had come to Chaptico to begin with. Al Senior may have been a good samaritan, and maybe he was senile. But there was a reason he'd chosen Tori's family. There was a reason her family was given that land and not anybody else. And she was determined to find out what it was. "I don't need your help. And I don't need a date!"

Jesse looked disgusted. "Tell me you're not seriously going out with that Nathaniel guy. He doesn't know anybody. He can't help you. Not like I can."

"How is *any* of this helping me?"

"I can introduce you around. You'll make friends."

"I've got friends."

"You sure about that?" he asked, letting the silence draw itself out.

Any minute, the bell would ring. Drew would be on his way to History upstairs, and Magda would be heading to English on the far side of the courtyard. She knew their schedules. She knew where they lived and their favorite foods and what they did for fun. That made them friends, didn't it? But who was she kidding? Friends were polite, easy to be with, and just as easy to get over. True friends were the ones you shared everything with. They'd tell you the things you needed to hear, even if it made you bleed.

Students began filtering toward their classrooms. Jesse looked back at Tori over his shoulder as he drifted along with them. Tori stopped in the middle of the hall and watched as they absorbed him. As they maneuvered to avoid her, muttering "What the hell are you doing here," Tori stood there, disoriented and lost, asking herself the same damn thing.

Tori left school through the side door by the gymnasium so no one in the office would see. She walked the two miles to the senior center, hoping she'd make it in time, and that her mother hadn't already left for her appointment with Bernie Wells. She waved at the desk attendant without stopping to sign in, and headed for the social center, where her mother taught her painting classes. The room was empty, so Tori jogged down the long, sterile corridor to the resident rooms. Sometimes her mother taught individual lessons or visited with the patients just to have something to do. She passed door after door, most of them open, the antiseptic hospital smells and the sound of daytime talk shows spilling into the hall. Tori listened for her mother's voice, peeking inside each room as she passed, glancing at the brass nameplates posted outside that all held familiar surnames from school.

And then she saw one that made her pause. Room 213.

M. RICE.

"What are you doing out of school?"

Tori spun to find her mother wearing a smock and a look of surprise. She smelled like paint thinner and concern.

Tori pushed Matilda Rice from her mind. "I want to go with you to see Bernie Wells."

Her mother's face fell. She led Tori down the hall, away from the patient rooms. "Why the sudden interest in Bernie Wells?"

Tori's cuts felt raw and her bandages itched. "Because I'm tired of having to go to school every day and justify my existence. I want to know why we're really here. I still have questions. Same as you."

Her mother's wedding band was too loose around her finger since her father's funeral. She fiddled with it absently, scrutinizing Tori. Her ratty smock hung slack around her too. It was splattered and smeared from work, a brightly colored palette that didn't entirely manage to hide the hopelessness underneath. A splotch of red paint caught Tori's attention, high on her mother's cheek, probably where she'd brushed her curls from her eye. She looked younger, frailer than she was, and Tori worried that Alistair Slaughter and Mr. Schiller would try to walk all over her. Tori reached up and wiped the past away.

Her mother stripped off her smock. "Are you missing any tests?"

"No."

"Any big assignments?"

Tori cocked an eyebrow. "None critical to my future as a well-adjusted, employable adult."

Her mother looked at her watch and dropped her smock on her art cart with a sigh. "Let's go."

*   *   *

Bernie Wells was a soft-spoken man with kind eyes. Not at all what Tori had expected. He had a snowy comb-over and a hawkish nose, and his bushy eyebrows seemed to reach across the desk sympathetically. His tan suit jacket showed signs of wear at the elbows, and a small stain (probably ketchup) stood out between the buttons of a dress shirt thin enough to reveal his undershirt beneath.

Tori wasn't with her mother the first time she'd met with Bernie, after he'd sent them a certified letter saying the Burns had inherited a portion of Al Senior's estate. And Tori didn't attend the closing when he'd given her mother the papers to the farmhouse and declared it officially theirs. The first time Tori had laid eyes on the house was the following day, when they'd packed their apartment in the city into a U-Haul and driven to the house on Slaughter Road.

"About what we discussed on the phone . . ." Tori felt her mother's anxious sideways glance. "Is there anything else you might be able to tell us?" Her mother skirted the question, speaking in vague terms.

"I'm very sorry, Mrs. Burns, but there's nothin' more I can tell you about the estate." He folded his age-spotted hands over a messy mahogany desk, covered in law books and loose scraps of paper, no evidence of a single computer or electronic tablet in sight. The phone had an actual cord in it. Tori fidgeted in her seat, imagining the hundreds of ways Mr. Schiller might crush him.

Her mother leaned forward in her chair. "There must be *something* else you can tell us. Something that can help us justify our right to be here. A person doesn't just leave a house and twenty acres of land to a complete stranger for no reason at all."

Bernie smiled politely, his mouth turning up at the edges but revealing nothing. "Attorney-client privileges don't die just because the man does," he said gently. "I've known Al Senior longer than you've been alive. He was a good man. He was fair in his dealings. Always did right by folks. It was his dying wish that your family have that house, Mrs. Burns. It was his land, to do with as he saw fit, and the law doesn't require a reason . . . only a will."

Tori bit her lip to keep from blurting out the question that had been eating her alive since her conversation with Jesse at school. The one her mother wasn't asking, because she was afraid to let Tori hear it.

So Tori asked it for her. "If there was a reason, why is Alistair Slaughter contesting the will?" Tori watched her mother sink back in her seat. The grandfather clock ticked in the corner. Bernie pursed his lips, and he and Tori's mother exchanged a heavy look. "Jesse says his grandfather was senile. That he was never supposed to give us the house. He says his dad's lawyer is building a case. He's going to prove we have no claim to the land and they're going to take it back."

Bernie peeled off his thin-rimmed spectacles and wiped them with a handkerchief he'd plucked from the breast pocket of his jacket. "It's a little premature to be filing a case just yet. The Slaughters are putting pressure on their lawyer to do it, is all. They're just a little sensitive right now, probably because of the timing, seeing as how Jack's running for county commissioner."

Bernie looked up as if he was expecting them to nod in agreement. Seeing the confused looks on Tori's and her mother's faces, he slipped his glasses back on and explained. "You see, a few years back, Al Senior gave a house to a particular woman—a close friend of his—and when he refused to tell anyone why, people started talking. Coming up with their own ideas about the nature of their relationship and stirring up a little bit of a scandal. At the time, Alistair was running for a seat on the board of county commissioners, the same post his brother's running for now. Some speculate his daddy's choice cost Alistair the election. I suppose it might be easier to stomach the idea that your father was an old codger who was losing his mind than to concede your loss to a better candidate. Alistair just can't seem to accept the fact that his father was a grown man with a mind of his own. And Jack's just worried about keeping the whole thing quiet, so things don't go the same way they did for his brother." Bernie sighed. "But it don't matter. Alistair Slaughter can run circles around that courthouse for the next four years for all the good it'll do him. Al Senior was no more senile than I am. And Alistair would do well not to open that can of worms." Bernie tapped the yellow legal pad on his desk. He looked from Tori's mother to Tori, and then back again. "Believe me when I tell you, your family has more legal claim to that land than he does. Will or no will."

The hair on the back of Tori's neck stood on end. "So it wasn't just some random gift. He had a reason for choosing us."

Bernie thought long and hard before answering, and for a moment Tori wondered if maybe he wouldn't. "He did."

"A reason that will hold up in court?"

Bernie pursed his lips. "Let's hope it doesn't come to that. At least, not yet. We just need to hold him off for a while."

Tori's mother held her curls back from her face, smoothing out the worry lines that had etched themselves deep in her forehead when Tori's father died. "I wish everyone else felt that way, Mr. Wells. You're the only person in this town that seems to think we belong in that house. Frankly, I'm tired of feeling like I need to validate our reasons for being here." She let the ringlets bounce back over her eyes, and Tori couldn't help but notice a few gray strands where they laced through at her temples. "I'm not trying to look a gift horse in the mouth, Mr. Wells. But this town has some sharp teeth, and I feel like this is all going to come back to bite us unless we can prove we have a reason to be here." Her mother rose to her feet, drawing her scarf tight around her neck. But Tori wasn't ready to leave. She still had so many questions. About why Al Senior had chosen Matilda and Tori's mother. About how Matilda knew Emmeline and Nathaniel. Somehow, she felt like the answer to why they were all here was buried in that cemetery. Tori followed her mother to the door. The bells tied to the knob jangled as her mother opened it, eager to go.

Tori paused. "Mr. Wells? How much do you know about our cemetery?"

"Oh, well, I..." He rocked on his heels. "I really don't know much. According to the survey in the will, it's pretty old."

"Then why doesn't it show up in any of the maps in the library?" Like the missing thirteenth floor in a hotel, Tori wondered if it had been erased to placate the superstitious, or if there was something there the Slaughter family had wanted to hide. Tori snuck a sideways glance at her mother. "Does it have something to do with Emmeline Bell?"

Bernie slipped his arthritic hands into the pockets of his golf pants, and looked down at his shoes. "Now, there's a name I don't hear so much these days. Not since I was a young man. Emmeline Bell. The Witch of Chaptico." There was a hint of amusement in his voice. Bernie clucked his tongue, thinking. "When I was your age, we used to tell that story 'round the fire this time of year."

A chill skated down Tori's spine.

"Do you know anything about her? What happened to her? Where she was buried?"

Bernie shook the loose change in his pockets. "I don't. No more than what you'd read in a book, but there may be someone who does. If I were new around town, and had questions...say, about local history and burial grounds...ghost stories..." he said with a playful lift of his brow, "... things of that sort...I might head over to the senior center. There's a lady livin' there by the name of Matilda Rice. She worked in the historical society for a lot of years. Before that, she worked over in the office of public records. She was real close with Al Senior before he died. As a matter of fact, she's the woman I was telling you about. The one Al Senior gave that old house to. It's a shame what happened to it," he said with a sad shake of his head. "Anyway, she don't talk much, except to herself these days. People say her health's been failing, but if you catch her on a good day, she might be inclined to speak with you."

Tori and her mother exchanged a look. "Thank you, Mr. Wells. We'll do that." Her tired eyes welled as she reached out to shake Bernie's hand. He held it a moment longer.

"Just be careful, Mrs. Burns. Once you dig up the past, you can't always put things back the way they were."

• • •

Her mother slumped in the driver's seat and stared out the windshield.

"Why didn't you tell me Alistair is taking us to court?"

"I didn't want to worry you or your brother. You heard Mr. Wells. He says we have nothing to worry about."

"Nothing to worry about? How about getting kicked out of our house? Again! We have no money! You have no job! Where will we go?"

Her mother shut her eyes. Tori knew it was a terrible thing to say. It wasn't her mother's fault they'd lost the apartment. It wasn't her mother's fault they hadn't been able to pay their bills after her father died. But they'd been lucky. Al Senior's will had made it through probate within a few months of her father's death. Bernie's letter had appeared a few days before the eviction notice had. And they'd been too relieved to ask any questions. Too desperate to doubt their right to a set of keys and the promise of a roof over their heads. If Alistair won, if they lost the house and the fields that supported them now, they'd have nowhere left to go.

"Alistair's entire case rests on his claim that his father wasn't legally competent when he drafted the will. They'll have to prove Al Senior was going senile."

"Did you see that man's office? There wasn't a single computer in it! He could have retired in the 1980s! Our *attorney* is probably senile. And Magda's dad has never lost a case."

"Bernie only has to prove that Al Senior had the mental capacity to make the decision to leave us the house."

Tori's thoughts ran to Matilda Rice, talking to herself in the grocery checkout and rambling about dead people as her life was being loaded into a truck. She had been Al Senior's friend. She was supposed to be Tori's best resource for answers about why they were here. "And what if he can't?" Tori thunked her head against the window.

"These kinds of cases can drag out for a long time. He only has to hold Alistair back for four years."

Alistair Slaughter can run circles around that courthouse for the next four years for all the good it'll do him.

"Then what happens?"

Her mother pressed her lips between her teeth.

"Mom," Tori said, sitting up. "What happens in four years?"

Her mother turned away and swiped a tear. "In four years, you'll be twenty-one. And if you decide to, you can petition the courts to open your adoption records."

"I don't understand. What does that have to do with . . . ?" Tori replayed Bernie's conversation in her mind, the little details she'd missed before coming back to her.

. . . your family has more legal claim to that land than he does.

He didn't say her *mother* had legal claim. He said her *family* did.

"You think this has something to do with me?"

Her mother stared out the windshield and took a deep, shuddering breath. "The estate is yours, Tori. The land, the house, all of it."

"I don't understand. . . . What are you saying?"

"It's under my care as your custodian until you turn twenty-one, but legally it belongs to you." She turned to face Tori, her eyes shining with tears. "I didn't tell you. I'm sorry."

Tori's insides felt like they were falling and her skin felt numb. "Are you saying I'm related to the Slaughters? Am I, like . . . Jesse's cousin or something?" she asked, not bothering to hide her disgust.

"I don't know," her mother said. "That's exactly the problem. No one but you can legally open your sealed adoption file. All we know is that the estate was left to you, in your name only. I can only assume that there's a specific reason for that. And since estates are usually passed from family member to family member . . ." She let her thought trail. But Tori knew the rest already. Jesse had said it himself. . . . Slaughter land stayed in the family. She could only assume Al Senior would have left his estate to another Slaughter. Even one his family had given away.

"No." Tori wrapped her arms around herself and shook her head, pinching her bandages. "No, no, no." All she could see was Jesse's blond hair and blue eyes, Dorothy's prim clothes and perfect skin, and Alistair's cynical face. She fit in less in that family portrait than she did in her own. "There must be some mistake. There's no way I belong to those people."

"You belong to us." Her mother closed a hand over Tori's and squeezed it tight. But her fingers weren't the same as Tori's father's. They didn't feel big enough to handle this. They didn't feel strong enough to hold her above water, and it was all crashing too fast over her head.

"They don't know, do they?" Tori's throat closed, suddenly thick and dry. "Alistair has no idea. That's why he thinks his father was crazy. That's why Bernie said Al Senior was keeping his reasons a secret. Because he didn't want to hurt his family. He wanted to protect them from the truth." He'd wanted to protect them from knowing about *her*. Like she was some big, dark family secret that could rip them all apart.

"I don't think they know," her mother said.

"So what are we supposed to do? Just wait for Alistair's lawyers to come up with some evidence that his father was crazy? Are we supposed to just wait for him to have us kicked out of our own house?" Tori couldn't hold back the rising panic in her voice. Her chest was caving in on itself. She dug her fingers into the bandages, but it didn't do anything to relieve the tightness in her throat. Magda's dad would never have agreed to represent the Slaughters if he didn't think he had a strong case. All the Slaughters needed were a few loyal neighbors and friends to come forward and tell the court that Al Senior had been behaving strangely. If Magda's dad could convince the court to reverse the decision, Tori's family would be homeless.

"I've never hidden anything from you, Tori. You've always known how you came to us. And if you want to know where you came from . . . if you want to know why that house has become yours . . . then we'll look for our own answers. We'll do what Bernie said. We'll talk to Mrs. Rice. Maybe she'll know."

"How's she supposed to help? Everyone thinks she's crazy too!"

"The symptoms of dementia come and go. It's not unusual to have moments of lucidity. I'll talk to her nurse and see if it would be okay to talk with her. We'll try to catch her on a good day and ask her what she knows. It's just . . ." She hesitated, as if weighing her words. "Remember what Bernie said, about digging up the past?"

Tori had never asked her mother about her birth family. She'd never wanted to make her parents feel like she was ungrateful, or that she wanted to be somewhere else, with anyone else. It felt like a betrayal, to admit to being curious about the people who had given her up. She didn't know how to ask for her mother's help without pushing her family away. And yet, if she'd been erased from the margins of another family's story, she needed to understand why.

"Let's go home," her mother said with a tearful smile. "We've got a lot of digging to do."

EM'S PUNISHMENT

"You wanted to see me, sir?" I pushed open the door to Slaughter's study. The first thing I saw was Emmeline's face, her eyes pinned wide over the top of his desk. Her skirts were hiked up across her lower back, and Slaughter stood behind her, his hand raised as if ready to beat her. Emmeline turned briskly away from me, a tear sliding down her splotchy cheek.

Slaughter's face contorted with rage. "I wanted to see you an hour ago! Now, I am otherwise engaged."

I looked down at the floor, afraid of embarrassing her any more than I already had. "Shall I come back, then?" I asked thickly. Emmeline's punishments were not unusual. At fifteen, she had developed a rebellious spirit, and Mrs. Slaughter was known to keep a switch in every room of their house, so as not to miss an opportunity to "beat the devil's influence out of the girl," careful never to leave a mark. Once, she'd made the mistake of taking a switch to Emmeline's cheek, and Slaughter had turned on his wife in a fit of rage the likes of which none of us had ever seen before. And I wondered what Emmeline had done to deserve such humiliation, to be bent over his desk bare-bottomed like a child.

"There's a leak in the shed roof. I want it repaired by nightfall," Slaughter growled.

"Yes, sir," I said, twisting my cap. My feet turned for the door, but my heart reached back for Emmeline.

"Sir?" I asked, my voice cracking on the word. "Shall I stay and repair the window you asked me to look at last week?"

"Why? You've already repaired it, have you not?" Slaughter demanded.

"I could mend the chair leg. I noticed it wobbles—"

"Go," Slaughter said through clenched teeth. "And close the door behind you."

He raised an open hand again.

She turned away from me, her face wet with tears.

I left and shut the door as Slaughter asked, but I couldn't make myself walk away.

"What are you doing out here?" Thomas asked in a gruff voice behind me. He listened to the persistent slaps and Emmeline's pitiful cries as they trailed through the door, his gaze landing pointedly at my knuckles, still white around the handle to the door. "Get on back to work, boy," he said, with a jerk of his head toward the fields.

"But Em—" I started, frustration giving way to anger inside me.

"There's nothing you can do for her. Best to let him get it over with quick. If you tarry here, you'll only draw out her suffering, and bring on some suffering of your own. Go on, then," he said quietly. "It'll be over soon."

Thomas nudged me gently, standing between me and the door. Something in the soft set of his jaw said he understood, but the breadth of his shoulders left little room for argument. I nodded, and headed for the shed. Needing to smash something. Needing to mend something. Needing to keep my hands busy before they did something I might regret.

It was nearly sundown when I climbed down from the shed roof and ran straight to Emmeline's quarters. She wasn't there. Instead I found her huddled on the floor of the scullery, crying into Ruth's arms. I ached to comfort her. To hold her close and whisper apologies in her ear for failing over and over again to keep her safe. For it seemed the stronger I had become, the less good I was able to do.

THE CUTTING

When they got home, Tori's mother hovered in the kitchen near the cutlery drawer, and Tori could feel her worrying, watching, waiting for Tori to run upstairs and shut herself in her room. The pressure was building in her chest, so she told her mom she was going out for a walk, and then she took off into the woods. She jogged to the barn, calling Nathaniel's name as she threw open the door. It echoed in the hollow space. The ashes had been swept from the fire pit, the barn cold and empty as if he hadn't been there for a while. Her blanket and pillow lay folded on the straw, and a handful of rusted and battered tools rested neatly on a table fashioned from two old sawhorses and a sheet of warped and splintered plywood from the shed. Breath held, she picked up a small nail and ran her finger over the point. She wondered how long he'd been gone and when he'd be back. She tucked the nail in her pocket, a seed of worry burrowing inside her as she wondered where he could be.

Nathaniel wasn't at the river either.

She ran the whole way back to the house. Then to the shed, seeing no sign of him. And then she heard it . . . a dull *pat-pat-pat*, coming from the cemetery. Tori took the path briskly, pausing halfway down the trail as something strange caught her eye. A large evergreen—or at least she'd thought it'd been green yesterday—stood brittle beside the path, its needles as dry as straw and the color of winter hay. She looked past it, toward the cemetery, where the blighted finger of dead, brown grass seemed to have begun stretching this way, leaving a pattern of lifeless undergrowth in its wake. The trail ahead of her was spotted with desiccated trees.

She hurried past them to the cemetery, only slowing again when she caught sight of Nathaniel's crisscrossed back between the trees. He stood hunched over the hole. *His* hole. Only it wasn't a hole anymore. He used the back of an old shovel to pat the last few mounds of dirt in place, then dropped it beside another pile of rusted tools from her shed. He wiped the sweat from his forehead before putting her father's turtleneck back on.

Tori started toward him, then paused when Nathaniel bent to retrieve Emmeline's figurine from the ground. He brought it briefly to his lips. Then, with his eyes closed, he held the doll over a small opening left in the dirt. Something inside Tori stirred. Breath held, she waited, watching, expecting him to drop the figurine in and bury her. Nathaniel held Emmeline suspended over the hole until his hand began to shake. Finally, with a muttered swear, he closed his fist and shoved the doll deep in his pocket.

Nathaniel grabbed a rock from the dirt over his grave and pitched it hard at the tree. It smacked into the trunk and Nathaniel grunted. His hand flew to the back of his head. He pulled it away and inspected his fingers, looking slowly up at the oak with the same mystified expression Tori had seen when he'd cut his hand at the river.

For a moment, he stood completely still. Then his chest heaved faster, and he reached for a saw. He leveled it against the trunk, pausing when the blade bit into the bark. With gritted teeth, he began to cut it.

Tori lurched out of the woods, screaming his name as Nathaniel pulled and pushed with quick, determined strokes. He cried out and sweat beaded down his face. Eyes squeezed shut, he forced the saw deeper into the trunk until he finally sank to the ground, leaving the saw anchored in the tree.

"Nathaniel!" Tori skidded to his side. He gripped his waist, moaning and writhing, and when she tried to help him sit up, he wouldn't be moved. She forced his hands out of the way, struggling to lift the hem of his shirt.

The cut was deep, gaping and jagged, exposing layers of skin and bands of muscle. The skin around it was slick with clear golden ooze.

Breathing hard, he groped at the wound. A trail of glistening sap dripped from his fingers and his whole body began to shake.

"It's okay," Tori said, trying to keep her voice steady. "You'll heal. You did it before." She gripped his hand tightly, waiting for his skin to sew itself back up. Nathaniel's head rested in the dirt, and his eyes shuddered closed. Thick yellow blood flowed from his side. It wasn't slowing. She looked back through the trees, to the porch lights of her house, down to the dusky edge of Slaughter Road across the field.

The oak tree rustled ominously overhead, and when Tori looked up, a handful of tiny leaves slowly began to unfurl. The saw hung poised in a deep crevice, sap dripping from its teeth.

She slid out from under Nathaniel and stumbled to her feet. Grabbing the saw with both hands, she pulled, leaning all her weight against it. Nathaniel cried out, but the blade didn't budge. She braced a foot against the trunk and tried again. Her arms began to shake, and sweat trailed down her back. With one final jerk, she ripped the saw from the tree, knocking herself to the ground with it.

Nathaniel arched with a scream.

Tori scrambled to his side, lifting his head and resting it in her lap. "Nathaniel?"

His body lay limp in her arms.

"Nathaniel, answer me! Wake up!" The crows in the field took flight with a chorus of shrill caws. A chill wind stirred, and the leaves that had bloomed just moments ago shivered and fell as the tree began to scab over with scaly new bark.

Tori yelped as Nathaniel's eyes fluttered. His hand crept to his waist, searching again for the wound. Clumsily, he pushed away the sticky fabric, revealing a deep pink scar that seemed to shrink as Tori watched. She hauled herself to her feet, dumping Nathaniel's head on the ground.

"You scared me half to death, Nathaniel Bishop! Are you trying to kill yourself?"

With a scowl, he pushed himself up against the trunk and muttered, "Would you blame me?" He made a face as he tried and failed to wipe the sap from his hands.

"That's not funny!" Tori remembered the look in her mother's eyes when Tori had woken up in the hospital after her mother had found her cutting in the bathtub. Terrified and helpless and utterly alone. She paced the length of the cemetery, digging her fingernails into the bandage on her arm and waiting for the pressure in her chest to ease.

"Victoria!" Nathaniel ran after her, taking her by the arm. "Whatever you may think of me, I didn't come here intending to harm myself." He released her, his voice falling soft. "Or to frighten you." He looked down at the saw, at the ground, at both of their hands ribboned with sap. "It's a very helpless feeling, staring into your own grave. When Slaughter tied me to that tree, I thought death..."

Tori's insides twisted, sickened by the fact that her own ancestors were the ones responsible.

Nathaniel rubbed the sap between his fingers. "Well... I don't know what I imagined death would be, but I never imagined I would spend it alone."

Tori didn't know what to say. There were no words that could erase what he'd been through. She looked away, at the blighted patches reaching out from the cemetery. At death pointing its finger at her. She wrapped her arms around herself and rubbed the chill from her skin. "I'm sorry," she said, feeling guilty for reasons she didn't want to think about. "It was terrible, what they did to you, but maybe..." She made herself look at him.

She made herself say the things she'd needed to hear when she'd thought she'd wanted to die too. "Maybe you're not alone. For what it's worth, I'm glad you're still here."

Nathaniel's eyes lifted to hers. "It's worth a great deal to me," he said softly. The color had come back to his cheeks, and he bent to retrieve the saw and the last of the tools in the awkward silence that followed. "I suppose I am indebted to you."

"Indebted to me? For what?"

"For saving my life. However strange a life it may be." A sad smile lifted the corner of his lip. They were both quiet, that awkward silence falling around them again. "I never asked for this," he said. "Most of the time, I think I'd rather be dead. But not now. Not in this moment. And maybe that's something."

"It's okay. I guess I owed you one." Their eyes caught again. Held. Every time she looked inside them, they seemed less strange to her.

"Is that what you were doing?" he asked. "That night I found you here?"

"It wasn't . . ." Her throat thickened with lies and excuses. She looked at the saw in her hand and pushed them back down. "It was an accident. I didn't mean to . . . at least . . . not that time." She'd never talked to anyone like this before. Not to anyone who'd actually understood. And she wasn't sure, but it felt like maybe he did.

"Maybe we could make a deal, then," he said, inclining his head to the oak. "I'll promise not to harm the tree if you promise not to harm yourself." He was serious. Waiting for an answer Tori couldn't give him. The nail she'd taken from the barn was cold and sharp in her pocket.

"I'll try." She started toward the woods.

"Tori, I—"

She scooped up the backpack she'd dropped at the edge of the cemetery and handed Nathaniel the shovel. "Come on. You're a mess," she said as he lumbered after her. "We can leave the tools at the barn and you can clean up in the river."

Nathaniel followed close behind. Or maybe it only felt like he did. Part of her wanted to put distance between them. The other part hoped he'd try to keep up. When they got to the barn, Tori dropped her backpack beside it. Nathaniel set down the tools. They stood beside the door in the dusky evening light, neither one of them ready to be the first to leave. He plucked a sticky pine needle from her hair with a wry smile. "Perhaps you should consider joining me. You don't look much better off than I."

"Whose fault is that?"

"Entirely your own," he suggested. "I never asked you to put your hands all over me. I was powerless to stop you."

Tori laughed out loud. "You wish!"

Nathaniel bit his lip and didn't argue. Tori felt her face grow hot. "Thanks, but I think I'll go clean up at home."

"I meant nothing untoward. I was only teasing you. I'm sorry," he said earnestly. "You look fine. More than fine. You look . . ." His mouth hung on the next word and he shut it before he could finish. Tori waited, wondering what he might have said if he had. "Please, come with me. The barn gets too quiet sometimes. And I . . ."

In the distance, Slaughter's dogs bayed and Nathaniel stiffened, abandoning the rest of his thought.

"It's okay," Tori said, watching the color drain from his face. "They can't hunt on our property. We're close to the edge of Slaughter's land. That's why they sound so . . ." They both paused to listen. Tori cocked her head as the barking grew louder. Closer.

"Come on. They shouldn't see you." She grabbed Nathaniel by the elbow, pulling him down the path toward the river. When the dogs grew louder, Nathaniel picked up his pace.

"What are you doing?" she asked as Nathaniel pushed Tori ahead of him. "It's not like they're looking for us."

But as the baying of the dogs rose to loud howls and she could hear the snap of branches under feet, she wasn't so sure.

Nathaniel pulled Tori off the trail, whispering urgently in her ear to go, go quickly. She picked up speed, dodging fallen branches, fighting the urge to look over her shoulder to see where the dogs were going.

It was nightfall when they reached the river. The darkness was disorienting; she wasn't even sure they were on her land anymore. A buoy light flashed in the channel and she ran toward it, bursting out of the trees onto the steep, muddy bank. Behind them, the dogs were barking, and Alistair's gruff voice cut through the dark.

"Git 'em! Find 'em, boy!"

The beam of a flashlight silhouetted the trees behind her. In front of her, the river was a dull black pool.

Poised to run, Nathaniel searched the shoreline. He jumped down to the water's edge, dragging Tori with him. They ducked and ran for a dark shape ahead . . . a wharf. The flashlight beams cut close over their heads, and they hunkered in shadow of the pier. Nathaniel pulled her in close, their backs pressed into the bank under the boards. Tori shut her eyes, listening as the dogs passed close. Nathaniel held her to him, staring up at the underside of the wharf. She smelled sweat and sap, blood and the river, and something else that Tori couldn't place. Something choking and putrid. She began to shiver. A buoy bell rang softly in the channel, and her whole body stilled as the sound of it echoed in some dark recess of her mind.

Moonlight sifted through a hole at the end of the wharf, casting a pale circle on the water.

A face stared back at her.

Bloated, distorted and blue. It bobbed half above, half below the waterline, two white eyes, wide in their rotting sockets. The boy's mouth gaped, filling and spilling over with the current, the rest of his body wedged under the pier. Tori sucked in a breath, catching Nathaniel's attention. He uttered a soft swear and covered her mouth, pressing her face to his chest, his lips against her ear, whispering for her to stay quiet. That it would be okay.

Nathaniel held her until the sound of the dogs faded. Then Tori tore herself out of his arms, out from under the pier, away from the boy's body. She stumbled through the shallows, her breath ragged and fast, aiming for a shoreline blurred by tears. She covered her mouth, fighting back sobs, clawing at mud and roots until she reached the top of the slope. Nathaniel caught up, winded as he reached for her.

"Don't!" she said, folding her arms and pinching them as she paced. She dug her fingers into her bandages until her cuts began to throb. Until her pulse began to slow. As the details of the dream she'd had the night she found Nathaniel bobbed, black and white and wavering, to the surface. "I had a dream. The night you came back." She was underwater. Her clothes were stuck. She'd fallen backward into the river. There had been a face above it, watching her. Had she dreamed of her own fear of the water, or had it been something more? "I dreamed of someone drowning. And now Will's dead!"

Matilda . . . That day they were packing up her house . . . Matilda's daughter had started to say it . . . that Matilda had known Will wouldn't come home. Matilda had been right. And the Slaughters had told everyone she was senile. Delusional. They'd driven her away.

"You saw it in a dream?" Nathaniel asked, bent over his knees, trying to catch his breath.

"I know it sounds crazy! But I swear, I . . ." Tori stared. "Your lip . . ." she said, struggling to make out the details of his face in the dark.

Nathaniel angled his face toward the shadows and wiped his mouth with his sleeve.

"It's nothing. Mud. We should go," he said, taking her gently by the shoulder. "They could come back at any moment, and they shouldn't find us here." He led Tori back the way they'd come, away from the river, toward the trail. In the darkness ahead of her, all she could see was Will's face. Her throat burned as she thought about what his last moments must have been like. How he'd died. Her porch light flickered in the distance like the light above the surface of the water in her dreams. All she could think about was getting home, the anonymous call she would have to make so the police could find Will.

She stopped at the break in the path.

"Will you be okay?" she asked Nathaniel.

"Don't worry about me." He paused. "But I think it's probably wise if you stay far from the barn for the next few days." Tori nodded. The police would be there, back and forth through the woods. The Slaughters too. As if he'd been reading her thoughts, he said, "I'll find you when they're gone. Once I'm sure they're not watching." But they were always watching. And she knew it was a promise he wouldn't be able to keep.

A STRANGER AMONG US

'm staring again through the black-and-white lens, down into a lap that isn't mine. Sunlight flickers over me, broken by shadows of the branches of a tree.

The oak. I recognize the gnarled and twisted shape of it. It's freckled with tiny buds, and the high grass around me bends with the wind, lush and healthy and green.

Spring.

My hands—her hands—hold a block of soft wood and a small knife. I whittle away at the rough exterior, then shape the carving with the fine point of the blade. My hands are steady. Like I've done this before. An etch here, a shave there. A woman's face. A cap. A long, bell-shaped dress, pulled tight around a firm, round belly.

I smooth the edges. Calloused fingers stroke the doll's face, tracing down the front of her dress without catching. I hold the wooden doll out in front of me, one hand drifting down to my own stomach, cupping a slight bulge beneath the heavy fabric.

With a quick dart of the blade, I slice my palm.

Blood trickles down over the doll. The pale wood is stained red with it. I massage it in and let the sun bake it dry in my lap.

Blackbirds sit close, pecking at lost grain in the dirt. They tip their heads and watch me curiously.

I touch the doll with a fingertip. The wood is smooth and evenly stained. I turn the doll upside down and poke its feet with the tip of the blade.

I yelp.

Pulling my bare foot into my lap, I twist it until I can see the blackened sole. A small drop of blood beads from a puncture.

I look up into the sky. Into the bright white light of it until the vision is gone.

Except for the haunting ring of a girl's laughter.

　　　　●　　　　●　　　　●

The slam of car doors chased any dreams from Tori's mind. The house smelled like coffee, and bacon frying, and the sun was already up outside her window, which meant she'd overslept her alarm. She slid out of bed and peeled back the edge of her curtain. A police car sat in the driveway, and two officers headed up the steps of her porch with Alistair Slaughter close behind them. Tori scrambled to throw on her clothes, the hazy events of the previous night coalescing as the men knocked on the front door. Walking home. Making an anonymous call through the crisis hotline to report Will's body. Falling numb and exhausted into bed.

Tori hovered, listening at the top of the stairs.

"Good morning, officers. Alistair." The tone of her mother's greeting suddenly changed. Tori could hear the precise moment when the plastic smile slid away. "Is everything all right?" Tori caught the note of panic in her voice. She descended the stairs with heavy steps and her mother's relief at seeing her was almost palpable. Kyle paused his video game in the next room and peered over the back of the sofa.

"May we come inside?" one of the officers asked.

"Where are my manners?" Tori's mother held the door open wide, sounding flustered as she ushered them in. "We can talk in the kitchen. Would you like some coffee?"

"No, thank you. We won't take much of your time."

A knot tightened in Tori's gut. Without a sound, she sat on the bottom stair in the foyer, watching through the railing as the officers and Alistair sat down at the kitchen table. She recognized one of them. He was the same one from last week, after the fire at Matilda's. The one who'd stood on her front porch, taking notes while Alistair drilled her mother with questions about Nathaniel. The other wore plain clothes, the gold badge on his belt visible through the lapels of his open jacket. Tori listened, barely breathing, so she could hear them all murmuring in the kitchen.

". . . caught up by his clothes under the pier. They found him close to the rear property line you all share with Mr. Slaughter."

"Oh, Alistair. I'm so sorry," her mother whispered, reaching to place her hand on his. He slid it to his lap before she could touch him.

"Understandably, the boy had been pretty upset, grieving the loss of his grandfather and all," the uniformed officer explained. He lowered his voice. "More than likely, it was a—"

Alistair slammed his hand on the table. "That boy was afraid of the water! He didn't know how to swim! He turned up in that river because someone put him there!"

The officers exchanged a brief look. The uniformed officer waited for the angry flush in Alistair's cheeks to settle. He cleared his throat and started again. "More than likely, it was an accident," he said with a quick glance at Alistair. "The pier is old, and isn't in good repair. But just to be sure, we do need to ask you and your family if any of you witnessed anything out of the ordinary around the time Will went missing."

Tori's mother was quiet. Tori heard the slow pour of coffee into her mug, then the others, even though they'd all declined. "Nothing I can think of. I mean, it's always quiet here. We're pretty isolated."

"What about that boy?" Alistair interjected. "Bishop. The one who's been hanging around with your daughter."

Tori's knuckles tightened around the banister. The plainclothes officer held up a hand to silence him.

"When we spoke last week," the uniformed officer continued, "there was mention of a young man by the name of Nathaniel Bishop who had visited with your daughter—"

"You can't possibly think Nathaniel had anything to do with this," her mother said.

"There's no need to be alarmed, ma'am. But it's possible Will might have known him."

"He did know him!" Alistair shouted. "His name was written all over Will's journal, and I want to know why."

The officers exchanged a significant look. "I don't recall any mention of a journal." The plainclothes one wrote something down in his notebook. "I'd like to see it. It might help us get a better understanding of what happened."

Alistair eased back, uncertain. "I guess you'll have to ask his momma about that."

The officer made another note and turned back to Tori's mother. "The boy's Aunt Dorothy said she remembered him mentioning someone named Nathaniel. Alistair seems to think this name is familiar too. It's possible he and Will were acquainted. And we are concerned that we've been unable to locate the young man. Alistair's son was under the impression this Nathaniel was staying with another student from the Academy, but apparently Jesse was misinformed. If you happen to know where we can find him, we'd like to speak with anyone who's been on the property recently."

"I really don't know." Her mother sounded ruffled. She was a terrible liar. "I haven't seen him in a while."

Alistair turned and spotted Tori where she sat on the bottom step.

He launched out of his chair, his finger pointed across the kitchen, making Tori scramble to her feet. "You ask her! You ask her right this minute! I want to know where to find this Bishop boy! This isn't a game, girl. My nephew's dead. And somebody set that damn fire to my fields. You tell this officer right now. I want to know where to find this Nathaniel Bishop!"

"Mr. Slaughter, maybe it'd be best if you wait in the car," the plainclothes officer said, resting a hand on his shoulder.

Tori's mother stood slowly, placing herself between the kitchen and the hall. But Tori didn't trust Alistair not to barrel right through her.

"Nathaniel is gone. He isn't here, and I haven't seen him," Tori said loudly. They all quieted. Alistair's eyes were still firmly on Tori. He reminded her of his hunting dogs, glaring and hungry, pushing up against the fence.

"Then you can bet your ass I'm gonna find him," he said, pulling against the officer's grip. "I'm gonna find him, and when I do—"

"I want to register a complaint against Mr. Slaughter," Tori said, channeling her inner Magda, wishing she'd had the sense to report it when Alistair had broken into her mother's room. "I want you off my land and out of my cemetery."

Alistair glared so hard at Tori, it felt like they were the only two in the room. "You oughta know by now that you can't keep me out, girl," he said in a low voice that made Tori shudder. "I know my rights. I've got a right-of-way to that cemetery."

"Only if you can prove the people buried there are related to you. And I heard you. . . . You said it yourself, when you were trespassing there last week. Nothing in that cemetery belongs to you. And nothing in this *house* either." Tori glared back just as hard. "This is *my* house. *My* property. If you don't stay off my land and leave my family alone, I'm going to petition the court for a peace order against you."

Alistair's face swelled red with rage. "You little bitch! I'd as soon see this house bulldozed to the ground than to see it given to you!"

The uniformed officer held Alistair back with both hands. "Alistair, I'm going to have to ask you to leave!"

Alistair clenched his jaw, looking between Tori and her mother. Tori's mother's mouth hung agape and all the color had drained from her face.

"This isn't over," Alistair said, shaking himself free from the officer's hand. "I promise you that."

The plainclothes officer followed him as he stormed out of the house, but Alistair made a beeline to his truck. He slammed the door and tore down the driveway, leaving a cloud of gravel dust in his wake.

The uniformed officer drew a long, slow breath and rested his hands on his hips, watching him go. "I apologize for disrupting your breakfast. I'll go ahead and register that complaint for you. But you'll have to follow up and handle the petition on your own." He added in a low voice, "Bernie can probably help you with that." Then he reached in his pocket and handed Tori's mother his card. "If you happen to run into this Nathaniel Bishop person, please give me a call."

●　　●　　●

Tori's mother waited until the officers were gone before she spoke. "Your brother told me Nathaniel was the one who fixed the window. Have you seen him this week?"

Tori stuffed her lunch in her backpack and zipped it hard.

"Why did you lie to the police?" her mother asked.

"Why did you?" Tori fired back.

"Because I'd hate to think that Nathaniel was involved in any of this. And I'd hate to think my daughter was involved with someone who could be! Is there something you want to tell me?"

No, there wasn't *one* thing. She wanted to curl up in her mother's lap and tell her everything. About what she'd learned about the Slaughters. About the color of a dead boy's lips and eyes in the dark. About Nathaniel . . .

"Where were you last night, Victoria? I checked your room. I know you weren't there."

Tori thumbed the nail in her pocket. She snatched her backpack off the floor and followed her brother down the porch steps.

"Can we talk about this? Please?" her mother called out behind her.

"Later," Tori hollered back. "I don't want to be late for school."

Tori paused at the top of the driveway, dumbstruck by the strand of discolored lawn stretching out from the cemetery woods, a crooked finger of brown grass like the one in Jesse's front yard. Only this one was cutting through hers, like a long, narrow shadow pointing toward her house. Feeling sick to her stomach, Tori ran past it to catch up with her brother. She would rather take the bus with her brother and a bunch of middle schoolers than ride with Magda to school.

Kyle walked fast, like he was trying to put distance between them. Probably because he didn't want to be seen with her. Tori wasn't sure she blamed him. She'd just threatened to file a restraining order against Alistair Slaughter in the middle of his own freaking farm. When word of this made its way around the Academy, she'd never live it down. None of them would.

"Kyle," she called after him. "Kyle, come on! It's going to be okay. I swear." He stopped at the end of their driveway, fingers hitched in his backpack like he was ready to make a jump for the bus doors the second it arrived. "Can you please just say something?"

He took a shuddering breath. "Mr. Slaughter's right. We shouldn't trust Nathaniel. He shouldn't come over anymore."

Tori rocked back on her heels, blindsided by his reaction. "But Alistair's lying. Nathaniel didn't . . ."

The bus pulled to a stop in front of them, its engine drowning her out. Kyle was through the doors before they even finished opening and when Tori stepped into the bus and climbed the steps, he had already crammed himself between two other kids in the front row. He wouldn't even look at her. As she walked down the aisle, every other kid on the bus stared, waiting for her to claim a seat. They set their backpacks and coats in the empty spaces on the benches beside them, like they hoped she wouldn't choose theirs, and she wished everyone else in this town would stop looking at her too.

THE CONTRACT

I stood in the open doorway to Slaughter's study, sweat trailing down the small of my back and soaking the armpits of my tunic. I should have cleaned up a bit before coming to find him. I should have—

"Don't just stand there hovering, boy. Come in." Slaughter dipped his quill and scrawled out a few figures, his attention more on the sheets of parchment spread across his desk than on me. I was a man of seventeen, yet he still insisted on calling me boy. Because men who rely on size as the source of their strength do well to make others feel small.

I stepped inside, whisking my cap off my head and holding it in my hands before him, hoping I hadn't trailed in mud from the field on my boots.

"Speak up, boy. I don't imagine much of your work gets accomplished while you stand here ogling me at my tasks."

"Yes, sir," I said, taking a step closer to his desk. "Two weeks from tomorrow marks the end of my seven years with you—both mine and Emmeline's. And I've come to inquire about our contract."

"What about it?" Slaughter asked without looking up.

I cleared my throat quietly, unsure of the best way to come out and ask. "Two years ago, I asked when our commitment to you would be satisfied. You informed me our contract had not yet been earned. But I've inquired with some of the men, and they tell me that the law limits a redemptioner's contract to seven years."

Slaughter continued to scratch out numbers with his quill, pausing not once to acknowledge that he had heard. My heart hammered beneath my ribs. Slaughter's thoughtful pauses rarely foretold anything good.

"And what makes you think you are worthy of redemption? You are lucky to be here, under my roof. You came to me with nothing. I should think you'd have the decency to show me more gratitude."

It was the same conversation we'd had when I was a boy of fifteen. But I was a man now, and without question, Emmeline was a woman. And I would not leave without the answers I came for. "I wish to see my contract."

Slaughter's quill paused, a mere fraction of a second, but long enough to reveal I'd struck a nerve. He did not answer. I put my shoulders back, gripping my cap in a fist at my side, refusing to cower to him anymore. "I will know what my contract entitles me to."

At this, Slaughter tossed his quill in its jar and put his hands flat on his desk, prepared to rise from his seat. But I was taller than I had been the last time I stood before him like this. And something in his eyes, the way he hesitated before rising, told me he was aware of this too. "You wish to know what you are entitled to?" He bit the words between clenched teeth. "You are entitled to nothing," he said, easing back in his chair again.

"How is that possible? There must be some—"

"Get back to work. I've no time for such nonsense." He resumed his work, taking his anger out on his parchment.

"I wish to ask Emmeline to marry me."

The quill snapped on the page and Slaughter cursed under his breath. He looked up at me slowly, thoughtfully, a crooked smile tugging at his lips. "You wish to marry her?"

"I wish to provide for her."

A muscle ticked in Slaughter's jaw. "Don't you understand, boy? There is nothing you can provide for her. You're a servant. And servants are not permitted to marry without their master's consent." He chuckled to himself, dismissing me with a pointed finger toward the door. "Get back to work, boy, and forget all this foolish—"

"Emmeline is already with child."

Slaughter's smile slid away. He glanced at the open door to the main house, his face ashen and tight. "I should like to marry her. To give her and the child a proper home. The men I've spoken with—"

"What men? What men have you spoken with?"

"Thomas and the others. He tells me a contract of indenture entitles us to land and provisions." Thomas was a felon, one of three convicted criminals released to the colonies under Slaughter's employment on the promise of a fresh start. Surely, if such men were entitled to land and provisions for their labor, then two innocents should have been worthy of the same, if not more. "The standard ten acres apiece is enough to sustain us."

Slaughter launched to his feet, throwing the contents of his desk to the floor. "How dare you! How dare you make such demands!"

"But our contracts! The ones the captain gave you! We are entitled to—"

"You are entitled to nothing! There are no contracts!" Slaughter was breathing heavily, his face red and swollen and furious.

"I don't understand—"

"Don't play daft, boy! You know as well as I do, your parents never signed any contract. They never sent you here, never made any arrangements for you. You were unwanted. An orphan. I spared you. The girl, I was willing to pay for. But you! You, they had to give away. And you belong to me until I say otherwise!"

The world rolled under me. No contracts. No papers.

"But the captain..."

"His papers were a forgery. They'll do you no good."

"But the law—"

"I AM THE LAW!" Slaughter pounded the desk with his fist. "And you have forgotten your place, boy!"

Dumbstruck, I backed myself toward the door. I had never forgotten my place. Slaughter had always been good at reminding me. I was his property. There was nothing here that belonged to me. And if I chose to leave, to run, there was only one thing that belonged to Slaughter I was determined to take with me.

ABSENCE AND THE HEART

When Tori got to school, she headed straight to the library to avoid bumping into Magda or Drew. Jesse and Bobby weren't there. Relieved, she sank into an empty carrel and checked her phone.

Where were you this morning? Magda had texted.

Tori put her phone away. For the rest of the day, she tried to focus on her schoolwork, but Will Slaughter's name peppered every conversation in the halls. Missing-person flyers were still hung on bulletin boards, stuck to restroom doors, as though taking them down was some kind of taboo. Jack Slaughter's election stickers were slapped on textbook covers and the insides of lockers all over campus, even though they weren't supposed to be. None of the Slaughters were in school, and yet she felt them everywhere.

When she got off the bus, police cars lined the short section of Slaughter Road where her property abutted Alistair's, closest to the point where she'd found Will's body. Fresh tracks cut through the field, and yellow tape draped along the trees to keep people out of the woods. Tori went straight home, resisting the urge to go looking for Nathaniel. Too many other people might be looking for him too. Instead, she spent her evening watching the smokeless sky over the barn from her bedroom window, wondering if he was cold or hungry, and hoping he was okay.

The next day was exactly the same. Tori woke up early and took the bus to school, turned the ringer off on her phone, and went out of her way to avoid running into Magda and Drew. The mood in school was unusually somber. Jesse's friends cut Tori sideways looks in the hall between classes. Kim didn't once kick Tori's seat, but Tori could feel her eyes boring into her back. Tori glanced back once at Lisa during third period and saw her scribbling in the margins of her notebook. At the end of class, she brushed past Tori's shoulder, dropping a piece of paper on Tori's desk that said *He's dead because of you.*

Will's death had been ruled an accident by the medical examiner and the police. But as far as everyone else was concerned, Tori's family had come to Chaptico and ruined his life, and that's what killed him.

In fourth period, Tori got another text from Magda: *I'm sorry.*

Tori didn't answer. True, they hadn't known each other long, but she'd thought Magda was a friend. She should have told Tori her dad was representing Jesse's family. That the Slaughters were trying to have Tori kicked out of her home. Instead, Magda had ridden with Tori to school every day, pretending not to know.

At least let me explain. Can we please talk?

Tori's fingers hovered over the screen. Her teacher turned from the whiteboard, looking over the rims of his glasses at the phone in her lap, and Tori tucked it away without answering.

That afternoon, she got off the bus at the end of Slaughter Road carrying a battered plastic violin case she'd borrowed from the music department at school, feeling lonelier than she had in a long time as Kyle's short legs ate up the winding dirt road ahead of her. She paused in front of Mrs. Rice's mailbox where her name had been scraped off, staring at the singed FOR SALE sign in the yard, her mind haunted by all the questions she never asked.

The lot looked so empty. All that remained was the pile of blackened cinder blocks that used to be the foundation of Matilda's house, and the burned stump of the old walnut tree. Al Senior had told Will that the answers were under the oldest branch of a tree. Tori could see straight through it now, to the charred earth that used to be Slaughter's soybean fields behind it, and she kicked herself for not talking to the woman. For not believing Matilda while she'd had the chance.

If there had been any answers here, there sure weren't any left.

She's been talkin' to you, even if you ain't been listenin'.

Tori wouldn't make that mistake again. She was listening now.

●   ●   ●

When she got home one afternoon, the yellow police tape was gone. The field was speckled with blackbirds, and the road alongside it was empty of cars. Tori cut through it to the cemetery. The budding leaves she'd seen dotting the oak just days ago had opened, green and shivering in the late afternoon sun, and she wondered what it meant.

She set the violin down beside the trunk and peeled off her sweater, letting cool lines of sweat trickle down the neck of her shirt. It had been too many days since she'd last seen Nathaniel. Enough time for Will's funeral. Enough time for Drew and Magda to stop coming to pick her up in the morning and to ease her brother's mind that Nathaniel wasn't coming back. Now, with the threat of a restraining order and a police report filed against Alistair, Tori hoped it might finally be safe to find Nathaniel. The cemetery was empty. As empty as it had been before Nathaniel had shown up here. And for the first time, that emptiness didn't feel like a reprieve.

She leaned against the tree and rested her head against the trunk, touching the bark Nathaniel had cut. Over the squawk of birds, she could just make out a rhythmic sound.

A dull echo through the trees.

Tori gathered up her sweater and the violin case, and followed it through the woods to the barn, toward the steady thunk of a hammer. She set the violin down just outside and cracked the door. Nathaniel perched high in the rafters, barefoot and shirtless on a makeshift ladder, securing a board across a hole in the roof.

Tori plugged her ears with her fingers and watched as he nailed the board in place, his teeth gritted around a handful of nails, and his hair tied loosely back. His pants were low on his waist, and she could see the outline of his ribs. A line of sweat trailed down his abdomen where the saw had split him open. Not so much as a scratch marked the smooth, hard skin there, even though his back was riddled with scars.

"Nathaniel?" Tori called out.

He swung the hammer down hard on his thumb, swearing loudly as he tipped off balance. With a terrible thud, he crashed to the floor.

"Nathaniel?" Tori knelt over him but didn't touch him, remembering how he had teased her after the incident at the tree. Aside from the dark rings under his eyes, he didn't appear too worse for the wear. And yet . . . his body was slow to rouse. Something felt off, and Tori couldn't quite put her finger on it.

His eyes fluttered open, a pale gray-green, his pupils swelling and shrinking as they came in and out of focus. "I should have known it was you," he said, turning his face away and pushing himself slowly to his feet.

"What were you doing up there anyway?"

"Mending the roof." He took a moment to steady himself before shaking out his fingers and inspecting his thumb.

"You should be more careful."

He looked shaken as he crossed the barn. Rolling his shoulder, he said, "I've suffered worse."

"I was talking about the noise. Someone might hear you."

Nathaniel shot her a resentful look and bent to retrieve the nails from the floor. Tori took in the scattered bed of straw, the dusty blanket tossed carelessly on top, and the mound of cold ashes in the fire ring. Beside it rested a small animal trap fashioned from washed-up fishing line and woven branches, the floor littered with shells and scraps of dandelion weeds and nuts, cracked oyster shells, and what looked like roasted animals, picked clean to the bones. Tori swallowed back guilt. She'd left him alone here for days with next to nothing.

"Are you okay?"

"I'm fine," he said pulling away with a jerk when she came up behind him and prodded a wound. His shoulder must have caught the edge of the beam when he fell. "I heal well enough on my own." The cut was as raw and as hot as his temper. They had agreed that she should stay away from the barn until things settled, but maybe more time had passed than Nathaniel had expected. With a pang, she realized the cut wasn't the only wound that would be slow to heal.

Nathaniel craned his neck to see it for himself, and his already pale face blanched even more. He snatched his shirt from the floor and drew it sharply over his head. "It will mend." He looked tired. Weary. From the work or because of her, she couldn't be sure. He rotated his shoulder, grimacing as he moved through the barn, his brow still furrowed and angry as he studied the underside of the slatted roof.

A pink stain began to seep through the fabric of his shirt. "You're bleeding."

"It's nothing that can't be fixed," he said roughly. But Tori wasn't so sure.

"No." Tori took Nathaniel's hand, surprising him. She turned it over to inspect his injured thumb. A pale purple bruise bloomed under the nail. "I mean you're *really* bleeding."

He twisted his hand from hers. "I said I know!"

The hammer lay beside a stack of salvaged boards. The saw rested beside it, and the sight of it made her queasy. Nathaniel's jaw tightened and he slapped a plank across the sawhorse. She caught the wince in his eyes—the stiff movement of his shoulder—when he drew the saw across it.

"Don't you think we should talk about this?" Tori said over the noise as he worked. She leaned around him when he didn't answer, trying to see his face and getting in his way. He dropped the saw on the table, refusing to look at her. "Don't you think we should talk about the tree? What it means? Don't you think we should—"

"I should have the roof patched by nightfall…" he said coldly. He shoved a handful of nails into his pocket and hefted the board to the ladder. "… in the absence of further insufferable distractions." His foot rested on the bottom rung, as if waiting for her to go.

Insufferable? Tori's face burned to the tips of her ears. She itched to watch him climb the ladder just so she could kick it out from under him. Insufferable? He'd spent the last three hundred years in a hole in the dirt. So she'd left him alone for a few days. Why should she feel guilty for offering him her barn to sleep in and putting her father's shoes on his feet?

"Insufferable? How about ungrateful! You can sleep in the river for all I care!" She grabbed her sweater and stormed out the door. Nathaniel dropped the board as he called after her, but Tori was already running through the trees. It was only after she climbed her porch steps that she realized she'd left the violin behind.

SOMEONE ELSE'S ROOM

ori threw open her bedroom door, hot and flustered and angry. Jesse Slaughter looked up, his blue eyes catching her horrified reflection in the mirror over her dresser where he was rummaging through her things. All her schoolbooks and papers had been shuffled around, and the framed photo of Tori and her father wasn't exactly where it was supposed to be. Jesse held a slip of paper between his fingers—a Lance Armstrong quote she'd cut from a magazine and stuck between the mirror and the frame. *Pain is temporary*, it reminded her. *Quitting is forever.* The same quote that had been printed on the T-shirt Nathaniel used to make her tourniquet in the cemetery. Jesse dropped it onto a pile of her things.

"What the hell are you doing in here?" She scanned the rest of her room for anything else that was missing or out of place. Her closet door hung open, her trophies turned face out so her name was showing. The cardboard box from the high shelf inside was gone—a loose collection of odds and ends left behind by the Slaughters when Tori had moved in. Tori's stomach dropped at the sight of it, lying open on her bed.

"I never knew you were a swimmer," Jesse said, watching Tori stuff the trophies deeper in her closet and slam the door.

"I'm not." Saying it out loud made it feel closer to the truth, and she hated him for making her do it. "Why are you going through my stuff?"

"I came to talk to you."

"You shouldn't be here."

"Whatever," he muttered, carelessly touching her things. "Your mom had to go to the store and she said I could wait for you inside."

"Inside my bedroom?" Tori followed him, righting picture frames he'd moved and closing books he'd opened, her hands trembling with anger.

He shrugged. "I got bored watching your brother play video games. I figured I'd check out the old house." He sat heavily on the edge of her mattress and took a deep breath through his nose. "It smells different," he said, leaning back on his hands. The porcelain doll Tori kept hidden in the box rested on the bed beside him.

"Get out."

"Relax," Jesse said through a laugh, as if any of this was funny. "I didn't mean anything by it. It doesn't smell bad. It smells like you. That's all. Just . . . different." The way he looked at her, punctuating the last word, the familiar way he reclined on his elbows across her bed, made Tori feel like she was the one out of place. He reached for her throw pillow. It was old and worn with a verse her mother had cross-stitched when Tori was little. Jesse's brows knitted, his lips moving as he read the words. Tori could almost hear her mother whisper them as his eyes moved back and forth across the pillow.

> *Not flesh of my flesh,*
> *Nor bone of my bone,*
> *But still miraculously my own.*
> *Never forget for a single minute,*
> *You didn't grow under my heart,*
> *But in it.*

She grabbed the pillow from his hands and clutched it to her.

"What do you want, Jesse?"

"I just came to see how your meeting with Bernie Wells went."

"That's none of your business."

He raised an eyebrow. "Fair enough."

"Can you please just go?"

He shook his head with a look of mild disbelief. "I'm *trying* to be the bigger person here."

"By barging into *my* house, the house your family is trying to kick me out of? And then asking how the meeting with my lawyer went? Like this is somehow okay?"

"Come on, Burns. Don't you think this is hard on me too?"

"Please, Jesse! Tell me how any of this must be hard on you!"

Jesse sat up slowly. "You want to know how hard this is for me?" A strange shine touched his eyes. His voice grew thick, and Tori's breath caught as he drew the old porcelain doll into his lap. She opened her mouth to tell him not to touch it. She started to reach for it, then stopped herself.

"I'll tell you a little something you probably don't know about this house." His jaw hardened as Tori tugged on her sleeves, wrapping her arms tightly around herself, feeling naked under his stare. "This house belonged to my granddaddy. That bedroom your mom's been sleeping in? That was his room. That bedroom Kyle's been camping out in? That was my daddy's. He grew up in that room. My Uncle Jack? He slept downstairs, in your *guest* room," he said through a choked laugh. "And *this* room belonged to my Aunt Francine, up until the week you got here."

Tori swallowed an angry lump in her throat, no choice but to stand here and listen to Jesse Slaughter explain all the reasons this house didn't feel like it belonged to her. All the reasons it shouldn't.

"These pink walls? Hers. This furniture? Hers. This doll," he said, squeezing it tightly in his fist. "Hers. She grew up here, in this room, in this house. Then she moved back in five years ago when my granddaddy got too old to take care of himself. Her son, my cousin Will? He lived in that bedroom," he said, pointing at the wall between Tori's brother's room and hers, his voice shaking with anger. "So don't think for a minute being in *your* house isn't hard on me."

Breath held, Tori watched as a trickle of blood dripped down the length of his arm, and the first deep red drop stained the quilt on the bed. Jesse looked down at the doll in his hand. At the stain blooming over her dress. "What the hell. . . . ?" he whispered, staring at the slice in his palm. He turned the doll over and peeled back her dress, exposing her stuffing. Horrified, he withdrew the razor blade hidden inside, tucked safely away the day they'd moved in. It was the only safe place. The only place Tori's brother wouldn't nose around. The only place her mother wouldn't think to look, in a box of things that had never belonged to her. A box her mother had packed up herself.

"You . . ." He rose slowly to his feet, his voice shaking with a quiet rage. "Your family . . ." He stared at the blade. At the red stain spreading over the doll's dress, like some horrific voodoo charm. "You ruin everything," he said. "The house, the fires, that goddamn blight, and now Will. . . . We've lost everything because of you." Jesse tossed the doll away from him and grabbed his sweatshirt, squeezing the fabric to stem the flow of blood. He stood over her, staring down on Tori until she couldn't breathe beneath the cold blue of his eyes. "I used to feel sorry for you. About what happened to your family. About what my family's trying to do. About the names people call you behind your back. But you know what, Burns? I don't feel sorry anymore. Not for a damn bit of it. It's all gonna come back around on you. I promise you that."

He tore out of her room and down the stairs, slamming the porch door behind him.

They tied Thomas to the tree the next morning. Slaughter's men marched me out to watch. Slaughter paced in front of all of his servants and slaves, a long switch held behind his back.

"It has been brought to my attention that Thomas has been offering some among you legal counsel, suggesting means through which you might avoid repayment of your debts. So I thought it best to make very clear the punishment for traitorous and ungrateful behavior." His gaze fell hard on Emmeline. "Nathaniel, step forward, boy."

I felt her head snap to mine, her panic almost palpable. I came to stand before him, my shoulders straight and my chin high, determined not to reveal the depth of my unease.

"Nathaniel has been discussing contracts and the law with some-one who knows a great deal more about them than perhaps he realizes. Thomas, tell the boy, how long have you been in my employ?"

"Eleven years, my lord," Thomas answered.

"Louder!" Slaughter shouted. "This is a lesson they all should hear." The side of Thomas's scratchy face was pressed hard against the bark, distorting the M-shaped scar on his cheek, his arms wrapped almost half-way around the tree, bound tightly enough to suppress the flow of blood to his hands.

"Eleven years, my lord!" he cried out.

"Did you not advise young Bishop that redemptioners need only work for a period of seven?"

"I did, my lord!" he cried out again, a tear sliding down his cheek.

"And why would a redemptioner such as yourself be bound to my service for so many years?"

"Because I ran, my lord!" Thomas's tears flowed freely then, the tree absorbing his wracking sobs.

Slaughter looked out across each of our faces. "Like a coward and a criminal, he ran to avoid his obligations. And he was apprehended. Tell them what happens to redemptioners who violate their contracts! Tell them what happens when they break the law!"

"We forfeit the time we've earned, my lord. And the contract commences again."

"And . . . ?" Slaughter grabbed Thomas by the hair and pulled his face from the tree.

Thomas sobbed, struggling to breathe in his bindings. "And we're punished, my lord."

"And how many strokes did your defiance earn you?"

"Nineteen, my lord. One for every day I was gone."

Slaughter shoved his face back against the tree with a look of disgust. "Clearly, I was too generous. Your punishment didn't leave a strong enough impression on you, and now, because you've forgotten the consequences, you advise others to follow in your shoes."

"No, my lord! Please, my lord! I never told anyone to run!" Thomas strained against his bindings.

"Nathaniel," Slaughter said, reaching out to me with his switch. "Thomas will be rendered unfit to oversee the fields. His responsibilities now fall upon you. It seems fitting, as you were the one who was ill-advised, that you should be the one to repay him." The switch wavered in the space between us. "You will deliver upon his back nineteen proper lashes. Let it be a warning to all of you not to follow Thomas's example."

I clenched my fists, my resolve. I looked past him and said, "I will not, sir." I would not beat a man for talking with me. Would not repay candor with deceit.

I braced for the blow, or for the grabbing hands that would strap me to the tree opposite Thomas. Instead, Slaughter looked at me and laughed.

"You do not wish to accept the responsibility? Very well, then. Samuel!" Slaughter shouted to the crowd of servants and slaves behind me. Samuel pushed forward to the front of the line. "You will deliver thirty-eight strokes upon Thomas.... Nineteen for Nathaniel, and nineteen for you." My stomach fell away. Thomas had stopped crying, his scruffy jowls slumped against the tree. His eyes were closed, his face pale and shaken, all the fight inside him gone. Samuel and I exchanged a brief glance. If Samuel refused, as I had, the burden would pass on to the next of us, and Thomas's suffering would grow by nineteen strokes more. Samuel took up the switch.

He gritted his teeth and began counting. The crowd gave a collective start at the crack of the first lash. Across the sea of mournful faces, I spotted Emmeline's turbulent gray eyes. Her hands rested on her belly, on the secret hidden under the loose fabric of her skirts. The longer we stayed, the greater the punishment. The more we resisted, the more others would suffer for our sins. Emmeline and I... We had lived through so much. We could survive more. But the child? I met her eyes, and in that moment, I made her the same promise I'd made when I took her hand on that wharf.

I will not let you go. I will not let harm befall you. And when I go, I will take you with me.

THE MENDING

Tori stood on the paint-peeled porch after dinner, breathing in the crisp night air, struggling to shake off what Jesse had said when he'd left her room. The farmhouse smelled like old secrets, choking and oppressive, and a pressure had been building inside her, a wave of anxiety rearing up over her head. She was shaky, thinking back on the conversation. On the way his hands had touched everything in her room. On the way he'd looked at her when he'd discovered the razor in the doll, as if Tori were responsible for every nightmare his family had endured.

She slung the trash into the open cans, making them clatter against each other. Through the screen door came the rapid-fire artillery of Kyle's video game, then the rattle of dishes in the kitchen and the answering bark of Jesse's dogs. He was upset. Grasping at straws. And Tori had been an easy target for his anger. Because Jesse didn't know what Tori knew . . . that she might be part of his family too.

She jammed her hands into the pockets of her jeans and shivered under her sweatshirt, her chest tight at the thought of going back in.

"I'm going for a walk," she called through the door, pulling it shut before anyone could answer. Her feet kicked up the first fallen dry leaves as she crossed the yard, out of the glow of the porch lights. The night was clear, the stars thick and close overhead, and the ground was awash in moonlight. A breeze blew across the grass, rolling over it like waves, and in the distance, Tori heard the river lapping at the shore.

She lifted her head, taking in gulps of air, wondering if any of this would ever feel familiar or comforting. Wondering if any of this would ever relieve the pressure inside her. If it would ever not feel like she was drowning here.

Across the yard, something shimmered against the trees. She walked toward it, trying to make out what it could be in the dark. An oyster shell. It hung from a low branch by a loop of rough twine, the mother-of-pearl inside polished to a high shine that caught the porch lights and reflected them back at her in iridescent shades. A tiny irregular growth protruded from its smooth surface, maybe the beginning of a pearl. Tori held it in her hand. The outside edges were rough, ugly and sharp, but the center . . . the inside glistened soft and bright, making it hard to look away.

A quiet melody reached Tori's ear, a haunting tune barely audible over the rustle of leaves. She took the oyster shell from its branch and followed the sound into the woods. The melancholy note of a violin hovered on the wind, lifting goose bumps over her skin. Tori stood listening beside a pile of cracked shells just outside the open barn door.

Light flickered between the boards and smoke swirled from a hole in the roof. The weathered wooden husk of the barn, gray and lifeless a week ago, felt welcoming and warm. She drew the oyster necklace over her head and tucked it under her shirt before she peered into the opening.

A small fire crackled in the ring of river stones on the floor. Nathaniel sat beside it with his eyes closed, the school violin tucked under his chin, his song filling every shadowy inch of the room. A smile touched his lips, and the hostility that had settled deep in Tori's chest earlier began to loosen, filling the space behind her lungs with some unidentifiable emotion. His skin glowed with the firelight, and the turtleneck covered the scar at his throat. He looked real. So human and alive. Both happier and somehow also sadder than she had ever seen him before.

The last inch of the bow pulled across the strings. Nathaniel opened his eyes. They were circled in dark rings, and his smile was weary when it found her waiting in the open door.

"I didn't think you'd come," he said, standing by the fire. When Tori stepped inside, he lowered his head and fidgeted with the bow. "I'm grateful."

"I know it's not much." She gestured to the beat-up plastic violin case. "I borrowed it from the school. It was the best I could do."

Nathaniel flushed. "I'm grateful for the fiddle too." His smile was self-effacing. "I was worried you meant what you said earlier, about me sleeping in the river."

"I thought I was an insufferable distraction."

Nathaniel's hair fell like a curtain over his eyes as they dropped back to the floor. "Not an altogether unpleasant one." He tipped his head, looking up at her cautiously. Tori felt her cheeks warm. "Will you stay?"

The fire snapped with tiny sparks. The air in the room was drowsy and warm. "Maybe just for a little while." She eased down beside the fire, tucking her legs beneath her.

Nathaniel lifted the fiddle. He closed his eyes and began to play. His fingers danced quickly over the neck, the bow skating over the strings.

"You weren't kidding when you said you knew how to play," she said over his rousing jig. He raised an eyebrow and a slow smile spread over his face as he changed tunes.

"And what about you?" he asked without missing a beat. "What is your great talent?"

"Me?" Tori stammered. "I . . . I don't really have one."

Nathaniel's bow paused in the middle of a note and he lowered his violin. The barn felt smaller in its silence. "Don't be modest. You're too quick not to have a gift of your own." He leaned closer, the firelight playing on his skin. "Tell me."

"I *did*," she said, feeling stupid for the weakness that had settled into her rusty muscles. "I don't have a talent. At least, not anymore."

"I see." Something in the way Nathaniel watched her made her feel like he knew. Like he could see every day she hadn't spent in a pool reflected in her eyes. "You know," he said, resting the fiddle in his lap, "once you love something enough—enough to let it consume you completely—it becomes part of you, even when it's buried and quiet."

The fire hissed and sputtered. Tori looked down at her hands. Hands that hardly remembered holding her father's. Hands that hadn't stroked the water in a long, long time.

She watched Nathaniel raise his violin to his shoulder with a stinging envy, the way she sometimes watched Drew carry his swim bag through the halls at school. Like it was comfortable. Effortless.

Nathaniel waited a breath before settling into a piece Tori recognized. He performed it slowly, drawing out the notes until each one sounded like a tear about to fall.

"'Greensleeves,'" she said through a lump in her throat.

"You know this song, then?"

"A little," she said. "My father used to sing it to me."

Nathaniel raised his eyebrows. "Do *you* sing?"

"He wasn't my real..." She pressed her lips between her teeth. He'd been gone for over a year and it still felt like a betrayal to say it out loud. "I was adopted."

"Not all things come to us by blood."

But Tori wasn't so sure. Swimming had always felt like it came from somewhere inside her. Like she'd been born to it. Like the water was the only air she could breathe. And yet, her father used to stand on the side of the pool, far enough from the lip so he wouldn't fall in, shaking his head in amazement as he timed her. Inhaling and exhaling with her, as if they shared every victory and breath.

"Who taught you to play?" Tori asked.

"A man by the name of Thomas, another indentured man—a redemptioner branded for murder from England, contracted to oversee Slaughter's slaves." Nathaniel massaged the scar on his thumb. "I guess I was a boy of ten, or maybe eleven, when I started lessons. Thomas handed me an old fiddle and said, 'Here, boy. You'll need to learn so you can play for the master's parties when I'm gone.' We'd practice every night after we'd finished our work, all the while Thomas kept saying, 'Soon, boy. Soon I'll be a free man and that fiddle will be yours.'" Nathaniel grew quiet, his thoughts lost somewhere in the fire. Tori didn't know if it was the smoke or nostalgia that made his eyes shine.

He swallowed hard and picked up his fiddle. "I'm sorry. You didn't come to listen to me tell stories." And before Tori could find the words to tell him she liked hearing him talk—that when he spoke, something inside her was listening—he began playing again.

Faster and lighter, the notes filled every inch of the barn, plugging the holes with wood smoke and laughter. Nathaniel's whole body responded to the music, and she thought this might be the first time she'd seen him truly alive. His smile became wide and contagious, and Tori clapped out the rhythm even though she didn't know any of the words. When the last jig wound to an end, Nathaniel held the bow and the neck of the fiddle in the long fingers of one hand, and plucked Tori up off the floor.

"Maybe you can't sing," he said, breathless, his sweat-slicked skin shining in the firelight. "But everyone can dance."

Tori's face was tight and sore from laughing, but she couldn't seem to stop. "I don't dance!"

"Not even with Jesse Slaughter?"

Her laughter calmed. She wondered if he'd seen Jesse leave her house tonight. If he'd gotten the wrong idea. "Especially not with Jesse Slaughter."

Their eyes caught at the familiarity of the moment . . . his hand around her wrist, the firmness of his grip—the same as at it had been at the river, when he'd tried to see under her sleeve. But this time, Tori didn't pull away. Nathaniel's eyes were hazel and honey, and her mouth became dry when they fell to her lips. "I told you. I don't dance."

His hand slid from her wrist to her fingers, drawing her close. "Tonight, you do."

Nathaniel's hand was warm—warmer than it should have been. He held hers for a long moment, then tucked the fiddle under his chin and raised the bow, his deeply shadowed eyes never once leaving her as he began to play.

Tori crossed her arms over her chest, unsure of what to do with them and determined not to try.

He laughed. "See? You've already got the knack of it."

She stood there awkwardly, her feet planted to the floor as he fiddled a slow box step around her, keeping them shoulder to shoulder and back to back. It reminded her of a do-si-do she'd suffered through during square dance lessons in middle school. He disappeared behind her. When Tori turned her head the other way to find him, his face was there . . . close to hers, making her breath catch as he stepped slowly around her, backward to his first position. The narrow distance he kept between them felt intimate. A tease, the way his eyes seemed to want to touch her, but his body never did.

He paused close to her. Closer than before. The bow froze on the strings and the last vibrations of the final note simmered between them.

"Is it hopeless," he asked, "this desire I feel to accompany you to the dance?"

The oyster shell felt suddenly heavy around her neck. There could never be enough silk and sequins to cover up the pieces of her she didn't want to show him. Because she didn't trust herself not to fall in love with him if she did. And because if she stripped herself bare of all her secrets, her flaws might be the only thing he'd be able to see.

"I don't think it's a good idea."

He lowered his violin and nodded wearily. "I understand. It was foolish of me."

Tori rushed for something to say, some way to put back the pieces. "It's not that I don't want to. It's just . . . people will notice you're different. That you're not from here—"

"But I am from here," he said softly.

"But not *now*. If anyone figures out what you are . . ." Nathaniel winced. The words were out before she could take them back. Suddenly, Tori wasn't sure which one of them she was talking about. "If anyone figures out how you got here, before we figure it out for ourselves . . . It's just safer here. For you. For now. For both of us." She took his hand and gently squeezed it, tilting her head to catch his eye, searching for a glimmer of hope in it. "Besides, I already told Jesse I have other plans."

He nodded again, this time pressing his lips between his teeth to hold back a smile, turning before she could catch it widening over his face. He knelt to put the violin back in its case, and Tori's eye leapt to the dark stain seeping through the back of his shirt.

"Nathaniel." Something in the sound of her voice made him still. "Your back. It's still bleeding."

He rose slowly, not bothering to try to look at it.

Tori gently brushed his hair aside, revealing a mix of russet-brown blood and sap. He tensed as she pulled up his shirt. The wound was open, pink and hot around the edges.

His eyes—the change in their color—in *his* color. The dark rings beneath them. The rise in his temperature. In his appetite. The change in the tree...

"Have you ever heard of a woman named Matilda Rice?" she asked, trying to mask the tremor in her voice.

He shook his head.

"I think there's someone you should meet."

can't move. I jerk my arms hard, but they're bound tightly against my body. I can't see. I'm wrapped in something. Kicking. Screaming.

I'm dumped on a hard surface. I hear a latch snap shut. . . . A lock . . .

The black-and-white vision clears as a cover is pulled from my eyes. I'm lying on a rough wooden floor. Women in long skirts and caps surround me. They're staring at my body. I look down at myself. I am naked. My stomach is swollen and hard.

"The girl has been consorting with the devil," one of them says. She has thin lips and sharp eyes. She stands alone, blocking the door. "It is the task of this committee to seek out his mark. And then the devil's concubine and his seed will be destroyed."

The vision becomes blurry as the women converge. I'm thrown down on a long wooden table. They poke and prod me, lifting my arms and peeling apart my legs. Their hands twist and pinch and pull every inch of me. Then, they roll me over while they pull at my hair, my scalp, and pry at my bottom.

"She has no marks, missus," one of them says.

"Then the devil has hidden it, and we look until we find it," the thin-lipped woman snaps.

A long silver needle—long like the ones my mother used to knit with— slices the periphery, ominously distorted by the black-and-white lens as it crosses my field of vision and comes to rest in front of me. I stop thrashing, unable to see anything but the sharpened tip.

"The mark of the devil will not bleed." She tests the point on her finger. The women lie across me as I thrash and scream. She pierces my skin, over and over, blood smearing as the women fight to hold me. With a scream, I kick the woman by my foot, hard on the side of her head, knocking her to the floor. Two women rush to help her. I swing my fists. My knee catches a nose and someone cries out. I roll from the table to my feet and bolt for the door. The thin-lipped woman stands in my way and I tackle her to the floor. Wrestle the needle from her hand. I push her cap off her head and grab a fistful of her hair, pulling her to her feet.

I press the point into the side of her neck.

Two of the women cower, injured on the floor. Two others hover over the one with a broken nose. My arms are smeared with blood. I back out the door, dragging the thin-lipped woman with me.

"I will curse every last one of you! If you harm my child, you will suffer a witch's wrath for all eternity!"

I throw the thin-lipped woman to the ground. Then I run for the shelter of the trees.

●　　●　　●

Tori woke with a start the next morning. Her right arm tingled where she'd been sleeping on it. She took a moment to get her bearings, shook the pins and needles from her hand, and checked the time on her phone. It was early, but at least it wasn't a school day. She sent a text to Magda. *Whose side are you on?*

The silence in the moments that followed seemed to drag on indefinitely.

Tori set the phone on her nightstand. She should have expected this. Tori wasn't only asking Magda to choose between her or the Slaughters. She was asking Magda to choose between Tori and Magda's dad. And suddenly, Tori regretted being so tough on—

Yours.

A spark of hope dared to flicker inside her. Tori picked up her phone.

Then help me? Please?

Another long silence. Longer this time. And Tori wondered if she was asking too much.

Drew and I will be there in an hour.

*　　　●　　　●　　　●*

An hour later, Nathaniel and Tori waited in the trees at the bottom of Tori's driveway. Tori adjusted Nathaniel's turtleneck to cover his scar. A feverlike flush replaced the pallor he'd worn when he first came out of the ground, and the shadow of a beard bloomed around his jaw. She looked up into a pair of tired, soft gray-green eyes and opened her mouth to speak, but words failed her. She'd spent the last half hour trying to figure out how to prepare him for this—for the things he was about to see that would make no sense to him, and things he might not even believe. But it was all too much. It was impossible to cram three hundred years into thirty minutes, so instead, she reminded him that no matter what he saw, he shouldn't react. Shouldn't gape. Shouldn't ask any questions until they were alone, when she promised she would do her best to explain it all.

Drew pulled his Mazda to the side of the gravel road, and Tori took Nathaniel's hand, checking for other cars before walking him out of the trees. When they were close enough for the exhaust to warm their legs, Tori snuck a glance at Nathaniel. He didn't so much as flinch, but Tori could feel the shift in his posture, the sudden rigidity of his hand in hers. It was warm. Warmer than last night when they'd danced.

"He's hot," Drew mouthed through the window. It took Tori a moment to register what he meant as she opened the back door to let him in.

Magda twisted in her seat, extending a hand to Nathaniel. "I'm Magda and this is Drew. We are so excited to finally meet you. Tori hasn't told us nearly enough about you!"

"Which is probably for the best," Tori muttered. She still wasn't sure she had forgiven Magda. And Tori wasn't ready to trust her with something as big as Nathaniel's story. Not until she knew how it connected with her own.

Drew put the car in gear and pulled onto the road. Nathaniel's knuckles turned white on the armrest and Tori put her hand on his with a light squeeze as a reminder. He gave a barely perceptible nod of his head.

Magda softened her voice, turning to Tori. "I really am sorry. I didn't know my dad was taking Alistair's case until it was too late." Her eyes welled, her apology tumbling out on shaky breaths. "And by then, I was too ashamed to tell you."

"Well, *I'm* glad we got all this out in the open so we can put this little shit-storm behind us," Drew said. "This whole thing is ridiculous! You can't evict someone from their own house."

Tori knew better. Her family had been through it before. It had started the same way, with a letter, a ticking clock in an envelope, counting down the days until their home would be taken away. "You can if you can prove they don't legally own it," she said. "Alistair's trying to prove his father wasn't competent when the will was drawn."

"Tell her, Magda," Drew said without taking his eyes from the road. "Tell her that's never going to happen."

Magda turned, but not far enough to look Tori in the eyes. "I'm sure everything will work itself out."

Nathaniel's hand tensed under Tori's. "The Slaughters, they're trying to take your home. Why didn't you tell me?"

Tori didn't answer, hoping he would let it go.

"They're the worst kind of people," he said under his breath. "Ruled by selfishness and greed."

The words cut deep, leaving a lingering sting and making her feel ugly inside. Tori fingered the oyster shell under her sweater. "Maybe not all of them."

All three of them turned to look at her. They looked like they weren't really sure who she was anymore. For that matter, neither was she.

Drew pulled into the drop-off lane in front of the senior center. "We're going to get some coffee. We won't be far. Text us when you're ready for a ride home." He hesitated before pulling away from the curb. Magda wore a grave expression as she waved good-bye.

"Come on," Tori said, turning for the door. "Maybe we can figure out what one of us is doing here."

* * *

Tori rapped softly on the door to Matilda Rice's room and pushed it open.

"Mrs. Rice?" She poked her head inside. Matilda sat in a recliner beside the bed, the handle of her cane curled in one arthritic hand and an old bible resting in her lap. She looked up, poised to stand. But then her milky-white eyes locked on the doorway behind Tori and she slumped back in her chair, her jaw slack with surprise.

"You was right, Emmeline," she whispered. "All this time, you was right."

The hair on Tori's neck stood on end. Tori pulled Nathaniel inside and shut the door. He approached Matilda slowly, as if trying to place her.

"Come closer, boy." She rested her cane on her lap and reached out to him. Her arm shook with involuntary tremors. Nathaniel knelt beside her. Matilda took him firmly by the jaw, her gnarled fingers digging into his skin as her other hand reached for the collar of his turtleneck.

He tried to stumble out of her grip. "What are you after?"

She fixed him with her cloudy eyes. Something he saw inside them made Nathaniel hold still. She pulled back the neck of his shirt, running her fingers over the mark around his throat. A cold breeze stirred the curtains.

"Nathaniel Bishop." She drew his name out slowly, clucking her tongue against her remaining teeth. "I've been waiting for you. 'Bout damn time."

"How do you know my name?" he asked, straightening his collar and rising to his feet.

"Emmeline's been talking about you since I was a child. Before that, she talked to my momma. Before that, she talked to *her* momma. Emmeline's been driving my family crazy since she passed on back in the 1730s. And frankly, I'm tired of listening. Tired of dragging her 'round with me just to spare my daughter from having to hear it too. 'Bout damn time." She shook her head and gestured to an empty chair. "You know why you're here, boy?"

"Emmeline," he said.

Matilda nodded.

"So the stories are true. She escaped Slaughter's people." He pulled the chair in front of her and eased down into it, letting go of some invisible burden. "And what of the child?"

"Emmeline's baby girl? Don't know much about her except that she lived long enough to start a family of her own. Emmeline and her friend, Ruth. They ran that night. After Slaughter hanged you, the fires started." The mention of a fire tickled at Tori's memory. The dream she had of the night Nathaniel had died. As Matilda told Nathaniel the story, the dream began to unwind like a movie in Tori's mind. And she could see it all, as though she had been there.

"Everything burned," Matilda said, gazing off across the room. "The house, the barns, the fields. Everything but that damned tree burned to the ground. The fire never touched it. Never touched you," she said, looking at Nathaniel. "And everyone was so busy running around, trying to put out the fire, no one noticed that Emmeline, Ruth, and Sam were already gone. Took what they could and ran. Crossed the river and built a camp in the woods. Later, they met up with a few other runaways. Took 'em in and made 'em all family. Changed all their names and gave 'em all new papers. Emmeline got real good at forging papers. Somehow, they all made do." Matilda sighed. "Emmeline figures Slaughter's people were too afraid to go looking real hard for her. She figures they were all just glad she was gone."

Nathaniel's face was haunted as he bore the news of losing them all over again. And Tori hated it . . . the guilt she knew he was feeling. The pain of being alive when your reason for living is gone.

"How did this happen? Why isn't Nathaniel dead?" she asked.

Matilda blinked, turning to look at Tori as if she was only just realizing Tori was in the room. "Because Emmeline saved him."

"Because Emmeline *cursed* me," Nathaniel scoffed.

"Not you, boy," Matilda said. "She cursed that tree."

"I don't understand," Tori said, but Matilda's attention was fixed on Nathaniel.

"She magicked that tree to take care of you. To keep you from rottin'. To give back the life it took from you. That tree ain't bloomed in three hundred years. Because it's been giving all its life to you." She pointed a finger at Nathaniel. "Like it or not, that tree is part of you now."

"But why?" Nathaniel shot to his feet, pacing the room.

"Because she loved you."

Nathaniel's whole body stilled. "Then why . . ." His voice broke on the words. "Why bring me back? To what end?"

"Because you made a promise, boy. A promise you gotta keep."

Nathaniel sunk into his chair and scrubbed a hand over his face.

"What promise?" Tori asked.

"You ain't got much time, boy," Matilda said. "That Slaughter boy got curious and started diggin' around. Won't be long before the rest of 'em start doin' the same. And if they find what's hidin' under that tree, then you're in danger, boy. You both are."

"Wait," Tori said, stepping between them. "What do you mean?"

Matilda didn't answer. Nathaniel got up and began pacing the room.

"What does she mean, you don't have much time? Time for what?"

"She means I'm dying," Nathaniel snapped.

Tori sat down on the edge of the bed, any arguments left inside her knotting into a tight ball inside her throat. Nathaniel squeezed his eyes shut and whispered an apology.

Dying . . . It shouldn't have surprised her. Inside, she must have known. . . . The change in his color, the shade of his eyes, the change in his blood . . . It all had to mean something. But it didn't seem fair that it should mean this.

"I don't understand. If the tree is supposed to protect him, why isn't he healing anymore?"

"Because he ain't under it," Matilda said matter-of-factly. "And the longer he stays up here, the less time he's got left."

"Then what's the point? Why bother saving him if he's only going to die anyway?"

Matilda shook her head. "Honey, we're *all* gonna die someday. Ain't a spell gonna stop that. We all just got to use the time we got in this world to do what we're meant to do. We were all meant to do something. Just got to figure out what it is. But you already know, don't you, boy?"

Matilda fell quiet, her head tipped toward Nathaniel. Nathaniel pulled the small wooden figurine from his pocket and held it, his thumb gentle as it moved over the doll's belly.

"She saved me because I wasn't the only one she intended to protect."

Matilda reached for him. "That magic Emmeline made for you before you died . . . she did it because she cared for you, because she knew her child was gonna need you. And you made her a promise—her and that child.

"That spell she cast on you . . . it came from in here," she said, pressing her gnarled hand against his chest. Then to his forehead. "Not from in here. She knew you were gonna die, and she was angry, and young, and scared. And without thinkin' it all the way through, she did the only thing she could to save you. She cast that spell hoping you would come back. That if she did it right, you might rise up on your own. Only she was careless and somethin' went wrong."

Nathaniel shut his eyes. He closed his hand around the doll and pressed it to his lips, as if he was searching inside himself for some way to forgive her.

"After Slaughter hanged you, Emmeline went into a rage. She lost her mind and put a curse on every one of his people. Not just one generation. She cursed 'em all. Every generation of Slaughter to come. And without realizing, she tangled you and that tree all up in it. It wasn't no protective spell that brought you back. It was—"

"Dark magic." Nathaniel and Matilda turned to stare at Tori. "That's what you told me. I remember. I know the curse. I heard it. In a dream." Black and white flashes of it came back to her in a rush. "*Warned be the wicked who would harm those bound to me. Should the blood of Slaughter spill the blood of mine own, the tree will bear witness against him. Tragedy will befall him, suffering and fire. And my curse will not quiet until Slaughter blood is shed.'"* Nathaniel stared at the floor, dumbstruck, taking it all in.

"So that's it?" Nathaniel rose to his feet, pacing the room. "This is the reason I'm here? To fulfill her curse on Slaughter's people? To shed their blood and end it all? No, there has to be another way."

"Only one way," Matilda said. "Might be Emmeline's blood brought you here. But only Slaughter's can send you back." Matilda's milk-white eyes slid to Tori, and Nathaniel froze.

"Send who back? Back where?" Tori demanded.

"No." Nathaniel shook his head at Matilda. "I won't go back."

"Back under the bosom of that tree," Matilda said.

Nathaniel set his jaw, looking as livid as he'd been the day he'd tried to cut the oak down. "And what if there is no tree?"

A cold wind stirred, rustling the curtains. The blinds rattled against the window glass, and the flower vase on Matilda's night table tipped and fell to the floor, shattering like an exclamation. All three of them fell silent, watching the water spread across the floor.

"If there is no tree..." Matilda said, turning to Nathaniel. "Then there is no boy."

Nathaniel took Tori's arm and pushed her abruptly toward the door.

"Wait!" Tori argued. "I have questions."

"We should go."

"But I don't understand—" The door shut behind them. Nathaniel walked fast, eating the length of the hall with long, angry strides, pulling Tori along with him until they were outside on the sidewalk.

"What does she mean, it was Emmeline's blood that brought you back? If Emmeline's been dead for three hundred years, there's no way she could have..." Tori reached for the bandage, touching it through her sweatshirt.

She'd cut herself.

In the cemetery.

She'd bled on the ground. Right before Nathaniel climbed out of it.

"This is why," she whispered, trying to make sense of her racing thoughts. "This is what brought you out of the cemetery. My blood. It's Emmeline's, and . . ."

Nathaniel sank back against the brick wall and pressed his palms into his eyes. "I sacrificed everything, *everything* to protect her. Because I swore that I would. I gave my life to save her and Slaughter's bastard child. And this is how she repays me. With sap in my veins and a life that withers come winter."

"Slaughter's child? But I thought . . ." The words stuck in Tori's throat. *The girl has been consorting with the devil.*

Nathaniel wasn't the father of Emmeline's child. The child was Archibald Slaughter's.

"You thought what?" Nathaniel rose, his head tipped curiously toward her. "You thought Em and I . . . ?"

Suddenly, her circumstances made a perfect twisted sort of sense.

It was supposed to be a seven-year contract. . . . We were to have ten acres each plus provisions. . . .

Emmeline was entitled to land. To property she and Nathaniel had been promised, property they had *earned*. Al Senior must have discovered the truth, that Tori was Emmeline and Archibald's descendant. He'd honored his family's broken contract with his own will, and never told them why, and the land had never left the family.

Nathaniel reached for her.

"Don't," Tori said. She didn't know how to be with him now. *Who* she would be to him now that they both knew who she was. It was as if Matilda Rice had opened a door to a pitch-dark room and shoved Tori inside. And now she was stuck in this place—this place she had always imagined being filled with light and answers—and she couldn't feel her way through it.

Just an hour ago, she'd wanted desperately to know where she'd come from. How she'd gotten here. And now? "I don't know who I am anymore."

Nathaniel took her by the shoulders, lowering his head to look at her until his eyes were all she could see. "If you believe nothing else right now, believe this." He gripped her tightly, making her look at him, making her hear. "You are Victoria Burns. And nothing that happens to you—nothing they do or say to try to make you believe you are anyone else—will ever change that. You are the same person you were before this place. You are the same person you will be when it's over. And you are a better person than all of them." He brushed a tear from her cheek, and Tori rushed to wipe it away herself. She took a deep, shuddering breath.

"Come on," he said, taking her hand. "There's something I want you to see."

THERE MUST BE SALT

t was nearly dusk when Drew and Magda dropped them off at the foot of Tori's driveway. Nathaniel's gait was sluggish as he led Tori by the hand up the hill.

Nathaniel didn't stop when the grass changed color under his feet, even as Tori tried to slow to see it. The blight had encroached on her front yard, the tip of it stopping a few yards before her front porch. Nathaniel's gaze traveled the length of it, but he kept his pace, drawing her away into the woods.

"Where are we going?" she asked when they passed the footpath to the barn.

"To the shore."

"Why?"

Nathaniel's toe caught on a stick and he stumbled, the heaviness in his steps mirroring her own. Tori felt raw and stinging and weary inside.

"You'll see." Tori followed him until the shimmering surface of the river cut like diamonds through the branches of the trees. Nathaniel stood on the embankment looking out over the river, a faraway glassiness like longing in his eyes. Tori wondered what he was remembering. Who he was missing. Why he'd brought her here.

"'Whosoever then first after the troubling of the water stepped in was made whole of whatsoever disease he had,'" he said, barely loud enough for

Tori to hear. His cheeks flushed pink. "The book of John." He picked at a long blade of dry grass, squinting out over the rippled shine. Tori stood quietly, a little behind him, discomforted by the thought of getting too close to the shore.

Nathaniel inhaled deeply. He plucked a small stone from the muddy ground and sent it skipping out over the river's surface. "The water . . . I've always had such a love and loathing for it. On one hand, it was this great, terrible thing that divided me from my family. As a boy, I ached to cross it, but even if I dove in and swam, or stowed away with a captain and sailed, the distance was so vast and I was already so changed, it felt like nothing would be the same had I returned. And yet . . ." he said with a bittersweet smile. "And yet, some days, the water was the only place that felt like it could heal me. There were days when it seemed to wash me clean of this place, the blood and the sweat and the rage. It cooled the burn in my heart. Made my weariness weightless." Nathaniel turned to Tori. He looked at her. Through her. "Being here, in the river, made me feel closer to the person I was before all this."

Nathaniel pulled his shirt over his head and tossed it over a piece of driftwood.

"What are you doing?" she asked as he kicked off his shoes.

He waded out into the autumn-cold water and crooked a finger at Tori, grinning like a fool. "I'm reminding you who you are. Now get in before I have to drag you in myself."

He disappeared under the surface, then popped up again, brushing his wet hair back from his face. His cheeks flooded with color and his eyes flew open wide. Icy water slid over his arms and his chest, every muscle tensed with the cold.

"I can remember who I am from up here," she told him, trying to look everywhere else.

"What are you so afraid of?" He splashed her, missing by inches.

She touched the oyster shell hidden under her shirt. She hadn't stepped a foot in anything deeper than a bathtub since her father had died. Back then, there were only a few cuts. A few small, pale scars that she probably could have explained away. Now there were so many. Underneath her clothes, Tori wasn't sure she was still the same person anymore. She wasn't as strong as Nathaniel. She couldn't strip them off, wash it all away, and remember who she was before all of this. There was a piece of the Slaughters inside her. Her insides felt as ugly as her outsides now. And she didn't want Nathaniel to see.

"Very well," he said, surging toward the shore.

"What are you doing?" She backed away from him as he climbed the bank. He shook out his hair like a dog after a bath, spraying her with freezing cold droplets. She covered her face against them, and in that moment when her eyes were closed, he scooped her up, throwing her over his shoulder.

"Put me down!" she shouted, slapping his back, feeling the scars beneath her fingers. He plunged into the water and didn't let go. When they were waist-deep, he threw Tori in.

The water was a shock of ice down her spine. She held her breath against a yelp and scrambled for the surface. When she broke it, his laughter was the first sound Tori heard. She sputtered, her shoes catching in the mud, pulling her down, and she lifted her feet to paddle farther away from him. Nathaniel swam after her with a self-satisfied grin.

"That was a shitty thing to do!" Tori said. But as the words came out, Nathaniel rolled over onto his back, staring up at the sky with an expression more content than she'd ever seen him wear. And suddenly Tori ached to feel what he was feeling. That weightlessness. The muted sound the world took on when her ears were submerged. The numbing cold on her skin. It was why she'd stopped swimming. Because after her father had died, she'd needed to *feel* something. She'd needed to *hurt* so she wouldn't forget him. Because if she didn't feel the pain of his loss . . . if she let herself numb to the fact that he was gone . . . then who was she becoming?

Her clothes were lead drapes on her skin, an anchor to hold on to while she drifted beside Nathaniel. She eased back, daring to let herself float, but her shoes pulled at her feet. She tipped her head farther, closing her eyes against the warm, prickling sun, reminding herself to breathe. Nathaniel's fingertips brushed hers, and when she turned, he was watching her, the light catching droplets of water on his skin, his chest rising and falling, perfect and unmarred by scars. Tori wondered what his body must have looked like once, before the Slaughters broke him.

"Who were you . . . before all this?" she heard herself ask.

"The same person I am now," he said, squinting peacefully against the sun.

"But how can you be, after what happened to you?"

Nathaniel thought about that for a moment, long enough that Tori worried she'd said something wrong. "Who I am," he finally said, "has nothing to do with my scars. It runs deeper than that. Who I am is in my blood. It's in my soul." He turned to Tori, tentatively. "In my heart."

Below the surface, she felt his fingers curl around hers and tug ever so gently until she was drifting closer to him, unaware of her shoes and her clothes, of anything but the touch of his hand. The lightness was back, that terrifying buoyancy. Suddenly she was feeling far too much.

Tori tipped forward, letting her feet sink to the mud. She wiped the water from her eyes and wrapped her arms around herself, shivering.

"Aren't you cold?" she asked, breaking the silence.

"A bit," Nathaniel said quietly, his hand outstretched and empty, the contentment gone from his face.

It didn't matter who they were before. *This* was who they were now. And no matter how deep they swam, or how he pulled at her, Emmeline's curse was a dam between them. The river couldn't fix that. And it couldn't fix him. The longer he was away from the tree, the more vulnerable he would become.

"Matilda said we don't have much time. We shouldn't be wasting it here."

"Shouldn't I have a say in the matter?"

"Not if it involves giving up."

Nathaniel stood, scrubbing the water roughly from his face. "I never said I'd go quietly."

Tori grimaced. "Matilda said that if the Slaughters find what they're looking for, we're in danger. Whatever it is, I'm pretty sure they're already searching for it."

"What do you mean?"

"Before Al Senior died, he told Will that the answers were buried under the oldest branch of the tree."

Nathaniel looked at her curiously. "What kind of answers?"

Tori shrugged. "Probably the same answer we're all looking for. Why is my family here? Why did Al Senior leave the land to me instead of his own family?"

"We know why. Because you're Emmeline and Archibald's descendant."

"But we have no proof."

"And you think that's what they're searching for."

"It has to be. Jesse said Will had been digging holes all around Slaughter Farm. That Alistair was angry and made him fill them all in."

"You think that's why they're so interested in the cemetery."

Tori nodded, her mind racing.

"But Will didn't make the hole in the cemetery."

"The Slaughters don't know that. What if they thought Will was onto something?"

Nathaniel thought for a moment. "It would explain the broken window. Your mother's room is located directly under the longest branch of that old mulberry tree."

"And the fire . . . The Slaughters were the ones that complained about Matilda. They were the reason her family decided to send her to the senior center. The fire started in her house right after she left. But if they thought the answer might be in her house, why burn it down?"

"Unless the goal isn't to find the answer at all. But to destroy it." Nathaniel stood chin-deep in the water, thinking. "That begs the question, how far would they go?" he asked gravely.

The truth sank inside her like a stone. Nathaniel's name had been erased from the margins of that book. The cemetery had been erased from all of the maps and land records except the property survey Al Senior had left in his will. Matilda's house had been burned down, essentially erased from the estate. And now Will . . . "Will didn't jump off that wharf because he was upset. He was pushed. I know it. The dream I had the night Will died . . . it can't be a coincidence."

Nathaniel's expression was grim. "If Alistair is willing to kill his own kin to keep anyone from discovering his father's secrets, what's to stop him from harming you? If you're right about this, then the only way to ensure your safety is to find those secrets first, before Alistair does. It's easy to silence a child, but he can't silence a village. We have to show everyone why that land is rightfully yours."

"This is insane! I don't know what the hell I'm supposed to be looking for!"

"Maybe someone else does. These dreams you mentioned," Nathaniel said. "Tell me about them."

Tori thought back to what she could remember of the dreams. "It's like I'm seeing things through someone else's eyes. I think it's Emmeline."

Nathaniel brushed his wet hair from his face, thinking. Tori slouched deeper in the water and shivered. Nathaniel was right about the river.

Being in it cleared her mind, and made her feel closer to the answers. To finally understanding who she was, and why she was here.

"It makes sense," he said. "You share Emmeline's blood. You're connected to one another. And she's using that connection to communicate with you, the same as she's able to communicate with Matilda."

"I don't understand."

"Emmeline... She was..." Nathaniel took a long breath, as if trying to figure out how to explain. "Emmeline was very close with a girl named Ruth. They cared for each other... very deeply. There was a time when I thought maybe Emmeline and I could love one another. But Emmeline... she didn't feel the same... not about me."

Tori thought back to the memories Emmeline had shared with her. Of her interactions with Nathaniel, contrasted with the brief flashes of moments she'd spent with Ruth. And Tori couldn't believe she hadn't seen it before. "They were in love with each other."

Which made everything Matilda had said that much clearer.

Emmeline had never returned Nathaniel's love. She couldn't. Not the way she had loved Ruth. And Nathaniel had promised to care for her child anyway. "I understand," she said. He looked relieved not to have to explain. "But how is Emmeline able to communicate with Matilda if Ruth and Emmeline don't share..." The words drifted from her as flashes of a dream pushed their way to the surface. Images of a knife and two hands holding. "They shared blood."

Nathaniel nodded, his eyes closing briefly. "Emmeline bound them to each other with a blood ritual. It must have created a connection powerful enough to enable Emmeline to communicate with Ruth, as well as her descendants, the same as Emmeline is able to communicate with you. If you're sharing visions with Emmeline, she must be trying to tell you something. Once you know what that is, all you have to do is break the curse."

"No! You heard what Matilda said. Once Slaughter's blood is shed, you go back to the tree." The thought left a painful ache under her ribs.

"Whether it be today or a fortnight from now, I'm going to die anyway, Victoria. And if the curse isn't satisfied before that, what then?" She refused to look at him. He moved closer, leaning into her space, making her acknowledge the one truth she didn't want to think about. "You heard Matilda. The two spells are tangled. The same as your lineage. The fact that you are Emmeline's descendant doesn't negate the fact that you share Slaughter's blood. The curse Emmeline inflicted is on all of Slaughter's people. After it's done consuming Alistair and his family, eventually it will come for you."

Inside, Tori knew. "The blight." That insidious stain creeping up from the cemetery. First it reached out for Slaughter's house, and now it was reaching for hers.

"How much misfortune?" he asked quietly. "How many people will die at Emmeline's hand because of her mistake? You heard Matilda. Suffering and fire. Will was an innocent. A child. Alistair may have been the one to force him off that wharf, but it was Emmeline's curse that pushed his hand. And the fire . . . That fire turned, Victoria. It might have started in Matilda's house, but it was Emmeline's curse that drew it to Alistair Slaughter's land. It could have burned more than just fields," he said, taking her chin gently in his hand and bringing her eyes to his. "You—your home and your family—the things and people you love most, will be next. And if I hide in that barn as though my hands are tied—if I fail to protect you, to honor my promise—I'm no better a man than Slaughter."

The house, the fires, that goddamn blight, and now Will . . . We've lost everything because of you.

"But what about you?" She cared about him. If they were able to break the curse, why would she have to lose him too? It wasn't fair.

Nathaniel set his jaw. "I know who I am. I've made my decision." His hazel eyes softened on hers as he let her go. "I know what kind of man I want to be."

Tori nodded, her throat too thick to speak. She waded back toward shore, needing to feel the earth under her feet. "How do we do it?"

Nathaniel splashed softly through the water behind her. "The curse only said we have to shed Slaughter blood. I watched Emmeline cast a spell once. The language was all symbolic—it's all about intent. So it stands to reason, a small amount of Slaughter blood would probably do."

Tori didn't like where he was going with this and she pushed the thought away, refusing to acknowledge her connection to the Slaughters, no matter how small. She was Emmeline's descendant, and the spell would surely preclude her. If the power of the spell really was about intent, she knew who she wanted to be too. "Fine. I'll think of a reason to invite Jesse to the tree, and then I'll punch him in the nose. Problem solved." The thought of punching Jesse pushed a reluctant smile to Tori's face, and she rolled sideways as she stroked to see if Nathaniel was smiling too.

He treaded water a few yards behind her, his face ghost-white.

"I thought that was pretty funny," she said, kicking water playfully in his direction. He didn't react and her smile slid away. Nathaniel stared down at the water, confused. "What's wrong?"

"I don't...I don't know," he said haltingly. "I feel odd. I feel..." Nathaniel winced and touched his face. He pulled his hand away and a trickle of blood stained the tips of his fingers. He sucked in another sharp breath. A long gash opened slowly as she watched, as if cut by an invisible knife, high across his cheek. Thick red streams of blood spread down his face into the water.

Tori struggled, fighting against the mud to get back to him.

Nathaniel clutched his chest. He gasped and slid under the water. She kicked up her feet and stroked to his side, catching him under the arm and heaving him up until his face was above the surface.

"What's happening?" She spit water from her mouth, struggling under his weight as dark red clouds of blood bloomed all around them.

Tori swam hard to shore, one arm dragging Nathaniel until their feet touched the bottom. Fighting the heaviness of the water and their clothes, the sediment dragging at their heels, they staggered through the shallows to shore. Nathaniel looked down at himself with gritted teeth. Thick streams of blood poured from his chest, down his stomach. Tori's heart pounded wildly at the sight of the winding gash in Nathaniel's chest. As she watched, a new line began to slice down, then sideways, opening a second deep cut in his skin.

"No. No, no, no!" she said, helpless as another formed, diagonally up and then down, carving him open. She didn't know how to stop it. "What's happening?" she asked, scrambling to drag him onto the shore.

He dropped to his knees in the mud, crying out as the cuts began to take shape, forming a word. S-L-A . . . U . . .

Nathaniel collapsed to all fours, his blood spattering the riverbed.

"The tree!" Tori grabbed Nathaniel's hand and heaved him to his feet. She climbed up the embankment, dragging him with her as she ran for the oak. Nathaniel lumbered weakly behind her. Tori rushed through the woods, sticking to the path to avoid the grabbing brambles and limbs, but Nathaniel was slowing her down. He groaned. Stumbled. Then he fell to his knees. Tori hesitated a fraction of a second before leaving him and breaking into a sprint.

When she finally flew out of the trees and into the cemetery, Jesse, Mitch, and Bobby were standing under the oak, their shoulders shaking with laughter. Mitch braced his foot against a shovel while Bobby worked at digging a hole, jabbing the sharp end of his spade hard against a root.

"What exactly are we looking for, Jesse?" An empty case of beer lay on its side in the weeds, the ground littered with empty cans. Bobby crushed one and tossed it away from him.

"I don't know." Jesse took a long drag off a cigarette and looked up into the gnarled arms of the oak. "This is the oldest tree on the whole damn farm. Whatever Will was looking for, it's gotta be here." He gripped a pocketknife and brushed his fingers over the splintered wood, halfway finished carving his name. All Tori could see was Nathaniel's body, the scars they would leave if he didn't heal.

"What are you doing?" Tori shouted, angry and breathless, dripping river water at the edge of the cemetery.

Jesse and his friends whipped around. For a moment, they just stared, their eyes traveling in turn over her hair and her face and her clothes.

"What the hell happened to you?" Jesse asked. Tori was drenched, covered in mud and blood and shaking from the cold. Let him make his own assumptions.

"Get away from my tree!"

Jesse flicked his cigarette ash to the ground, looking sideways at his friends, like he was trying to decide who he needed to be right now.

He choked out a laugh. "What are you gonna do? File a restraining order?" He turned his back on her and began to carve another letter, and somewhere in the woods behind her, Tori heard Nathaniel moan.

"I said stop it!" Tori stood behind him, ready to launch herself at his back. She wanted to scratch him, to hit him. She wanted to make him bleed.

Bobby jammed the shovel into the ground and worked it back and forth with the heel of his boot.

"I'd invite you to stay, Burns, but we're out of beer," Jesse said around his cigarette as he kept carving. Mitch laughed. Bobby poked the blade of the shovel into the hole a few times, then tossed it aside.

"Hey," Bobby said, kneeling to reach into the dirt. "I think I found something. Is this what you're looking for?" He unearthed a brown jug, or maybe it was an urn. At first, Tori didn't care. She was just relieved Jesse wasn't cutting anymore. But then Jesse's eyes slid to hers. Was this it? Was this the answer? The secret Will had been looking for? Tori's fingers itched to touch it. More than that, they itched to punch him. She could do it. She could draw his blood and take the jug and end it all right now. She took a hesitant step toward him, her hand fisted at her side.

Bobby pitched it to Jesse, and Jesse caught it in the crook of his arm with a smug smile. Tori tried to see over Mitch's and Bobby's shoulders as Jesse brushed the dirt from its sides. It was old and irregular, coated in dirt. And yet, something about the jug seemed familiar. It made the hair on her neck stand up, and she was filled with a fiercely protective need she couldn't understand—to take it . . . and put it back.

"That's mine," she told them. "You can't just go digging in my yard."

Jesse wiped a finger around the mouth of the bottle, revealing a cork.

"What is it, Jesse?" Mitch asked.

"What's it look like?" Jesse snapped. "We're digging in a cemetery. It's probably somebody's ashes."

"Put it back, Jesse!" Tori shouted. "It doesn't belong to you."

"I don't know. . . ." Bobby squinted down at the hole where he'd found it. "There's no headstone. And the hole's too shallow to be a grave. Maybe we should open it and see what's inside."

Panic flared inside her. "No!" Tori made a grab around them, but they stood close together, blocking her out.

Jesse turned the jug, studying it from every angle.

"Put it back!" She didn't know why she said it. She should *want* to open it . . . to reveal the answers . . . the secrets, even if it meant Jesse and his friends saw them too. But something inside her was screaming that they shouldn't open it. That they shouldn't stir whatever was inside.

"Open it, Jesse. Let's see what's in it," Mitch prodded.

Jesse started prying at the cork, but it was stuck deep in the mouth of the bottle and wouldn't budge. While they were all focused on it, Tori came from his other side and grabbed it out of Jesse's hands.

"Give that back, Burns!" he said, his voice rising as she walked backward toward the trees. An empty beer can crunched under her heel and she cradled the jug, struggling for balance.

Jesse jerked his knife out of the tree and followed Tori into the woods.

ori bolted for the trail, clutching the jug to her chest. Once she was in the thick of the woods, she changed direction, away from Nathaniel. Away from the tree.

Tori ran until the three boys' footsteps were muffled, lost somewhere behind her. Then she changed direction again, away from the barn, toward the river. Their voices carried through the trees; she heard the crunch of brush behind her. She pushed herself faster against the pull of her wet clothes.

A hand shot out of the shadows and closed over her mouth. Tori struggled to breathe as she stared up into Nathaniel's face. He pressed her tightly to his body, the dirt-caked bottle wedged between them. She could feel his blood on her skin, the coppery smell of it thick in her nose. He put a finger to his lips before letting her go. Then his gaze fell to the jug in her arms and his whole body stiffened. Even in the dark, Tori knew Nathaniel had seen it before. His eyes, pinched with pain before, were suddenly alert and fearful.

"Okay, Tori! You made your point! " Jesse hollered. "If you don't give it back to me, I'm gonna have to tell my dad. You don't know what you're getting yourself into, Burns. He's gonna come after you."

"She can't have gotten far," Bobby said, somewhere close, shaking Nathaniel's attention from the bottle.

Nathaniel took Tori's hand and they crept silently through the trees, away from Tori's property toward Slaughter Point.

"Give it back, Victoria! It doesn't belong to you!"

"This is stupid. What do you want with an old piece of pottery anyway?" Bobby's voice wasn't far behind Jesse's. Tori could hear him huffing, stomping through the brush as though he was trying keep up. "Why not just let her take it?"

"Because it's not hers! And I'm sick of her taking everything!"

Suddenly, Tori heard a snap and a shriek. It sounded like Mitch was screaming. "Jesse! Bobby! Help me!" There was a loud scuffle. Nathaniel and Tori squatted in the brush, their breaths held.

"What happened?" Jesse shouted.

"Oh, shit."

Mitch groaned, breathing hard. "It was a hole. I turned my ankle."

"Goddamn Will and his fucking holes!" Jesse growled. "We've got recruiters coming next week!"

"It's not my fault. I didn't see it!"

Jesse let loose with a long string of swears. Tori could feel him looking for her, listening and waiting for her to reveal herself. She didn't move.

"You listening to me, Burns?" Jesse called out. "Whatever that thing is, it came out of *my* field! It belongs to *me*!" Jesse was loud, his footsteps close.

"Come on, Jesse. His ankle's broken, man. We've gotta get him home. You can talk her into giving it back tomorrow. Let's go."

Tori waited, listening to the sound of Jesse and his friends' slow retreat. When they were gone, Nathaniel winced, easing to his feet. He extended a hand to Tori, but she didn't take it, her hands shaking too badly to let go of the jug.

Nathaniel was staring at it. At the swollen cork and the chipped handles and the cracks in the finish.

"Where did you find that?" His hoarse whisper felt fragile, vulnerable. As if he was afraid of it. Tori clutched it tighter it to her chest.

"I think this is it. This must be the answer Al Senior buried. Jesse dug it up from under the..." Something in Nathaniel's expression made her pause. He shook his head. His eyes were filled with the same foreboding she'd felt when Jesse tugged at the cork. "You know what's in here, don't you?" she asked. "You've seen it before."

"I'll explain everything, but not here," he said quietly. And he led Tori back to the barn.

• • •

It was past nightfall when they finally made it to the barn. Nathaniel paused at the door, barefoot and bloody, the wet hem of his jeans caked with dirt. He glanced down at the jug in her arms, the way he had throughout the long walk to the barn, with fascination and revulsion, as if he longed to take it from her, and at the same time, as if he never wanted to see it again.

"It's late. You're cold," he said, dragging his eyes from it. "You should go home and get some rest."

Tori's teeth chattered, but she held the jug tighter. "You promised you would tell me what this is. I'm not leaving until you do."

Nathaniel hesitated, his lips pressed tightly together as if reconsidering that promise. Then he held the barn door open, gesturing Tori inside.

"Very well. But I won't stand by and watch you catch your death of cold." Nathaniel set to work, making a small fire from kindling, dry pine needles, and twigs. When it began to smoke, he turned his back to her and Tori looked away as he stripped off his wet jeans and draped them over the sawhorse. He slid quickly into an old pair of her father's khakis, then turned to Tori expectantly, holding out his hand for the bottle. But Tori's fingers were frozen around the cold stone. She couldn't set it down even if she'd wanted to. Everything, inside and out, was numb.

He reached hesitantly, taking the bottle and laying it carefully on the floor. Tori's frozen fingers curled as if the bottle was still in them, and her chilled clothes stuck to her skin. Nathaniel held his hand out to her again. This time, she realized, for her wet clothes.

"I'll wear this," she said. Tori draped the heavy blanket over her damp sweater, but it only managed to push the cold deeper into her bones.

"You won't get warm this way." Gently, Nathaniel took the blanket from her. He held it like a curtain, open and wide, averting his eyes. "Go on, then. Take off your clothes and we'll hang them by the fire. Cover yourself with this for the time being. I promise, I won't look."

She could hardly feel the tips of her fingers, and her whole body was shuddering. She knew he was right. But she didn't want him to see her under all this.

He waited, his eyes closed and his head turned away. Over the top of the blanket, the deep red letters carved in his chest caught the firelight. His chest, smooth until this afternoon, had been the only part of him that had been free of scars. The only piece of him that had been untouched by Slaughter's family.

Tori kicked off her sopping shoes and peeled away her socks. Her jeans stuck stubbornly around her ankles and she had to fight to pull them off. She tugged at her heavy sweater. It was long enough to cover her underwear, but not long enough to cover the rows of fading pink scars on her thighs. She checked again to make sure Nathaniel wasn't looking. Then she lifted it over her head, clutching it to her body while it dripped on her feet.

She stood in her bra and underpants, vulnerable and naked—angry that her shame felt stronger than everything else. Stronger than her anger at Jesse and her fear of Alistair. Stronger than her feelings for Nathaniel, and the way those feelings confused her. She grabbed the blanket and pulled it around her, high around her neck. It was gritty with dust and pine needles, but it was dry and warm.

Nathaniel picked up her clothes from the floor and hung them beside his. Then he stepped in close, tucking the edges of the blanket tightly under her chin.

"Are you all right?" he asked.

She wasn't. She wasn't all right at all. "That jug. If it's not what Al Senior was talking about, what is it, Nathaniel? What's in it?"

Nathaniel looked up from the bottle, his face full of doubts, as if he was trying to decide how much to tell her.

"It's a witch's bottle," he finally said. "The one Emmeline made and buried before Archibald Slaughter hanged me. It holds the spell she used to bind me to the tree. I'd wager that if you opened that cork, you'd find something of Emmeline, something of me, and something of that tree inside it." Nathaniel scratched absently behind his ear, pulling at a section of short-clipped hair Tori hadn't noticed before, hidden behind the longer strands that fell around his face. "I'd thought it all nonsense the first time I watched her make one for herself and for Ruth. The nails, the heart, the bird bones . . . It all seemed so foolish."

"But why would the Slaughters want it? How would they even know what it is?"

"I don't think they do. Em would have buried it in secret. She never would have told anyone. It would have been too dangerous if anyone found it. Even I didn't know where it was."

Too dangerous.

. . . if they find what's hidin' under that tree, then you're in danger, boy. You both are.

Matilda's words awakened the chill in her bones. "What would happen to you if someone opened the cork?" Tori heard herself ask.

Nathaniel blanched. "If you believe the lore to be true, then the protective spell would be broken. The power would turn against the one who cast it, in favor of the one who opened it, destroying its maker. And destroying me."

"You have to hide it," Tori said quickly. "You have to hide it before they figure out what it is!"

If Jesse had opened that cork, Nathaniel would have been gone forever. And the power would turn against Emmeline—against her descendants—in Jesse's favor.

"Tori, I can't—"

"You have to! If anyone finds it—"

"I want you to do it."

The words sucked all the air from the room, the heavy silence broken only by the crackle of the fire. Nathaniel stood close, his face half-shadowed in the dim light of it. "I want you to bury it. Don't tell me where. I'm afraid I can't be trusted not to destroy it myself. And I can't leave ... not yet. Not until I know you're safe." He tugged up the blanket where it had fallen around her shoulders, and her heart clenched.

"I should have broken the curse. Jesse was right there, in front of the tree. I should have hurt him, but I ..."

She'd wanted to, hadn't she? Watching him cut the tree, listening as he tortured Nathaniel. She'd wanted to lash out. To make him bleed. She could have ended the curse before he'd found the bottle at all.

"But what?" Nathaniel asked.

"I couldn't. You heard what Matilda said! Everything will go back to the way it was. You'll go back to the tree. And I ..." And she wasn't ready to let him go yet. He was the only part of this place she felt connected to. The only place she felt like she belonged.

He held the blanket around her shoulders and pulled her closer, brushing a thumb over her cheek, tipping his forehead to hers until their noses were touching. Until their lips brushed. They were warm and soft and Tori pulled away before any of this cut her too deeply to fix.

"This isn't right. I should go."

"Why?" he asked angrily, following her to the door. "Because I'm cursed? Because no matter what happens, I'm going to die?"

"Yes! Because you're going to die!"

"There are worse things than death, Victoria!"

"Like what?"

"Like spending a lifetime alone!" Nathaniel's voice cracked. "Will you please just look at me?"

She turned around slowly, to the spell bottle on the floor and the pile of straw he slept on. To the rusted saw against the wall in the corner and the fresh cuts in his skin. Everywhere but at his face. Until she couldn't not look at it anymore.

"I'm not dead yet, Tori. I feel this! I feel *all* of this," he said, clutching his chest. "I feel cold. I feel hungry. I feel completely alive when I'm with you!"

Tori's eyes welled, tears blurring the name written in blood and scars on his chest. She backed toward the barn door, away from the cracked and chipped witch's bottle that was holding him together—the curse she was now responsible for.

"I have to go," she said, racing for home, taking his blanket with her.

●　　●　　●

It was late. Tori didn't even know what time it was. The light in her mother's bedroom was on, and Tori hoped she'd gone upstairs for the night. She snuck in the back door, careful not to let it slam behind her, and tiptoed to the foot of the stairs. The hallway smelled like lasagna and burned garlic bread, and her stomach growled loud enough to wake the dead.

"You missed dinner," came her mother's voice from the darkened kitchen. "Want to tell me where you've been?"

Tori took two steps backward and stood in front of the entry to the kitchen. Her mother sat at the table in the seat closest to the window, silhouetted by the glow of the porch light outside.

Tori pulled the blanket tighter around herself. She could tell her. About her visit to Matilda's room. About Emmeline and the child she'd had by Alistair Slaughter's great-great-gazillionth grandfather. How they were related . . . But then she'd have to tell her mother about everything else. About Nathaniel and where she'd been and why he'd been staying in the barn. And those were secrets Tori wasn't ready to share yet. Because once you speak a secret out loud, it's not just yours anymore.

"Not really," she said.

Her mother looked down at Tori's bare, muddy feet. "Were you with Nathaniel?"

When Tori didn't answer, her mother nodded to herself and stared into her coffee mug. "Are you at least being safe?"

"It's not like that."

"Then tell me, what's it like?" her mother asked, her voice rising. "And don't tell me I wouldn't understand!"

"You won't understand! Because you can't!"

"And Nathaniel does? Do you even know this boy, Victoria?"

Tori's face crumpled. It was as if her mother had put words to every jumbled thought in Tori's head. Nathaniel understood. He felt everything she'd been trying so hard not to—alone, forgotten, and completely out of place. In the barn, in the river, in the cemetery . . . These places they'd been together . . . they were the only places where she didn't feel different. Because she and Nathaniel felt the same.

But Nathaniel would be gone soon.

And then, there would be no place left in this world where she fit.

"I want you to see that therapist we talked about." Tori's eyes snapped to her mother. "You've been through a lot this year. There's no shame in asking for help."

Her fists tightened around the blanket. "I don't need help."

"I think you should talk to someone."

"I don't want to talk to anybody!"

Her mother sighed deeply. It rattled in the dark, as if she'd been crying, and Tori felt a stab of regret. "Go clean yourself up. I left you a plate in the microwave. Have something to eat and get some sleep. We'll discuss this in the morning."

Tori raced up the stairs to her room and leaned back against the door, sliding to the hardwood, thinking about what her mother had said. She stared at her phone and started a text to Magda. Her fingers hovered over the screen. She bit her lip, deleted the text, and dialed Magda's number instead. When it rolled to voicemail, Tori called Magda's landline at home. After three rings, Magda's father answered. There was an awkward pause when Tori told him who was calling. The connection muffled as if he'd covered the receiver with his hand.

"Tori?" Magda finally answered.

"I need your help," Tori said.

"What's going on?"

"Not over the phone. Can you come to my house?"

"It's almost nine—"

"Please? It's important." Tori swallowed painfully, fighting the overwhelming urge to cry. Magda was quiet for a moment. "I'll be there as soon as I can."

Tori disconnected and buried her head in her hands. The pressure that had been steadily growing in her chest crested. Tori felt it rise up the back of her throat. The room blurred with tears and Tori bit her lip hard, but the pain wasn't big enough. She scrambled up and crossed the room, reaching high in her closet for the box containing the Slaughter family's abandoned things. She felt inside the bodice of the doll for the razor she'd hidden the day she'd moved here. That night had been a night like this, when the room and the walls and her mind and her throat closed in until she could hardly breathe. She'd made Nathaniel a promise, that she would try not to hurt herself. But she was already hurting. And he was already dying. And those promises felt more like wishful lies, impossible to keep.

Francine's doll was covered in Jesse's blood. Her porcelain-dead eyes stared at the ceiling as Tori used Nathaniel's blanket to wipe the blade. She leaned against her bedroom door and slid back down, sitting against it with the razor cupped in her hand. Then she pressed the blade to her thigh, waiting for the crashing tide to ebb, for the flood to recede, for her head to break the surface so she could breathe.

THE PLAN

I stood in the wood in the dark, my hands blistered and shaking from fatigue. Thomas had died a few hours before sundown, but Slaughter made Samuel and me wait until cover of dark to bury him, deep under the shadow of the tree. He would tell anyone who asked that Thomas succumbed to a fever, but it was Slaughter's sentence that had killed him. After Thomas's whipping, Slaughter had forbade me to cut his bindings, demanding he be left overnight, half-naked and bleeding. A lesson, he'd called it, lest any of us wish to follow in Thomas's footsteps.

It was near midnight when Sam and I had packed down the last shovels of dirt over Thomas's body. Too overwrought to return to the barn loft, I'd tossed pebbles at Emmeline's shutters until she roused, and when one cautious gray eye peered down from between them, I'd gestured to the wood, where I waited for her, restless and pacing.

I started at the crackle of feet on fallen twigs. Emmeline's long black hair was impossible to see, but her shift glowed white as she weaved her way through the trees, and her eyes were wide with fear.

"What's happened?" she asked, breathless and shaken.

"Thomas. He's dead." Her pale hand reached for her belly, making the roundness of it visible through the fabric. She had a month, maybe two, before it would grow too large to hide. This morning, I had been all too ready to take Emmeline and leave this place. Now, I wasn't so sure. "It's all my fault."

"How? I don't understand."

"I went to Slaughter yesterday. I told him..." Her eyes narrowed on me, two honed blades glittering in the dark. "I told him you were with child, and I wished to marry you."

Emmeline took an unsteady step away from me. "Why would you do such a thing?" Emotions were at war on her face. Judgment and anger that I'd revealed her secret. Shock and relief that I'd claimed responsibility.

"What choice do you leave me? You're all I have left in this world, and I will not let you suffer alone."

Emmeline threw her arms around me, her hot tears falling down my neck. She kissed my cheek, pressed her forehead to my lips. We stood like that for a while, both of us trembling. "What will we do?"

"He says we have no contracts."

Emmeline reeled back. "That's a lie!"

"He said they're forgeries. Useless. He said..." I didn't have the heart to say the words out loud. That we were stuck there. "He said he will not honor them."

"If he's telling the truth and they are forgeries, then he's guilty of at least that much. We'll present ourselves before the magistrate and demand our release."

"If they release us from Slaughter, they'll only sell us off to someone else! We're seventeen, Em! Not old enough to claim exemption under the law. At the very least, we'll be split up and indentured to new masters for another five years!"

"And if we run?"

"Then he'll claim our contracts are valid and have us hunted. Like he did with Thomas."

Emmeline dragged her hands through her hair. I could see the darkness scratching at the walls of her mind as she paced in tight circles, her eyes becoming fierce, chilling in their focus. A cold breeze stirred. It billowed the hem of her shift and lifted the ends of her dark and tangled hair, making her look every bit the witch the captain's men had thought her to be. "If he can claim those contracts are valid, then so can we. You remember as well as I how he insisted upon them. If they're forgeries, then they're convincing enough for him to use them against us. Which means we can do the same."

"What are you suggesting?"

"I will not stay, Nathaniel. I won't." Her eyes welled with angry tears.

"If he catches you, he will kill you."

"If I stay, I'm as good as dead anyway! There has to be another option! There has to be a way." Emmeline rested her hands on my chest. She looked deep in my eyes like she was reaching for my heart, even though she knew it had always been hers. "I'll make sure to tidy his study tomorrow. I will find those contracts. Then you and me and Ruth . . . we'll—"

"No," I said, gently pushing her hands away. "She's a slave, not a servant, Emmeline. She belongs to Slaughter. There's nothing we can do for her." Not without further risk to ourselves and the child.

"I will not leave her behind!"

"We cannot take her!"

"I need her!" Emmeline clasped a hand over her mouth, as if stifling a cry. Her eyes brimmed with tears. "And when this child is ready, I'll need her even more."

"Ruth is his property, Em," I said in a low voice. "She has no contract—forged or otherwise."

"Then we'll pretend she's ours!" she implored. "We can do this, Nathaniel! Look at us!" She took my head in her hands, looking up at me with those shining eyes until all I could see was her face. "By appearance, we're the perfect family. You're handsome and well-spoken, and I'm with child. We'll have papers, and we can tell anyone who asks that Ruth belongs to us."

"But she doesn't, Em."

"She belongs to me! And I to her! In the only way that matters!" She took a deep, shuddering breath. "All we have to do is get far enough from here that no one recognizes the name Slaughter."

"He has a long reach," I said softly. I could not imagine any world where the name Slaughter did not exist, but it was no use arguing with her. She was of one mind now, a steadily building storm, and it would take a mountain to break her will.

"We'll travel at night."

"And go where?"

"Anywhere! Across the river to Virginia. North to Annapolis. I don't care where we go, Nathaniel. But this child and I..." She shook her head with a mournful smile, the way I'd always imagined she might look at me if we ever said good-bye. "We will not stay."

I nodded, taking her hands in mine. "Then nor shall I."

A half hour later, there was a soft knock on Tori's bedroom door. Magda cracked it open and poked her head inside, which meant her mother was still awake in the kitchen. Tori was bandaged and dry, dressed in layers of shirts and sweatshirts and sweatpants and thick winter socks. But underneath it all, she was still chilled to the bone.

Tori couldn't shake the image of Jesse with his knife, carving his name into the tree. She couldn't shake the fact that his blood ran through her veins. She wished she could open them all and bleed until every last ounce of whatever connected them to each other was gone.

Magda stood beside her bed, her car keys still in her hand. Tori wrapped her arms around herself and shivered, trying to figure out how to say what she needed to say.

"I know why Al Senior willed us the land," Tori said.

"But I thought you couldn't petition the court to open your adoption file for another four years?" Magda bit her lip.

Magda knew. She knew Tori's adoption played a part in this. Which meant her father had figured that much out too. Tori hesitated, second-guessing herself. It was a risk, confiding in Magda. But it seemed more of a risk not to.

"This is going to sound crazy, but hear me out." Magda nodded and sat beside her. "In 1699, a man named Archibald Slaughter owned the plantation that became Slaughter Farm. He bought an indentured servant named Emmeline Bell from a captain who had kidnapped her from England."

"Wait..." Magda said, her eyes lighting up. "You mean *the* Emmeline? The Chaptico Witch?"

"She was ten years old at the time. I'm pretty sure he abused her for years. But when she was seventeen, Archibald Slaughter got her pregnant. She escaped with a contract that entitled her to a piece of Slaughter's land. Ten acres, plus provisions. There were two contracts, actually. One for Emmeline and one for...a friend. An indentured boy. He didn't make it."

"And the Slaughters didn't honor the contract," Magda said, piecing the rest of the story together on her own.

"Al Senior must have known. He must have had access to old family documents or journals. And he granted us the twenty acres plus the house."

"But why give it to you?"

Tori hesitated. She took a deep breath and touched the oyster shell through her shirt, wishing she didn't have to say it. "Because Emmeline Bell was my great-great-gazillionth grandmother."

"Which also makes you...Oh, man." Magda looked like she might be sick.

"So here we are. Now, what do we do?"

Magda scratched her head, her mouth still gaping. "I have to tell my dad. If you're related to the Slaughters, then all we have to do is prove it."

"I've been thinking about that," Tori said quickly, her mind working through all the ways Magda could help find the information she would need. "There must have been a birth record. Emmeline probably declared Slaughter as the baby's father, even if she never told anyone else."

"Why would she, though? If she was afraid enough to run from him, why would she connect him to her child with a birth record?"

"To secure her daughter's future? It's the only explanation that makes sense. Emmeline would have known Slaughter would never honor her contract. Not in his lifetime. And who was to say Slaughter and his wife wouldn't outlive her? Maybe giving her daughter the Slaughter name, even if it was only on paper, was the only way to make sure she would have a legitimate claim to the land that was owed to her mother. How else would Al Senior have figured it out?"

"How did *you* figure it out?"

Tori tugged on the cuff of her sweatshirt. She needed Magda. She needed her to know about Emmeline, so she could give her father enough information to dig up the truth about how the land had ended up being passed to Tori. But she wasn't sure if she could trust her with Nathaniel's secrets too.

"Matilda Rice told me."

Magda slumped. "The same Matilda Rice who was just admitted to the senior center because she's not *competent* enough to live by herself? Come on, Tori. If you want me to go to my father with this, you've got to give me something solid. Something that will hold up in court. Otherwise, it's just fodder for Alistair's case."

Tori rested her head in her hands. Magda was right. It didn't matter that Matilda was once a historian or what records she'd had access to. Throwing Matilda's name around while Magda's dad was trying to prove that Al Senior was senile would only make things worse.

"You wouldn't believe me if I told you."

"Try me." Magda was wearing the same expression she'd worn for weeks, every time Tori had lied to her or Drew. The one that said, *I can see right through you.*

Tori took another deep breath. "The other indentured servant . . . the one who died . . . His name was Nathaniel Bishop."

Magda tipped her head. Blinked. Blinked again. "So...he's an... ancestor of your friend Nathaniel?"

"Not exactly."

"What aren't you saying?"

"You remember what Drew said, about a kernel of truth?"

Magda nodded.

"Emmeline Bell was real. She lived here on Slaughter Farm. And she *was* a witch."

"Okay...?"

"And Nathaniel...my friend Nathaniel...he lived here too. They grew up here. On Slaughter Farm. Together."

Magda's mouth fell open. She laughed awkwardly, then shut it again. She stood up. "You know, it's late. I should really go—"

"Magda, I'm telling the truth!" Tori whisper-yelled so her mother and brother wouldn't hear her. "Nathaniel came out of that hole in my cemetery. The one the Slaughters were so eager to fill! It was Emmeline's fault. She made a curse. Or a spell. Or some—"

"You're asking me to believe that a three-hundred-year-old dead guy crawled out of your cemetery and told you all this. I've *seen* Nathaniel, Tori. He isn't exactly *Walking Dead* casting material."

"I thought of all people, you and Drew would believe me."

"Maybe Drew will," Magda muttered.

"But you don't," Tori said, standing in front of the door.

"You haven't exactly been honest with me lately," Magda whisper-yelled back, narrowing her eyes at Tori as if she were the only guilty one in the room.

"Me?" Tori struggled to keep her voice down.

"You want me to believe you? How about we start with something easier? Like why you haven't gone to any of Drew's meets?" Blood rushed to Tori's cheeks, and the fresh cut on her thigh burned. "You want to talk about honesty? Let's talk. What haven't you been telling me?"

Tori felt Magda's eyes all over her. On her arms and her legs. On every scratch and every scar Tori had hidden from her. Except Magda's eyes never left Tori's face. They were hard on Tori's, daring her to prove herself.

"Fine. Don't believe me." Tori turned her back on her, and gestured to the door. She heard the click when it opened, and Tori held her breath, waiting for it to close. For the creak of the floorboard on the other side of the door, telling her Magda was gone. But it didn't come.

"My dad," Magda said softly. "I can ask him to check with the state's department of vital records. Maybe we can find something there." Tori didn't say anything. She didn't move, too afraid she would say or do the wrong thing and Magda would change her mind. "You don't have to tell me what's really going on with you. Or with Nathaniel. Not if you're not ready. But Drew and I ... We care about you, you know?"

After a moment, Tori heard the telltale creak in the hall and she looked over her shoulder. Magda had left the door open behind her.

THE TIME WE HAVE LEFT

I am kicking. Thrashing out. I am being carried somewhere. Four men. One on each ankle. One on each arm. Moving fast. The sun is blinding, a bright white sky. Black trees pass by in a blur, and my long white skirts tear and pull as the men trip over them. The scenery moves too quickly, granular and shaky. The river ahead is shiny, silvery-gray, and topped with small white crests. Panic flares inside me. I snap my foot hard in the air, catching one of the leaders in the chin. He swears loudly and his hands dig hard into my ankle.

"Keep the witch still."

I am dropped hard on the bank. One of the men holds me around the throat. Another grips my hands. I kick and shout. I spit at their faces as the others tie stones into the folds of my dress and knots around my ankles. I holler all the ways I will make them suffer and pay.

It takes all four of them to lift me to my feet. To carry me onto a small wooden barge. I stop fighting. My arms and legs are tired. The rocks in my dress are too heavy. I take long, deep breaths. I feel my heart begin to slow. I focus on a single point on the horizon, following the direction of the current.

Suddenly, one of the men steps into my field of vision. I know this man. The one with the long plait and the buckles on his shoes.

He raises his voice loudly, so the crowd gathered on the shore can hear. "If you are innocent, the water will embrace you, and you shall be accused *of welcoming the devil into your heart no more." His eyes glimmer, black and wicked. "Good-bye, fair servant," he says in a low voice meant for me. "For I have no doubt this is a test you shall pass."*

He shoves me hard. I am falling backward, my arms pinwheeling. I hit the icy water with a crash.

It pours over me as I sink down below the surface, the man's face silhouetted by the circle of light above my head wavering farther and farther from reach. I can't get any air. My limbs are like lead, my skirts weighed down with rocks. I can't kick my way to the surface. The walls of my chest pressing in until black and white stars twinkle in front of my eyes. I reach down into my skirts. I feel something sharp in my hand. And I start cutting, shedding everything that weighs me down, tearing my clothes away.

⊛   ⊛   ⊛

Tori sat up fast, gasping for air. Bright sunlight spilled across her bed. Her lungs burned and her wrists ached, and her pajamas were drenched in sweat. She sank back against her pillow, trying to orient herself. Sunday morning. She'd come in late last night, wrapped in Nathaniel's blanket, looking like something that had washed up out of the river.

Nathaniel...and that damned witch bottle.

She listened to her mom and brother move through their morning routine downstairs. If she stayed in her room long enough, they'd leave. Her mother would drop Kyle off at soccer practice and head to the senior center for most of the afternoon, and she could forestall the inevitable conversation with her mother. Tori would have the house to herself. Her house. Alone. The thought wasn't even remotely comforting.

Her phone flashed awake on her nightstand and Tori rushed to answer it.

"Magda?"

"I told my dad. . . ." Magda sounded sullen. "Well, not everything, but enough. But there's a problem."

"What kind of problem?"

"We checked online. The state only has birth certificates dating back as far as 1895. So my dad called a friend at the historical society this morning. They couldn't find any record of an Emmeline Bell ever having given birth in the state of Maryland around that time. And the only child on record for Archibald Slaughter was a son, born in 1707 by his wife, Elizabeth."

"What does that mean?"

"It means we're at a dead end. Without the information inside your adoption records, there's no way to trace your lineage backward. And to trace Emmeline's descendants forward, we need a starting point."

Tori sighed, rubbing her eyes, struggling to sift through the flood of information in her head. It was all beginning to feel hopeless. "If Emmeline didn't report her daughter's birth, then my adoption file won't matter. I won't be able to trace it back far enough to prove anything."

"I'm sorry, Tori."

"It's not your fault." She forced herself to smile so Magda could hear it in her voice. But her throat felt thick and she couldn't manage to pull it off. Tori said good-bye and disconnected. She lay in bed another minute, listening to the silence in the house. When she was sure her mother and brother were gone, she headed to the kitchen. She filled a grocery bag with sandwiches, apples, bottled water, and chips, grabbed Nathaniel's blanket, and snuck into the guest room to find another pair of her father's old clothes before heading to the barn. As she walked, she sniffed the air for the scent of wood smoke. But the crisp breeze smelled like pine and river mud.

The barn was quiet. No violin. No hammering. No firewood crackling. A pile of animal scraps had been scattered in the dirt a few yards outside, the bones brittle and dry.

Tori knocked lightly before opening the door.

Nathaniel woke with a start, the witch bottle cradled protectively in his arms. He rubbed his eyes, looking disoriented as he started to get up. Naked to the waist, the rest of him was buried under the pile of straw he'd been sleeping in. His clothes hung over the sawhorse, stiff with dried mud from the river.

"I brought your blanket back," she said sheepishly, turning to give him some privacy as she dug the items from the duffel bag. "And fresh clothes. And something to eat." She held the clothes out behind her without looking, and a small fraction of her guilt was relieved when she felt him finally take them.

Nathaniel shook out the pants with a hard snap and Tori flinched.

"If Jesse tells his dad I took the bottle from him, they'll probably come looking for it. We shouldn't stay long. We should find another place to hide you," she said as he took the shirt from her.

Tori turned cautiously. Nathaniel had dark bags under his eyes and a scab across his cheek. "Whatever we do, we should do it soon," he said. "There's not much time."

She hated the resignation in his eyes. It scared her, how little green was left in them. "There's still time."

"I'm tired, Victoria," he said quietly, as if he'd already given up.

"What are you saying?"

Nathaniel scrubbed a hand over his face. There were bruises under his skin. "I think you should take the bottle . . . and destroy it."

"No!" she said, vehemently. "It would destroy *you*."

"And the protection of the spell would become yours. Whatever magic is in that bottle will turn in your favor. It will protect you. Regardless of what happens to me."

Tori gaped at him, incredulous. "What happens to you? Have you even stopped to consider what that means?"

"I was up all night thinking about it if you must know."

"What happened to not going quietly and knowing what kind of man you want to be? What changed between yesterday and today, Nathaniel?"

Nathaniel gritted his teeth. He unbuttoned the top three buttons of her father's flannel shirt and opened it wide. Most of Slaughter's name was still etched in angry red letters across his chest. The skin around it was inflamed, some of the cuts still weeping. Tori swallowed hard.

"My choices seem fairly straightforward," he said, his voice shaking with controlled rage. "I can lie in this barn and wait for death to find me, leaving you no safer than before." He counted off on his fingers. "I can break the curse and go to my grave, leaving you with no more answers than you had before. Or you can break that bottle. I'd rather you destroy me than have to lie in wait for Jesse's family to return to the cemetery with that green monstrosity and dig me up in their desperate search for whatever they think is buried there!"

Her eyes welled. "I would never let that happen."

"You saw Jesse in that cemetery, Victoria. His family will not let this go! If you don't find his grandfather's secrets before he does—"

"Then we will! We'll keep looking! We'll find them first. And once we find them, we'll satisfy the curse and you'll be safe. We both will."

"Destroying that bottle is the best protection I can offer you! That was my promise to Emmel—"

"No!" Tori snatched the bottle away from him and held it to her. "You don't get to use me as your excuse for giving up. You made a promise to me too!"

Nathaniel looked stung. "It's no use, Victoria. The woods go on for miles. Alistair's father could have written a dozen copies of those records, preserved them under any one of a thousand trees. In a million years, we might still never find them."

Tori dropped into the pile of straw, hugging the bottle. "Maybe the Slaughters were right. Maybe Al Senior *was* senile. The whole idea of burying documents is archaic! Who even does that anymore?" Nathaniel winced. "I'm sorry. I'm just frustrated! My lawyer is so old, he doesn't even have a computer. And we're looking for legal papers *underground*. It all feels completely ridiculous."

Nathaniel eased down beside her, as close as he'd been the day she'd shown him how her headphones worked. His gaze was sharp, curious. "Ridiculous, how? Tell me."

"People don't hide valuable things underground anymore. We use banks. Or computers. If you want to preserve an important document, you save it to a cloud."

Nathaniel made a dubious face and pointed at the ceiling. "A cloud?"

She raked a hand through her hair, reminding herself she'd have to be patient with him. There was so much he didn't know. "Not a real cloud. A figurative..." Her voice trailed away and she cocked her head, thinking. "A figurative one. They're looking under the wrong tree. We all are." Tori shot to her feet. "The answer was never buried under a real tree. It's buried under a metaphorical one." And Will must have figured out where it was.

This was it. This was what Jesse had been looking for. He just hadn't figured out where to look. "But where? Where would Al Senior have hidden records from his family, where none of them would know they existed?"

Tori paced the barn. She knew this answer. Better than anyone. If you wanted to keep a record safe from your own family, you safeguarded it with someone who wasn't in your family at all.

Bernie Wells knew who this person was. And he'd tried to tell her.

She worked in the historical society for a lot of years. Before that, she worked over in the office of public records. She was real close with Al Senior before he died.

"Matilda. She's the one. The one who's hiding the answers."

"Matilda?"

"Stay here. Don't leave the barn." She pressed the witch bottle into Nathaniel's arms as she scrambled for the door.

Tori opened the door to Matilda Rice's room. Matilda sat on the far edge of her mattress, her cane dangling over the edge and her hunched back to the door. A tray of uneaten food rested on a table beside the bed, the plate and mug still covered in plastic wrap.

"I ain't eatin' any more of that no-sugar-no-salt-no-good hospital food," she said. "It's dry and it smells funny."

"Mrs. Rice?" Tori stepped into the room. "It's Nathaniel's friend, Tori Burns."

Matilda stiffened. "I'm done talking with you." Then she looked up at the ceiling and said, "I'm done talking with all of you. I already told you what I know 'bout that Nathaniel boy."

"But I have questions about me."

"And I told Al Senior before he died, I wasn't gonna talk about it." Matilda poked her cane against the floor, punctuating the end of the conversation.

"But—"

"But nothin'! I talked to that little Slaughter boy and look what happened to him!"

Tori's throat went dry. "What Slaughter boy? Do you mean Will?"

Matilda didn't answer.

Tori backed out of the room. She sprinted down the hall for the vending machines, pulling every bit of change from her pockets and jamming it into the machine. She pounded the E4 button and waited for the package of Ho Hos to drop to the bottom of the machine, then she ran back to Matilda's room.

Tori opened the wrapper and set the Ho Hos onto the comforter beside Matilda, breathing hard, waiting to see what she would do. Matilda turned at the sound and raised an eyebrow.

"Alistair Slaughter is trying to take away my house," Tori said. "And I really need to talk to you."

After a moment, Matilda's gnarled fingers curled around the wrapper.

"I told you she'd come back when she was ready to talk to me," Matilda said to no one in particular. But Tori wasn't so sure. She remembered the way the vase had fallen over the last time she'd been here. The way the curtains had rustled as if moved by a breeze even though the windows were shut. She wondered where she should sit. It felt like the room was already full of people—an entire history Tori couldn't see.

She watched Matilda pull a chocolate roll from the wrapper and take a slow, luxurious bite. A smile crept over Matilda's lips and she licked at the crème in the corners.

"My family says I ain't allowed to have these," she said with a congested chuckle. "Too many preservatives, they say, like they're trying to get rid of me. Like them Slaughters've been trying to get rid of me. Trying to get rid of my house," she said with a knowing nod to Tori. "They've been calling it an eyesore, sayin' it needs to come down. But there ain't nothing wrong with me or my house. And a little bite of cake never hurt nobody." She smiled wide around the chocolate stuck in her gums. "You won't tell nobody, then. It'll be our little secret."

Secrets. Tori was buried in them already. Matilda patted the space beside her on the bed and Tori sat down. She didn't have the heart to tell Matilda her house was already gone. And she didn't want to frighten her by telling her how. She just needed to let Matilda get comfortable—to get her talking before she changed her mind.

"You mentioned you talked to Will Slaughter," she said, steering the conversation back to things Matilda already knew. "What did you talk about?"

Matilda chewed on her cake thoughtfully. "He used to come by my house sometimes after school. He liked the dish I kept on my porch, with them ribbon candies in it. Used to sit and eat 'em all up while his granddaddy came to talk to me. Then, after Al Senior died, the boy just kept on coming. He liked my stories, see." Matilda took another nibble of cake.

"What stories?"

"His favorite was the one about how Emmeline escaped from the river. He liked me to tell it over and over. So I did."

"Would you tell me?"

Matilda worried her hands on her cane. "Oh," she said with a cautious glance toward the ceiling. "I don't know. I s'pose one little story couldn't hurt nothin'." Matilda gummed her lip. "Well, see, Archibald Slaughter knew Emmeline was with child, and it was only a matter of time before his wife found out he'd been abusing the girl. He had two choices. He could give Nathaniel and Emmeline all that land and let 'em out of their contracts, or he could get rid of his problem altogether. Greedy and proud as he was, he couldn't bear the thought of giving up a piece of his farm, and letting Emmeline go off with another man. So when everybody started talking 'bout she was a witch, he saw his chance.

"He had his men drag her down to the river. They bound up her ankles and tied rocks in her dress. It was a test, see. If she was a witch and there was evil inside her, the water would reject her and she'd come right up on out of it. And then Slaughter could hang her. Or burn her. Get rid of her that way. And everyone would be glad the witch was gone. But if she was pure, the water would take her. And she'd be gone just the same."

"She would drown," Tori whispered. A black-and-white vision pushed its way to the front of Tori's mind. The dream that had haunted her since the day they'd moved to Slaughter Farm. Water rushing into her lungs. Daylight bubbling through the surface over her head. These were Emmeline's memories. And she'd shared them with Tori the night Will drowned. As if Emmeline were trying to tell her. . . . "What happened next?"

"Emmeline was smart. Strong," Matilda said with a wry, toothless smile. "She knew what Slaughter meant to do and she was prepared. She hid a knife in her dress. Cut herself right out of her clothes and swam hard as she could. But Slaughter and his men caught her up on shore, and when his wife saw Emmeline come out of that river naked with that swollen belly, she knew what Archibald Slaughter had done. And she'd be damned if anyone else found out."

"What did she do?"

"She set out to prove Emmeline was pregnant by the devil. They dragged Emmeline inside that house and held her down on a table, searching for a birthmark or a scar . . . somethin' unnatural they could point to as the devil's mark."

"The needle," Tori whispered, remembering the flash of a knitting needle and the prickle of pins in her arm when she awoke from the dream.

"You know this test, then," Matilda said, raising a thin eyebrow.

"I dreamed it. Emmeline fought them off. She used the knitting needle to escape."

Matilda gave a slow, knowing nod. "So you been listenin' after all. That's good. 'Cause Emmeline knows things. Important things. Things that might save you and that boy."

"I don't understand. Save us from what?"

"I told Al before he died, secrets are dangerous. Not small secrets, like this one," she said, setting aside the cake wrapper. "I'm talking 'bout the big ones. We try to hide things, to bury our own shame. But it ain't the nature of secrets to lay down quiet. Shame's gonna find its way to the surface. It don't matter. . . . You can cover secrets in more secrets. . . . You can bury 'em deep. But the more you try to hold 'em down, the harder they're gonna fight to come out. And the Slaughters got a lot of history to wrestle with. They got a lot of shame scratching at their back door. And they're not gonna let no one open it and let it all come rushin' in."

"Is that what happened to Will?"

Matilda's soft jowls sagged at the mention of his name. "That boy never did come home, did he?"

Tori shook her head.

Matilda drew a heavy breath. "I'm afraid it might've been my fault."

"I don't understand."

"I told him the same stories I'd been telling his granddaddy for years. Told him about Emmeline and Nathaniel and Ruth. About the history of the Slaughter people, and mine. Didn't think nothing of it. Al Senior and little Will . . . They were working on a project together. Al said he needed my help, because I had worked for the historical society. That's why he believed me at first, when I told him the stories. 'Cause I had credentials. But we didn't need none of that. I got all them stories and papers handed down through the family from Ruth. Al started listening to the stories, and coming more often. Always asking to know this or that. Little Will liked to come and listen to the stories too."

"You said they were working on a project together. What kind of project?" Tori held her breath. This had to be it. She had to be right.

"A genealogy project. It was a family tree," she said, a smile wrinkling her face. "A real big one. Went back all the way to the sixteen hundreds. To the arrival of the first Slaughter people here in Chaptico."

Tori fought the urge to leap to her feet. "Do you still have it?"

Matilda looked up at Tori as if Tori had dragged her from a memory. "Have what?"

"The family tree? Is it here? With you?"

"Oh, no," she said, her smile shaking away. "After Al Senior died, I gave all that to Will."

"To Will?" she asked, her limbs suddenly heavy.

"It seemed right he should have it. Since it was his family and he'd worked so hard writin' it all down. I told him it would be our secret, since his granddaddy made me promise not to tell nobody. If I'd known what would happen to him . . ." She trailed off, her cloudy eyes looking haunted.

Tori thought about the missing maps of the cemetery and Nathaniel's unmarked grave. She thought about the short passage about Emmeline in the history book—how it told such a narrow slice of her story. The Slaughters had been silencing their history for generations. They had driven Matilda away, burned her house so she could never come back, and told everyone she was crazy, so no one would believe her. Someone had pushed Will into the river to keep him from telling these stories. The same person who'd filled up all his holes, trying to keep the stories from surfacing. The same person who'd served her family with a lawsuit to get rid of her. And Alistair would keep pushing away the facts, burying the stories—the debts, betrayals, murders, and scandals . . . the truth of how Tori came to inherit this land—until Tori was gone.

She rested a hand on Matilda's. "I won't let him cover this up."

I t was nearly sunset, and the tobacco fields were awash in pink and pale yellow sunlight. My tunic was soaked through with sweat, the first breaths of an evening breeze cooling my skin as I loaded the last of the harvested leaves into the wagon.

I heard them before I saw them approach. The steady clink of metal on metal and three sets of boots crunching over the dry field. Slaughter walked briskly, flanked by two of his largest men.

I tossed an armful of tobacco into the wagon and wiped my brow on my sleeve, squinting against the low sun behind them, unable to make out the expression on Slaughter's face. A cold unease settled under my skin. His men carried shackles.

"Sir?" I asked, looking to the men's faces. One of them had an *R* branded into his forehead. The other's ears had both been cropped. They had been criminals, redemptioners like Thomas. Thomas had been a good man, merciful and kind. But now Thomas was gone, and these men's hard, scarred faces were heavy with fear.

"Take Mr. Bishop to the shed," Slaughter said without pause for greeting.

"To the shed?" I took a reflexive step away from them. The shed was for containing criminals. A makeshift prison since the jail had been moved with the State House to Annapolis, too far to transport lawbreakers for petty crimes. And Slaughter, a sheriff by the will of the governor, for lack of any oversight was free to do with his people as he pleased. "Why?" I asked, as the men removed the shackles from their belts.

"You are under arrest," Slaughter said, carelessly plucking a fat worm from a leaf on the wagon and flicking it away while the men snapped the heavy irons around my wrists and ankles.

"For what?" The men nudged me forward, but I refused to be moved. "What crime am I accused of?"

"You are accused of stealing."

"Stealing? And who is my accuser? I should like him to look me in the eye and tell me what I stole!"

In three long strides, Slaughter stood before me, his dark eyes piercing and his nose nearly touching mine. "I am!" I flinched against the spittle as he shouted in my face. "And if you do not return to me what you've taken, your punishment will be severe."

"I've taken nothing from you, I swear," I said, swallowing a knot of guilt. I hadn't stolen anything. Not yet. But I had committed the crime clearly in my mind a million times while I'd slept last night. In my dreams, I had taken Emmeline. Taken her and run.

"You will return those contracts to me, or be charged as a thief and a conspirator."

The words were like a rush of blood to my head. Emmeline. She'd found our contracts. We were one step closer to leaving this place. I squared my shoulders against the weight of his chains. "I am falsely accused. You told me yourself, those contracts do not exist."

Slaughter balled his hands into fists. "You will return them immediately!"

"I cannot return what I did not take, sir," I said in a low voice, throwing Slaughter's own words back at him. "As you've always been careful to remind me, I am entitled to nothing of yours."

"Take him to the stocks," Slaughter commanded the men. "You'll have the night to reconsider your options. I'll spare you the knowledge of what awaits you tomorrow if you fail to change your mind."

*   *   *

A soft scratching roused me, the gentle clatter of metal against wood. I blinked and lifted my head, struggling to make out my surroundings in the dark.

Night.

Only a few more hours of torture before Slaughter's men would release me. Only a few more hours until—

"Bloody hell!" a voice whispered behind me.

"Em?" I croaked through parched lips. "What are you doing here?" The chains at my ankles rattled as I shifted in the stocks, trying to catch sight of her. My back and shoulders screamed in agony and my arms and legs tingled, numb.

"Trying to get you out!" she whispered. "The lock. I can't manage it." Emmeline fell silent. In my mind, I could see her pacing, staring at the lock, chewing on a thumbnail while her mind churned, her dark hair wild and her gray eyes furious.

"If you're caught here, it will only make things worse for both of us."

"I don't think they can get much worse," she said through an angry sigh. "Ruth overheard Slaughter talking at dinner. He plans to flog you if you don't confess to stealing the contracts come morning. If he doesn't get them back, he'll—"

"The contracts. Are they well hidden?"

"Yes."

"You're certain? You haven't told anyone?"

"Only Ruth and I know where they are."

But if Slaughter suspected Emmeline enough to put pressure upon Ruth, we could all be in great danger. "Then go back to the house. Say nothing to anyone, no matter what happens."

"But if I don't return them, he'll—"

"He'll kill me even if you do!" There was no escape. Not for me. But maybe there was still a way for her.

"But, Nat—"

"Tell no one, Em. Do you understand?"

There was a sorrowful hitch in her breath.

"Em, please," I whispered. "Come where I can see you." Slowly, she came to stand in front of the stocks, pressing a warm hand over mine.

"Oh, Nathaniel," she said through her tears. "You're so cold." She brushed my hair back to kiss my forehead, her lips tender against my skin.

"Why didn't you run?" I asked, wishing all this was a dream. That she was already gone. Safe.

"I would leave you here no sooner than you would leave me." Emmeline cupped my bruised cheek and I let my head rest heavily in her hand. Her other hung at her side, her fist clenched around the hilt of a knife. The blade glimmered in the moonlight, filling me with a cold unease. "He will pay for what he's done to you. To all of us."

She took a step back, and suddenly I could see all of her so clearly. Her black-and-blue cheek and her split lip, the bruises circling her neck ... Slaughter. He was so willing to disfigure me, to leave permanent scars on my face and my body. But this ... this was the first time Slaughter had ever left such a mark on Em's skin. She might as well have plunged that blade into my gut.

"You have to go, Em. You have to run. Now. Take the contracts. Take Ruth if you must. Just leave before he is of a mind to kill you. You saw. You saw what he did to Thomas. You know what he'll do to me. Take to the woods and find a place to hide."

"I won't leave you. Not like this."

"I'll be no more than a day behind you. I'll find you. I swear. Just go! Please!"

"He will never let you live. He told me as much!" A tear slipped down her cheek and she brushed it roughly with her sleeve. She shook her head, her knuckles white around the handle of the knife. "And I will not watch you die by Slaughter's hand."

Emmeline came closer, her face pinched with anguish, the knife outstretched toward me.

"Em! What are you—?"

The knife slashed close behind my left ear, then...

Cautiously, I opened my eyes. Emmeline stood watching me, gripping a fistful of my hair, her chest heaving and tears sliding over the bruises on her cheek. She sheathed the blade. Then she lifted my shirt, tucking the knife into the inner pocket of my trousers beside the small wooden carving I carried there, checking to make sure it was snugly in place before drawing my shirt down over it.

"I love you," she said, backing away from me, her head shaking as if she could hardly believe what she'd done. "I have always loved you."

She turned and ran, and I shut my eyes against a rise of hot tears, listening for the sound of her feet in the grass, praying she would run. Keep running. Until she was far, far from here.

But the only sound to reach me was the rustle of boots, drawing nearer. Men's shouts, growing louder. "We've found the witch!" one of them cried out.

And a numbing cold the likes of which I had never known spread over me as Emmeline began to scream.

WILL'S SECRET

ori spent the next three days searching every room of her house, starting with the one that used to belong to Will. Jesse had said that Will lived there with his mom and his grandfather when Al Senior had grown too old to care for himself, and had only moved out in the days before Tori's family had moved in. If Will had a family tree, it was possible he would have hidden it there.

Tori checked on Nathaniel every day after school, but he kept their visits short, insisting she keep looking for it. Each day, the circles under his eyes grew darker; each day, he seemed to bruise more easily. When Tori got home from school on Monday, she found him sitting on the bank of the river with his head on his knees. On Tuesday, she'd found him sleeping in the barn. Today, she was too afraid to wake him. She feared one d come home from school and he might not wake up at all.

She was running out of time. If she didn't find the a would force her hand and make her smash the bottle stand looking at it anymore.

Instead, Tori headed to the house after scho ing as hard as she should have been. She told tired too. Her dreams . . . visions, as Nat to repeat themselves. They were bec fying. Each time, she remember

285

Nathaniel's hanging was the most disturbing of them all. Part of her kept hoping that another solution would reveal itself, some new angle to this double-edged sword . . . one that didn't include Nathaniel leaving.

She sank down on her bed, forestalling the inevitable. Hugging her cross-stitched pillow, she thought back to that awful night when she'd found Jesse in her room. How he'd gone through her closet unpacking all her secrets. How he'd found her razor . . .

Tori had already looked in Kyle's room, where Will used to live, but she hadn't looked hard enough. She'd been looking in obvious places. She had checked the boxes of odd things they'd discovered during the move, emptying an old piggy bank and checking the pocket of a worn tooth pillow, in case Will had hidden something inside. She'd found no trace of any documents or papers. Not even so much as a folded note. But Will had known he was hiding so much more than that—it was his secret, the one he couldn't tell anybody. If she were a thirteen-year-old boy, where would she hide something dangerous? Something her family didn't want her to have?

Kyle's room was painted pale blue under the *Minecraft* and *Halo* posters that covered most of the walls. His sheets were piled in the middle of the bed, his feather pillow still impressed with the shape of him. Graphic novels littered the wood floor, along with Legos and action figures he claimed to be too old to play with. She kicked them out of her way, turning a slow circle in the middle of the room. It was the third time she'd searched this room this week.

She pressed her fingers to her temples and looked around her. toys and the floor and searched under the bed, pushing piles of dusty so she could dirty socks that reeked of her brother out of her way them. She wooden planks for signs of a hollow space beneath anything tap tress and looked again under the box spring for ten note from inside, finding nothing more than a handwritten mentioned from school.

Regardless of what Jesse thought, this wasn't Will's room anymore.

These spaces belonged to her brother now. To his clothes, his sheets, and his toys. Maybe Will had taken his secrets with him when he'd moved back to his own house, when Tori had moved in. But if that was the case, why would Jesse have been snooping around in her room, and why had his father broken into her mother's bedroom? Tori had to believe the secret was still hidden in this house.

If it was here, no one had found it yet.

Not her. Not her brother or her mom. Not Alistair or Jesse. Which meant Will had been good at hiding things.

Tori walked to the closet and opened the bifold doors. Battleship and Sorry came crashing to the floor from the top shelf, spilling markers and plastic ships to the floor. The floor of her brother's closet was piled with outgrown shoes, cleats and shin guards, sweatshirts and an old Halloween mask or two. The walls inside were plastered in *Star Wars* movie posters, strategically overlapped to cover every conceivable inch of wall space. She groped around the inside of the closet under her brother's things, pressing the floorboards and feeling the walls, when she accidentally tore a poster.

Her fingers pushed right through it into a hole in the plaster. Carefully, she plucked out the thumbtack and peeled back the glossy paper, revealing a small opening in the bottom corner of the wall. A mouse hole, she realized, finding nothing more than a trail of droppings inside, and a few tooth marks where something had gnawed on the paper's edge. Tori sat up on her heels.

And then she saw them.... Pencil marks, visible under the poster's torn corner.

Tori pulled back the paper, prying out the last of the thumbtacks that held it in place. Behind it, a list of names had been written on the wallboard. First and last names. Birth dates and death dates. Marriage dates connected by pencil lines. Her breath came faster and she yanked a handful of clothes from their hangers and tossed them to the floor, exposing the length of the wall. She slipped both hands under the next poster, tearing through it and ripping away the long sheets until the thumbtacks and a few torn edges were all that remained between her and Will's secret.

Slowly, Tori rose to her feet, stepping back far enough to see the entire thing.

"What are you doing?"

She turned abruptly to find her brother, standing white-faced and confused in the doorway to his room. She looked down at the shredded remains of his poster collection under her feet. "I'm so sorry, Kyle. I swear, I'll buy you new ones."

But he wasn't looking at his posters. And he wasn't looking at Tori. Kyle's eyes were glued to the closet wall, his face a mirror of every ounce of guilt Tori was feeling.

Tori turned to stare at it too. The forking history of the Slaughter family was as broad and tangled as the big dead oak outside in the field. Names. So many names. Tori wasn't even sure where to start looking. And there, near the mouse hole, was Al Senior, beside his wife, Beatrice. Below them, three names were connected by one long line . . . Alistair, Francine, and Jack. Tori's gaze shot to the top, near the ceiling, searching frantically, until she found them . . . Archibald and Elizabeth Slaughter. An odd broken line connected Archibald to Emmeline and another line connected her to Nathaniel Bishop. Tori looked under Emmeline's line, for the name of the child she and Archibald had conceived, but there was only a blank space. A question mark.

Al Senior's big secret. Had this really been it? A giant question mark was all Will had died for? The simple fact that their family tree had forks and knots in it, blank spaces they couldn't account for, names that weren't the same as their own—and someone might find out about it?

Tori's hands clenched into fists.

"I'm sorry," Kyle said in a quiet voice behind her. "I found it the day we moved in. I thought it might upset you." Tori followed his anxious glance to the top right corner of the closet where her name and date of birth had been written off to the side, in the margins with a question mark, a faint line connecting her question mark to Archibald and Emmeline's. "I didn't know what to do, so I covered it up." He wiped his nose with his sleeve. "I don't care what anyone says. Or what's on that wall. You're too ugly to be anyone else's sister except mine." His cheeks flushed bright pink and his gaze drifted down to the mess on the floor.

"Is this why you don't trust Nathaniel? Because of this?"

"He's related to Emmeline too, isn't he? That's why he has the same name as that boy on the family tree—Nathaniel Bishop?" Kyle pointed to Nathaniel's name, printed neatly beside Emmeline's. A line connected them and their dates were the same. Not birth dates, then. Probably the date they'd arrived at the Slaughter plantation together.

"No, he's not related to her. It's just . . ." Tori drew out a long breath, stalling while she tried to come up with an explanation he might believe. "It's kind of a long story."

"So he's not here to take you from us?"

"No," she said, taken aback. "That's not why he's here at all." Kyle's shoulders fell, like he'd just shed some invisible burden. All this time she'd thought he'd been pushing her away, wishing her gone, when all he'd been trying to do was hold on to her. "Face it. You're stuck with me."

This brought a reluctant smile to his face. And Tori was surprised how much it had changed in the weeks that had passed since she'd seen the last one. And how much she'd missed it.

He scratched his head at the pile of clothes hangers and poster shreds on the floor. "Did you really have to wreck my room?"

She laughed, choking on the lump in her throat. "Would you have let me in otherwise?"

Kyle shrugged. "Probably not."

The smell of something burning downstairs wafted into Kyle's room. It was creeping up on dinnertime; her mother must have come home.

"Has Mom seen it?" she asked.

"I don't think so. I covered it our first day here while she was unpacking the kitchen."

Good. If she looked too closely at Nathaniel's name, it wouldn't be an easy coincidence to explain. Anyway, Magda had already said there were no records of an Emmeline Bell giving birth in Maryland in the year she'd escaped Slaughter's plantation, which meant the search for the missing branches of her family tree had come to a dead end. At least until Tori turned twenty-one.

She brushed her hair from her eyes, ready to cover the whole thing back up. "Can we keep it our little secret for now?"

"Yeah," Kyle said, looking relieved. "But we'd better clean all this before Mom gets home."

Tori felt a stir of unease. "What do you mean? Where is she?"

"She dropped me off and went back to town. She said she's bringing takeout home for dinner."

"Then what's that . . ." The burning smell was growing stronger. In the doorway behind her brother's head, curling claws of black smoke scraped their way across the ceiling.

"Go!" Tori ran for the hall, pushing Kyle in front of her. But by the time they reached the top of the stairs, the foyer below was engulfed in flames, the fire licking its way up the walls toward Tori's bedroom. "Come on!" she shouted into her sleeve to keep from choking. She pulled Kyle the opposite way to her mother's room, shutting them inside. Tori threw aside the curtain. She tried to open the window, but it was nailed shut, still boarded from the outside after the break-in.

Tori ran to the opposite window. The front porch below was a mass of orange flames. There was no other way out.

"Tori?" Kyle cried. Smoke-blackened tears spilled down his face and he coughed into the neck of his shirt.

"Victoria!" She heard her name being shouted, over and over, muffled by the sound of the flames. "Stand back!"

"Get down!" Tori shouted, pushing Kyle to the floor.

A loud bang shook the room. Tori hugged Kyle tight at the sound of splintering wood and the crash of glass.

Then a hand yanked them from the floor.

"Come on!" Nathaniel shouted, grabbing them both and guiding them through the smoke back to the broken window. He pushed Kyle out first onto the roof of the back porch. "Down the tree! Go, quickly!"

Tori made a run for the hall, Nathaniel swearing and coughing behind her. "What are you doing?"

"My father's things!" She reached for the knob. The metal seared her hand and she snatched it away. Smoke poured through the gap underneath it.

Nathaniel took her by the shoulders. "They can't be saved. We have to go!"

With one last look at the door, Tori scrambled out of the window, reaching back to pull Nathaniel through before she climbed down the roof to the mulberry tree.

She ran to where Kyle sat in the grass, hugging his knees and coughing in fits. She could barely hear the scream of sirens over the sound of the fire chewing its way through their walls, their roof, their house, their everything, burning the last flimsy shreds of Slaughter's secrets to the ground.

AFTER THE FIRE

The sirens grew louder. Smoke poured thick through the broken bedroom window upstairs, and flames began licking upward from the house. Tori heard her mother's car door slam in the front yard. She began shouting for Tori and Kyle, her voice pitched high with panic. Kyle was already on his feet, running to meet her.

Tori turned to Nathaniel. Her breath caught at the sight of him. The scab on his cheek had opened. His face was smeared with blood, and he wavered, his shoulders heavy with fatigue. "You shouldn't let anyone see you here," she said, trying not to reveal the tremble in her voice. "Wait for me at the barn, okay?"

"Will you be all right?" he asked, wiping soot from her cheek.

"I'll be fine." She took his hand and squeezed. It was as hot as the fire. "I promise."

Tori waited until Nathaniel disappeared into the woods before racing after her brother. She found her mother, clutching Kyle tightly to her and rocking on the blighted stretch of grass, tears rolling down her cheeks as she watched the fire spread to the roof. She opened her arms, and Tori fell into them, all of them holding on to the last of what they had.

"What happened?" she asked as the lights of the first fire truck became visible through the trees.

"I don't know," Tori said, still coughing from the smoke. "We were upstairs when it started."

"We couldn't get down. Nathaniel rescued us through the window in your bedroom."

Tori cringed inside, wishing she'd had the forethought to tell Kyle not to mention that part. The fewer times Nathaniel's name came up around catastrophic events involving the Slaughters, the better.

And Tori had no doubt the Slaughters *were* involved in this. Somehow.

Her mother reached for Tori's hand. "Then I'm grateful Nathaniel was here," she said with a gentle squeeze. "Where is he? We should make sure he's okay."

Just then, the fire trucks turned up the driveway. And the police. The lawn erupted in chaos, and not long after, the last charred vestiges of Tori's house slumped, drenched and smoking.

"It's an old house," the fire marshal told them. "Old wiring. Not unusual for problems to develop, hidden behind the walls." It was the same thing the police had said about the fire at Matilda's. Tomorrow they'd come back when the house was cool, and open an investigation for the insurance company so Tori's family could recover the loss and rebuild.

But Tori wasn't reassured. How could they put a price on a cardboard box containing the last of her father's things? How could they write a claim for the security that came with having a roof over their head? Sitting in the dead grass, watching their house smolder, Tori wasn't sure it was possible to rebuild these things they'd lost. And when she looked at her mother's and brother's empty stares, she wasn't sure there was anything left inside them to brace.

"Where will we go?" Kyle asked when the sun began to set, the last of the smoke blurring with the dusky colors of the evening sky. The question pinched her mother's eyes. It was the same question he'd asked the day they got their eviction notice at the apartment, after their father died. And Tori regretted every time she'd told them they couldn't understand what it was like to feel out of place. They were all out of place. They were all ungrounded, trying to find somewhere they belonged.

"I called the senior center," her mother said, brushing Kyle's bangs from his eyes and planting a kiss on his forehead. "A patient passed away this afternoon. That's why I had to run back to town earlier. Anyway, I've asked the center if we can use the room tonight. They're packing up her things and cleaning it for us now. It'll be a little cozy, but the director said we can use it for a few days until we figure something out."

Kyle whined. "We have to sleep in a dead person's room? That's creepy."

"It's a warm bed. And they're very generous to let us use it." Her mother tucked Kyle closer into her side.

Tori stood beside them, rubbing her arms against the cold. Close by, three police officers talked in low tones, and she moved a few steps toward them, trying to hear. She recognized one of them as the officer who had come to her house after Matilda's fire and after they'd found Will. He pulled a notepad from his squad car, flipped pages backward, and showed it to the others. They all wrote something down in notepads of their own. Tori hoped it wasn't Nathaniel's name.

A pickup truck idled at the bottom of her driveway. The driver's door hung open as Jesse took a few steps closer, his expression unreadable as he watched the smoke rise from what used to be his grandfather's house. Tori locked eyes with Jesse across the lawn and he glared back. His mother said something to Jesse from the passenger seat and he got back in his truck, slamming the door hard enough to make Tori shudder. His wheels kicked up a cloud of dust as they peeled down Slaughter Road. The officers looked up, but hardly seemed surprised, and their heads dipped back to their hushed conversation.

Tori went to sit with her mother and Kyle, her stomach growing sick at the sight of the blighted grass that surrounded them, as if the curse were holding them in the palm of its hand. In her gut, she knew Alistair had started the fire in her house, the same as he'd burned Matilda's. And yet, she couldn't deny that Nathaniel had been right. The curse was coming for her. Closer to her house and the people she loved. She couldn't help but wonder if it had pushed Alistair's hand. If it had made him light the match. And she was grateful her family would have a place to stay where Alistair couldn't touch them.

As sick as Nathaniel was, she couldn't leave him alone here. It was all she could do to stand there waiting for everyone to leave. Tori took her mom's phone and dialed Magda's number.

"Mrs. Burns?" Magda shrieked on the other end of the line.

"It's me."

"Tori! Thank God!" she said before Tori could get in a word. "Drew called and told me. He just heard the news. Are you okay?"

"We're fine. We're all okay."

"But the house . . . ?"

"There's not much left of it," Tori said as a charred piece of what used to be her front porch crackled and fell. "That's kind of why I called. Can I tell my mom I'm staying with you tonight?"

"I'll have my mom make up the guest room for you. You can stay as long as . . ." Tori waited through a heavy pause. "You're not really coming, are you?" Magda asked, catching on.

"Right," Tori said with a quick look toward her mother. "Just for the night. My mom and my brother have a bed at the senior center, but it's a little crammed for the three of us, and I'm sure she'd be more comfortable knowing I'm staying with you."

"You're going to be with Nathaniel, aren't you?"

"Yes."

"Are you sure that's a good idea?"

"Great, thanks, Magda," Tori said quickly. "I really appreciate it and I won't be any trouble at all. Promise. I'll see you soon." She disconnected and handed her mother the phone. "That's Magda's cell number in your call log. She said I can stay with her tonight. You can call Magda if you need anything."

Her mom rose to her feet, pulling Kyle up with her. He leaned against her, his face filthy and his hair a mess, his eyelids growing heavy. "I'm going to get Kyle settled at the center. I don't think there's anything more we can do here. Will you be okay?" she asked, squeezing Tori's hand.

Tori nodded. "Magda's on her way to pick me up."

Her mother hesitated.

"Go, I promise. I'll be fine," Tori insisted, blowing into her hands and bouncing on her heels to keep warm.

Her mother roused Kyle and directed him into the car, where he curled against the door and closed his eyes, his sooty forehead pressed against the glass as they drove away.

THE SUFFERING TREE

I searched the faces in the crowd for Ruth. For Sam. If they were gone—if they had taken the contracts and run like we'd planned—Emmeline must be with them. It was all I could hope for as Slaughter's men loaded me, bound and weary, onto the horse-drawn cart beneath the tree. And yet, her scream still echoed in my mind, chilling me.

A stone smacked into my cheek. Another into my forehead. Shouts and cries and jeers bellowed all around me.

When the noose lowered over my head, I was that ten-year-old boy, wandering the dark streets of Bristol all over again. My world suddenly dark, surrounded by the voices of strangers, completely alone.

I would die here a liar and a thief. They would bury me without a casket, without a marker. The grass would soon grow over me, and the man I was would rot away, nameless and forgotten.

And the thought of spending eternity alone terrified me more than the threat of any pain I'd ever suffered under the witness of this tree.

The hangman cinched the rope about my throat, forcing my chin high. I saw her then. . . . Em, vengeful and defiant across the field, looking so much like she had the first time I'd seen her on the ship when they'd pulled the sack from her head. Wild black snarls of hair and eyes like a turbulent sky, scratched and bruised and barefoot in a filthy, bloody shift, her fists clenched, daring the world to touch her.

I failed. I'd failed her. I told her she would escape. That her child would be safe. I was supposed to be a brother, an uncle . . . the man she needed. But I was worthless, a servant boy bought for less than a barrel.

"Forgive me!" I called to her, my shout breaking on the words as the cart lurched out from under me.

Tori waited until her mother's car was out of sight before slipping off into the woods with the firemen's blankets tucked under her arm. Maybe she should have felt relieved. The insurance money might be enough for a fresh start. Her family could take the money and move someplace else. Back to the city. And when Tori turned twenty-one, she could sell her land back to the Slaughters and be rid of this place for good. That is, if the curse didn't follow her.

But the thought of leaving . . . the idea of abandoning Nathaniel and Will and Matilda. Of letting their stories be buried. And never seeing Nathaniel again . . . The faster Tori ran, the more the burning walls of her chest felt like they were caving in.

The barn was a shadow against the trees up ahead. No sign of life. No firelight in the window.

Tori pushed her legs faster. She threw open the barn door. It was pitch-black inside. A small square of the dirt floor was illuminated by a pale beam of moonlight through the smoke hole in the roof.

"Nathaniel!" she called out, tossing the blankets to the floor. The barn was silent. Motionless. A lump hardened in her throat. Then something moved in the shadows.

Nathaniel rushed toward her, and it was only when his arms were around her that Tori felt like she could breathe again.

"I thought you were gone," she said into his chest. He was bundled in one of her father's thick knit sweaters. It smelled like smoke and cedar and faintly, the river.

"I'm sorry. I didn't want to risk building a fire. I was afraid someone might see. Have they all left?"

"I think so."

"You're cold." He started to pull away, toward the stack of firewood, but she held him in place, her arms locked around him as she stared at the frail witch's bottle, half-hidden under a pile of straw. For a moment, neither of them moved. Tori didn't want to tell him about the tree in her brother's closet. That Slaughter had won. That her home was unlivable, and soon, they'd both be gone. Slowly, he wrapped his arms around her and pressed his lips to the top of her head.

"I'm sorry," he whispered into her hair. "About your home. And your father's possessions. I would have saved them for you, if I had come sooner."

"It's okay," she said, pushing herself gently from his arms, from her father's sweater. The truth stung and she blinked it away. "It's time we let him go."

"It's not okay." The urgency in his tone startled her. "He was your home. And you . . ." His eyes pinned her in the dark. "You have become mine. You're the reason I came. You're the reason I've stayed."

His hand was on his scarred chest, begging her to need him. To remember him. He was afraid, she realized, not of death, but of being forgotten.

"I won't let you go." She brushed the tips of his fingers with her own, the way he'd touched hers in the river. He closed his eyes and swallowed hard. Tori stepped into him until she could feel his heart beating, memorizing the moonlit shadows on his face—the cut of his jaw, the small knot at the bridge of his nose, and the stray lock of hair that fell across it.

She cupped his cheek, following it down across his lower lip, feeling his warm breath against her finger. Then she leaned in until her lips were close enough to feel it too.

Tori felt Nathaniel's heart leap. His hand found the small of her back and pressed her closer as their mouths brushed.

Tori kissed him back deeper, until she was breathless and shaking. She pulled back slowly. His eyes fluttered open and came to rest on Tori's hands where they gripped the hem of her shirt.

She held her breath and pulled it up over her head. Clutching the fabric at her side, she stepped into the dim square of light, until she was little more than moon-white skin in a plain cotton bra and row after row of pink and purple scars, as naked as she'd ever been in front of anyone.

His gaze locked on the oyster shell around her neck, then traveled over the rest of her. She swallowed hard, aching for him to see past it, to find something beautiful and shining beneath that she wasn't entirely sure was there. Tori grew cold all over under the weight of his stare, blood rushing to her cheeks. Then, in a burst of three quick strides, he was all she could see. His mouth fell on hers, their lips and teeth colliding. His hand tangled with her fingers through the fabric of her shirt, and without breaking the kiss, he tossed it away.

Clumsy and hungry, they pulled each other close. Tori's hands slid under his sweater, over the scars on his back, pushing the fabric up with them. Nathaniel yanked it over his head, a few long strands of his hair coming loose from the knot at the nape of his neck and falling against Tori's cheek. His forehead rested on hers, his chest rising and falling in the pale light of the barn. Tori trembled as she caressed his cuts with the tip of a finger, wishing she could erase every terrible thing the Slaughters had done to him without changing him at all. He was strong, beautiful in ways the moonlight couldn't see.

His fingers weaved into hers. He kissed her, softer, carefully this time, as if he were asking permission. She pulled him down with her into the straw and whispered that it was okay.

That she was safe. That this is what she wanted. And that she would not let him go.

My hands are shaking. But these hands aren't mine. The fingernails are dirty and chipped, the pads thick with calluses.

I'm struggling to remove a cork from a stone jug. Wet grass, rocks, and tree roots press into my knees. Around me are a rusted spade and several small objects I can't make out in the dark. I hear wind, the rustle of leaves. I smell rain and the brine of the river.

The cork pops free.

I fumble with the small bits on the ground, bending them to fit inside the narrow mouth of the bottle. A handful of bent nails and tiny pins, a heart cut from rough cloth... My fingers frantically skim the ground, closing on a long lock of hair, and I shove it inside.

The black-and-white funnel of vision moves frantically, as if I'm searching for something. It turns upward and focuses on the tree above my head.

I push myself to my feet. I leap, reaching for a low-hanging branch and breaking it off. I cry out as I drag it across my palm. My hand shakes, and a dark line of blood rushes to the surface. I curl my fist over the mouth of the jar, funneling the blood inside. When the bleeding slows, I snap the branch into pieces and drop them in the bottle.

I draw a trembling breath. Rocking back and forth, I whisper fast.

"In death, may the iron strengthen you. With life may the oak sustain you. May the heart stitch yours forever to mine. My blood will call you home."

I force the cork back into the jug and use all my weight to press it firmly in place.

Then I take up the spade and start digging.

●   ●   ●

Tori's eyes flew open at the caw of a crow.

Her skin was coated in straw dust. Outside the barn, morning birds chattered and shrieked.

A pile of red embers smoldered in the stone ring on the floor. Tori laid her cheek back down against Nathaniel's chest as he slept, listening to the steady rhythm of his heartbeat, and willing hers to slow. She was fine. Her hand was fine. No cuts. No blood. It was only a dream.

He was still here. They were safe.

Beside them, buried in the straw, was Nathaniel's witch bottle, the sunlight illuminating the countless hairline cracks in its surface.

Tori closed her eyes and thought about curling deeper into the crook of Nathaniel's arm, drawing the scratchy blanket higher over both of them, and letting the soft sound of his breathing chase away the remnants of the dream.

But it wouldn't let go.

Something didn't fit. Something didn't match between these visions Emmeline had been showing her, and Nathaniel's memories. And it wasn't until Tori closed her eyes and held them up side by side in her mind that she knew for certain what was different.

The nails, the heart, the bird bones . . . It all seemed so foolish. . . .

Bird bones. There had been bird bones in Ruth and Emmeline's bottles.

But there weren't any in Nathaniel's.

She cast that spell hoping you would come back. That if she did it right, you might rise up on your own. Only she was careless and somethin' went wrong. . . .

Emmeline had never intended to trap him, or to curse him. She'd meant to save him. But she had been rushed. She'd panicked. And she'd made a mistake. She'd left out an ingredient when she cast the spell. Nathaniel couldn't survive away from the tree because he was still bound to it. And without the bird bones, he'd never be free of it.

One day, the wings of a bird will carry us from our bindings and we'll be free of this place.

That's what Emmeline had been trying to tell her.

Careful not to wake Nathaniel, she eased out from under the blanket and slipped quickly into her clothes, shuddering when the cold metal button of her jeans pressed into her skin. Carefully, she picked up the bottle and held it to her. Nathaniel didn't stir, his arm still curled around the empty space where Tori had slept beside him.

She couldn't save her house. She couldn't stop the Slaughters from trying to get rid of her. She couldn't bring Will back. But there was still time to save Nathaniel.

So with his life in her hands, Tori set out to fix it.

* * *

Tori smelled it before she reached the opening in the trees. The house . . . her house . . . what was left of it anyway. The closer she got, the more it choked her. She circled around the blackened remains, looking for a way in.

The grass around the burned foundation was still shiny with frost, the ground spongy from the shower of hoses it had taken to drown the fire. In the daylight, she was surprised to see how much of it still stood. The front porch and its eaves had completely caved in, and the front hallway, along with all of its contents—jackets, shoes, and backpacks, the credenza that ran the length of the stairs—was simply gone. But the second story, and most of the rear of the house and the roof were intact.

The mulberry tree out back was still standing, the siding around it stained in dark ribbons of soot where smoke had poured from the windows below, but the porch roof and her mother's bedroom window through which they'd escaped seemed hardly touched by the fire. Even so, without knowing what might be waiting for her inside, she didn't dare bring Nathaniel's bottle with her.

The sun was still low in the sky. She probably only had an hour or two before the police and fire marshal came to start their investigation, so she tucked Nathaniel's bottle in the shadows under the porch and climbed up the mulberry tree with both hands. Testing the porch roof with the toe of her shoe, she stepped gingerly onto it and held her breath as she crossed to the open window. The smell was awful as she ducked into her mother's room, breathing through her sleeve. Her mother's clothes still hung inside the open closet, but Tori doubted the stench of the fire would ever wash out.

She looked around at her mother's belongings—her books, her clothes, her sodden wood furniture—all soft, vulnerable things that wouldn't have lasted anyway. She searched the ruined room for something solid. Something time and fire hadn't touched.

In her mother's closet was a metal box, a fireproof safe where she'd kept their social security cards and birth certificates and other important documents—the title to the car and her parents' marriage certificate, a few precious photos and trinkets. Tori rose up on her tiptoes to reach where it sat on a high shelf. It was heavy and she had to use both hands to lower it to the floor. The keys hung from the lock, because her mother had always been too afraid to lose them. Tori withdrew a few of the contents. The crisp white edges of the documents inside were all perfect. They smelled like the inside of the safe, not like the choking air in the room.

Safe.

Dry.

Perfectly preserved.

Tori's mind raced as she shook out the last of the contents and placed them carefully on the shelf. With the safe tucked under her arm, she stood in front of the open window, giving her mother's sopping, dismal room one last look.

A cool breeze rushed through the window, making the heavy wet curtains snap against her legs. The latch of her mother's bedroom door popped and the door cracked open. A chill raced up Tori's spine as she listened to the room, waiting, half expecting something to come crashing to the floor. But the only sound was the occasional soft crack of burned and swollen wood.

She peered out into the hall, unsure of what might be left of the house on the other side of the door. Smoke stained the hallway walls, and the foyer and the railing down the stairs were charred black. She stepped cautiously, cold gray water squishing up around the toes of her sneakers through the carpet runner. The floor creaked, then groaned, and she clung close to the wall, the metal box tucked tightly under her arm.

Kyle's room was storm-cloud blue, the floor covered in the papery paste of what used to be his posters. The walls inside his closet were blistered and oozing gray water. There was nothing left of the tree but two dark question marks.

A creak downstairs made Tori stiffen. She listened for the sound of anyone else in the house. Wind whistled through the hole in the foyer, blowing a draft upstairs through the hall. The rest of the house was quiet.

She eased down the wall toward her bedroom. Her door was warped on its hinges. A gray film coated the walls, and her comforter dripped puddles of cloudy water to the glass-peppered floor. Tori stepped inside. The small embroidered pillow her mother stitched for her lay facedown in the middle of her bed where she'd left it.

The room was still. But Tori felt Emmeline here, lingering, her presence like a damp chill. Goose bumps raced over her skin and she turned fast to leave. Suddenly, the temperature in the room fell. The wind snapped the curtain. When she turned back again, the cross-stitched pillow had flipped over, faceup on the bed.

The silence in the room felt heavy, laden with expectation. Tori snatched up the pillow and held it to her chest. Behind her, the door creaked on its hinges, wavering in the breeze.

Quickly she stopped to recover the knife she'd hidden behind the dresser. Then she carried the safe and the pillow with her across the hall over the burned threshold to the bathroom, her mind racing as she dug through the hamper. Reaching under the pile of musty clothes, she found the dark turtleneck Nathanial had worn. A few long strands of honey-colored hair clung to the fabric. She grabbed three plastic bags from under the cabinet, the bottle of peroxide, and stuffed it all inside the safe.

●　　●　　●

Tori trekked to the cemetery field. The oak was spotted with blackbirds, and crows pecked in the frost-crusted dirt. After leaving the house, Tori had returned to the barn—careful not to wake Nathaniel—to grab the tin can full of loose nails and screws, as well as what she'd hoped was a wing from the pile of scraps that had been his hunted dinners. Now she set her load under the tree and searched under the outstretched branches for a fallen twig from the oak, but the wind had scattered a tumble of dried leaves and sticks from the forest into the field, and she needed to get this right. She couldn't afford to screw up.

She set down the metal box, looked up into the oak, and cringed. If she snapped a branch and tore it away, she would hurt him. But if she didn't do this, he would suffer far worse.

"I'm sorry," she whispered. Then she leaped and grabbed the end of a low-hanging branch, bending it toward her. "I'm so sorry." She shut her eyes and cut. Not slowly, the way she cut herself, making sure she felt every jagged bite of the blade. This time, she cut quick. If she was fast, maybe he wouldn't hurt for long.

Tori spread the contents of the safe on the ground. She unscrewed the plastic bottle and emptied the nails from her pocket, choosing the heaviest ones and tossing them inside, along with the bird bones.

She unsheathed the knife and lifted the cross-stitched pillow into her lap with a pang at the thought of ruining it. Gritting her teeth, she turned it facedown and plunged the blade into the fabric, sawing it in the shape of a heart. When she was done, she stuffed the front panel of the pillow with the stitched lettering inside her pocket and tucked the heart inside the bottle with the nails. She closed her eyes, trying to recapture the dream.

The hair. Nathaniel's hair.

She unrolled the shirt, careful not to shake loose the strands that clung to it. She plucked as many as she could find . . . four, five . . . She searched every inch of the fabric for another, praying the few she had were enough. Pinching them between her fingers, she dropped them into the bottle.

Tori pressed the blade of the knife to her palm, but something didn't feel right. Changing her mind, she took the cutting from the tree and whittled the end into a sharp point before returning the knife to her pocket. The knife would have been easier. Less painful. A cleaner cut. Instead, she did exactly what Emmeline did in the dream. Biting her lip, she pushed the stick deep into her skin, dragging it down her palm and leaving a long, ragged wound. The blood came fast. Faster than Tori was used to. As fast as it had that night Nathaniel had come out of the ground. The sight of the first few drops trickling down her arm brought a sickening rush of déjà vu. All she could hope was that she'd gotten this part right.

Curling her hand like a funnel around the lip of the bottle, she let the red stream pour inside. She thought back on the dream, trying to hear it inside her head. Emmeline had recited something as she'd corked the bottle. Tori whispered the beginning of the incantation exactly as she remembered it.

"In death, may the iron strengthen you. With life may the oak sustain you...."

She stopped herself. There was something missing. Something she needed to add to make this right.

"May the wings of the bird raise you up and carry you from your binds. May the heart stitch yours forever to mine. My blood will call you home."

She screwed the lid back on the bottle and listened to the air. To the slight breeze that made the dead grass shiver. She wrapped the bottle inside the plastic bag, carefully knotting it twice. Then she put it inside the safe and turned the key.

Tori waited, watching the sky for a gathering of clouds. For the low rumble of thunder. For the tree to shed its new leaves. She waited for the birds in the field to take to the sky. For some sign that she'd gotten this right. That Nathaniel might be healing.

But the air was still.

●   ●   ●

Tori checked to make sure no one was around before stripping down to her bra and underwear. The river churned, brown and green and daunting in front of her. If there was any chance she'd gotten this right, it was best to hide the bottle quickly. As long as it was out in the open, Nathaniel's life was at risk.

A cold wind rippled over the water, licking her skin and giving her the shivers. The safe was clunky and awkward, difficult to hold. She stood in the murky water up to her ankles, waiting for her feet to numb. Emmeline had been wrong before. What if this wasn't right? What if someone found it? What if the water found a way inside? Maybe there was a better place.

She heard Nathaniel's voice in the soft splash of the waves against the shore.

. . . the water was the only place that felt like it could heal me.

She swore to herself, or maybe to Emmeline, and with a deep breath, she charged in.

The box was heavy, pulling her down below the surface, and Tori had to fight to keep her head above water. Suddenly, it was as if she was back in the pool, in a drill, her arms bound at her sides, the coach hollering at her to use her legs and kick. She steadied her breathing, feeling her muscles begin to loosen, her chest start to open, her pulse rate even out and slow. When she reached the channel buoy, she clung to the edge, giving herself a moment to catch her breath. Her muscles and skin were numb.

An oyster boat puttered north up the river toward her. She slouched under the water, peering out from the buoy to watch it pass. When it was gone from sight, she drew a few long, deep breaths and dove headfirst toward the muddy bottom.

The water was a dark and cloudy green. Tori swam toward the center of the channel before kicking her way down to the deepest point. She set the safe on the bottom, her lungs burning for air, her mind screaming for the surface already.

Being here, in the river, made me feel closer to the person I was before all this.

Using her hands, she carved out a hole in the mud and dropped the metal box into it. She gave it one last tug, making sure it was stuck good and deep before shooting for the surface.

She broke free of the water, gasping for air. Filling her lungs again, she swam to shore, dragged a heavy rock from the muddy bank, and dove back under the water. She made two more trips to the cold, muddy river bottom, laying the stones on top of the box until it was concealed. When she finally surfaced, her lungs were on fire and her muscles burned with fatigue. She gripped the base of the buoy for support before kicking away from the channel.

What are you doing? It was the question she had asked Nathaniel when he'd tossed her into the river. And now, she was asking herself.

Her skin stung, her cheeks prickled with the needling wind every time she turned her head to breathe. A stab of longing cut deep in her chest as she swam for the shore.

Nathaniel's voice was a whisper in her mind. *I'm reminding you who you are.*

She closed her eyes and breathed in, cutting a perfect line in the water. She felt hope kicking its legs to the surface. She felt love taking root someplace deep. She felt all of it, everything. And for the first time in a long time, she knew she was completely alive.

THE DISCOVERY

Tori climbed up the embankment with cramped muscles and burning lungs. She reached down for her jeans. And stopped.

Magda and Drew stood a few yards away, their mouths agape. Tori wrapped her arms around herself, trying to cover as many of her scars as she could. The wind blew cold over her wet skin, and her knees refused to stop shaking. Drew's eyes moved between Tori and the channel marker, gauging the distance. Then down at his watch and back again, as if he might have actually been timing her. Magda's eyes were watering.

"What are you doing here?" Tori asked, breathing hard. She grabbed her jeans and rushed to put them on. Then quickly dragged her shirt over her head.

"Your mom's been calling, leaving messages all day. She was worried about you. And we thought..." Magda cleared her throat. She couldn't seem to look Tori in the eyes. Tori bent to put on her shoes so Magda wouldn't have to. "We thought maybe we should check on you."

Drew pulled off his letter jacket and wrapped it around Tori's shoulders. "It's forty-five degrees out here! What the hell are you doing in the river?"

"Taking a bath."

"More like taking a lap!" Drew said. "You want to come clean? You've been holding out on me." Magda was focused on Tori's arms, like she couldn't make herself unsee what was under Tori's sleeves.

"Tori... tell us what's going on," she said.

Tori caught a few more breaths. "Fine." She brushed her wet hair from her eyes and turned to Drew. "I'm the illegitimate descendant of the Chaptico Witch, and I just cast a protective spell over my boyfriend—"

"Right, the three-hundred-year-old dead one—" Magda muttered.

"And I dumped it in the river so the Slaughters won't find it."

"You weren't kidding," Drew whispered to Magda. She shook her head. Drew turned back to Tori. "Anything else?"

"Yeah," Tori snapped, bristling at the way they were both staring at her. Probably the same way she'd stared at Nathaniel when he'd climbed out of the river and told her all about him and Emmeline. "Your butterfly sucks and your coach is wrong. You want a faster time? Try working your back."

Drew shook his head and smiled.

"And I'm okay. I promise," Tori said to Magda, hoping she'd read between the lines. "So, you believe me?"

Drew scratched his head. "Which part? That you could lap my ass in the pool if you wanted to? Or the zombie boyfriend part?"

"Both."

Drew stuffed his hands in his pockets and looked her up and down. She was dwarfed by his heavy jacket, drenching the collar. Her feet were filthy with mud and her lips were blue. She wondered if she looked as pathetic as Nathaniel had the day she had found him wandering in the cemetery, talking about dead people. If Drew was only going to agree to pacify her. Because he felt sorry for her. Because he didn't know what else to do.

"Let's just say I believe *in* you," he said.

Magda handed Tori a rumpled fast-food bag. "We thought you guys might be hungry," she said. "We've been worried about you." As far as olive branches went, Tori guessed this was probably the best she could ask for. She reached for the bag. It smelled like burgers and fries, and Tori's stomach growled as she tore into it.

Drew wrapped his arms around her while she ate and gave her a noogie, planting a kiss on her wet hair. He reeked like fancy aftershave. Tori glanced at Magda. Her blond hair was pulled back in an updo, layers of short blond waves hanging loose around her face. Homecoming. It was tonight.

Her stomach did a nosedive and she pushed the half-eaten burger back in the bag. "What are you guys doing here? Shouldn't you be getting ready?"

Magda freed a loose strand of hair from the corner of her lip. Her makeup wasn't done yet. "I know you said you didn't want to go, but we wanted to give you one more chance to change your mind. You can come to my house to get ready. Your mom already thinks you're there anyway and—"

"I can't. Nathaniel and I—"

"Nathaniel can borrow a jacket and tie from my house," Drew said. "And you can wear Madga's dress from the last spring formal."

Tori opened her mouth, groping for an excuse Magda wouldn't skillfully argue her way around. Their eyes caught, and for the first time, Tori hoped Magda would see through them.

"She'll be cold in a strapless," Magda said with a tight smile, trying not to look at Tori's sleeve. "I have something else that might work."

"Thanks, but I'm not really in a dancing mood." Tori hitched a thumb toward what was left of her house. "Thanks for dinner. We'll be okay here."

Magda reached for her hand, awakening the pain where she'd cut her palm to make the spell. Magda turned it over so Drew could see it too. She looked Tori deep in the eyes. "We're here, if you need to talk about it."

A lump formed in Tori's throat. All she could do was nod. Magda's hand still held hers. And when she finally let go, it felt like she'd left a door open.

Part of her wanted to ask them to stay. Maybe if they saw Nathaniel ... what was happening to him ... they'd believe her. But she wasn't sure Magda and Drew could handle much more honesty today. She started to take off Drew's jacket, when something fell from the pocket. It was the cross-stitched face from the throw pillow.

"Here," Drew said, picking it up for her. "We saw this on the path to the river. Magda recognized it from your bedroom. We figured you must have dropped it." Drew held it out to her, reading it to himself as he did.

Not flesh of my flesh,
Nor bone of my bone,
But still miraculously my own.
Never forget for a single minute,
You didn't grow under my heart,
But in it.

"I like that. It reminds me of us." He put an arm around each of them, pulling Magda and Tori closer together. The trimmed edges of the cloth ruffled in Tori's hand.

After a moment, Magda said, "Come on. Let's get back to the car. It's freezing out here. I brought you a change of clothes and some bottled waters and a toothbrush. "

Tori stood on the shore, transfixed by the fraying square of cloth while Magda and Drew made their way back to the house. The sun shimmered white on the dark water, like something out of one of Emmeline's dreams. Her mind raced. Why had Tori needed *this* pillow? Emmeline had turned this one over. She'd made sure Tori had picked it up. She'd made sure Magda and Drew had found it on the path.

"Not flesh of my flesh," Tori said, reciting the words of the pillow over and over. She wasn't related by blood to her mother or her brother. As far as biology was concerned, she was more Slaughter than Burns. But nobody but Al Senior and Will had known that. She pictured her name, Victoria Burns, scribbled on the Slaughter family tree with a question mark. The curved line connecting her to Archibald and Emmeline ... and Nathaniel Bishop ...

Emmeline's voice came to her as if from one of her dreams. *They are only names. They mean nothing.*

Emmeline ... She'd had no family name. The line on the family tree had connected her to Nathaniel Bishop, as if they were siblings.

He's related to Emmeline too, isn't he? That's why he has the same name....

Tori's heart picked up speed. "Magda!" she called out, sprinting after her before she could get too far ahead. "Emmeline's name ... I was wrong. I need you to try again."

"Tori," she moaned. "We've been through this. We didn't find anything."

"Please! This is important," Tori panted, catching up with her. "Her name would have been Emmeline Bishop."

"Bishop?" Magda paused on the path to grimace at her. "But isn't that Nathaniel's—"

"I'll explain everything later. Just try the search again. Please."

Magda looked at her watch. Then at Drew. She heaved a sigh. "The historical society is probably open for another hour or two. I guess I can try. While I do that, you should call your mom. She's called about a dozen times wanting to talk to you." Magda pulled her cell phone from her jacket and tromped off.

Drew rubbed his arms against the cold. "You want to wait with me in the car?"

"Go on without me," she said with a smile. She looked over her shoulder to the blackened dirt around her house. "I'll come say good-bye in a minute. There's something I need to do."

Tori walked around the house, to the rear corner of the porch where she'd hidden Nathaniel's old spell bottle that morning. When she ducked low, she could just see it through the slats between the singed boards. But she couldn't open it now. Not until she knew for certain the new bottle had worked and Nathaniel was okay. And she couldn't do that until Magda and Drew were gone.

She sat down gingerly on the blackened porch step and pulled out her cell phone. The screen flashed awake, silently informing Tori she'd missed eleven calls from her mother. She sent a quick text message to her mom. *I'm okay. Just tired. I'm staying at Magda's again tonight, but I'll check in soon.*

After a few minutes, Magda appeared around the corner of the house.

"I was only able to make a few calls. At first glance, all the lady could find was an old receipt for the sale of three hogs to an Emmeline Bishop in 1709 in Westmoreland County."

Tori brightened. "That's right across the river from here. That could be her."

"Maybe."

"When will you know for sure?"

Magda eased down on the step beside her. "All of their eighteenth-century records are saved on microfiche. It'll take a while. We'll probably have to make a few trips. But if we go on the weekends, maybe we can find a birth record for Emmeline's baby. If we do, we can track Emmeline's line as far as we can, and try to connect it back to you."

"That could take months." And Tori didn't have that kind of time. Nathaniel couldn't hide in the barn much longer. She didn't have a house here anymore, and who knew where her family would go? A month ago, Tori thought it would have killed her to stay in this place. But now she'd do anything not to have to leave. "There has to be a faster way to prove it."

Magda carefully scratched at a bobby pin in her hair, looking frustrated. "I don't know," she huffed. "Maybe if we had a copy of the original indenture contracts? Something in writing connecting the Slaughters to Emmeline, proving she was entitled to the land?"

Tori buried her head in her hands. There was no way she'd be able to find Emmeline's and Nathaniel's contracts, assuming they still existed at all.

"It's getting late. You should let us take you over to the senior center." Magda's voice fell soft. "Your mom's worried about you. You should at least check in with her and have a hot shower."

The senior center.

Something elusive slid around in the back of Tori's mind as she stared at Magda's phone.

That's why he believed me at first, when I told him the stories. 'Cause I had credentials. But we didn't need none of that. I got all them stories and papers handed down through the family from Ruth.

Tori stood up too fast, pushing Magda off-balance and knocking the phone from her hand.

The family tree ... Matilda had given it to Will because it belonged to the Slaughters. But the stories ... the papers passed down from Ruth ... those had belonged to *her* family. Those she would have kept for herself.

"You're right. I should check in with my mom."

Magda looked relieved. "Drew and I can drop you off."

Tori cast a furtive glance into the trees. Toward the barn. Then the river. No sign of Nathaniel. The old witch bottle was a nagging pressure she'd have to deal with. And soon. "Can you give me a ride back here after?"

Magda checked the time on her phone and bit her lip. "I've got to get home and get ready. We have to leave at seven for the dance."

"I'll hurry," Tori said, heading for Drew's car. "Hopefully, this won't take long."

THE HEART CHOOSES

On Sunday morning after the bonfire, Em and I lay on our backs in one of Slaughter's fallow fields. The sun was bright against my closed eyes, provoking the return of the headache I'd awoken with after finishing off the last of Thomas's stolen rum. I'd taken his flagon to the shed roof, my clothes still smelling like wood smoke and salt fish and sweat, and drunk until I was numb. Until the night before was all but a swirling memory in the back of my mind. I threw an arm over my face, shielding it from the light.

"I know you're not sleeping," Em said, poking my rib with a finger.

"I should very much like to be," I muttered, the words muffled in my sleeve.

"Aren't you going to ask me?"

"Ask you what?"

"About the child?"

And there it was, the words giving flesh to thoughts I hadn't dared speak out loud.

"Did Slaughter do this to you?" I asked, taking my arm from my face to look at her. Though in my heart, I already knew the answer.

Her jaw hardened as she looked at the sky. The sunlight shone into her eyes, narrowing her pupils to knifelike points. They would get her in trouble someday, those eyes. I'd said it first on the ship, and thought it every day since. Em's eyes were as bright and as dark and as changing as the moon. Every whim in her heart and grudge on her mind shimmered against their surface, and even when they were unable to look away, most people who met her feared them.

"It matters not who planted the seed. It only matters who cares for it," she said, stroking her fingers absently over her belly. "The child is mine. Mine and Ruth's."

I scrubbed my face. It was stubbled and tired, weary with worry. "The secrets you're keeping are too big for you."

"But they're not too big for you," she said, sitting up and sliding close enough to lean over me, her elbows perched on my chest.

"What's that supposed to mean?"

"It means I trust you, Nathaniel." Her eyes were dark then, looking down into mine. Her hand was soft on my heart. "You're my brother—"

"Don't be foolish."

"Slaughter's papers even say it, Nat! You're my brother, maybe not by blood, but in my heart, you're my family. The only family I have left. And I need you to be an uncle to this child."

My mouth was suddenly dry, all of my protests forming a painful lump in my throat. "An uncle . . ." I said, testing the word on my tongue.

Em reached into the folds of her skirts and withdrew a wooden figurine. A doll in her own likeness. She pressed it to my chest. "I cannot give you my heart. The heart is stubborn. It chooses for itself, and it isn't mine to give. It hasn't been for a long, long time. But I would give you my life, and the life of my child. I would place them in your hands, into your safekeeping."

Hesitating, I picked up the doll, turning it over to study Em's tiny face and swollen belly in my fingers. It was both the lightest and heaviest thing I'd ever held, and I wondered if she felt the same, carrying the weight of the world beneath her bosom. She and Ruth.

I could not give it back, this precious piece of her she was willing to give to me. More now than before, I needed to be the man I had once promised her I would be. Her family. Her protector. "I am to be an uncle, then. Uncle Nat," I said, smiling if not for myself, then for her.

I wrapped my fingers gently around it. Em eased down to lay her head against my chest, listening to my heart. A heart she couldn't take, though she cupped it in the palm of her hand.

THE EMPTY FOLDER

Magda and Drew dropped Tori off in front of the senior center. Drew left the car idling and Magda checked the time again on her phone.

"We can only stay a few minutes."

"I'll be as quick as I can. If I don't make it back in ten minutes, go ahead without me." Tori leapt out of the car before they could answer.

The front desk attendant looked up from her computer as a chill wind blew in behind Tori, ruffling the pages of the attendant's logbook. Tori could still feel the woman's eyes on her as she reached the end of the corridor to Matilda's room.

She paused before pushing open the door. Matilda's nameplate was gone.

Voices carried from inside.

Filled with a deep sense of unease, Tori cracked the door open and peered into the room. It smelled like pine and lemon disinfectant. Her mother lay in the hospital-style bed, the back adjusted at an angle so she was almost sitting up. Kyle curled in the crook of her arm, listening as she read to him from a book with peeling library stickers on its spine. As Tori stepped inside, their russet heads snapped up together. Her mother's eyes took in Tori's confused expression, her river-dulled hair, and the mud on her shoes, but it felt like they were seeing much deeper.

"Where's Matilda?"

Her mother shifted Kyle's weight and angled herself out of bed. "I've been trying to call you all day. Magda said you were sleeping. Are you feeling okay?" she asked, holding Tori by the elbows and examining every inch of her face. Tori nodded, averting her eyes so her mother wouldn't see the lies hiding inside them.

"This was Matilda's room," Tori said, disoriented. Tori was just here a few days ago, listening to her stories about Will. . . .

Tori's mother gave her a sorrowful look. "I know. We were all shocked when we heard the news. It was very hard on her family. She had only just arrived here."

"How?" Tori heard herself ask hoarsely. "How did she die?"

"I don't know exactly. She was old, honey. I didn't mention it last night because I didn't want to upset you." She hugged Tori close. "Are you sure you're okay? You look flushed. Maybe you should stay here tonight. I can have them wheel in a cot and we can have the doctor on call look at you."

"No." Tori pulled herself gently out of her mother's arms, acutely aware of the knife that was still tucked in her pocket and praying her mother hadn't noticed it. "Magda can't stay long. She's waiting for me outside. I told her mom I'd stay another night." Tori looked around the room. At the place where Matilda had sat on the bed the last time Tori was here. "I just wanted to make sure you're both okay."

Her mother was quiet. Too quiet, as if she were listening for the things Tori wasn't saying.

"Did they feed you?" Tori asked, quickly changing the subject. She crossed the room toward the half-eaten dinner tray on the bedside cart so her mother wouldn't see her wipe her eyes. Some gowns and slippers, a few socks and random sweatshirts—probably pulled from the lost and found in the lobby—had been piled on the chair Matilda used to sit on. Tori pulled open the closet. "Did they give you enough blankets and pillows?"

She faced the closet. Made herself focus. Matilda was gone, but maybe her things weren't. Tori steeled herself as she searched for signs of Matilda's packed belongings, but nothing of Matilda's had been left here. Even her picture was gone from the wall.

"We're fine," her mother said with a thoughtful tilt of her head. She pointed to the tray. "There's a little leftover turkey, and what's left of my roll. You can have it if you're hungry." She waited, watching, and it felt to Tori like some kind of test. Tori's hair was stiff and gritty from the river. Her clothes still smelled faintly of smoke and Nathaniel, and she wondered how long it would take for her mother to figure out that she hadn't slept at Magda's last night.

"Thanks, but I ate at Magda's." She pushed the idea of food away. It wasn't hard. She couldn't have choked anything past the lump in her throat anyway. "So," she said awkwardly. "Is it weird staying in Mrs. Rice's room?"

Her mother raised an eyebrow.

Kyle made a face and curled back into his book.

"I just mean, it's weird being in her room and not seeing her stuff here." The quiver in her voice was real. Just days ago, Tori had been in here, feeding Matilda Ho Hos and coaxing her for information. Today, she was gone. And something about that felt more than shocking or painful. Something about that felt very, very wrong.

Her mother rested a hand on Tori's back. "I didn't realize you knew her."

"I didn't. Not really. I talked with her once, when she lived in the house on Slaughter Road." She cast a guilty glance at her mother. "And once while she lived here."

Tori caught the flicker of surprise on her mother's face. The brief flash of Kyle's eyes over the top of his book. "Oh, I hadn't realized . . ." Her mother cleared her throat. "Did she . . . ? Did you . . . ?" She shut her eyes, flustered, and pressed her lips tightly shut, as if torn between wanting some scrap of proof they belonged here, and not wanting to know anything at all.

"It's okay," Tori said, sparing her mother having to ask. "Mrs. Rice wasn't able to tell me much."

"I'm sorry," her mother said, pulling her in close.

"It's just weird. She seemed fine."

"I know. It happened so quickly. But apparently Mrs. Rice hadn't adjusted to the idea of being here, and sometimes with elderly patients, that's all it takes." Tori's mother sniffled and sighed. She looked at Tori with a sad smile. "A lot of visitors came to pay their respects to her family yesterday when they heard the news. Her daughter will be back tomorrow morning to pick up Matilda's things. You could stay tonight and pay your respects when they come," she suggested hopefully. "There's a movie playing in the dining hall in a little while. The three of us could go."

"I can't stay," Tori said. "I told Magda I'd go home with her." It wasn't entirely a lie. It just left room for interpretation. But if Tori was going to catch a ride back to the farm, she needed to hurry. Matilda's belongings were still here in the senior center, but where? "Do you think I could write Matilda's family a letter and put it with her things?"

Her mother reached up to stroke Tori's hair. "That would be nice," she said, her smile breaking as she rubbed at the grit Tori's hair left on her fingers. "We put her things in the art studio. You can ask the front desk attendant for a key."

"Thanks." Tori gave her a quick kiss on the cheek and left before her mother could ask the questions Tori saw brewing under that stare.

She ran back to the desk. "Hello, I'm Sarah Burns's daughter. We're staying in Room 213. My mom needs the key to the art room." The receptionist handed it over and started to give Tori a lecture about not signing in, but Tori dashed off for the studio with a breathless "Thank you" before the woman could finish.

She fumbled with the door and switched on the light, locking it behind her. The inside of the studio smelled like her mom. Like turpentine and chalks and the acrylics that stained all of her shirts. Easels with brightly colored paintings hugged the walls, making the room feel claustrophobic, their legs threatening to trip her as she navigated past them toward two small boxes stacked behind her mother's desk. RICE #213 was written in bold letters on the sides. Tori pried open the first box. It smelled like the senior center, hardly distinguishable from the air out in the hallway. Pajamas, hat, extendable cane, socks, the picture frame Tori recognized from Matilda's wall—things her mother had probably helped to pack up after Matilda had died.

Tori folded it all back inside and opened the second box. The breath this one blew into the room was different, musty and old, like the box in Tori's guest room closet of almost-forgotten things no one was ready to let go.

The first thing Tori saw inside was a folder stamped with the historical society's logo. It rested on top, as if it had been waiting there for her to find it, and she reached for it greedily.

This was it, she told herself, peeling it open, every hope she had hinging on its contents.

Tori dropped to her knees beside the box. It was empty. Had the contents fallen out, or had they been taken?

She tore into the box again, digging through the disorganized objects inside. It was a mess, everything carelessly tossed inside, as if someone else had gone digging in it before she had. Old lockets, a few crinkle-edged photos, Matilda's husband's obituary clipped from a yellowing newspaper, and a tattered family bible. Random scraps of her life all thrown together.

Tori's hand froze, her fingers suspended over a Ho Ho wrapper. Its brightness and shine stood out from the rest of the dull and brittle hodge-podge. Like a buried message, just for her.

The wrapper was pressed flat, as if it had been squeezed between the pages of a book. Tori turned it over and peeled back the wrapping, revealing the small white slip of cardboard underneath. One side retained the sugary outline of the two cakes Tori had fed her. On the other—the side hidden from prying eyes—were wavering letters and numbers, written as if by shaking hands. Matilda's hands. A message left behind in ballpoint ink.

11:29

What did it mean?

Was it a time? A birth date?

Tori texted Magda. *11:29 . . . What's the first thing that comes to your mind?*

A pause.

The approximate elapsed time since you got out of the car. You've got two more minutes. Then we've got to go or we'll be late to the dance.

Tori texted back an apology. It was stupid to think Magda could give her insight into Matilda's head anyway. They couldn't be more different. Magda was pragmatic, grounded in logic and facts. And Matilda talked to ghosts about witchcraft and curses. She believed in things she couldn't see. . . .

Tori picked up her phone and texted Drew. *11:29. First thing you think of. Go!*

A pause. *My thousand yard freestyle time.*

Tori shook her head. Of course he'd think of swimming. *Try again.*

Another pause. *IDK. My Aunt Helen's birthday? A bible verse?*

"The bible," Tori whispered. She set down her phone to dig Matilda's heavy hardback bible from the bottom of the box. It was the same one she'd seen Matilda holding on her front porch the day they'd moved her to the senior center. The same one she'd seen on the table beside Matilda's bed.

She flipped through the pages until they seemed to stop turning on their own, as if the page had been bookmarked by more than just the pencil lines underlining a portion of the section called Proverbs. The lines were uneven, drawn in the same shaky hand.

> . . . *he that seeketh mischief, it shall come unto him.*
> *He that trusteth in his riches shall fall:*
> *but the righteous shall flourish as a branch.*
> *He that troubleth his own house shall inherit the wind:*
> *and the fool shall be servant to the wise of heart.*
> *The fruit of the righteous is a tree of life . . .*

Tori turned the page to read the rest.

> *Behold, the righteous shall be recompensed in the earth. . . .*

A slip of paper fell into her lap. Two sheets, folded in half. She peeled them open.

A scanned photocopy of an indenture contract, dated 1699, under the name of Emmeline Bishop. And signed by Archibald Slaughter.

And another photocopy, this one of a handwritten list in loopy, hardly legible scrawl. A list of births, all dated in the winter of 1706. Tori's heart picked up speed as she scanned the names and found her. Katherine Bishop, born to Emmeline Bishop and Archibald Slaughter on December 6, 1706, recorded by a town clerk in Monrovia, Virginia.

Tori sank back on her heels. For a moment, all she could do was stare at them. This was it. Her history. Her identity laid out in black and white in front of her. Everything she'd ever wondered about herself, everything she'd felt she needed to know. It was the culmination of every childhood fantasy she'd ever feared and daydreamed, these papers in her lap.

She was elated to have finally found them. And yet somehow she felt no different.

You are Victoria Burns. . . . Nothing that happens to you—nothing they do or say to try to make you believe you are anything or anyone else—will ever change that.

She laid the pages over each other and folded them gently back along the crease. More of Matilda's handwriting covered the back side of the outer page.

"Al's secrets aren't safe with me any more. Give these to Bernie. He'll know what to do." A long series of numbers and letters had been written below it.

Matilda had known.

The Slaughters had burned Matilda's house down, not to drive her off their land. They'd done it to destroy evidence of whatever Matilda knew. They'd burned Tori's too. And now, just like Will, Matilda was dead.

Something must have happened after Tori's last visit. Matilda had known she was out of time, and that someone would come looking for these. And she had left the Ho Ho wrapper for Tori to find.

Tori considered the combination of letters and numbers written on the back of the copies. They reminded her of the Dewey numbers on the spines of the books in the library at school. Matilda had worked in the historical society. This number probably corresponded with a volume in the society's library. Most likely, that's where the original documents had been stored.

Tori fumbled with the wrapper and the photocopies, stuffing them in her pockets before putting the boxes back in place. Her hands were still shaking with adrenaline when she returned the studio key to the front counter, and she pressed them flat on the high surface of the desk.

"You just missed your mom, hon," said the desk attendant as she dropped the key back in the drawer. "The movie just started. She and your brother are in the dining room watching with everyone, if you'd like to join them."

"I have to go. I don't want to disturb the movie."

"I understand. Before you go, you can go ahead and sign in the logbook like you're supposed to. Don't forget next time, hon," the woman said with a pointed look that made Tori shrink behind the tall counter. Tori grabbed the pen and quickly scrawled her name.

"You know," Tori said through a frog in her throat. "I came to visit someone yesterday and I forgot to sign into the visitor log then too." The woman grunted as Tori flipped backward a few pages to yesterday's date, skimming the names. Her mother was right, an entire page of visitors for Rice – Room # 213, not all of them entirely legible.

But if someone had scared Matilda enough to make her leave the coded message for Tori, it would have been after Tori had last visited with her, and before her mother had returned to the senior center yesterday afternoon. Before Matilda's family had all begun arriving.

Tori flipped to the previous page, searching for the right block of time. For a familiar name.

There it was.

Slaughter. No first name. No initials. No room number to visit.

"When I come to visit my mom, what do I write for room number?" Tori asked the woman, an ominous feeling creeping up the back of her neck.

"You don't need to put down a room number." She shuffled through the loose papers on her desk and gave Tori a warm smile. "Not if you're a volunteer."

HOMECOMINGS

Tori's mind spun over the logbook. *Jesse.* Jesse was a volunteer. His mother had told them herself.

Suddenly, it all made perfect sense. Why Jesse had been rummaging in her room and digging in the cemetery. Why he felt so guilty about what had happened to Will. The house—it was supposed to be his. His entire future had been tied up in it. He'd said it himself. He was tired of losing to her.

Tori raced out the front door, eyes peeled for Drew's car, but it was gone. The sun had already set, the purple horizon dotted pink and orange and the parking lot lights already flickering on. Magda had warned her they couldn't wait around long.

The dance would be starting soon.

The bonfire. It was supposed to be tonight, after the dance. Jesse and his friends would be there soon, and she'd left Nathaniel alone. He didn't know. He was still as convinced as Tori had been that Alistair was behind all of this.

Tori ran back to Matilda's old room and dug around in her mother's purse for her car keys. She hadn't been behind the wheel since she'd gotten her learner's permit when she was fifteen, and she felt a flutter of panic as she crossed the parking lot to the car.

Knuckles white on the steering wheel, she tried to remember everything her father had taught her. She released the emergency brake, put the car in reverse, and rolled slowly past the first of the parked police cars, hearing her father's voice in her head. *Breathe.*

The police were everywhere, or maybe it just felt that way as she took the car at a crawl through the center of town. As she passed the turnoff to the Academy, two squad cars were setting up cones for a DUI checkpoint on the opposite side of the road.

Tori fought the urge to press down on the accelerator. Soon she would have the proof she needed to show everyone that land was rightfully hers. To expose Alistair's family's secrets. And if she was right, all she'd have to do was destroy the old bottle and shed Slaughter blood to untangle Emmeline's spells and break the curse. If Nathaniel was right and Tori was the one to break the bottle, it would turn the protective spell in her favor. Then, she would tell Magda's dad and the police what she knew about Jesse, and hope someone believed her.

After what seemed like an eternity, Tori rolled slowly up the driveway to her house, barely able to distinguish the gravel from the grass. No porch lights, no ambient glow drifted from the kitchen or the bedrooms. The house sagged like a dark, rotting corpse, the breeze off the river blowing the choking smell of it right to her. She shut the car door, and the hollow sound echoed back to her.

Tori ran to the back of the house, to the opening under the porch where she'd hidden Emmeline's bottle that morning. She reached tentatively into the hole, waiting for a spider to crawl across her knuckles, or a snake or a possum to jump out and bite her. But all she felt was chilled, wet ground. Her groping became panicked, her hands scraping the dirt inside the lattice and coming away empty. She ducked her head inside, her eyes burning from a smell like wet charcoal and struggling to see in the dark. She stretched as far as her arms would reach and felt nothing.

The bottle was gone.

Tori pulled her head out from under the house, sucking the cold, fresh air into her lungs while she tried to figure out what to do. But something about the air smelled strange. The wind had shifted. Instead of coming off the river, it was blowing from the west. From the field. It carried the smell of smoke—not the charred reek of the house, more like fresh poplar and pine. As Tori followed it toward the path to the cemetery, the steady pulse of bass thudded through the ground and she walked faster until she was stumbling through the dark at a run, her jeans and sleeves catching on thorns and brambles as the music grew louder. The crackling bonfire blazed orange through the branches, casting a wide halo of light close to the oak.

Tori paused in the shadow of the tree line, her fists clenched at the sight of the cemetery littered with coolers and crushed cans. Familiar faces from the hallways at school laughed in frilly, sequined gowns. Guys in crumpled tuxedos leaned against grave markers, drinking from red plastic cups, their suit jackets slung carelessly over the headstones. Jesse's pickup truck had been backed up to the edge of the field, its stereo blasting, the keg pushed to the rear of the open tailgate where red cups spilled out onto the dead grass.

If Jesse and his friends had gone to the dance, they hadn't stayed long. Tori scanned the faces for Jesse, but he was nowhere in sight. Mitch leaned against the tree, sucking down the last of his beer. His leg was set in a heavy cast, and a pair of crutches rested by his feet. He was the only one at the party who wasn't smiling, and he cast anxious glances in her direction, as if he were expecting something to come bursting out of the trees.

Tori stepped forward and their eyes caught across the cemetery. Mitch crushed his can and tossed it as he called out to a group of his friends. Tori saw his lips form the words "Burns is here."

A few people sipped their beers, watching her over the tops of their cans and cups. The music died as someone leaned into the cab of Jesse's truck to turn it off. Suddenly, the only sound was the snap and hiss of the fire as the sparks leapt toward the branches of the oak.

"Where's Jesse?" Tori asked through a tight throat.

"He isn't here." Mitch's eyes flicked to the path to the tobacco barn.

Tori's heart lurched. Without thinking, she ran headlong into the trees. Crashing through the thicket, she was moving too fast to stumble, ignoring the twigs as they scraped across her face.

A dim light shone in the barn's window, but when Tori threw open the door, the coals inside were cold and gray, the soot scattered as if someone had kicked them across the floor. A flashlight lay on the ground, shining a beam into the straw. It was strewn everywhere. The sawhorse had been knocked down, along with Nathaniel's bucket of nails. A dark stain spattered the dirt floor.

Blood.

Thick and red.

"No!" She took the flashlight out with her, pointing it into the trees, listening for the sound of feet in the brush. They couldn't have gone far.

"Your boyfriend's got a few things to answer for," a cold voice called out. Tori spun around, searching for Jesse's face. "Like all this weird shit that started happening as soon as he showed up here."

Jesse and Bobby stood about ten yards away at the trailhead to the cemetery. Nathaniel hunched between them, his chin resting on his chest and his hands hanging loosely together, bound at the wrist. One of them had been bandaged with scraps of torn fabric, probably from the wound she'd given him when she'd taken the cutting from the tree, and a fresh wave of fear crested inside her. The blood in the barn. The bandage on his hand. What if her bottle hadn't worked? And where was the old witch bottle now?

"You let him go!"

At the sound of Tori's voice, Nathaniel raised his head.

"You can have him after I get through with him. My dad and I . . . we've got a few questions for him." A slur smudged the ends of Jesse's sentences.

"I know you have the bottle, Jesse. Where is it?"

Tori could feel Nathaniel's eyes on her in the dark, the questions rising off him. She was supposed to have it. She was supposed to have hidden it where no one would find it. He had trusted her. And she'd screwed it all up. Nathaniel dropped his head. They could kill him, right here, right this minute. Her stupid plastic witch bottle didn't work, and now Jesse was holding Nathaniel's life in his hands like it was some kind of present he was just waiting to tear into.

Jesse's mouth hung open, his face a shadowed mask of disgust and disbelief. "You're asking me where the bottle is after you stole it? Is this some kind of a joke?" He stared at Tori like she was the crazy one. "That's all you people are. Fucking liars and thieves."

Tori raised the light to Jesse's face. He reeled to cover his eyes, but not before she saw the thick red stain under his nose. Blood streamed over his lips and down his chin. It stained the crisp white collar of his shirt. The blood in the barn . . .

"Get that thing out of my eyes!" Jesse shouted. Bobby started forward, his arm outstretched to snatch the flashlight from her. Suddenly, Bobby lurched, falling facedown in the underbrush with a swear.

"Son of a bitch tripped me!" he shouted, clamoring to his feet and rounding on Nathaniel. Nathaniel's head snapped sideways as Bobby cuffed him hard in the cheek.

Slowly, Nathaniel opened his eyes. They were a livid emerald green, as bright as they had been the night Tori had pulled him from the dirt. He dragged his sleeve across his mouth and checked it for blood. The yellow streak stopped him cold. He licked his lips and glanced up at Tori, a smile curling into his cheek.

Suddenly, Nathaniel kicked out sideways, toppling Bobby backward as he swung his fists into Jesse's ear. Tori charged into Bobby, throwing him to the ground, her flashlight wound back and ready to swing.

The metallic snap and click came from somewhere close.

Everything fell silent, all of them frozen by the sound of a bullet being chambered.

Alistair Slaughter stood a few yards away, sighting them down the length of his hunting rifle.

Tori eased off Bobby. Nathaniel slowly raised his hands.

"Is this him? Is this Bishop?"

Jesse nodded, rubbing his ear and scowling. He grabbed Nathaniel by his collar, making a show of it for his dad. "This is him."

"You, boy!" Alistair's eyes narrowed down the barrel at Nathaniel. "Where'd you come from?"

Nathaniel licked his swollen lip, stalling. "I already told your son. I'm from England. I'm here to visit a friend."

Nathaniel's eyes flashed to Tori's, betraying him.

"He's lying. He's been living in the old tobacco barn the whole time he's been here. Tori's been hiding him." Jesse spit, freeing one hand to wipe the blood from his upper lip.

"Which would put you pretty damn close to every god-awful thing that's happened 'round here. What did you do to my nephew Will? That boy couldn't swim. He'd never've gone into that river like that. Not unless someone pushed him! And how 'bout that fire that started at Mrs. Rice's house?"

Alistair started talking faster. There was a hint of hysteria in the rise of his voice. "And how 'bout my house, boy!" Alistair was shouting now, spittle flying with every word. "That house has been in my family for generations! It was gonna pay for my son's college. Did the girl put you up to it? Did she tell you to do it?" Alistair jerked his chin at Tori. "Why'd you do it, girl? So you could claim the insurance and move someplace else?"

Tori looked to Jesse. Why wasn't he confessing? But it wasn't guilt or pride she saw in his eyes. They were glassy. Pinched with pain. It was as if all of his cockiness and bravado had slipped away, revealing the hurt and loss underneath.

The hair bristled on the back of Tori's neck.

Something wasn't right. Not right at all.

Suddenly, Tori's mind broke the murky surface and her chest filled with an icy truth.

The murders, the fires . . . Tori saw all of Emmeline's dreams anew, as a backdrop to Matilda's words. Together, they fit to form a clearer picture.

We try to hide things, to bury our own shame. . . . But the more you try to hold 'em down, the harder they're gonna fight to come out.

Tori knew who was behind this. She knew who was holding down the truth, protecting the family from shame. Covering up their scandals.

Alistair's booming voice startled her back to the moment.

"Why'd you do it, boy?" Alistair's face swelled with rage. The color drained from Nathaniel's cheeks as Alistair's finger tightened on the trigger. "Answer me! Why'd you do it?"

Tori looked to Jesse and Bobby, her eyes pleading for help, hoping one of them would talk Alistair down. Neither of them looked at her. They were transfixed on Alistair's gun. On the vein bulging in his sweaty forehead. On his trembling trigger finger.

In one quick motion, Tori brought the flashlight up and pointed the beam straight into Alistair's face.

"Run!" she shouted to Nathaniel. Nathaniel hesitated a fraction of a second before crossing in front of Jesse for the shelter of the woods.

A deafening crack pierced the night. Tori ducked and covered her ears, and for a moment they rang so loudly it was as if she was being held underwater. Alistair's gun smoked. Bobby's mouth hung open and he stared wide-eyed into the brush, his chest heaving. He backed up, scrambling for the trailhead, tripping as he shot quick, terrified looks over his shoulder.

Tori ran to Nathaniel's side. He and Jesse lay motionless in a tangle of limbs. The blow had thrown them backward, leaving Nathaniel resting on top of Jesse's legs.

"Nathaniel!" His skin was cold and pale, and when she pried open one of his eyelids, the emerald-rimmed pupils were large and lifeless. Frantic, she ran her hands down the length of his shirt. They caught on a hole in the fabric, no bigger than the width of her finger. She drew up his shirt, exposing a small entry wound.

Using all her strength, she rolled Nathaniel onto his side and a cry escaped her. The skin of his back was roughly torn, open and angry where the bullet had gone through. A wide ribbon of sap streamed from it, clinging like webbing to Tori's fingers. Under him, Jesse's blue eyes stared vacantly at the sky. As Tori watched, a stain soaked through his dress shirt, blooming like a dark red rose.

Alistair had shot through Nathaniel. He'd killed his own son.

Tori eased Nathaniel back to the ground and his eyelids fluttered open. "Matilda..." he muttered, barely loud enough for Tori to hear. "Did you see her? Did you find the contracts? Do you have the proof you need?"

Tori nodded, stroking his hair back from his face and holding his head in her lap, waiting for some magic to heal him. He flinched with pain. His skin was slick with sweat and his chest moved up and down irregularly.

"Where's the bottle?"

Hot tears welled in Tori's eyes, blurring her vision. "I hid it. But it's—"

"Then it's time," he said, fighting for breath. "You have to break the curse."

"No!" she said urgently.

Behind her, Alistair roared and fell to his knees, the gun pointed skyward.

"It's done," she said, her voice breaking. "It's done, isn't it? He killed Jesse. He spilled Slaughter blood! It's all over now. It has to be." Even as she said the words, she knew they weren't true. Something was wrong. She felt Emmeline's anger simmering everywhere. In the cold wind rustling along the belly of the woods. In the ghostly damp chill that clung to her breath and made it curl from her lips.

"It's the only way," he said. "You have to be the one. The one to satisfy the curse. The spells are tangled and you're the common thread between them. It has to be you. The bottle and the blood. You have to spill them together."

Tori panicked. She didn't even know where the bottle was. Or what would happen to him if she couldn't find it. "I can't! I can't do it!"

"Look at me, Tori." He gritted his teeth and winced through the pain as he reached into his pocket. "This isn't like before, when I cut myself. I know. I feel it. I'm not strong enough to heal from this." He searched for Tori's hand and pressed something into it. Emmeline's doll. His fingers were cold and weak when they closed over hers. "Finish this."

"But—"

"Victoria," he whispered. "Do not let your grief make you forget who you are."

Tears streamed down her face. She knew what she had to do. She knew this was what he wanted. If she let him die here—if she let the police or the Slaughters or anyone else find him—he'd be painted into history as some kind of deranged drifter.... The strange boy with no identity who systematically tore apart Slaughter Farm and all its residents. He deserved better than a phony legacy. He deserved more than to be labeled a liar and a thief. She could give him that. She could exhume the truth. She could tear the lid from the coffin of lies Archibald and Elizabeth Slaughter had nailed shut over him.

She pressed her forehead to his, their noses brushing, his last few breaths mingling with hers. "I'll remember you, Nathaniel Bishop," she whispered against his lips.

A resounding crack split the night. Tori spun just in time to see Alistair's eyes roll back in his head as he fell sideways. Drew stood behind him, his tie askew and the jacket of his tux loose around his cummerbund, a rock clutched in his hands. Magda peered around him, her corsage hand gripping his shoulder and her high heels sinking in the dirt.

"What are you doing here?"

"We were late to the dance. Jesse and his friends had already left by the time we got there. We asked around and heard that Jesse was planning to have the bonfire even though you told him he couldn't. We came to try to get rid of them."

When Tori turned back to Nathaniel, his eyes were closed. His chest was still. She pressed a hand to it, but couldn't feel his heart beating.

"What the hell happened?" Drew asked, reaching for Magda's hand as they took in Jesse's and Nathaniel's limp bodies.

"Alistair ... he shot Jesse. I think it was an accident." Tori's breath hitched, her mind reeling over what to do next. "Where's Bobby? He ran for help and he—"

Drew looked incredulous. "Bobby didn't run for help. He just ran. Magda was arguing with Mitch, and she threatened to report them. Then we all heard the shot, and everyone at the bonfire scattered. Everyone's gone, except us."

Nobody had called for help. Nobody was coming. She looked down at Nathaniel's pale face, unsure what to do, all their voices echoing in her mind. Nathaniel and Matilda and Emmeline.

Finish this.

Her grip tightened around Emmeline's doll. It was all she had left of Nathaniel. And she knew what he wanted her to do. She shoved it in her pocket with the knife and ran for the tree. She heard Magda and Drew running behind her. When she reached the old oak, it was empty. Everyone was gone. She pulled the knife from her pocket and sank into the dirt.

"Um . . . Tori?" Drew's voice pitched high with concern. He probably thought she was insane. She wouldn't even know where to begin to explain. But Drew and Magda weren't looking at her. She wasn't even sure they were listening. Their eyes were fixed behind her.

Tori turned.

Across the field, Dorothy Slaughter walked fast toward the fire, pausing every few steps to take in the abandoned bottles and cups that littered the ground, then the deep tire ruts left behind by Jesse's truck where Bobby and Mitch must have peeled out. As she neared, Tori saw the old stone witch bottle cradled in the crook of her arm.

"Go," she whispered to Drew. "Check on Alistair. Keep an eye on his rifle and make sure he doesn't run." She turned to Magda. "Go with him. Call the police."

They both hesitated a moment, then took off into the trees. Tori didn't have long.

She stepped out from around the fire and pointed to the bottle. "What are you doing with that?"

Dorothy started. It took her a moment to find Tori against the light of the fire, and Tori came closer so she could get a good look. Tori fingered the knife through the fabric of her pocket. A cold wind stirred, tossing empty cups and dead leaves across the brittle grass.

The fire hissed. Sparks and flames reflected in Mrs. Slaughter's eyes. Her long hair was coming loose from her bun. It blew across her lips, catching in the corners of her crooked smile. "This?" she asked, holding up the bottle.

"It's mine. You took it from my property. Give it back." Tori flexed her fingers, itching to take it.

"Yours?" she spat. "You entitled little brat! Nothing about this place is yours!"

"The house is mine. The land too."

"That's a lie!"

"I can prove it. I'm a descendant of Archibald Slaughter and Emmeline Bishop. She was an indentured servant, and Archibald owed her and her brother twenty acres of land. Al Senior knew it. He had proof. And he wanted to do the right thing."

Mrs. Slaughter's smile twisted into a sneer. "That's what's in this bottle, isn't it? This is where the old man hid them." She shook the fragile stone jug. "This is where Alistair's father buried the secrets he was determined to keep from us."

Lightning flashed, thunder clapped. The wind swirled harder, rattling the branches of the tree.

Tori couldn't let Dorothy open that bottle. Not if it shifted the power of the bottle in Dorothy's favor.

"Was it worth it?" Tori eyed the fire, reaching into her pocket. "Killing your nephew and an old woman to keep everyone from learning the truth? Ironic, isn't it? The things you were willing to do to keep people from discovering what a terrible person you are."

Mrs. Slaughter's step faltered less than ten feet from the fire. She clutched the bottle to her chest and her smile crumbled and blew away. "What did you say?" Her eyes hardened.

"I know everything," Tori told her. "I know what you did."

"I didn't do any of those things!" Dorothy's face was a smug mask of false innocence. "It was that boy, Nathaniel Bishop. The one the police are looking for. The strange boy that's been hanging around here."

"I don't know what you mean. Nathaniel doesn't exist."

"Of course he exists! Just ask Jesse. He'll tell you—"

"Have you ever seen him?"

Dorothy scowled, growing annoyed. "Will wrote about him. In his journal. The boy worshipped him like he was some kind of hero! He kept writing about him, saying Nathaniel was coming back to Slaughter Farm to seek revenge for what happened to Emmeline. Clearly, the young man is disturbed," she said disdainfully, "to be consumed by such a ridiculous legend. I hope the police find him before he can hurt anyone else."

"Nathaniel's dead." Hot tears prickled Tori's eyelids and she blinked them back. It took everything inside her not to scream.

Mrs. Slaughter stared at her, her mouth parted.

"Nathaniel Bishop was murdered, hanged from this tree by Archibald and Elizabeth Slaughter three hundred years ago. He couldn't be the one who pushed Will into the river. Or the one who set the fires. Or the one who murdered Matilda Rice. The Nathaniel Will wrote about in his journal? He died a long time ago."

Mrs. Slaughter blanched. She stared into the flames with a vacant expression, as if she were seeing the pages of Will's journal anew, watching her alibi burn. "Don't be foolish. No one would ever believe a ghost did those things," she muttered, almost to herself.

"No. They'll believe you did." Dorothy's eyes snapped to Tori's. "It was you, wasn't it? You were the one who pushed Will into the river, because he knew why Al Senior left me this land. You knew he'd found proof, and he wouldn't tell you where it was. And the deeper you dug into your family's past trying to find it, the worse all that history started to look."

"No!" She shook her head, hugging the bottle. Her eyes darted around them into the woods.

"You'd figured out who your family was by reading Will's journal. You read the books he brought home from the library about Emmeline."

"I was only concerned! The boy was obsessed! He wouldn't stop digging!"

"What were you afraid he would find? That the stories about Emmeline were true? That your pristine estate was built on the backs of kidnapped children and abused girls? That you have all that you have now because your ancestors broke contracts and murdered slaves?" Dorothy grimaced. "Or were you most afraid of finding out that you were related to me?"

She charged at Tori, her finger pointed like Alistair's. "You're no Slaughter! You have no proof!"

Tori could feel her blood begin to boil. "That's it, isn't it? You couldn't find the proof Al Senior had hidden. So instead, you tried to erase it. You got rid of the journal and you killed Will to keep him from telling anyone. You burned Will's old house down, hoping to destroy it. Matilda's too. And then you killed her, to keep her from telling her stories to anyone else. And when Jesse came home complaining about some stranger named Nathaniel, you thought you'd found your scapegoat. But you never figured out who Nathaniel is. That he doesn't exist anymore." It was the truth. Tori could see it all over Dorothy's face as Dorothy advanced on her. Her eyes weren't mournful or shocked. They were calculating and aware.

"My father-in-law had no idea the poison he was inviting into our lives. That stupid hobby—all that ridiculous research he was doing behind closed doors, all those stories he was filling the boy's head with—it all would have ruined us! And I won't let that happen." Dorothy's expression was wild, feral in the firelight. Her hair had come loose from her bun. It whipped around her face, dark smudges of mascara sliding below her eyes. Sparks blew across the small space between them, and she stared into the fire with a maniacal focus. "Sometimes," she said coldly, "when invasive weeds get too thick, we have to burn our fields to rid ourselves of competition . . . to encourage growth." She reached down, grabbing the end of a piece of long kindling from the fire. She brandished the smoking orange end with one hand, cradling the bottle in the other. "And that's all you people are—weeds! Rooting where you don't belong and choking out my family! When you're gone, we'll be healthy again."

Dorothy snarled. She sliced the air with the searing wood, close enough for Tori to feel the heat of it. She backed away, unable to retaliate for fear of hitting the bottle. With a grunt, Dorothy swung again, hard and fast. Tori sidestepped, but Dorothy pressed in, edging her closer to the fire until Tori could feel the heat of it at her back. Dorothy lashed out again with an angry shout, the scorching tip of the wood whistling past Tori's face.

"I'm sorry Jesse is dead," Tori shouted, narrowly avoiding the blow. "But hurting me won't bring him back!"

Mrs. Slaughter stumbled, her face registering the words before her body did. She righted herself and took a step backward, the kindling poised in her hands as she looked around her at the abandoned coolers of beer and the freshly built fire. The wood slipped from her fingers.

"What happened here? Where's Jesse?" she demanded, still clutching the bottle tightly against her, her breath coming in rapid pants. "Whose blood is that?" she shouted, pointing at the red smear on Tori's sleeve.

Tori eased a safe distance from the fire, her eyes fixed on the bottle.

"Alistair came here with his rifle, looking for the person who killed Will. He was angry and confused. He made a mistake. And he shot Jesse—"

Dorothy's face contorted with rage, and she dropped the bottle. Tori held her breath as it fell and rolled off Dorothy's shoe.

"Liar!"

Tori leapt for the bottle, but Dorothy charged and tackled her to the ground, knocking the knife from Tori's hand. She closed her fingers around Tori's throat. Tori twisted sideways, and they rolled together toward the heat of the fire while Tori struggled to breathe. One hand fumbled in the grass for the knife, the other pushed against Mrs. Slaughter's chest. Finally, her fingers closed around the handle and Tori brought it up to Dorothy's arm in one quick motion, slashing her skin.

Dorothy screamed, releasing Tori like a hot coal. She clutched her arm, baring her teeth. The wind threw a cascade of sparks from the fire, and a cold rain started to fall. Dorothy launched for Tori again, and Tori dodged her, putting the bonfire between them. They circled it, staring each other down over the flames.

"There is no proof, you bastard child!" Dorothy yelled. Lightning flashed and thunder rocked the ground. Rain pelted her face and dripped off her chin. "Nobody knows who you are!"

The rain was as cold as the river, and Tori's clothes were heavy on her skin.

Who I am is in my blood.

She wiped the rain and tears from her eyes.

Dorothy feinted once across the fire, then launched around it for Tori again. Tori darted around the other side, snatching the bottle from the ground.

"You're wrong." Tori pressed the blade to her own forearm, making Dorothy stumble and pause. Blood ran fast down the length of her arm, ushered by the rain down her fingers and over the bottle. She didn't wait to see what Emmeline would do. Didn't wait for signs that the curse had lifted. She knew who she was, who she'd been before all of this. She knew exactly what she needed to do. She took a deep breath and raised the witch bottle over her head.

"What are you doing?" Dorothy shouted, her voice cracking.

Then Tori threw it down and watched it shatter in the flames.

D rew and Magda raced down the slope from the trees, calling Tori's name. Tori was sitting on the ground, wearing the scratchy gray blanket given to her by the EMTs and a bandage around her wrist. The police were there. They'd taken Dorothy Slaughter away in handcuffs moments before, while she'd muttered incessantly about all the ways she wanted to kill Tori Burns. How she wasn't guilty. How it was all the fault of a boy who no one could prove existed. The police officer had scratched his head, and Tori shrugged. Then she'd sent them up to the woods to find Alistair, who had been loaded into an ambulance, wearing handcuffs and a bandage around his head.

It all felt too easy, the fact that they'd both been taken into custody and Tori was still sitting here in her cemetery, under her tree. Worry needled at her mind.

Winded, Drew dropped to the ground beside her. Magda stood behind them in her torn and muddy stockings, bent at the waist with her hands on her knees, trying to catch her breath.

"We found Alistair stumbling around in the woods. He's got a bad concussion. Didn't even know what day it was," Drew said. "I stayed with him until the police came, while Magda went to check on Nathaniel, but it was weird...."

"He was gone," Magda said, dropping to the ground in a puddle of torn satin. "I looked everywhere. It's like he just disappeared." Tori nodded numbly. She should have felt relieved that his body wasn't waiting in the woods for the medical examiner to cart away. It had all happened the way he would have wanted it. The curse was broken, and Emmeline's spell over him was lifted. Everything was back as it should have been. And yet, she couldn't help wishing he wasn't gone.

"I know," she told them through a shaky sigh. She lifted her chin, keeping her head above the surface. "He'll be fine. He's gone home."

Drew and Magda cast each other doubtful looks.

"Just . . . if anyone asks, Nathaniel was never here. Okay?" Tori said, wiping away a tear.

They both nodded, watching Tori with cautious expressions. Tori began filling in the blanks for them, everything Mrs. Slaughter had done and everything Tori had learned during her visit to Matilda's room. Drew offered to drive Tori to Bernie's office in the morning. Magda offered to call her dad in case Bernie needed help. They both offered to stay until the police dismissed her, and drive her to the senior center.

She shook her head and stood, giving each of them a long hug before they headed back to Drew's car. Needing a minute alone, she walked the length of the cemetery, beyond the halo of the police floodlights. She wove through the headstones, treading cautiously in the dark. And when she came to the place where Nathaniel was buried, she reached out a toe, not surprised to feel the dirt was slightly mounded.

She knelt down. A cold wind gathered and the branches of the old oak shivered. Then its leaves let go and slowly began to fall, blowing across Nathaniel's grave.

There was no pain.

Something held me buoyant, like a gentle hand at the small of my back lifting me to the surface. Weightless and floating under a light as bright as the sun, my fingers reached out for another's, brushing skin and pulling it close.

And in my head, I heard her whisper, "You will heal. You are not alone."

THE OTHER SIDE OF THE RIVER

I am standing on a shoreline.

The tall man with deep brown skin in front of me hands a sack to the ferryman who eyes it warily. The ferryman checked our papers twice before letting Sam and Ruth step into his skiff, only handing them back after closely inspecting the signature and the raised wax seal. He hefts the sack up and down, testing the weight of it again, same as he had done back on the opposite shore.

Sam...No, we must call him Thomas now....He wears deep worry lines, unwilling to let his guard down while he's wearing this free man's skin. He squares his broad shoulders and looks down at the ferryman, his deep voice assuming a tone of authority when he thanks him for the ride.

As the ferryman tends to his boat and his lines, we all stand on the bank, staring across the water, back to the Maryland shores.

"We should go," I hear myself whisper. "We should keep moving."

Ruth adjusts her cap, making sure it covers her missing ear. She gathers up our belongings, slapping my hand away when I try to offer help. Maybe because she knows I'm exhausted from the burden I'm already carrying. Or maybe because she's terrified the ferryman might grow suspicious. I let her carry the bundles, maybe to ease her mind. Or maybe because I am tired, all the way through to my bones. The black-and-white image seems to grow more muted and cloudy.

Sam and Ruth gather up the last of our supplies and walk briskly toward a trail up ahead, disappearing into a thick stand of trees, but I don't turn away from the river. Not yet.

Instead, I lay a hand on the swell of my belly.

"You are strong," I hear myself say, the words little more than a whisper in my head. "No matter where you are raised or what name you are given, you will endure. You will swim, you will dance, and you will love without fear. Nathaniel and Ruth and I . . . we will protect you. That, my child, is my promise to you."

And with one last look back across the water, I close my eyes and Emmeline disappears.

BEGINNINGS

I t was late spring.

Tori sat inside the iron fence after the last day of school, under the old oak next to Nathaniel's grave. She talked to him sometimes. Maybe that was silly. She knew he couldn't hear her at all. She should probably worry that someone else could. But sometimes, when all the pressure of home and school and being without him felt like it was too much, this was the only place where she could breathe.

A balmy breeze blew across the dead grass and the sun was hot on her cheeks. After a few minutes, Tori peeled off her sweatshirt and lay back in a patch of sun, letting it warm the skin below her short sleeves and her neck where the oyster shell necklace settled between her collarbones. She drew a long breath through her nose, inhaling the faint scent of the river, and she smiled up into the branches of the oak. They were twisted, tangled and dry. Deep scars still lingered in its trunk. On the outside, it was easy to see why everyone assumed it was dead. But inside, Tori was pretty sure they were both healing. And most days, she thought they were going to be okay.

More than six months had passed since Dorothy was arrested for her crimes and Alistair was arrested for killing Jesse. It seemed like everything had changed. Francine never got over the death of her son, Will; she had overdosed on painkillers and antidepressants on Christmas night. Alistair's brother, Jack, had suffered a stroke not long after. Emmeline's curse may have been sated, but something else was still eating away at their family. Tori knew better than anyone that shame has its own set of teeth.

Magda's father had helped the Burnses petition to have the old tree protected as a recorded historic property, creating an ordinance making it illegal to harm it or cut it down. The historical society put up the fence and a placard, but the buds never grew back in the spring, and the grass underneath remained brittle and brown.

No one came through the old cemetery anymore. The Burnses had collected the insurance money on the house, and at Tori's insistence, they had decided to stay and rebuild it. Tori had painted her new room green, and her mom stenciled the sentiments from her lost cross-stitched pillow on her wall. There were shiny new locks on all the doors, but they rarely used them. Aside from Magda and Drew, her family didn't get many visitors anymore.

They were still here. A family of transplants slowly taking root. Tori went to school. She studied. She passed her classes. She volunteered at the historical society with Matilda's daughter, and at the senior center with her mom on the weekends. Tori's mother had been offered a paid teaching position there and her paintings had started to sell.

Drew nagged Tori tirelessly about joining the swim team. Tori wasn't quite ready for that, but she coached him on his butterfly and went to his meets and cheered with Magda. And sometimes, when she wasn't feeling herself or she was missing Nathaniel, she'd swim a few laps in the river after school.

Tori didn't have Emmeline's visions anymore. She had other dreams now. Some, but not all of them, were her own. Others seemed to pull at her fingertips while she was sleeping, letting her know he was here with her.

Tori spent a lot of time in the cemetery with Nathaniel, waiting for Slaughter Farm to settle and still. For the name Bishop to disappear from everyone's lips. Today, the only sound came from the winding branches above her head, peppered with chattering blackbirds.

Tori stood, brushing the grass from her legs. She jumped to grab a low-hanging branch. Pulling it toward her, she bent it over and over until it tore loose. Then she stripped away the bark and rolled up her sleeve. It felt strange. She hadn't cut in a long time. She had finally talked to her mom, and together, they'd found a counselor—a kind woman with a private practice in the next county, far enough away so no one from school would find out. Magda had accompanied her to her sessions those first few weeks until Tori had finished her driving lessons with Drew. Now, Tori was able to drive herself.

Her chest was full, her body light as she dragged the switch across her arm. She'd made Nathaniel a promise that she'd try not to hurt herself—and even in her darkest moments, she'd kept that promise. But she'd also promised not to let him go.

Slowly, red droplets fell to the ground.

She listened to it spatter, like the beat of a heart.

Her head snapped up at the thunder of wings as hundreds of blackbirds rushed from the tree. The ground beside her began to shudder. Then crumble and shake. A choked laugh escaped her throat and she watched, her heart racing, as cold white fingers sprouted up through the earth. This time, when he reached for her, she took his hand and she pulled.

Emmeline and Ruth's story had come to an end.

But Nathaniel and Tori?

Their story was just beginning.

ACKNOWLEDGEMENTS

I am first and foremost grateful for my tireless agent and champion, Sarah Davies. Thank you, Sarah, for your wisdom and for advising me to put this story back in the drawer until I had the voice to tell it. As always, you were right.

Thank you to my editor, Emily Meehan, and her team at Disney • Hyperion, for placing their faith in my stories. This book would not be what it is today if not for the patience of Hannah Allaman, who coached me through every painful revision with kindness, honesty, and care. I am grateful to the following people who worked together to bring this story to life and then to library and bookstore shelves—Maria Elias, Brandy Colbert, Dina Sherman, Frank Bumbalo, Holly Nagel, Jackie DeLeo, Sara Liebling, Guy Cunningham, David Jaffe, and Amy Goppert.

My critique partners, Megan Miranda and Ashley Elston, have been a source of support, sanity, and laughter throughout the development of this book (and all my books). I appreciate you both more than words can express. Thank you to Romily Bernard, Tamara Ireland Stone, Heather Ezell, and Tessa Elwood for offering feedback along the way.

One of the things I loved most about writing this book was the research involved. My thanks go out to the brilliant staff and educators of Colonial Williamsburg, Historic Jamestowne, and Historic St. Mary's City, who bring the early colonies to life.

While rooted in real landmarks and historical facts, this book is a work of fiction. Chaptico, Maryland, is a real town, and Chaptico Wharf is a real part of colonial Maryland's history. Moll Dyer, Mary Lee, and Rebecca Fowler are thought to have been real women, persecuted as witches during that time period. And children were sold into servitude in the colonies throughout the late sixteen hundreds and into the early seventeen hundreds, some at the bequest of their parents, but many forcibly and against their will. While the backdrop of this story is real, the individuals, families, and events depicted in this novel are entirely fictitious. There is no Slaughter Farm. There was no Chaptico Witch. And, sadly, Nathaniel and Tori are products of my own imagination.

I would like to thank my family, for their sacrifices and patience during the writing of this book. Without their support, it would never have been possible. My parents have believed in this book since the very first pages, and have waited years to finally know the rest of Nat's and Em's stories. This book (and all the pages that never made it into the final version) is as much theirs as mine, and I love them for it. I'm thankful for my children, who amaze me with their imaginations, and who still let me read them fairy tales every night. And for my husband, who breathes inspiration into my life in so many ways, but especially this story. Tony, you are my home.

Finally, I would like to thank my readers—the librarians and booksellers who put my stories into the hands of people who'll love them, the fans who leave thoughtful and passionate reviews, and students who e-mail to tell me they ditched class to finish my books because they had to know what happened next. A book doesn't come to life for me until you've read it. My characters don't really breathe until you've met them, and these places I write about don't exist until you've stepped into them with me. Thank you for making them real.